GONE AGAIN

GONE AGAIN

A JACK SWYTECK NOVEL

JAMES GRIPPANDO

31652002938901

HARPER

An Imprint of HarperCollins*Publishers*

GONE AGAIN. Copyright © 2016 by James Grippando, Inc. All rights reserved. Printed in the United States of America. No part of this book may be used or reproduced in any manner whatsoever without written permission except in the case of brief quotations embodied in critical articles and reviews. For information, address HarperCollins Publishers, 195 Broadway, New York, NY 10007.

HarperCollins books may be purchased for educational, business, or sales promotional use. For information, please e-mail the Special Markets Department at SPsales@harpercollins.com.

FIRST EDITION

Library of Congress Cataloging-in-Publication Data has been applied for.

ISBN: 978-0-06-236870-6

16 17 18 19 20   OV/RRD   10 9 8 7 6 5 4 3 2 1

FOR TIFFANY

GONE AGAIN

Welcome Home, Jack!

Jack Swyteck was standing outside the Freedom Institute, and the handwritten greeting on a Post-it was stuck to the front door. It was Monday morning, and Jack had moved in his office furnishings over the weekend. The doormat at his feet displayed a less welcoming message, but it summed up the sense of humor of the lawyers who worked there: COME BACK WITH A WARRANT.

It made Jack smile, even if this wasn't the full-blown homecoming that his former colleagues wanted.

More than a decade had passed since Jack's resignation, but a four-year stint with the Freedom Institute had been his first job out of law school. At the time, "law-and-order" governor Harry Swyteck—Jack's father—was on his way toward signing more death warrants than any chief executive in Florida history. Their public clash was a political embarrassment. Harry might not have taken it so personally if Jack hadn't aligned himself with a ragtag group of former hippies who were under the mistaken impression that the state flower was cannabis and the national anthem was "Kumbaya." There was Eve, the only woman Jack had ever known to smoke a pipe. Brian, the gay surfer dude. And Neil Goderich, their fearless leader, a ponytailed genius who had survived Woodstock. To outsiders, Jack was the odd man out. But they became friends, and his resignation didn't change that. The split was more about style than substance. Forcing the government to prove its case beyond a reasonable doubt was enough for Jack. Getting another guilty man off death row didn't make him want to break out a three-dollar bottle of cold duck and throw a party. Or issue a press release.

Jack pushed open the door and stepped inside.

"Jack is *back*!" shouted Hannah. Neil's daughter was as young and idealistic as Jack had been when Neil had taken him under his wing. It was hard to believe that his mentor was gone forever, walking on over the hill with Abraham, Martin, and John.

"I guess you could say I'm back," said Jack. "Sort of."

Hannah was a foot shorter than Jack, and she raised up on her toes to give him a big hug and a peck on the cheek. Eve and Brian were standing right behind her, each with a small suitcase in hand. Jack would have bet money that Brian's corduroy jacket was the same one he'd worn on the day of Jack's resignation. Maybe the elbow patches were new.

"Sorry to say hi and bye," said Hannah. "But Governor Scott signed two more death warrants last night. We're off to FSP to see our client."

Jack remembered those trips to Florida State Prison. That was how he'd met his best friend, Theo Knight, the only innocent man Jack had ever defended at the Institute. "Safe travels," said Jack.

"You wanna come with?" she asked.

"Nope."

"You sure?"

Jack almost said "Dead sure," but caught himself. "I'm positive."

"Okay, then. You know where Mr. Coffee is. Be sure to lock up when you leave. Three of our neighbors had break-ins this month."

"Is there an alarm I should set?"

She chortled. "Have you been gone *that* long? We're lucky if the lights go on when we flip the switch."

He knew money was tight; it was the reason he'd returned.

They filed past him and out the door, looking less like the talented lawyers they were and more like something from the Island of Misfit Toys. It wasn't really necessary for them to travel all the way to Florida State Prison; the sojourn was a holdover from the old days, when Neil would organize a vigil outside the prison gates before an execution. Back in the days of an old electric chair that was prone to misfire, resulting in flaming heads and contorted purple faces, they might draw a hundred impassioned protesters or more. Lately, it was basically Hannah, Eve, and Brian.

The door closed, and Jack was alone. He'd requested no fanfare to mark his return, and his old friends had more than honored the request, thanks to Governor Scott.

Jack put down his briefcase and looked around. The historic house on the Miami River had changed little. The foyer doubled as a storage room for old case files, one box stacked on top of the other. The bottom ones sagged beneath the weight of denied motions for stay of execution, the box tops having warped into sad smiles. The old living room was the reception area and secretarial work station. The dining room, Florida room, and a downstairs bedroom served as offices for the lawyers. The furniture screamed "flea market"—chairs that didn't match, tables made stable with a deck of playing cards under one leg. The sixties-vintage kitchen was not only where lawyers and staff ate their bagged lunches; it also served as the main (and only) conference room. Hanging on the wall over the coffeemaker was the same framed photograph of Bobby Kennedy that had once hung in Neil's dorm room at Harvard.

It saddened Jack. Neil was the first friend Jack had ever eulogized, and his widow had taken Jack at his word when he'd pulled her aside after the funeral and said, "If there's anything I can ever do for you . . ."

"Well, there is one little thing," she'd said.

Sarah's mission was for Jack to fill Neil's shoes. Jack wasn't interested. He was a sole practitioner with a thriving practice. But when it became a matter of survival for the Institute, Jack made an accommodation. His lease was up in Coconut Grove, so he moved "Jack Swyteck, P.A." into the old digs, taking Neil's office. He wasn't officially affiliated with the Freedom Institute, just a subtenant, but Jack's monthly rent check would keep the Institute from going completely broke.

His cell rang. It was his wife.

"When are you coming home?" asked Andie.

"I just got here."

"I spilled a protein shake all over my gun-cleaning mat. Can you cut through midtown on the way home and buy me a new one? Johnson Firearms is the only shop that carries that mat with all the parts diagrammed for the Sig Sauer P250."

Jack chuckled.

"Why is that funny?"

"I don't know. Doesn't a pregnant wife usually send her husband on a run for ice cream or salt-and-vinegar potato chips?"

"Mmm. That sounds good."

"Which?"

"Both."

"Okay," Jack said. "Ice cream, potato chips, and a gun-cleaning mat. Anything else?"

"If I lie here long enough, I'll probably think of something."

"You're bored, aren't you?"

"Out of my mind," she said, sighing.

FBI Agent Andie Henning was seven months pregnant and four days into a short medical leave from the Miami field office. Her first and second pregnancies had ended in miscarriage. That history, together with high blood pressure, had prompted her doctor to order five days of bed rest.

"Tell me everything is going to be okay," she said.

"It's all going to be okay."

"You promise?"

"Yes. And you are going to be a great mother."

"No, I'm not. What if my next undercover assignment is six months long and I never even get to see my little—"

"Stop," said Jack. "The Bureau isn't going to send a new mother on a six-month undercover assignment."

"Well, that's a whole 'nother problem, isn't it? What if the boys at headquarters say to themselves, 'Oh, Henning's doing the mommy thing now,' and I'm stuck doing background checks on single young women who are angling for my job?"

"Andie, this is why you have high blood pressure. Breathe, okay?"

Another sigh crackled over the line. "You're right."

"You better now?"

"Triple fudge swirl."

"What?"

"That's the ice cream I want."

Jack smiled. "Triple fudge it is."

Jack worked all morning in the kitchen, which was the only room where the AC seemed to be blowing cool air. He was without his secretary, having given Bonnie the day off after a weekend of overtime on the office move. The old refrigerator emitted an annoying buzz, which Jack silenced every so often with a quick kick to the side panel. The overall ambience didn't exactly convey the image of powerhouse legal representation. Jack wondered what his paying clients would think.

Should've thought of that before you moved in, dummy.

A car pulled up in the driveway. Jack probably wouldn't have noticed, except that the tires skidded to a crunchy stop on loose gravel. The car door slammed, and the patter of footfalls on the sidewalk bespoke a brisk pace. An urgent knock on the door followed, which continued until Jack could open up. A fortyish attractive blonde was standing on the front porch.

"Can I help you?" he asked.

In the moment she took to catch her breath, Jack noted that her car was a Mercedes and that her designer jeans and cotton blouse, though casual, probably weren't from Target.

"I'm looking for Neil Goderich," she said.

"Unfortunately, Neil passed away last year."

She seemed confused by the news, though not particularly sorry to hear it. "This is where he worked, right?"

"Yes. For twenty-eight years."

"I need to speak to someone in charge. Mr. Goderich was the lawyer for Dylan Reeves."

"Who's Dylan Reeves?"

"Governor Scott signed his death warrant last night."

That jibed with the sudden exodus of Hannah and crew. "Do you know Mr. Reeves?"

"Yes. I mean, no." She paused, as if suddenly aware how incoherent she sounded. "Actually, he was convicted of raping and murdering my seventeen-year-old daughter."

Jack took a half step back, sympathetic, but cautious. A part of him would forever find it amazing that the families of victims didn't beat the crap out of criminal defense lawyers more often.

"I'm very sorry for your loss."

"You don't have to be," she said.

"I am. Sincerely."

"No, you don't understand. Sashi isn't dead."

Jack did a double take. "What?"

"My daughter is *alive*."

"Where is she?"

"I don't know. But Sashi is alive. I *know* she's alive. And I need you people to help me prove it, before they execute this man for killing her."

"I don't actually—" Jack stopped himself.

"You don't what?"

Jack was about to say that he didn't actually work for the

Institute, which was exactly what he'd told Andie when he'd promised that he wasn't going back to death-penalty work. But he'd checked that line at the door.

"I don't know your name," said Jack.

"Debra. Debra Burgette."

"Come inside, Debra. We should talk."

CHAPTER 2

Jack led Debra to the kitchen, talking as they walked. "I honestly don't know anything about Dylan Reeves' case," he said. "But I assume the police never recovered a body, if you're telling me that Sashi is alive."

"That's right," said Debra. "When the prosecutor told me they were bringing murder charges against Dylan Reeves, I was frankly pretty surprised. I didn't know you could do that before finding the victim."

"It's difficult," said Jack, "especially with all the CSI shows on TV. Jurors want physical evidence, and they want a forensics expert to tell them when, where, and how the victim died. That's why you have cases like Natalee Holloway, the high school girl from Alabama who disappeared in Aruba. Nobody was ever charged. But a missing victim doesn't necessarily mean a conviction is impossible."

Jack offered her a chair and cleared his work from the table. The fridge was buzzing louder than ever, and Jack silenced it with a swift kick. "Sorry about that."

Her gaze swept the room. "No problem. This is about what I expected."

Jack took a seat opposite her. "I don't want to make this painful for you, but can you start at the beginning?"

Debra collected herself, and the look in her eyes was one that Jack had seen before: the desperation and disbelief that attended a mother's recitation of what had happened to her child.

"Sashi went missing on a Friday. I drove her to school, like I did every day. Traffic was backed up much worse than usual. We just were not moving. Sashi was afraid she was going to be late, so she got out about four blocks from the school to walk the rest of the way." She took a breath, then continued. "That was the last time I saw her. That was a terrible mistake."

She was playing that deadly game—blaming herself.

"Would you like some water?" he offered.

"No, I'm okay."

"Did she ever get to the school?"

"No. The administration called around mid-morning and left a message that she was marked absent at homeroom. Unfortunately I didn't get the message till after lunch. I called her cell, but she didn't answer. I drove around to a few places that are within walking distance of the Prep. I was hoping maybe that she wasn't ready for a test or hadn't done her homework, so she decided to cut school. I didn't find her anywhere. Dismissal for the upper classes was at three, and that's when I started calling her friends. Nobody knew where she was. What scared me more is that none of them had even seen her on campus—which told me that she never got there."

"Did Sashi have her own car?"

"No. Sashi was seventeen but never got her driver's license, which was never a problem. We live in Cocoplum. There are jogging paths and cycling lanes that go on for miles."

"I know the area. I used to run along Old Cutler Road."

"Nice and shady, right? Sashi could easily have walked home from school if she wanted to kill an hour. She did like to go for long walks. I spent the whole afternoon checking her favorite places. The coffee shop, the park, the pond down by Matheson Hammock. If something was bothering her, or if she just wanted time alone, it was normal for her to find one of those places and do whatever teenagers do on their phones for hours on end. When it was getting dark, and still no Sashi, I really started to worry."

"Did you call the police?"

"I called my husband. He was on his way home from a business trip. I was pretty unnerved at this point, so he told me to calm down and that he'd handle it."

"So he called the police?"

"No. Sashi had been gone less than twelve hours at this point. This wasn't a four-year-old who had suddenly vanished."

Jack could have told her that seventeen is still a child, that most police departments had protocols that kicked in at four hours or less, and that the archives of the National Center for Missing and Exploited Children were filled with tragic examples of parents who had thought they needed to wait eight hours, twelve hours, twenty-four hours. But like all those other parents, she probably felt guilty enough. "So what did you do?"

"I couldn't just sit still till my husband got home. I took a photo with me and started going door to door in the neighborhood around the school, asking people if they'd seen Sashi. No leads. Around eight o'clock I met Gavin at the house. We searched one more time for any clues as to where she could have gone. We walked the whole neighborhood again, asking if anyone had seen her. We got back around ten o'clock. I went upstairs and checked her room one more time. I found her cell. Sashi *never* left the house without her cell. That's when the panic set in. It was more than twelve hours at this point. I called the police and made an official missing-person report. We enlisted friends to drive around, looking. That lasted all night, no sign of Sashi. By morning, MDPD had thrown everything they had at it: patrol cars, rescue dogs, helicopters, you name it. We had dozens of volunteers combing the neighborhood. The whole community stepped up. We looked everywhere."

"I seem to recall seeing this on the news."

"Yes, by six o'clock Saturday morning the local media was all over the story. For the next twenty-four hours, it was all about finding Sashi. Twenty-four god-awful hours. Then the headline changed."

"What happened?"

"About three a.m., Sunday, the police pulled over Dylan Reeves for driving drunk. They searched his car and found a pair of panties in the backseat. Sashi's DNA was on them. So was Dylan Reeves'."

"So he did sexually assault your daughter?"

"Yes. And for that, he should be in prison. But he didn't kill her, so he doesn't deserve to die."

"How do you know Sashi is alive?"

She hesitated, as if anticipating Jack's reaction. "Sashi calls me."

"What do you mean she *calls* you?"

"This isn't a flaky telepathy kind of thing. Every year on Sashi's birthday I get a phone call. Three times this has happened since she disappeared. It's always from a number I don't recognize. I answer, and no one talks. But I can tell someone is on the line. 'Sashi,' I say, 'is this you? Talk to me, sweetie. Can you say something? Anything? Please, baby girl. Talk to me.'"

Jack felt chills. "And the caller says nothing?"

Debra shook her head. "Not a word. This goes on for about two minutes. Then the call ends."

"When was the last call?"

Debra looked away, her eyes welling. "Two months ago. July twenty-first. Sashi turned twenty."

Jack wanted to offer a tissue, but a paper towel from the kitchen counter was the best he could do. "Have you told the police about this?" he asked.

"Of course," she said.

"Did they check the incoming number?"

"Yes. It's one of those disposable cell phones that are impossible to trace."

"Burn phones," said Jack. "Prepaid minutes, no service contract. A law-enforcement nightmare. Drug dealers love them."

"Do you think it's drug dealers who have my daughter?"

"I wasn't implying that," said Jack.

"Because drug dealers would be a relief, compared to what I have imagined. I keep thinking of those poor girls in Cleveland who were held for years as sex slaves in the basement of that monster—what's his name."

"Ariel Castro," said Jack. He remembered only because in Miami it wasn't easy to forget a sociopath who shared a surname with Fidel.

"Right. I try not to let my mind go there, but I lie awake at night thinking of a sadistic psychopath who lets Sashi call me on her birthday and hear my voice, but he won't let her talk."

Jack had met monsters like that—several, in fact, when he was a young lawyer with the Institute—but he didn't want to feed her fears. "What do the police think?"

"That I'm the victim of a hoax. A sick, cruel hoax by someone who gets off on this sort of thing and calls me on my daughter's birthday. Maybe a friend of Dylan Reeves. Maybe some perv who became obsessed with Sashi by following the murder trial on the Internet."

"But they've ruled out the possibility that it's someone holding Sashi against her will?"

"Yes."

"They don't think there's any chance that Sashi is alive?"

Debra shook her head. "They don't. As far as they're concerned, her killer is on death row and the case is closed. I don't know where else to turn. Except to you."

"You want Dylan Reeves' lawyer to prove in court that Sashi is alive. Is that it?"

"Yes. Unless you want your client to die by lethal injection for a murder that never happened."

Jack took a moment. The cell-phone calls on Sashi's birthdays might well have been a hoax. This whole thing could turn out to be a sad case of hope without end and a mother without closure. But, sitting across the table from the victim's mother in that old kitchen with the cranky refrigerator and the faded photograph of Bobby Kennedy on the wall—in Neil's "conference room"—Jack could only respond as his mentor would have wanted.

"I'll do what I can," he said. "But time is not on our side."

CHAPTER 3

Jack reached Hannah on her cell and caught up with her at a gas station on Coral Way.

The Freedom legal team had rolled out of the driveway two hours earlier, but Hannah was only ten minutes away. The "Neil-Mobile"—a beat-up Chevy van that Hannah's father had purchased when Gerald Ford was president—had broken down before they'd even reached the expressway.

"It's karma that the van went kaput and we're still here," said Hannah. "This is a huge break in the case."

She and Jack were standing in the garage. Neil's old van was high on the hydraulic lift, and the mechanic underneath was tightening the bolts on a new muffler. The old one had fallen off somewhere between the gas station and the Miami River.

"It could be," said Jack.

"*Could be?* Come on. We have the victim's mother saying that her daughter is alive. I'll do the legal research, but there has to be a judge out there who will say that's grounds for a stay of execution."

Jack recalled a night long ago, in the governor's mansion, when his father had seemed unmoved by Jack's insistence that an innocent man was about to be executed.

"It's the totality of the evidence that matters," he'd said. "I need to review the record. Then I'll decide."

Hannah glanced up at the Neil-Mobile. They had packed up

the record in the case, including the trial transcripts, for the meetings with their clients. The "totality of the evidence" was in cardboard evidence boxes inside the van.

"How much longer on that muffler?" Hannah asked the mechanic.

"Almost done," he said.

"That's what he told me an hour ago," she said under her breath.

"I can wait," said Jack.

"Not everything you need to know is in the printed transcript, anyway," said Hannah. "The prosecutor had a really strong rapport with the jurors, and she did a very effective job of convincing them that Reeves was the last person to see Sashi Burgette alive. Her mother testified that she drove Sashi to school, but Sashi got out of the car about four blocks from campus and was going to walk the rest of the way. She never made it, and the defense couldn't produce a single witness who had laid eyes on Sashi after that. Reeves' semen was still wet when the police found Sashi's panties in the back of his car early Sunday morning."

"I presume Reeves didn't testify in his own defense."

"Not a chance. Trial counsel advised against it. It would have been one thing if Reeves had wanted to take the stand and deny that he'd killed Sashi. But he also wanted to deny that he'd sexually assaulted her. There was no way the jury was going to believe that this was consensual sex and not a sexual assault. If he was lying about the rape, they surely would've thought he was lying about the murder as well. The best strategy was not to testify."

"Did you challenge the sexual assault conviction on appeal?"

"No. You know the drill. We're trying to stop an execution, not get a man elected to Congress. The evidence of sexual assault here is pretty solid."

"Even without a body?" asked Jack.

"The prosecutor put a psychiatrist on the witness stand. Sashi had psychological issues and an aversion to physical intimacy of any kind. She didn't even like to be hugged by her own parents. The very notion that she would engage in consensual sex with a convicted felon and lifelong loser like Dylan Reeves was something no jury would believe."

"Interesting," said Jack. "Her mother didn't mention any psychological issues to me."

"All done," said the mechanic. He punched the button, the hydraulic lift hissed, and the van began its descent.

Eve walked up behind Hannah, her unlit pipe clenched in her teeth. "It's good to have you back defending the guilty, Jack."

Jack knew she was kidding—sort of. "Would be nice if this one's innocent. But remember: even if he is, this is a onetime engagement for me."

"We understand," said Hannah.

Four tires simultaneously kissed the concrete floor, and the van clunked as it settled into equilibrium. "You need new shock absorbers," said the mechanic. "A new set of tires, too."

"We need new everything," said Hannah. "Just a muffler today, thank you."

The mechanic wiped his hands on his coveralls, then stepped away to write up the invoice. Another mechanic backed the van out of the garage, and Eve followed. Hannah hung back with Jack for a moment.

"I don't want to beat this point to death," said Jack, "but my conversation with Debra Burgette doesn't change the arrangement I made with you and your mother. I promised Andie that I was just subleasing space from the Freedom Institute to help you guys out financially."

"So . . . but for Andie, you would be back at the Freedom Institute?" asked Hannah.

"I didn't say that. Andie would never come out and tell me what to do with my career. This just isn't my season in life to go back to capital cases."

"Is it about the money?"

"Not entirely. But, hey, money matters. It's taken me a long time, and finally I've figured out how to make a decent living as a sole practitioner. Good thing, too. I'm about to start a family. You said it yourself: the Freedom Institute can barely pay its electric bill."

"Dad worked at the Freedom Institute my entire life. I turned out okay. Smith College. Harvard Law. A year of Barnyard."

"You mean Barnard?"

"No. Barnyard. Mom insisted that I work on a kibbutz in Israel after college. I raised chickens for a year."

They shared a smile. "I loved your father, and your mom is an amazing woman. But the Freedom Institute was *their* life, Hannah. Andie and I are in agreement about this. I've worked long and hard to build a successful practice, and I can't just give it all up."

"Okay. I respect that. But I need to know where you and I stand in the short term. Are you in this case, or are you out?"

"Right now, let's just say I'm *interested* in this case. But only because I was the guy who answered the door when the victim's mother said there was no homicide."

"Got it, chief."

"Good."

Hannah started toward the van. "Come on," she said. "I want you to take a good look at the evidence. In the interest of full disclosure, box nine is probably the best place for you to start."

"What's in box nine?" he asked.

Hannah's eyeglasses darkened as she stepped out of the garage and into the sunlight. "Your innocent client's confession," she said.

CHAPTER 4

Naturally, box 9 in the capital case of *State of Florida v. Dylan Reeves* was buried at the bottom of the pyramid of boxes and suitcases in the back of the Neil-Mobile. The day had turned hot and muggy, a typical weather pattern that made September Jack's least favorite month in south Florida. As the rest of the country enjoyed crisp autumn days and cool nights, Miami was at the peak of the hurricane season and the daily onslaught of tropical waves of sticky air. Jack's shirt was soaked with sweat by the time he finished unloading and reloading the van. He carried the evidence box to his car, and Hannah rode with him back to the Freedom Institute. Jack cranked the AC to high, and the cold blast from the dashboard felt good. The relief was short-lived, however. The office was like an oven.

"To the kitchen," said Jack. "It's cooler in there."

"Not really," said Hannah.

"Watch and learn."

He placed the evidence box on the kitchen table, opened the refrigerator, and basked in the chilly air. "Ahhh."

Hannah shot him a look of playful disapproval. "Surely my father didn't teach you that energy-inefficient trick."

"No," said Jack. "In fact, this was the one offense he thought worthy of capital punishment."

Hannah powered up her laptop and inserted the DVD from box 9. "MDPD homicide interrogated Reeves for about seven hours," she said. "All of it was video recorded. This three-minute segment is from the very end. It was, by far, the most powerful evidence presented at trial."

Jack pulled up a chair. Hannah cued up the video and hit PLAY. The case caption and an exhibit number appeared on the screen. The image flickered, and the video followed. It was the typical arrangement. A windowless room. Bright fluorescent lights. A suspect seated on one side of a rectangular table. A seasoned detective seated on the other side. Another detective was standing, his palms on the tabletop, his body language a bit more intimidating than his partner's. Jack assumed he was the "bad cop" in this tag team.

Hannah hit PAUSE, freezing the image on the screen. "Note the time: ten-fourteen a.m. Dylan Reeves is six feet tall and two hundred pounds. His blood alcohol content was three times the legal limit when the police pulled him over at three a.m."

"So, seven hours later, he's still legally drunk."

"Definitely," said Hannah. She hit PLAY again and turned up the volume. "Listen."

Jack focused, taking in the video as well as the audio. Reeves' BAC may have been over the legal limit, but the guy looked more hungover than drunk. His hair was a mess. He needed a shave. It required far more energy than he could muster to keep his chin off his chest. He was sinking in the hardwood chair, and his body language was screaming, *"I just want to go to bed."* He blinked slowly, and it took a verbal cue from the detective to get him to reopen his eyes.

"Dylan," said the detective. "Dylan Reeves."

"Huh?"

"You hungry?"

"Yeah."

"Corrigan here is gonna make a run to the drive-thru. You want something? How about some pancakes?"

"Okay."

"Some OJ? Fresh-squeezed?"

"Sure."

"Comin' right up, son. All we gotta do is wrap this up, and we can all have some breakfast. How's that sound?"

"Good."

The detective leaned closer, looking Reeves in the eye. "Did you hurt Sashi Burgette? You can tell us."

"No."

"It's okay. It'll be better if you tell us the truth."

"I didn't hurt her."

The detective shook his head. "I want to believe you, Dylan. I really do. But I know you're lying to me."

"I didn't hurt no one."

"A seventeen-year-old girl doesn't just drop her panties in the backseat of your car and then vanish. Poof."

"I didn't know she was seventeen."

"I'm sure you didn't. No one is saying that's your fault. None of this is your fault. We just need to know what happened. Tell me what happened to Sashi."

"For the hundredth time," he said, groaning. "I gave her a ride, and we had sex."

"She was a virgin, you know. A seventeen-year-old virgin."

Reeves sat up. His shoulders started to heave. Then his head rolled back, and his whole body trembled. He nearly fell off his chair but managed to right himself.

He was laughing.

"What's so funny?" the detective asked.

The laughter continued. The detectives watched in silence, but Reeves had lost all self-control.

"You think this is a joke, son?"

Reeves struggled to pull himself together. The laughter turned to wheezing, and in another minute he could breathe again. His interrogator was staring from across the table, but Reeves met his stare. He suddenly seemed sober, or at least alert.

"A virgin, huh?" asked Reeves.

"That's right. Seventeen years old."

He nodded slowly, and even though the camera wasn't positioned to catch a close-up, the smugness came across in the video. "Do you think God will forgive me?" he asked, his voice dripping with sarcasm.

The detective answered in a deep, serious tone. "He will if you ask him to. But you gotta ask him, son."

Reeves sank in his chair. The detective's words and skillful delivery were having a visible effect. Reeves' smugness slowly drained away.

"I understand your daddy was a preacher. Is that right, Dylan?"

The kill shot. It was as if a cold wind had just blown through the interrogation room, palpable even as Jack watched on video. Clearly, Reeves had finally given the seasoned detective the opening he'd been waiting for, the chance to play that ace he'd been holding for seven hours.

" 'Therefore, confess your sins to one another and pray for one another, that you may be healed.' You know that scripture?"

Reeves' eyes closed, but he didn't answer.

The detective let him stew another minute, then continued in the same preacher-like tone. "Do you need to be healed, Dylan?"

The question hung in the air for several seconds, and Reeves seemed to shrink in the silence.

"You do need it," the detective said gently. "You need forgiveness. Don't you, son?"

Reeves didn't move. Thirty seconds passed. Then, finally, in slow but discernible fashion, he lowered his chin, raised it, and then lowered it again.

A nod.

The video ended. Hannah hit STOP. The screen went black.

Jack had been watching so closely that he was literally on the edge of his chair. He settled back and took a deep breath.

"What do you think?" asked Hannah.

Jack didn't answer right away. He looked off in the middle distance, and then his gaze drifted back to Hannah.

"I think we all need forgiveness," he said.

CHAPTER 5

Jack left the Freedom Institute around six and headed home. The first stop was Johnson Firearms in midtown, where he purchased Andie's gun-cleaning mat. The next stop was supposed to be the Food Mart for potato chips and ice cream. A call from Debra Burgette sidetracked him.

"Can you meet me at the Travelodge on U.S. 1? It's right across from the University of Miami."

Jack had driven past it a million times, but he'd never been there. "Right now?"

"Yes. It's important."

"What is it?"

"Just come. I need you to see something."

Jack had spent all afternoon reading the trial transcript from *State v. Dylan Reeves*, and he had plenty of questions for Debra. He would have preferred to check in with Andie first, but there was urgency in Debra's voice; and once a death warrant was signed, there was no such thing as moving too fast, even if the execution date was still thirty days away.

"I can be there in twenty minutes," he said.

He got there in ten. Debra was waiting for him in the lobby. "You want to grab a coffee and talk?" asked Jack.

"No," she said, taking him by the arm. "Follow me."

Her voice had that same urgency that Jack had detected on the phone, but the look in her eyes was not a worried one. It bordered on excitement. She led him down the long hallway on the ground floor, past the business center and several meeting rooms. They stopped at a set of double doors, which were closed. It was the entrance to "Ballroom B."

"I've been working on this all day," she said as she pulled open the door.

Jack stepped inside and stopped. It was small for a "ballroom," more suitable for a Rotary Club lunch than, say, a wedding reception. Instead of the typical round dinner tables with white table cloths, however, Debra had brought in a dozen rectangular folding tables. Leaflets, flyers, and posters, each with a yellow ribbon of hope fastened to it, were spread out across the tables. Jack picked up one of the flyers. It wasn't the photograph that he'd seen in the case file earlier that afternoon, but it was the same beautiful seventeen-year-old brunette with the flawless olive skin and mysterious dark eyes. The identical three-word message was on the flyers, the posters, and the banner that hung on the wall behind the tables:

FIND SASHI BURGETTE

"We'll put laptop computers over there," said Debra, indicating. "Volunteers can work social media, send e-mail blasts—all the virtual-world stuff. That table by the door with the cash box is for people who want to contribute to the Find Sashi reward fund. And on those tables in the back we can put out coffee and snacks. Bagels and such in the morning. Maybe some finger sandwiches in the afternoon. If folks are kind enough to donate their time, the least you can do is feed them."

Jack was speechless. Of course he felt sorry for a woman who'd lost her daughter, but he couldn't hide his concern.

"Debra, is this all your idea?"

"Not entirely. I have you to thank."

"Me?"

"Yes, *you*. For three years, no one would help me, Jack. Not the police, not my church, not even my husband. Ex-husband. Gavin and I are divorced now. Did I mention that?"

"No. You didn't."

She breathed in and out, her gaze sweeping the room. "I feel like I'm forgetting something. There's just so much to think about."

"Debra, is anyone coming?"

"Yes, of course. I e-mailed at least a hundred people. I was hoping the room would be buzzing when you got here. But traffic is so bad this time of day. I'm sure they're coming, though. They'll be here. It's the traffic."

Jack didn't mention that his trip from midtown had taken just half the time he'd estimated.

"I invited the local news stations, too," said Debra.

"They're coming?"

"Yes."

"Did they say they would come?"

"Well, no. But I left a message on the voice mail. I'm sure they're coming. Darn traffic."

They stood in silence—awkward silence. Then the ballroom door opened.

"Ah, see! They're here," said Debra. She hurried to the door.

Jack stayed where he was. A woman about half Debra's age entered. Debra took her by the hand and led her straight to Jack. She was a younger version of Debra, the same strawberry-blond hair, blue eyes, and high cheekbones.

"This is my daughter Aquinnah," said Debra.

She shook Jack's hand and smiled politely, but there was a hint of embarrassment in her expression. "Very nice to meet you."

"Aquinnah is premed at Barry University."

"Impressive," said Jack.

"Not really," said Aquinnah.

"Don't be modest," said Debra.

"It will be impressive if I pass organic chemistry."

Debra smiled awkwardly, as if not sure what to do with that remark. "Did you bring any volunteers with you?"

"No, Mom. Just me."

"Well, that's a start. Let's see. Why don't you sit over there at the ribbon table. I tied about twenty already, but they all need safety pins so folks can fasten them to their lapels."

"Sure thing," said Aquinnah. She stepped away, catching Jack's eye as she passed behind her mother. Aquinnah's expression didn't exactly say "crazy," but it was close.

"How old is Aquinnah?" asked Jack.

"Twenty. Same as Sashi."

Jack glanced again at Sashi's photo on the flyer. Aquinnah was by no means unattractive, but Sashi was definitely the prettier one, even without a smile.

"They don't really look alike. Are they fraternal twins?"

"No, no. Sashi is adopted. Did I not mention that?"

"No. You didn't."

"Not that it matters. I love both my girls equally. We adopted Sashi right before her fourteenth birthday, and her younger brother, Alexander, when he was two—almost three. They're from Chechnya. Gavin wanted a boy, and if it had been up to him, the adoption would have gone through that way. But how could anyone break up a brother and sister? *I* sure couldn't."

Debra fell quiet. The energy she'd radiated since meeting Jack in the lobby was suddenly gone.

"Are you okay?" asked Jack.

"Funny," she said. "I always felt as though we had done a good thing by adopting Sashi. You know, in her country they kick the kids out of foster care at age sixteen. Chances are she would have ended up a prostitute or a drug addict. We gave her a . . . ," she said, swallowing her words, "a better life."

Debra's hands started to tremble. Jack didn't know what to say. He didn't want to give false hope. "You did the right thing."

"Yes," she said, sniffing back tears. "It was the right thing. And this time it is all going to work out. I know it is. And I am so grateful to you, Jack. So, so grateful."

"Debra, I—"

She took a quick step closer, squeezed his hand, and kissed him on the cheek. "Thank you."

She stepped away, and Jack took a breath. Their eyes met for a moment, and Jack saw a hint of gratitude in Debra's. But it was mostly desperation.

"You're welcome," was all he could say.

CHAPTER 6

Jack was halfway home, standing at the checkout counter with a bag of potato chips and a carton of triple fudge swirl ice cream, when Andie phoned him.

"Honey, Dr. Starkey wants me to meet her at the hospital."

Jack gripped his cell but dropped everything else, including his wallet, as he ran for the exit. The automatic doors parted on his way out.

"Sir, your wallet!" the bag boy shouted.

He did a quick one-eighty, but the doors closed suddenly. He slammed into the glass, his forehead taking the brunt of the beating. "Ow, shit!"

"That's gonna leave a mark," the bag boy said.

Jack checked for blood. There was none. He thanked the bag boy for the wallet and groceries and ran to his car. Andie was still on the line.

"What was that noise?" she asked.

"Nothing. Is the baby coming?"

"No, it's my blood pressure. It's too high."

Jack jumped into the driver's seat and started the engine. "I'll pick you up."

"The ambulance is on the way."

"Ambulance?"

"Dr. Starkey says it's only a precaution. Just meet us in the ER."

"Okay. I'll drive straight there."

It took Jack forty minutes to reach the hospital, thanks to an accident on the Dolphin Expressway. The ice cream was a total loss, so
he ditched it in the trash receptacle outside the ER entrance, wiping
his hands on his pants as he passed through the automated doors to
the waiting room. It was packed. The only available seat was the one
next to an old woman holding a plastic bucket that reeked of vomit.
A tattooed biker with road rash on his bulging arms was stretched
across three seats, but no one seemed inclined to make him share.
Jack saw no sign of Andie, but priority for a pregnant woman who
passed the time by cleaning her semiautomatic pistol would have
made sense, even if she hadn't come in by ambulance. Jack hurried
past the mayhem and went straight to the intake desk.

"I'm looking for my wife. Andrea Henning. She's very pregnant and came in by ambulance."

"What happened to you?" the nurse asked.

"Nothing. I'm trying to find my wife."

"Looks like you've got a big purple mango stuck to your forehead."

"I banged my head."

"When?"

"About an hour ago."

"Well, you came to the right place. We specialize in head
trauma."

"I'm just trying to find my wife. This isn't about me."

"It is now. Get in the wheelchair."

"No, you don't understand, I—"

"It's protocol. If you black out and hit the floor, I'll lose my
job. So get in the wheelchair, get some ice on that knot, and I'll
take you to your wife. Or go sit out in the waiting room next to
the woman with the bucketful of vomit and wait your turn. The
choice is yours."

Jack settled into the chair, and the nurse pushed.

"Smart move. By the way, your wife is one of the most beautiful pregnant women I've ever seen."

"Thank you. And she's probably the only one whose husband ended up in a wheelchair."

"No, sir," she said with a chuckle. "Not by a long shot."

They made a quick stop at the nurses' station and entered the ER through the pneumatic doors. Jack rolled up to patient bay number 3, peeked out from under the ice pack on his forehead, and saw Andie lying on a gurney. She was connected to an IV and a blood-pressure cuff, but she looked more concerned about Jack.

"I'm okay," he said, and that was all she needed to hear. It was as if the emotional logjam had broken. The heartbreak of two previous miscarriages, the stress of a difficult pregnancy, a week of bed rest, and the ambulance ride to the hospital—all of it found release in laughter. Uncontrollable laughter. If she laughed any harder, she would have needed a catheter.

The doctor intervened. "Sir, I can't get the patient's blood pressure under control if she has the giggles. You're going to have to leave."

Jack could only assume that he looked even more ridiculous than he felt. "I'll wait in the hallway," he said, and wheeled himself out.

Around ten o'clock Andie's doctor decided that she should be admitted to the hospital and stay the night "for observation." Jack asked why. The doctor told him. Jack didn't like the answer. He ditched the wheelchair and went up to room 311 for a moment alone with Andie.

"Hi," he said as he entered the room.

Andie was awake and semireclined in the adjustable bed. "Hey, Schleprock," she said with a warm smile.

It was a private room, and even though the door remained open, the hallways had quieted down for the night. Soft lighting gave Andie's hair a bluish-black sheen. A visit to the ER had taken some of the sparkle out of her eyes, but the supervisory nurse had been right on the money: she was beautiful. Jack leaned over the bed rail and kissed her. Only then did he notice that there were two heart monitors on the other side of the bed. It made him happy and concerned at the same time.

"Everything looks good with the baby," she said.

"I heard."

"What else did you hear?"

"That they finally got you to stop laughing."

She smiled again, and then it faded. "Seriously. Did Dr. Starkey mention the increased protein levels?"

"She did." And then some. Jack had shifted into cross-examination mode to get details. Preeclampsia can cause fetal complications: low birth weight, premature birth, and, yes, Mr. Swyteck, even stillbirth. It can affect the mother's kidneys, liver, and brain. When preeclampsia causes seizures, the condition is known as eclampsia. Jack didn't have to ask: he knew eclampsia could be fatal for the mother.

Andie reached over the rail and took his hand. "Jack, I'm sure your mind is running wild."

"No, it's not."

"It must be. Let's not ignore the elephant in the room. Your mother died from eclampsia. But just because I have preeclampsia doesn't mean it will develop into eclampsia."

"You're right."

"And even if the condition does get worse, Dr. Starkey is on top of it."

"You're right again."

"Medicine has come a long way since you were a baby and your mother got eclampsia."

"You're absolutely right."

"Will you stop saying I'm right?"

"Sorry." He breathed in and out. "What's the next step?"

"They'll do urine tests over the next twenty-four hours to determine how severe my condition is. We'll know more then."

"So yours could be a mild case?"

"Could be. They'll run tests on my liver and kidneys. They'll make sure the placenta is doing what it's supposed to do. The good news is that all this goes away when the baby is born."

"That is good news," said Jack.

"So don't be a doggy downer, okay? I don't want to turn the countdown to what should be the happiest day of our lives into a pity party."

"You got it."

"Oh, and I don't think we should tell your father about this. Don't you agree?"

It was the Swyteck way, actually, to keep quiet about such things. Never had Jack and his father even nibbled around the edge of a conversation about what it had been like for him to bring his newborn son home from the hospital. Alone.

"I agree," said Jack. "He and Agnes are in North Carolina till after Columbus Day and the Woolly Worm Festival anyway."

"And the same goes for your grandmother. She was lighting three candles a day and praying to Saint Anne for a healthy baby even before I started peeing on a stick."

"Abuela definitely doesn't need to know."

"Oh, and we probably shouldn't mention it to—"

"Honey, we'll keep this between us. How's that for a plan?"

She nodded and smiled weakly. Then she fell quiet, and Jack didn't feel the need to make her talk.

"I'm really tired," she said.

"I'm not surprised."

"I'm going to fall asleep soon."

Jack looked around the room. The armchair in the corner looked reasonably comfortable. "I'll stay here till you do."

"I'd like that," she said.

"I love you," he whispered, but her eyes were already closed. "And I'll be here when you wake up."

Jack felt a strange vibration in his pocket. His eyes blinked open, and slowly he realized that he was still in Andie's hospital room. He'd fallen asleep in the armchair. He pulled his cell from his pocket. It was 5:20 a.m., and Hannah was calling from the Freedom Institute. Andie was asleep, so he stepped into the hall.

"Good morning, chief," said Hannah.

Jack massaged the bump on his forehead. "Do you know what time it is?"

"Sorry, but we've been working all night on Dylan Reeves' emergency motion for stay of execution. The plan is to file at nine a.m. sharp. Do you want to read it first?"

The nursing station was in a shift change. Jack walked down the hall to a quieter place. "Sure. E-mail me the latest draft."

"Okay. I got a question for you, though. Last we talked, we were going to focus on procedural issues and our challenge to the so-called confession. You told us to downplay the argument that Sashi is still alive."

"I did."

"Well, have you seen today's *Miami Tribune*?"

"No. Have you?"

"I have a Google alert for Dylan Reeves. There's an article that just posted on its Web edition. It quotes you."

"What?"

"I got it right here. '*Lawyer Says Death Row Inmate Faces Execution for Murder That Never Happened.*'"

"I never spoke to anyone," said Jack. "Are you sure they're talking about me?"

"Yeah. I'll read it to you. Blah, blah, blah. Here we go. 'Twenty-eight-year-old Dylan Reeves has denied any involvement in the death or disappearance of Sashi Burgette since he was convicted of first-degree murder and sentenced to die by lethal injection. His lawyer, Miami attorney Jack Swyteck, now takes that argument one step further. The defense has uncovered significant new evidence that Sashi Burgette is still alive, Swyteck said in a press release.'"

"I didn't issue a press release. Did you?"

"No, Jack. I would never do that without your approval."

"Then who—" he started to say, but he stopped himself.

"I guess the possibilities are pretty limited, aren't they?"

Jack recalled his talk with Debra at the "Find Sashi" headquarters, and her mention of phone calls to the local media. "Unpleasant as it may be, I need to have a firm talk with Sashi's mother."

CHAPTER 7

Jack called Debra Burgette. She didn't answer. Either she knew he was angry and she was avoiding him, or she was still in bed, like most of Miami. He drove home to shower and change clothes.

The sun emerged from the Atlantic as he cruised across the causeway to Key Biscayne. Andie had initially resisted moving into his "bachelor pad," but she came around. Jack had a sweetheart lease on waterfront property, one of the original "Mackle houses" that were built mostly for World War II veterans who were brave enough to live in what was, at the time, little more than a mosquito-infested swamp. The house sold for $12,000 in 1955, and if Jack managed to hit the lottery before his lease expired, he and Andie could purchase it for about seven million. If not, the house was theirs to enjoy for another two years. It was basically a two-bedroom concrete shoe box, but it came with a dock. Dozens of Jack's friends begged to keep a boat there. Only one got his wish.

Theo Knight was Jack's best friend, bartender, therapist, confidant, and sometime investigator. He was also a former client, a onetime gangbanger who easily could have ended up dead on the streets of Overtown or Liberty City. Instead, he landed on death row for a murder he didn't commit. Jack literally saved his life. With his civil settlement from the state, Theo went on to open his own tavern—Sparky's he'd called it, a play on words and double-barreled flip of the bird to "Old Sparky," the nickname for the electric chair he'd escaped. Sparky's had done well enough to get him a second bar, and even a fishing boat. Theo was hosing down his gear in Jack's backyard as Jack pulled into the driveway.

"Got six beautiful dolphin," said Theo.

Jack enjoyed fishing, but it had been a very long time since he'd stayed out all night to bring home a half dozen fish. "Nice," he said.

"You look like hell. Did Andie finally come to her senses and kick you out last night?"

"No. She went into the hospital."

Theo dropped the hose, and Jack filled him in. They both needed coffee, so the conversation moved inside to the kitchen. Theo wasn't much help on medical matters related to pregnancy. He was a pretty quick study, however, when it came to Debra Burgette.

"The woman sounds fucked up."

Jack wasn't entirely comfortable with the diagnosis. "She's been through a lot."

"She's fucked up."

"So, you think I shouldn't get involved?"

"You *should*, if there's a chance this Dylan Reeves ain't guilty. Just know the bitch is crazy."

"She isn't crazy."

"That's what you said about your first wife."

He had a point.

Theo poured himself more coffee. "Let me shower off the fish smell and we can go talk to her. I'll tell you what I really think."

"It's pretty clear what you really think."

"Maybe I'll change my mind."

"Maybe pigs will fly."

"Maybe the sick son of a bitch who really made Sashi Burgette disappear has his eye on another teenage girl."

Jack bristled. "That's not funny."

"Nothing funny about an innocent man on death row."

Jack stared right back at him over the top of his coffee cup. For a moment, he was looking into the eyes of that teenage boy he'd met through the Freedom Institute, Florida's youngest inmate on death row.

"All right," said Jack. "You can shower in the guest room. Then we'll go see Debra."

They drove south against rush-hour traffic toward Cocoplum, one of south Florida's tony waterfront communities.

It was a breezy ride through Coconut Grove until they reached Cartagena Circle, a busy roundabout that was the Coral Gables version of the vehicular insanity surrounding the Arc de Triomphe. Traffic entered from multiple directions, almost no one understood the right-of-way rules, and even the ones who did were too busy texting to avoid a collision. Fortunately, it wasn't Saturday morning, when the Circle—*the* meeting place for hundreds of weekend joggers and cyclists— transformed into the world's greatest concentration of bulging blobs of jelly who had absolutely no business wearing form-fitting clothing.

"Bear left," said Theo.

"Where do you think we are, London?"

Jack followed the circle counterclockwise in the shadow of sprawling banyan trees, exiting at the twin royal palms that marked the gated entrance to the Cocoplum community. A security guard checked them in and let them pass. The Burgettes' address was programmed into Jack's GPS, which guided them past one Mediterranean-style mansion after another. Jack stopped when the mechanical voice said, "You have arrived." It was a pink tri-level house with arched windows, a barrel tile roof, and a fountain in the front yard. A manicured hedge with purple cocoplum berries lined the horseshoe driveway, which was empty—no sign of Debra's Mercedes. Jack parked on the street. He and Theo climbed the steps to the front door, rang the doorbell, and waited. No answer.

"Well, this was a waste of time," said Jack.

"Wait. Did you hear that?"

"Hear what?"

"Inside. Screaming."

"What—"

"Shhh. There it is again: *'There's a black man at the door, there's a black man at the door!'*"

"No comment," said Jack as he started down the stairs. The Burgettes' neighbor happened to be at the curb, picking up his morning newspaper, so Jack walked over and struck up a conversation. Theo followed.

"Excuse me. Is this the Burgette residence?"

The man stopped and looked Jack over. He looked Theo over, too—twice. "Who's asking?"

Jack introduced himself, as well as Theo—"my assistant"— and handed the man a business card. He was a balding, overweight man who confirmed his middle age by holding Jack's card as far away as possible to read it.

"Are you related to former governor Harry Swyteck?"

"He's my father."

He returned Jack's card. "Never did like that guy. Sorry."

"Well, that's politics."

"At least he didn't sign your death warrant," added Theo.

Jack left that one alone, focusing on the neighbor. "Debra Burgette asked me to take a fresh look into the disappearance of her daughter."

He shook his head. "Poor woman. Yesterday she gave me a stack of 'Find Sashi' flyers to distribute. How long has it been now? Three years? Long time to be in denial."

"Did you know Sashi?"

"Not really. The other girl—Aquinnah—I knew since she was

born. Sashi came much later. Adopted. Pretty girl. Real pretty. But not an easy kid to get to know."

"Because of the language barrier?"

"That's what I thought it was at first. She and her little brother came from Russia."

"Chechnya," said Jack.

"Right. But, no, it wasn't a language problem. Debra had those kids in private school, English-immersion classes, the whole bit. Alexander's a nice kid. Really a good boy. But Sashi. She . . ."

"What?"

"She had a screw loose. I don't know how else to say it."

"How do you mean?" asked Jack.

"Well, if you followed any of the news coverage of Sashi's disappearance, you would think it was the first time her parents had no idea where she was."

"You're saying that's not the case?"

"Not even close. Sashi must have run away from home a half dozen times before disappearing for good. Maybe more."

"I wasn't aware of that," said Jack.

"Oh, yeah. There was a stretch when Debra and Gavin were knocking on my door every other week, asking if I'd seen Sashi. They had a real problem on their hands."

"It sounds like it."

"Yeah. Sad situation. Anyway, I have to get to work. Nice talking with you fellas. Good luck with whatever it is that Debra wants from you." He turned and walked away.

Jack and Theo started toward their car.

"That was interesting," said Theo.

"Yeah. Also interesting that I read the entire transcript of Dylan Reeves' trial. I didn't see a single mention of any of those other times Sashi ran away from home."

"Maybe the judge kept it out."

"And normally I would agree with that. It smacks of victim assassination. But this is a murder case, and the body was never recovered."

"What difference does that make?"

"The prosecution has to prove that a homicide was committed. A jury might not jump to the conclusion that Sashi is actually dead if they know she ran away from home a half dozen times before."

"So you're saying Sashi might be alive."

"I'm saying . . ."

Theo finished the thought for him. "Maybe what crazy Debra is saying isn't so crazy. That's what you're saying."

Jack considered it. "Yeah," he said finally. "I guess I am."

CHAPTER 8

Breakfast was by far the best thing about her motel, but Debra wasn't hungry.

"Just coffee," she told the waitress. She was alone in a booth. A tall, cylinder-shaped pie display spun round and round behind her.

"The buffet looks awfully good today," the waitress said as she filled Debra's cup.

Debra didn't doubt it. Virtually every customer in the restaurant was in line at the omelet station.

"Coffee is all I need, thank you."

The waitress wrote up the check and tossed it on the table. "No rush, sweetie. Whenever you're ready."

It had been a lonely night at the Find Sashi command center. The high point had been Jack's visit. Aquinnah stayed for a couple of hours, but she turned out to be part of an ambush. Debra's two closest girlfriends had shown up, and, together with Aquinnah, the threesome mounted an "intervention" of sorts. It wasn't anything Debra hadn't heard before. More talk about "closure" and the need for Debra to find it. As if it were any other woman's business.

Debra glanced across the restaurant. Aquinnah was haggling with the motel manager. She was trying to get a refund of Debra's deposit on the ballroom. Debra had reserved it for two weeks. Debra could only imagine what, in the name of negotiating strategy, Aquinnah was saying to the manager about her "poor mother."

Hopefully, it was kinder than the words she had screamed at Debra on her way out of the ballroom last night.

"Warm up your cup for you there, sweetie?" asked the waitress.

"Yes, thank you."

The waitress finished the pour and stepped away. Debra stared down into her cup. She couldn't be too angry at Aquinnah. For nearly thirteen years, her life had been perfect. An only child. Mommy's best girlfriend. Daddy's princess.

And then everything changed.

T he patter of Aquinnah's bare feet filled the master bedroom, and Debra was suddenly wide awake. Aquinnah jumped into the bed and tucked herself beneath the covers at her mother's side. Her tiny voice shook, and she sounded much younger than a girl who was just two weeks shy of becoming a teenager.

"Mommy, I'm scared."

Debra pulled her close. It was like old times, when Aquinnah would stay up to watch an age-inappropriate movie that would keep her eyes open all night.

"What's wrong, baby? Did you have a bad dream?"

Gavin grumbled, half-asleep. Then he rolled over to the far edge of the king-size mattress.

"No," said Aquinnah, trying to whisper, but she was too shaken to keep her voice low. "It's Sashi. She scares me, Mommy."

"Oh, honey. There's nothing to be scared of."

"For *you* there isn't. You get to sleep in here next to Daddy. I'm at the other end of the hall. You say we have separate rooms, but we really don't. She can walk right through the bathroom and get into mine."

Debra had put Sashi in one of the adjoining bedrooms of the

"Jack and Jill" suite. "Sashi is not going to come in your room, Aquinnah."

"Yeah, she *does*. She waits till she thinks I'm asleep. Then she opens the door a little crack, and she looks at me."

"Aquinnah, you are imagining things."

"I'm not making this up, Mommy!"

Gavin grumbled again, then propped up on his elbow. "I have to be at the airport in four hours. Can I get some peace and quiet, please?"

"Sorry, Gavin," said Debra, and then she gave her daughter the shush sign.

Aquinnah lowered her voice, but it was filled with no less urgency. "Have you seen what Sashi does when she comes into a room? Her eyes are so weird, Mommy. It's like . . . like a cat."

"She's getting used to us," said Debra. "This is all new to her."

"And she walks around naked. She won't wear the pajamas you bought her."

"When her English gets better she can tell us what she likes."

"Just because she doesn't like them doesn't mean she has to rip them to pieces."

"She didn't rip them up."

"Yes, she did, Mommy! And no offense, but she *smells* bad."

"Be nice, Aquinnah. Sashi isn't used to bathing every day. We'll fix that."

Gavin was awake again. "That's it. Aquinnah, get back to your room."

"No, no, no, please, Daddy. Let me stay, please, please. I'll be quiet. I won't make another sound."

Gavin fell back onto his pillow. "All right. But that's it: no more warnings."

Aquinnah nuzzled against her mother. Debra put her arm around her and kept her close. The bedroom fell quiet. The air-conditioning cycled on, then off. Aquinnah was sound asleep. Gavin was snoring. Debra was wide awake.

Then she heard a noise from somewhere outside the bedroom—a thud of some sort.

"Gavin, what was that?"

He kept snoring. Debra heard it again. The noise was from downstairs. *The kitchen?*

Debra pried herself away from Aquinnah carefully, so as not to wake her, then slid out of bed and started carefully across the room in the darkness. The door creaked as she opened it, and she winced, fearful that she had woken Gavin. He didn't stir. She took her robe from the wall hook, slipped it on, and stepped into the hallway. Her bare feet glided across the carpet to the stairwell, which was bathed in the yellowish glow of a night-light. She walked softly down the stairs and stopped in the foyer. She definitely heard something again— more of a rustling than a thud this time, and it was definitely coming from the kitchen.

She started down the hallway and stopped. The noise was from the pantry. She crossed the kitchen, stopped at the open pantry door, and switched on the light.

Sashi gasped, but she said nothing. Debra didn't mean to stare, but she was so confused by what she saw that she couldn't help it. Sashi was completely naked. She was holding a pillowcase. It appeared to be stuffed with food.

Debra's heart sank. "Oh, honey. No. You don't have to do that here. You don't have to steal food. Come here, please."

She removed her robe and offered it to her, but Sashi didn't move. Debra stepped toward her and wanted to wrap the girl in her arms, which drew an immediate reaction.

"*Noooo!*" screamed Sashi. She pushed Debra away, hitting her squarely in the chest with both hands, and then ran right past her. It wasn't a little push. It knocked Debra backward and off her feet. She took down an entire shelf of canned goods and other nonperishables as she fell to the floor. She landed on her hip, but managed not to bang her head. She lay there for a moment to get her bearings and make sure she was okay. Her hip bone throbbed as she pushed herself up from the floor.

She took a breath and started to back away from the broken shelf and the mess all over the floor. Then she noticed the stuffed pillowcase that Sashi had left behind. Debra picked it up and looked inside. Several cans of soup. A pack of crackers. A half loaf of bread. And something that sparkled, which made her reach for it.

My earring.

It was half of a pair of tricolor gold earrings that she wore almost every day and kept in a jewelry dish in her bedroom. It had been missing for a week. Debra had thought she'd lost it.

She switched off the kitchen light and walked back to the stairway, taking the stuffed pillowcase and the earring with her. The climb up the stairs took longer than usual, and she knew that her hip was going to be killing her in the morning. She finally reached the top of the stairwell, but rather than go to the master, she went in the opposite direction, toward the Jack and Jill bedrooms. Sashi's door was closed. Debra stood outside it for a moment, but she didn't knock. She took the earring from her robe and put it back in the pillowcase with the food that Sashi had stolen.

She laid it on the floor outside Sashi's door.

"Good night, Sashi," she whispered. Then she turned and walked to the other end of the hallway, quietly entered the master bedroom, and climbed back into bed.

O kay, it's all settled," said Aquinnah, rousing Debra from her memories. She looked up from her cup and at her daughter on the other side of the table.

"What's all settled?" asked Debra.

"The refund. The motel is going to charge you only for one night, as long as we have everything out of the ballroom before noon today."

"Your father always said you should be studying business, not premed. Maybe he's right."

"Mom, do you have to turn everything I do into a question of whether you're right or Dad's right? A simple thank-you would be nice. I just saved you a two-week rental for nothing."

"It wasn't for nothing."

Aquinnah took a breath, then let it out. "I'm sorry. I know it's not for nothing. And I'm sorry I yelled at you last night."

Debra looked up from her cup. Aquinnah had delivered some pretty "tough love" the night before in the ballroom, but her morning-after apology seemed sincere.

"Apology accepted."

"But your friends are right. It's time to let go."

Aquinnah's words hung in the air. The tag-team trio—Aquinnah and Debra's two girlfriends—had covered this ground and re-covered it several times in the Find Sashi command center. The fact that Aquinnah would circle back and replow old ground, after an apology, made Debra's blood boil all over again. "*They* say it's time, do they?"

"Everybody does, Mom. Because it is."

Debra bit down on her lower lip. It was all she could do to avoid another shouting match like the one in the ballroom.

"Listen to me, Aquinnah. I will tell you when it's time for me to let it go," she said, rising.

Aquinnah looked right back at her from the other side of the booth, and their eyes locked.

"It is time," said Debra, "when *I* say it's time. When *I* say it."

Debra rose and walked away, her pace quickening as she crossed the restaurant. She stopped near the elevator, reached inside her purse, and dug out her car keys.

Attached to the key ring was a single tricolor gold earring.

She squeezed that earring so tightly that it left a mark in her palm. Then she hurried through the lobby, out the sliding doors, and into the parking lot.

CHAPTER 9

Jack dropped Theo at his apartment in the Grove and continued on to the Freedom Institute. He took the backstreets, which were surprisingly smooth sailing. Traffic planners had finally given up all hope that south Florida drivers would actually stop at stop signs. Throughout Miami's suburbs, four-way stops were being replaced with tiny traffic circles—embryonic Cartagena Circles of a sort, *sans* the spandex-clad cyclists. The idea was to at least slow down the guys who would otherwise race through stop signs. Fat chance. Like everyone else, Jack was weaving through the new traffic circles like a test driver through racing cones. He slowed down a little when Debra returned his call. He had her on Bluetooth.

"Jack, I just got your message. I am *so* sorry about the mix-up with the *Tribune*."

At least she wasn't denying that the press release was hers. "We need to straighten this out and get them to issue a retraction."

"Please, don't do that."

"I've already e-mailed the managing editor. If the story isn't down from the *Miami Tribune* website by nine o'clock, I'm personally walking into the newsroom and raising hell."

"Jack, I'm begging you. Don't make Sashi pay for my screw-up."

"This is not about Sashi, and this is not a 'screw-up.' I haven't even decided for certain that I'm going to represent Dylan Reeves, but you used my name and quoted me on something I never said. You're making things up."

"I'm sorry about the quote. But I swear: I tried to reach you on your cell last night at least five times. You didn't answer. And I told the reporter to call you and confirm the quote before running a story."

"Hold on a second." Jack pulled over to the curb and checked the call history on his cell. Five missed calls from Debra's number. Two missed calls from a number that he didn't recognize, which he presumed were from the *Tribune* reporter. All were during his "alone time" with Andie in the hospital, when his phone was off.

He got back on the line but left the car in park. "Okay. I found them in my call history."

"See? I wasn't lying."

"But you can't put my name in a press release, send it to the newspaper, and then tell the reporter to confirm it. That's why they call it a *release*."

There was silence on the line.

"Debra? You still there?"

"Yes," she said in a voice that quaked. "I apologize. Last night was awful. Aquinnah and I stayed in that empty ballroom for two hours after you left. Just the two of us. It ended in a total shouting match, with Aquinnah telling me to wake up, Sashi's dead, and no one was coming to help me find her."

"That's not an easy thing to hear."

"No. It was beyond painful. Because Sashi is alive. I know it in my heart. That's when I drafted the press release. I didn't mean to hurt you. I honestly thought you were on board. I've lost friends over this. I destroyed my marriage. Now Aquinnah and I are screaming at each other. If I lose you . . . then I've lost," she said, her voice cracking. "Then I've just lost everything."

Jack gripped the steering wheel and took a breath. There was a chance that Dylan Reeves was innocent—that he didn't kill Sashi. But that didn't mean Sashi was alive. It was a distinction he chose not to verbalize. Not yet.

"You haven't lost me, Debra."

Jack gave one final read to the emergency motion for stay of execution. It was filed electronically at 9:01 a.m.

"Really good work," he told Hannah.

"Thanks, chief."

It wasn't cause and effect, but at 9:02 there was a knock on the front door. Jack's secretary popped from her chair like a jack-in-the-box and answered it.

"My name's Gavin Burgette," the man said, "and I need to see Jack Swyteck."

It was Debra Burgette's ex-husband, and he didn't look happy. Jack introduced himself and invited him back to the kitchen.

Gavin was a private-equity manager in the Brickell Financial District, and he looked the part, dressed in a perfectly fitted suit that Jack guessed was Savile Row. The resemblance between Gavin and his biological daughter was strong, though the square jaw and Roman nose that made him the classically handsome type were probably features that Aquinnah fretted about when she looked in the mirror.

"How can I help you?" asked Jack.

Gavin dropped his copy of the *Miami Tribune* on the kitchen table. It was folded open to the article about Sashi. Jack noticed that his unauthorized quote was underlined in fountain-pen ink.

"What has Debra been telling you?"

Jack invited him to sit, and they took chairs on opposite sides of the table. Jack didn't try to hide anything, even if it was the two-minute version.

Gavin leaned forward, looking Jack in the eye. "Sashi is dead. Dylan Reeves raped and murdered her. Executing him won't bring my daughter back, but I've made peace with that. I'll never know exactly what happened to Sashi. But I'll know *exactly* what happens to the man who took her away. I damn well plan to be there when they stick the needle in his arm."

"You and Debra are in very different places."

"Yeah. We are. I don't owe you a marriage counselor's insight into what happened between us, but Debra self-destructed over this. You're aware, I'm sure, that she blames me."

"I've never heard Debra blame you."

"You will. She'll tell you I was too strict with Sashi, I wasn't understanding enough, I lacked patience, and that's why Sashi ran away like she did. The first ten times we brought her back home safely. This last time was different. She ran into Dylan Reeves, and the result was catastrophic. Debra wants to believe that Sashi is alive, that this time is going to turn out like all the other times Sashi ran away but finally came home, unharmed. It's not totally Debra's fault. The silent phone call she gets every year on Sashi's birthday messes with her head."

"Who do you think is doing that?"

"Talk to the police. They say it's a hoax. Who's evil enough to do something like that? I don't know. Could be anybody. I'm in private equity. I make a lot of enemies. We raise capital, we buy a company that's in trouble, we strip it down and fire two hundred employees, and we sell it for a profit. Maybe some guy in a deal I did lost his job, lost his house, lost his wife. He hates my fucking guts. Who knows? But I do know this: you, Mr. Swyteck, are destroying what's left of my family."

"I'm not—"

"Yes, you *are*. Do you think it doesn't tear my guts out to pick up a newspaper and see some lawyer making shit up about my daughter being alive just to get some scumbag off death row?"

"It's a long story," said Jack, choosing not to throw Debra under the bus. "But that was a complete mix-up."

"Fuck you, a mix-up! Do you think Aquinnah doesn't suffer

with this? How about my son? Alexander's nine years old now.
Do you think it's healthy for Debra to be telling him that his sister
is coming home?"

Jack didn't answer.

"*Do* you?"

"I know this is difficult for—"

"Oh, *please*. You know, I've punched a lot of walls since Sashi
went missing. I haven't punched anybody in the face yet. You're
close."

He pushed away from the table and started for the door. Then
he stopped, turned, and pointed his finger at Jack. "I want you
to stay away from Debra. Do your damn job if you have to and
file whatever fucking papers you lawyers file for walking pieces
of shit like Dylan Reeves. But stop messing with me and the two
kids I have left. That's not a request. That's a threat. Got it?"

Jack said nothing. If he'd learned anything from Neil, it was
to respect the victim's family—and "Never, *ever*, try to get the
last word."

Burgette turned and left, his footfalls pounding on the old
wooden floors, the door slamming on his way out.

Jack stayed seated. He couldn't disagree with anything Mr.
Burgette had said. He was still processing it, and it would probably change some things. It didn't change everything.

"Hannah?" he called out.

"Yeah?" she said as she appeared in the doorway.

"Call the warden's office at FSP," he said. "I want to meet
Dylan Reeves."

CHAPTER 10

Jack and Hannah flew into Jacksonville, an hour's drive from Raiford, and they reached Florida State Prison after lunch. A correctional officer escorted them to Q-Wing, their footfalls echoing in the long prison corridor.

Florida had 404 convicted murderers on death row, the male inmates divided between FSP and Union Correctional Institute across the river. All executions were carried out at FSP, so as soon as the governor signed a warrant, the inmate was moved to a cell on the ground floor of Q-Wing, the same floor on which he would die by lethal injection. Dylan Reeves was one of three on "death watch." Each temporary resident was detained in his own twelve-by-seven-foot cell. Reeves was in Cell No. 2. The other "newbie," a Pensacola man convicted of killing his ex-wife and her eight-year-old daughter, had his death warrant signed two minutes after Dylan Reeves', so he was in Cell No. 3. After each execution, inmates were moved to the next cell, working their way down the pipeline to Cell No. 1, the "bad luck cell," the launching pad to the gurney next door.

In Cell No. 1 was Elmer Hudson, whose crime fell into the category of "unspeakable," even by Freedom Institute standards.

"How's your daddy doing, Jack?" the guard asked.

Jack had been thinking about his father, who'd signed twenty-four death warrants in his two terms, resulting in twenty-one executions. Even at that pace, more inmates died of natural causes than at the hand of an executioner who, by law, would forever be anonymous.

"He's just fine," said Jack. "Doing a lot of fishing these days."

"That's good," the guard said. "Fishing's good for the soul."

Small talk. It felt awkward in a place where the stakes couldn't be higher and everything was done according to established procedures, from the initial cell-front interview—"Burial or cremation?"—to the last meal: "Sorry, no lobster; forty bucks is the limit, and it has to be locally available." Jack had always thought it was the ritual that lent a numbing comfort to those who labored in the business of state-administered death. But maybe it was the small talk.

"The governor probably won't remember me, but tell him Bud from DR says hello."

DR. Most Miamians would immediately think Dominican Republic. The former governor would know it was death row. "I will," said Jack.

A private room at the end of the cell block was for attorney visits. The electronic lock buzzed, the door opened, and the officer directed the lawyers inside.

"Age before beauty," said Hannah, allowing Jack to enter first.

Dylan Reeves was in the center of the room, seated at a small rectangular table and flanked by a pair of stone-faced guards. Reeves wore the same blue pants that were standard-issue at FSP, but his V-neck T-shirt was the bright-orange color that distinguished death-row inmates. Purple tattoos crept up both sides of his neck to his earlobes. He was slouching in his chair, as if to create the impression of cool indifference, but his eyes told a different story. Jack was still feeling the effects of having slept in the armchair in Andie's hospital room. Reeves looked as though he hadn't slept at all. It was one thing to contemplate death in the abstract, to acknowledge that "someday" we all must die; it was quite another to lie alone at night in a prison cell, counting down the exact number of hours you had left on earth.

"Get up," said the guard.

The chains rattled as the prisoner rose. The correctional officers removed the shackles from his hands and ankles, and Reeves
returned to his seat.

"I'll be right outside the door," the guard told Jack. "Buzz if
you need anything."

"Thanks," said Jack.

The guards left, and the door closed behind them. Jack and
Hannah seated themselves in the hard wooden chairs across the
table from their client.

Jack had read enough of the file to know that there was virtually nothing to recommend this life that was scheduled to end soon
on death row. High school dropout. In and out of juvie for drug-
related offenses. Fired from his last job at a loading dock for stealing
electronics. Arrested for armed robbery at a convenience store and
served two years on a plea bargain for naming his accomplice. He
had been out on probation when the police stopped him for drunk
driving and found Sashi's panties in the backseat of his car.

"So, you two are gonna save my life. Is that it?"

"That's the plan," said Jack.

"What if it doesn't work?"

Jack paused. That was the thing about capital cases: there was
no Plan B. "We're hopeful," said Jack.

Reeves sat forward in his chair, the cool indifference melting
away. "Really? Why?"

"Mostly a matter of procedure. You lost your direct appeals
and your state *habeas* petition. But you haven't been on death row
long enough to exhaust all of your rights in the federal courts."

Reeves rose and began to pace, suddenly energized. "That's
what really pisses me off. There's a guy I met in the yard two
weeks ago. He's been on death row for thirty-four years, I think
he said. I've been here less than three."

Jack recalled his conversation with Sashi's father, for whom
three years was way too long. "I'm sure that seems unfair to you."

"You're damn right. Why me? Why not the old guy?"

"The governor has complete discretion to sign a warrant for any inmate on death row. He's giving priority to any case involving an underage victim who was sexually assaulted."

"Oh, is that right?" he said, sniffing. "What about cases where there *was no victim*. Are those getting priority, too?"

"That point is made in the papers we filed with the court," said Hannah.

"Yeah, I skimmed through what you sent. Why isn't that the first argument? You've got an innocent client! Shouldn't that be on page one?"

"No," said Jack. "If we had DNA evidence proving that someone else committed the crime, yeah, that would be on page one. But we don't have anything close to that. We have a mother who thinks her daughter is still alive."

"That has to count for something," said Reeves.

"At this stage of the process, the goal is to keep you alive. Trying to convince a judge that you're innocent isn't necessarily the easiest way to do that."

Reeves shook his head, still pacing. "Now you sound like my trial lawyer. And he was a fucking alcoholic who came to court half-drunk and stinking of scotch."

Jack glanced at Hannah and asked, "Is that true?"

Hannah nodded. "I'm afraid so. Herb Graner is his name. Six months after the trial, he was suspended from the practice of law for substance abuse. He did a six-week treatment program to get his law license back, but he relapsed."

"We need to interview Graner," said Jack.

"Unfortunately, he's back in rehab right now," said Hannah, "and he hasn't returned my calls. Not sure he'd be all that keen about talking to us, anyway. We say some pretty unflattering things about him in our brief. Ineffective assistance of counsel is one of the major arguments."

Reeves stopped pacing and fired back. "That was in Leon's

brief, too. And in Tommy's brief, and in Clarence's. You know what? All those guys are dead. Ineffective assistance *never* wins. I could be represented by a fucking German shepherd and the Supreme Court would say that's not ineffective assistance of counsel." He stepped closer, palms planted on the tabletop. "What's the *best* argument? What's the one I'm gonna win on?"

"Errors at the sentencing phase of trial are usually the best arguments," said Hannah.

She was right, and it had been that way as long as Jack could remember. Phase I of a capital case was "guilt/innocence": Did the defendant commit murder in the first degree? The penalty phase followed: Were there special circumstances warranting the death penalty? Reeves' special circumstances were kidnapping and sexual assault.

"Even judges who are philosophically opposed to the death penalty are reluctant to override a jury's guilty verdict," said Jack. "That's just the way it is. Especially when you get to death watch."

"That's what Elmer told me—the guy in the cell ahead of me. You make it to death watch and it's, like, nobody wants to be the party pooper and stop the march to the gurney."

Jack had seen it firsthand. Issues that might normally get a court's attention, absent a death warrant, suddenly become "meritless" under the tension of a looming execution date.

"We have good arguments," said Jack.

"One is *very* good, in my opinion," said Hannah. "When there is no recovery of a body, the law requires more than a confession to convict the accused of murder."

"The better point is that I didn't confess to anything."

"It's on video," said Jack. "You clearly nodded your head. A confession doesn't have to be verbal."

"That detective asked me if I needed forgiveness. But I never said I killed anybody."

"Then why did you need forgiveness?"

"I was tired. I was hungover. I was still drunk from the night before. He started quoting scripture to me, and I nodded. I don't know why. Maybe it's because my old man was a preacher. A fucking hypocrite who was banging anything that moved, but still a preacher. All that matters is that I didn't kill that girl."

"But you did sexually assault her," said Jack, testing him.

"No, I didn't."

"You raped her, and that's why you needed forgiveness."

"No, *damn it*! I've said it all along. This was not a rape. That's why I wanted to testify at trial, but I listened to my lawyer and didn't say anything."

"You wanted to get on the witness stand and say that Sashi consented to having sex with you? Really?"

"Yes! It was her idea! She practically raped *me*."

Jack rose. "Let's go, Hannah."

"Wait," said Reeves. "Where you going?"

"The bullshit is about knee deep so far. I've been practicing law way too long to wait for it to reach all the way up to my eyeballs. We're leaving."

"You can't leave."

"Yes, we can. Meeting you in person is not an indispensable part of defending you. I have other things on my mind besides your sorry ass. My wife is seven months pregnant and in the hospital. I flew up here only to see if there really was some possibility that Sashi Burgette was alive. If you're going to lie, I'm getting on the next plane back to Miami."

Jack started toward the door, and Hannah followed.

"Okay, everybody just be cool," said Reeves. "Sit down and listen to me."

Jack stopped. "No more b.s.?"

"Fine. You want the straight story? I'll give it to you."

The lawyers returned to their seats. Reeves lowered himself into the chair across from them. He rubbed his face, as if coaxing the words out of his mouth, and then spoke.

"She got away," he said.

"Say that again?"

"I didn't pick her up in my car. We never had sex. Sashi got away from me. That's the truth."

Jack and Hannah exchanged glances. They were finally getting somewhere. "Start at the beginning," said Jack. "The cops brought you in to the station around three in the morning Sunday. When did you first see Sashi?"

"It was the Friday before that. Friday afternoon."

"Where did you see her?"

"There's a park on the north side of the canal just off Cartagena Circle."

"Ingraham Park."

"Right. Lots of joggers cut through there on the way into Coconut Grove or back toward Cocoplum. It's a steady parade of some pretty hot chicks. Not so much on the weekends, when all the fatties who exercise once a week come out. But on Friday evening, you get the hard-core fitness types who work out like maniacs and don't head over to South Beach till midnight."

"That's where you saw Sashi?"

"Yeah. Actually, I'd seen her there before."

"Exercising?"

"No. Never. She would walk there. If you wander a little ways off the trail, there's a rock ledge behind some trees and bushes along the canal. I'd seen her four or five times before. She would head over there and sit on the grass along the ledge, doing nothing. She'd just sit there for an hour or more, usually till sunset. Then she'd get up and walk back toward Cocoplum."

"Anybody with her?"

"No. Always alone. And she saw *me* there before, too."

"How do you know that?"

"She smiled at me. I know you think this is bull, but that girl was definitely interested. I could see it in the way she walked by me, sticking that little ass out."

"I'm gonna leave, Dylan."

"Okay, okay."

"No, not okay. You're talking about a seventeen-year-old girl who looked like the prom queen. Let me go out on a limb here, but I'm guessing you weren't the prom king."

"Still say she was interested."

"Last warning," said Jack.

"Fine. I *thought* she was interested."

"I'll accept that," said Jack. "So on this particular Friday afternoon, you decided to make your move?"

"Yeah. I had a toolbox in my trunk. There's a knife I kept in there."

"Toolbox, huh?" said Jack, translating in his mind: *rape kit.*

"Yeah. And you know what? I didn't even bother to go get the knife. Didn't think I needed it. She's there by the ledge all alone, layin' back on the grass and staring up at the sky. Knees up. She's wearing one of those little plaid skirts from the private schools. She's practically asking for it."

"I'm sure," said Jack, resisting the urge to slap him. "Then what?"

"I walked toward her, real quiet. She's still layin' on the grass. I know you call me a liar, but it looks to me like she's already spreadin' her legs a little. 'Don't move,' I tell her."

"Where was the knife?"

"In my hand."

"So you *did* have a knife."

Reeves glared. "Fuck you and your lawyer tricks. Yeah, all right. I brought it just in case."

Never failed. Details like a deadly weapon were memories these guys flushed when they got on death row. "Did you cut her?"

"No."

"Press the blade to her throat?"

"I don't know. Maybe. What I do remember is that things were going pretty smooth. Not much resistance. I get her panties off, then for two seconds I take the knife away to unzip my pants, which was stupid. I should have kept the knife right where it was and told her to do me. She kicked me right in the nuts. I mean bull's-eye. I'm hurtin' like you can't imagine."

"Then what?"

"That's it. She ran off, and I was in no shape to run after her. I kind of limped back to my car and got the hell out of there. I never saw the girl again."

Jack said nothing. The silence lingered. Finally, he spoke. "Nice story," said Jack. "It fits really well with Debra Burgette's hope and wish that her daughter is still alive. Too bad it doesn't hold water."

"It's the truth," said Reeves.

"Can't be," said Jack. "This was Friday, you said. You were stopped by Miami-Dade police Sunday morning at three. Your DNA was found on Sashi's panties. They were still wet. It's not possible that your semen was still wet thirty hours after the fact."

"Look, genius, here's the deal. I spent five hours getting shit-faced drunk at a strip club Saturday night. Naked dancers shaking their pussies in my face all night long."

"So?"

"Sometime after two in the morning, I walk to my car. I reach for my keys, and guess what I find? I still have the girl's panties in my coat pocket. Do I have to spell this out for you?"

"You sprayed her panties," said Hannah.

Reeves glared, wholly unappreciative of her statement of the obvious. "Like I'm the first guy to do it," he said.

There was a knock, and the door opened. The guard entered.

"Sorry to interrupt, folks. But I need to borrow the prisoner for about fifteen minutes. We need to take measurements for the burial suit."

"Burial suit?" said Reeves, looking at Jack. "They don't just bury me in what I'm wearing?"

"No," said Jack. "You get a burial suit."

Reeves shook his head, muttering. "It's okay to kill me, but it's a crime if my clothes don't fit. Can you believe this place?"

Jack didn't mention the legally required autopsy—would the cause of death really be a mystery? "We'll wait right here," said Jack.

Reeves rose. The guard refastened the shackles and led him away, leaving Jack and Hannah alone in the room.

"Do you believe him?" asked Hannah.

"He's a punk. He's probably stupid enough to stick to his story that he had consensual sex with Sashi if his only alternative is to admit to the world that he jerked off on her panties. So, yeah. Maybe I do believe him."

"Me, too."

Jack sat back and folded his arms, thinking. "Remind me of one thing, though, would you?"

"What?"

Jack breathed in and out. "Why is it that we want to save this guy?"

Hannah chuckled. "Good one, boss. You are so funny."

"Yeah, a riot," Jack said. "A regular prison riot."

CHAPTER 11

Three o'clock was pickup time for the elementary and middle school students at Grove Academy. Debra Burgette was right on time, but as any Grove parent knew, "on time" meant the back of the line. Debra would spend the next thirty minutes trapped in her Mercedes, inching her way up the palm-tree-lined driveway to the campus entrance, where a teacher would pluck Alexander from a line of well-behaved third-graders and buckle him into the backseat of his mother's car.

The SUV ahead of her moved up a car's length, and Debra rode its bumper. Purely out of boredom, she reached for her cell phone, but then she thought better of it. Debra was already on driver probation for two previous offenses in the cell-free zone, and security guards roamed the campus and parking lot like Secret Service agents.

Miami had its share of distinguished private schools, but for anyone who wanted the one-stop option of "pre-K through 12," Grove Academy was of singular distinction. The wooded five-acre campus was in Coconut Grove, right on Biscayne Bay, and students who didn't come to school each morning in a Lexus or BMW might arrive by boat. No class had more than twelve students. Mandarin Chinese was offered as early as age three. Classrooms had the latest SMART Board technology, and any student who didn't have a brand-new tablet every September was living in the Dark Ages. About once every decade, someone made it through the fifth grade without being named a "Duke TIP kid," but the best of the best weren't aiming for Duke, or any other college south of Cambridge, with the possible exception of that one in New Haven.

Debra would never forget the day Alexander had started there.

Or the day Sashi was expelled.

It happened on a warm and sunny April afternoon, just three months after Sashi's command of the English language had improved enough for her to enter the freshman class.

M r. and Mrs. Burgette, the headmaster will see you now," said the administrative assistant.

Debra and her husband were seated on a leather couch in the waiting area. Debra held a four-inch expandable file in her lap. In it were copies of e-mail exchanges with Sashi's teachers, disciplinary reports, appeals of disciplinary decisions, and an assortment of letters and pleas in which Debra had begged the administration to give Sashi another chance.

Gavin rose first, seemingly resigned to the inevitable. Debra followed, clutching her file and hoping for a miracle. The assistant led them into a cherry-paneled office, and then she retreated into the hallway and closed the door. Headmaster Avery McDermott and Associate Head of School Karen Feinberg greeted them politely but without smiles. McDermott offered his guests the matching striped armchairs and took his seat behind a massive and beautifully carved desk that was worthy of the Oval Office. The associate head pulled up a Winsome side chair and sat to the head's right.

"Well," said the headmaster. "Here we are again."

McDermott had been headmaster at Grove Academy for more than ten years but still spoke with a New England accent. He was a distinguished academic type whose salt-and-pepper beard made him look a little like Ernest Hemingway—without the turtleneck, of course, in the Miami heat.

Debra scooted to the edge of her chair, knees together, and with the bulging file resting atop her thighs. "Thank you so much for this opportunity to meet," she said in a voice that sounded overly obsequious, even to her own ears. "It's so, so very kind of you."

"I'm afraid I don't have happy news for you," said McDermott. "The number of second chances granted to your daughter in her short stay is unprecedented in the school's history. The terms of Sashi's latest probationary period were very specific. One more violation of our code of conduct would mean expulsion."

"What did she do this time?" asked Gavin.

"What is she *alleged* to have done?" asked Debra, correcting him.

"Well, let me walk you through it," said McDermott. "Sashi typically spends her lunch hour alone on the lawn in the Quad."

"That's her comfort zone," said Debra, "her cocoon. She puts in her earbuds, finds a quiet place outdoors, and lies in the sun. It makes her feel safe. She does it all the time."

Gavin cut her a sideways glance, telling her to cool it. When it came to defending Sashi, he called her "the fountain of TMI"—too much information.

"Yes," said the headmaster. "But today she assumed an inappropriate pose."

"How do you mean inappropriate?"

"She was on her back with her knees up."

"She's fourteen," said Debra. "Part kid, part woman. I'm sure she didn't realize what some of the older boys might be thinking."

"Her skirt was riding down her thighs. Her panties were visible. Some of the students who witnessed it say that she intermittently spread her legs."

"Which students? There are a lot of kids who don't like Sashi."

"I can't provide names, Ms. Burgette. But the Quad is an area on campus where the lower school and high school overlap. Some of the children who witnessed this were first- and second-grade boys who got their first look beneath a teenage girl's skirt. I can assure you that their parents will not be happy."

"I understand," said Gavin. "As you know, our Alexander is just a kindergartner, so I totally get it. We will personally apologize to those families if that will resolve this matter."

"It won't," said the headmaster. "There's more."

Debra closed her eyes, absorbing the blow. Somehow, however, she'd known it was going to get worse.

"One of our second-grade teachers, Dennis Jenkins, approached Sashi and told her to stop. She ignored him. When he bent down to tap her on the shoulder, she struck him."

Silence. Then Debra spoke. "Maybe he startled her. Like I said, if she was parting her legs, she was probably dozing off."

"She didn't strike him just once," said the headmaster. "It was vicious. We're talking repeated blows. She bloodied the man's nose. It may be broken."

"This is really bad, I know," said Debra. "But you have to understand. Sashi and Alexander were adopted from an orphanage in Russia. We don't know the whole story. Sashi is only beginning to open up to her psychiatrist. I'm sure that when she looked up and saw this strange man standing over her, something probably snapped. Some memory came to her. She must have thought that—"

"Ms. Burgette," he said, interrupting, "I'm well aware of the difficult circumstances. We've been over this before. If this were a first offense, I might feel differently. But Sashi was already on probation for stealing another student's cell phone. At some point, the academy must enforce its rules."

"How can we clear this up?" asked Gavin.

"We're handling it," said the headmaster. "Our legal counsel has been put on notice. The law requires us to report an altercation between a student and a teacher to the Department of Children and Family Services. I'm sure Mr. Jenkins will be exonerated, but our school policy requires that he be suspended until the evaluation is completed."

"Is all that necessary?" asked Debra.

"You don't know the half of it," said the headmaster. "The grapevine is fully engaged, and I've already gotten one call from the media. These stories get twisted, and I'm doing the best I can to keep this from spinning into a story of 'teacher attacks student.' The chairman of the board of trustees has called a special meeting for tonight. It goes on and on."

"What can we do to help?" asked Gavin.

"First of all, if you are contacted by the media, please do not talk to them."

"You have my word," said Gavin. "Again, I'm very sorry about this."

"I'm sorry, too," said the headmaster. "But the bottom line is that your daughter can no longer stay at Grove Academy."

"But . . . why?" asked Debra.

Gavin did that thing with his hand, waving off her question. Debra hated when he did that. It was really becoming a bad habit.

"Can Alexander stay?" asked Gavin.

"Yes, of course. This is about your daughter. Alexander is clearly GA material."

"*Material?*" asked Debra.

"There is one condition to Alexander's staying here, however," said the headmaster.

"Name it," said Gavin.

"Our lawyers have asked that you sign this agreement," he said as he handed it to Gavin. "It basically acknowledges the promises that you made in the application materials upon enrollment: all matters relating to student discipline shall remain confidential."

Gavin gave it a quick read. "Sure," he said, signing. Then he handed Debra the pen.

She hesitated.

"Ms. Burgette," said the headmaster, "it is in no one's interest for this incident to become public information. The DCFS investigation is strictly confidential. There will be a buzz around the campus for a few days, but our IT director and her staff have spoken with every single student who witnessed this incident, and they have made it absolutely clear that any postings to social media will result in immediate suspension. My hope is that we have this under control and that it will soon be forgotten."

"Sign it," Gavin told her.

"But—"

"*Sign* the document, Debra," said Gavin.

She did.

Gavin rose. "Thank you, Mr. McDermott. Let us know if there is anything more you need from us. We will be happy to cooperate. Debra, let's go."

"We're really not finished here," said Debra.

There went that dismissive wave of the hand again. Gavin really needed to stop doing that.

"Debra. Let's *go*," he said.

There were quick handshakes all around, and then Gavin whisked Debra out of the headmaster's office, through the lobby, and into the sun-baked parking lot. Debra did most of the talking on the walk to their car.

"You gave up too fast," she said as she fumbled to put on her sunglasses. It wasn't easy with a purse over her shoulder and the four-inch "Sashi file" tucked under her arm.

Gavin kept walking. "It's the best result we could hope for. At least Alexander can stay."

"We didn't bring a brother and sister halfway around the world so we could split them up."

"Lots of brothers and sisters go to different schools."

"And what private school is going to take Sashi after this?"

They reached their car. Gavin walked around to the driver's side. "It's all confidential. Can't you read between lines? That was the deal I just made with McDermott: sign this confidentiality agreement, and this incident won't follow your daughter around for the rest of her schooldays. He's happy to make Sashi somebody else's headache."

"But people talk. What if word gets out?"

"There's always public school," he said. "You're looking at a graduate of Gables High."

"Sashi can't be in a classroom with thirty or forty kids."

Gavin unlocked the car and got behind the wheel. Debra climbed into the passenger seat and held her Sashi file in her lap. "I'll write a letter to the board of trustees. That's what I'll do."

"Please don't."

"You don't even know what I'm going to say."

"If you make trouble, you're going to get Alexander kicked out, too," he said.

"Sashi is as much our child as Alexander. We have to help her. We *especially* have to help her."

Gavin pounded the steering wheel so hard it startled her. "Damn it, Debra! Sashi is beyond help."

Debra paused, and her eyes were suddenly like lasers. "Don't ever say that."

He breathed in and out, staring out the windshield. "She's beyond any help this school can give her," he said in a much calmer voice. "That's what I meant."

"I hope so."

He still didn't look at her. "No," he said finally. "That's not what I meant. I hate to say it, Debra. But it's time to be honest with ourselves. The problem isn't just school. Look at yourself in the mirror. When's the last time you had a good night's sleep? A year ago? When you're not worrying yourself sick about Sashi, you're making excuses for her. Oh, she was dozing off. Oh, the teacher must have startled her. Oh, she spent most of her life in a Russian orphanage. Honestly, honey, I'm beginning to think that Sashi is beyond any help we can give her." He glanced over at Debra in the passenger seat, then looked away again. "Way beyond."

There was a tap on the passenger-side window. Debra glanced over and saw the friendly face of Alexander's third-grade teacher on the other side of the glass. Debra had made it all the way to the pickup line, lost in her memories. She popped the lock, and Alexander jumped into the backseat.

"Hi, Mommy."

"Hi, big boy."

The teacher checked Alexander's seat belt, wished them a good day, and closed the rear door. Debra sniffled and pulled herself together.

"What're you crying for?" asked Alexander.

"I'm not crying."

"Yes, you are."

She checked herself in the rearview mirror and discovered that he was right. She dabbed a tear away.

"Are you sad?" he asked. "Is that why you're crying?"

"No, honey. I'm not sad. I'm crying because I'm happy to see you," she said, forcing a little smile. "I'm just so happy."

CHAPTER 12

Jack's flight landed at Miami International Airport in time for a late dinner, but he didn't eat. He went straight to the hospital. Andie was standing beside the bed, clipboard in hand and signing her discharge papers, when Jack entered the room and kissed her.

"How are you feeling?"

"Much better," she said.

"Eight o'clock at night is a weird time to be discharged, isn't it?"

"They needed twenty-four hours for the urine tests. My protein-to-creatinine ratio is a little out of whack, but not by much. I have mild preeclampsia, if I have it at all."

Jack smiled and hugged her. Andie was signing the last of the papers as the nurse rolled a wheelchair into the room.

"I don't need it," said Jack. "I swear."

"It's for your wife, sir. It's protocol for discharge of pregnant women."

"Oh, sorry. My bad."

Andie felt the bump on Jack's forehead. "Hardly noticeable. You heal quickly."

The nurse checked Andie's signatures. The paperwork was in order. Andie got in the wheelchair, and Jack pushed her down the hall to the elevator. Jack peppered her with questions all the way down to the ground floor, through the lobby, out the main entrance, and across the parking lot. She had mostly good news. Blood and urine tests could be done on an outpatient basis. No more bed rest: the risk of blood clots outweighed any possible benefit. Keep an eye on the blood pressure: 140 over 90 is too high. More frequent ultrasounds: need to monitor the baby's development, especially the lungs.

They were in the car when Jack got the "less good" news; Andie refused to call it "bad."

"If it gets worse, we'll have some decisions to make," said Andie.

"What kind of decisions?"

"The only cure for preeclampsia is to deliver the baby."

"When will it be safe to do that?"

"I'm twenty-eight weeks now. If we had to, the doctor says we could induce."

"And both you and the baby would be fine?"

"I would be, for sure. The baby would have better than a ninety percent chance of survival. But it would involve a long stay in the neonatal intensive care unit."

Ninety percent. Pretty good odds—until you thought about the last ten people you said hello to and imagined one of them dead. "That's better than what I thought you were going to say."

"It is. Unfortunately, at this stage, there's about a one-in-four chance of developing permanent disabilities, possibly serious ones. And about a fifty percent chance of milder problems, like learning and behavioral issues. That's why the doctor would like to see me get to thirty-two weeks, if possible. That's kind of the magic number."

Jack did the math, and Andie noted the expression on his face.

"What's wrong?" she asked.

"Nothing."

"You made a face. I know you, Jack. It wasn't 'nothing.' What's wrong? Did the doctor tell you something that she didn't tell me?"

"No, it's not that."

"Then tell me."

"I just realized: our baby would be born the same week Dylan Reeves is scheduled to die."

"Shit, Jack. Why do you even make an association like that?"

"I don't know why. Just a bizarre day."

"It's been a pretty stressful day for me, too. Get over it. In with the good, out with the bad."

"Andie, come on."

"Sorry. I don't mean to be flip. But capital punishment is one thing you and I will never see eye-to-eye on."

Jack stopped at the traffic light. A few raindrops splattered on the windshield, and Jack cleared them away with one pass of the wiper. "Are you mad that I got on a plane this morning?"

"No. There was nothing for you to do here. That's why I told you to go."

"I know you did. I have to say, though, that I didn't like being up there while you were down here in the hospital."

"It's okay, Jack. It's your job."

"Actually, it's not my job. I don't work for the Freedom Institute."

"You don't have to work for the Institute to defend a death-row inmate."

"That's true. In fact, the whole time I was away, I kept asking myself: What am I doing here? I just don't feel the passion it takes to do this kind of work anymore."

"No way, Swyteck. I don't believe that for one minute. You were just feeling guilty about me being in the hospital."

"No—I mean, yes, I did feel guilty. But it's more than that. I'm going to call Hannah and tell her I'm bowing out."

The traffic light changed and Jack hit the accelerator.

"Can you just withdraw like that?" asked Andie. "I thought once a criminal defense lawyer makes an appearance in a capital case he's kind of stuck."

"I haven't made a court appearance. Hannah signed the brief on behalf of the Freedom Institute, so I was never officially in the case."

They rode in silence. A few more raindrops gathered on the windshield, and beams from oncoming headlights made them sparkle in the night.

"I don't want you to drop out," said Andie.

Jack blinked, confused. "I thought you would be happy."

"Which is exactly why I don't want you to quit."

"I see."

"Does that make sense to you?"

Uh, no. "It makes perfect sense, honey." He reached across the console and took her hand. "Perfect sense."

The drive home across the causeway was a familiar one, but Jack was finding it difficult to keep his eyes on the road. It was the lighting—absolutely perfect lighting. Andie's profile was a silhouette in the passenger seat, and the distant glow of the Miami skyline seemed to highlight the perfect lines of her face. Views of downtown Miami and the financial district were killer from the Key Biscayne Causeway, especially at night—the south Florida version of Manhattan as seen from the Brooklyn Bridge.

"What are you looking at?" she asked.

"You," he said.

They were home by ten o'clock and went right to bed. Andie spent the longest time trying to get comfortable. The adjustable hospital bed had spoiled her. Finally she was asleep, and Jack dozed off not too much later.

Around midnight the phone rang. It was Hannah.

"We won, Jack! We won!"

Jack jumped out of bed and stumbled through the darkness to the master closet. He spoke softly behind the closed door, trying not to wake Andie.

"That was fast," he said. "What's the relief?"

"Thirty-day stay of execution."

A temporary stay. Dylan Reeves was new enough to the process for it to feel like a victory. Jack had defended others who had ridden the roller coaster too long, who preferred death to the illusory hope of another twenty- or thirty-day stay.

"Is there an opinion, or just an order?"

"It's one paragraph. Basically the court bought our lead argument that Reeves has not yet exhausted all of his rights to review. That much we expected. But here's the interesting part," she said, then read verbatim: "'The court hereby directs the trial court to conduct an evidentiary hearing, without delay, on issue number six presented in the petitioner's motion, *to wit, the possible whereabouts of the alleged decedent, Sashi Burgette.*'"

Jack froze in the darkness.

"Jack, are you there?"

"Yeah, I heard."

"'The *alleged* decedent.' They're not talking about a search for a body. They want an evidentiary hearing on the whereabouts of a living and breathing human being. What do you think about that, boss?"

It took a moment, but finally Jack could speak. "Holy shit."

CHAPTER 13

Jack was in Criminal Courtroom 3 of the Richard E. Gerstein Justice Building all Wednesday morning, but it had nothing to do with Dylan Reeves or the death penalty.

Jack represented a wealthy Cuban exile who had taken the law—and a blowtorch—into his own hands and melted his neighbor's life-size bronze lawn statue of Marxist revolutionary Che Guevara. Jack had bargained the charges down to a misdemeanor, but, on principle, his client refused the deal and didn't care how much it would cost him in attorney's fees to fight it. Principle was a beautiful thing. So were paying clients. They kept the lights on and put food on the table. In the blink of an eye, they would buy braces for Jack and Andie's kids. In two blinks, they would put those kids through college.

"Thank you, counsel," Judge Garcia said from the bench. "You'll have my ruling by the end of the day."

The crack of his gavel cut across the courtroom at noon sharp. Judge Garcia never missed a meal, and lawyers could set their watches by his break for lunch.

Jack packed up his briefcase and stepped into the hallway to return messages. Debra Burgette was first on his list, if only because she had called him seven times in the previous two hours. The hallway was abuzz as jurors, lawyers, and scores of others headed toward the elevators. Long wooden benches lined the corridors, but of the few seats available, none offered privacy. Jack found a quiet spot at the end of the hall near the window. He was scrolling his contact list for Debra's number when he did a double take and put his phone away. Debra was walking straight toward him.

"I've been waiting here for an hour," she said. Debra was wearing a navy-blue power suit and heels, dressed more for a board meeting than for hunting down a lawyer at the criminal courthouse.

"I had a bench hearing," said Jack. "How did you even know where to find me?"

"I'm not stalking you, I promise. Your secretary told me which courtroom you were in. I heard about the stay of execution."

"The order came down late last night. I should have called you this morning, but I haven't had a free moment."

"It's okay. I was at the state attorney's office this morning. I met with the prosecutor in Sashi's case."

Technically, it was Dylan Reeves' case, but Jack understood the point of view. "How did that go?"

"Not well. Not well at all, I'm afraid."

"What's wrong?"

"Well, first, I need to know something. After that mix-up with the newspaper, you said you weren't sure if you were going to be Dylan Reeves' lawyer or not. Have you decided?"

"My wife and I talked about it last night, and I told Hannah this morning. I'm in."

"Oh."

"You sound disappointed. I thought you wanted me to represent him."

"I did. But—let me ask you this: Are you officially Dylan Reeves' attorney? Or can that be changed, if necessary?"

"Debra, what are you getting at?"

She took a half step closer and lowered her voice. "The prosecutor gave me some advice this morning."

"What kind of advice?"

She looked up at him, her eyes clouding with concern. "I need a lawyer, Jack. A good one."

CHAPTER 14

Jack escorted Debra to her car in the courthouse parking lot and then walked across the street to the Graham Building. He wanted to speak lawyer-to-lawyer with Barbara Carmichael, senior trial counsel at the Office of the State Attorney for Miami–Dade County.

Jack had tried a case against Carmichael only once, years earlier, when Barbara was cutting her teeth as a "pit assistant," a C-level prosecutor in her first year of adult felonies, working sixty-hour weeks under her supervising attorneys. She'd made a career of it and was now one of the elite go-to prosecutors in capital cases. Her conviction record was perfect, a tribute to her courtroom skills as well as her keen sense of when to offer a plea and when to take a case to trial.

Dylan Reeves was one of many convicted killers that she'd dispatched to death row.

"Good to see you again, Jack," she said, as he entered her office.

Jack had called ahead to confirm that Carmichael was available over the lunch break. She'd agreed to a short meeting, so long as Jack didn't mind watching her wolf down a quick sandwich at her desk. After a full morning in court, she needed to rush back for a one p.m. suppression hearing. The life of a trial lawyer.

"Likewise," said Jack.

Debra Burgette had been short on details and long on intuition about her meeting with the prosecutor. Jack needed a better understanding of her concerns.

"How can I help you?" asked Carmichael.

"You know I'm defending Dylan Reeves," he said.

"I assumed so. I didn't see your name on the habeas petition filed with the court, but I did see the article in the *Miami Tribune*."

Time was too short to get into Debra's "nonrelease" of a press release with Jack's name in it. "I met with Mr. Reeves yesterday. I made the decision to join the defense team last night."

"Clever."

"What do you mean, 'clever'?"

"The argument that Sashi Burgette is still alive is clearly specious and entered for no purpose other than to delay the execution. You left your name off the pleading so that the court can't slap you with sanctions for filing a frivolous pleading."

"That wasn't a strategic decision."

"I'm sure it wasn't. No more strategic than your leak to the *Tribune* about 'significant new evidence' as to Sashi's whereabouts. You know as well as I do that judges read newspapers, especially when the quote is attributed to a lawyer named Swyteck and they owe their judicial appointment to a governor of the same last name. Didn't expect *you* to come down with a bad case of typical defense-lawyer-sleaze disease, Jack. You disappointed me."

"That's quite an imagination you've got there, Barbara."

"Instinct. Not imagination." She took a bite of her sandwich, chewing roundly while she finished her thought. "So, what's up?"

"Debra Burgette came away from your meeting this morning with the distinct impression that she needs a lawyer."

"Why?"

"That's what I'm here to find out. Debra couldn't give me a specific reason. It's more a feeling she had."

"Like the feeling that her daughter is still alive?"

"No need to get snarky about it, Barbara."

"You're right. That was uncalled for. I'm extremely sensitive to the pain the entire Burgette family has gone through. But Debra's grief over the loss of her daughter is taking her in a very unfortunate direction. I told her that this morning."

"She was pretty shaken up when I spoke to her. There has to be more to it than that. She honestly thinks she needs to hire a lawyer."

"We did discuss her role as a witness at the evidentiary hearing ordered by the court."

"Her role as a witness for the prosecution?" asked Jack. "Or for the defense?"

"Both. I assume you will be putting Debra Burgette on the stand to testify about the phone calls she's received every year on Sashi's birthday since her disappearance."

"No question," said Jack.

"There you have it. I told her the same thing I would tell any witness for the defense who decides to walk into a courtroom, swear an oath, and try to undo a jury verdict of guilty three years after the fact. The giving of false testimony is a felony, and this office prosecutes the crime of perjury to the fullest extent of the law."

"You honestly think she's lying about these phone calls?"

"I didn't say that."

"Her cell-phone records confirm that she received calls from an unknown burn phone, and that each call lasted between one and two minutes. She's not making this up."

"I understand your position."

"I'm not sure I understand yours," said Jack.

"Well, that's why they call it the *adversary* system. And that's what tomorrow's hearing is for."

"*Tomorrow?*"

"Yeah, tomorrow," she said, searching beneath her sandwich wrapper. "The scheduling order came in about five minutes before you got here. "Ah, here it is," she said.

Jack read it. "Nine a.m. Clearly the judge gave a very literal reading to the appellate court's direction to move forward 'without delay.' "

"As he should," said the prosecutor. "With any luck, your motion will be disposed of before the death warrant expires, and justice will be done right on schedule. Now, if you'll excuse me, I have a one o'clock hearing to prepare for."

Jack rose, they shook hands, and Carmichael led him down the hall to the elevator.

"Oh, I meant to ask: How's your wife, Jack?"

"She's doing well, thanks. I had no idea you knew her."

"We met at a task-force conference on serial killers. Smart woman. Boy, I'd love to be a fly on the wall when you two talk about Dylan Reeves."

"To be honest, she's totally behind me on this one."

"She told you that?"

"Yes. As a matter of fact she did."

"And you believed her?"

"Of course."

She smiled and shook her head, as she pushed the call button for the elevator. "Typical husband."

"What do you mean by that?" asked Jack.

"It's like the wife who says, 'Oh, honey, fresh flowers are such a waste of money. You don't have to buy me roses this Valentine's Day.' Only a moron thinks that's a free pass and doesn't come home with *two* dozen roses. And they'd better be red."

Jack laughed, but she didn't.

"That was friendly advice, Jack. Not a joke."

The elevator arrived, and the metal doors parted. Jack stepped inside.

"See you tomorrow morning," she said.

"See you," he said as the doors closed.

Jack rode in silence, wondering if it was friendly advice, or if the prosecutor had been messing with his head before tomorrow's hearing.

Or both.

CHAPTER 15

I t was bedtime on Key Biscayne, but Andie wasn't sleepy. She stepped out onto the patio for a breath of cool night air, but even with a breeze blowing off the bay, late September in south Florida wasn't all that cool. Heat lightning flashed over the distant Atlantic. It was many miles away, no rolling thunder, just a festival of light. Andie used to think of it as nature's fireworks display. Tonight, it reminded her of Week 28 and the lovely sciatica that shot down the back of her left leg like a bolt of electricity.

"When are you due?"

The unfamiliar voice of a woman startled her. Andie knew that Jack was preparing at home for the nine a.m. court hearing, but she didn't expect to find the star witness sitting on their patio. Debra rose and introduced herself.

"Sorry, I didn't mean to scare you," Debra said.

"That's okay. Where's Jack?"

"On the phone," she said, indicating.

Andie spotted his silhouette on the dock, his glowing cell phone pressed to his ear.

"Sit, please," said Debra. "He's on with Hannah. Could be a while."

Taking a load off her swollen feet sounded like a good idea. The real problem was getting herself *out* of patio furniture, not into it, but she still had to mind what she was doing as she lowered herself onto the striped cushions.

"I really appreciate all of Jack's help," said Debra.

"It's what he does."

"I know Sashi appreciates it, too."

Andie noted the present tense. "Jack told me about your . . . situation."

"Oh, really?" she said with a nervous smile. "Does he think I'm chasing windmills?"

"No."

Debra's smile faded. "Do you?"

Not an easy question to answer, but Andie had handled tougher from grieving families and the victims of violent crime. She'd distinguished herself on a multijurisdiction serial killer investigation in Seattle and Washington's Yakima Valley before transferring to Miami to do undercover work. Her "life B.J."— before Jack.

"I can only imagine what I would do in your situation."

Debra nodded slowly and looked off into the darkness. "No, you can't. Don't take this the wrong way, but until it happens to you, it's impossible even to imagine what it feels like, or how you might deal with it."

Andie laid her hand on her belly. It might have been a kick. Or maybe she was just feeling some of Debra's pain.

"Did Jack tell you anything about Sashi?" asked Debra.

"Some."

"Sashi was adopted, you know. Jack tells me you were, too."

"That's true. I was."

"I don't mean to pry, but—"

"It's okay. No, never met my biological parents."

"That's not what I was going to ask. I was wondering about your adoptive mother."

"Wonderful woman. Both Mom and Dad were terrific people. They were an older couple when they adopted me. I miss them every day."

Debra looked away again. "I didn't mean to insult you

by saying you can't imagine what it's been like for me. Being adopted, and a mother-to-be, maybe you could relate, at least a little, to what I'm feeling. What I've *been* feeling, since Sashi went missing."

"I can try."

"I'm not going to pretend that I had the perfect relationship with Sashi. It was difficult, especially at the beginning. But I tried. I really tried. I even took a special trip back to the Russian orphanage to see if I could find out more about her."

"Did that help?"

"Honestly, it felt like a dead end at first. No one at the orphanage could tell us much of anything about Sashi before the adoption. But there was one caregiver who seemed to be holding back something. When I went back, I found her."

"Did she tell you anything?"

"She did. The woman was from Chechnya, and she was convinced that Sashi was Chechen. The orphanage was in Moscow. That's a long haul for a girl who's barely a teenager—and her little brother."

"How did they get to Moscow?"

"The woman couldn't say for sure. But she had some, shall I say, interesting views on it. Adoption doesn't have a long history in Chechnya. The tradition is for extended family or neighbors to care for orphans. When President Putin passed the law banning adoption by U.S. citizens, he pointed to Chechnya as an example of why international adoption is unnecessary. But Gavin and I adopted years before that law was passed. Things were different then. Two wars had practically destroyed the country and left thousands of orphans."

"So Sashi was probably a war orphan?"

"Possibly. But because she ended up in an orphanage so far from Chechnya, and because she was so absolutely beautiful, this caregiver had another theory."

Andie was almost afraid to ask. "Which was . . ."

"That Sashi was stolen from her parents."

"What a horrible thought."

Debra took a breath. "It haunts me. And here's what else she told me: Chechens believe in the power of dreams."

"What did she mean by that?"

"Here's the example she gave me. Thousands of people disappeared in the Chechen wars. Families never found out what happened. No confirmation of death. To this day, if you go there, there are hundreds, maybe thousands of families who will be outraged if you even suggest, let alone assume, that their brother, their cousin, their child is dead. And the reason is dreams. So long as anyone in the family goes to sleep at night and has a dream about a missing family member, they firmly believe that he or she is still alive."

"Why would she tell you such a thing?"

"She wanted me to know that if Sashi was stolen, and her parents are alive, they will never stop looking for her as long as Sashi is still in their dreams."

Andie felt chills, and then another thought jarred her. "Are you suggesting that Sashi was taken back by her biological parents?"

"No. I think her parents are dead. I *have to* believe that. But what I'm saying is this: *I* still have dreams of Sashi. Sometimes those dreams are nightmares. But she is still in my dreams. And as long as my daughter is there—and she is *my daughter*—I will keep looking."

Their eyes met and held. Andie felt crushed by the weight of Debra's stare—her determination.

"Sorry that took so long," Jack said as he returned.

"It's okay," said Debra. "Your wife and I were having a nice talk."

"Help me up, Jack," said Andie.

He knew the drill, but this time the rise from deck-chair abyss ended with a surprise. She hugged her husband tighter than he might have expected and kissed him a little longer than the usual kiss good night.

"What's that about?" he asked.

"I'm proud of you," she whispered. "Good luck tomorrow."

And then she said good night.

CHAPTER 16

Mr. Swyteck, call your first witness," said the judge.

Thursday's hearing began at nine a.m. sharp before Judge Frederick, a silver-haired ex-Marine who had served on the bench for nearly four decades. He was a smart jurist who stuck to the facts and followed the law, which meant that he infuriated liberals and conservatives alike. Jack considered that a plus.

"The petitioner calls Dr. Emmitt Pollard," said Jack.

The "petitioner" was Dylan Reeves, who was not in the courtroom. A habeas corpus proceeding is a civil action, not a criminal prosecution, in which the prisoner brings suit against the warden, claiming that he is imprisoned illegally. Hannah was seated at Jack's side, and it was their job to convince Judge Frederick that their client was wrongfully convicted in violation of his rights. Barbara Carmichael sat at the mahogany table to Jack's left; with her was a lawyer from the State of Florida Office of the Attorney General, Bureau of Capital Appeals, the specialized division that represented the state's interest in postconviction proceedings in death-penalty cases. The jury box was empty, of course, since this was not a trial; the judge alone would hear the evidence.

Dr. Pollard swore the familiar oath, took a seat in the witness stand, and stated his full name for the record. He was a tall, thin man with a head too large for his narrow shoulders, and as he leaned forward, he bore an odd resemblance to the long and spindly gooseneck microphone that would amplify his testimony. Jack questioned him from the lectern.

"Dr. Pollard, what is your profession?"

"I'm a psychiatrist."

"Have you ever treated Sashi Burgette as a patient?"

"No, I have not. But I have reviewed her medical records."

"How did that review come about?"

"Three years ago, the state attorney's office asked me to do so in connection with the criminal case against Dylan Reeves."

"For what purpose?"

"It was stipulated by the parties that the victim suffered from reactive attachment disorder. 'RAD' for short. I was asked to express an opinion as to the likelihood that a seventeen-year-old-girl with RAD would engage in consensual sex with a total stranger like Dylan Reeves."

"What was your opinion, Doctor?"

"In Sashi's case, highly unlikely. After reviewing her medical records, it was my opinion that she might well manipulate strangers with charm, and even inappropriate signs of affection, but that if a stranger acted on those signals, she would resist aggressively. Perhaps violently."

Jack made a note on his legal pad: *Smiled at DR/kicked in nuts.*

"Briefly, can you please describe to the court what RAD is?"

"RAD is a mental disorder rooted in childhood experience. The child exhibits markedly disturbed and developmentally inappropriate ways of relating socially. A false belief that he or she is incapable of being loved continues through adolescence and into adulthood."

"What causes it?"

"Generally speaking, severe neglect or abuse early in life. The most serious cases are orphaned children from war-torn countries. But it might develop in less dramatic circumstances where there is an abrupt separation from a caregiver, frequent change of caregivers, or a caregiver who simply ignores a child's needs and the child's attempts at communication."

"In the case of an adopted child, like Sashi, what are the main challenges faced by the adoptive family?"

He sighed, as if not sure where to begin. "That's a hard question to answer. There are so many."

"Let me break it down. What would likely happen if a mother tried to hug or kiss her adopted daughter?"

"A child with RAD would typically reject physical contact, even from those closest to her."

"In terms of disciplining, would it make sense to tell a girl like Sashi to go to her room?"

"No. Parents with younger RAD children make that mistake when they use a 'time-out.' Being alone gives a RAD child the emotional space he or she craves. It just vindicates their belief that they are alone in this world."

The prosecutor rose. "Judge, I feel compelled to point out that this hearing is limited to *new* evidence that has come to light since the trial and sentencing of Mr. Reeves. All I've heard so far is repetition of the testimony that the state of Florida presented at trial, which convinced the jury that the DNA found on the victim's clothing most certainly did not result from her consent to sexual activity with Dylan Reeves."

The judge nodded. "Yes, Mr. Swyteck. This hearing is not a 'second bite at the apple,' as the saying goes. It would better serve your client to stick to *new* evidence."

"I'll get right to the point," said Jack. "Dr. Pollard, isn't it true that before her disappearance, Sashi Burgette ran away from home numerous times?"

Carmichael was back on her feet. "Objection. Again, this is not new evidence. The fact that Sashi was a frequent runaway was made known to Mr. Reeves' counsel long before trial."

"Judge, I've read the trial transcript. Not a single witness testified that Sashi ran away from home."

"The fact that she ran away from home was clearly referenced in the medical records of Dr. Wurster, which Dr. Pollard reviewed before he testified."

"True," said Jack. "But those records were described in a very general way as background information that Dr. Pollard relied on to form his opinions. The actual records of Dr. Wurster were not offered into evidence at trial."

"Well, if they weren't presented to the jury, the only person to blame is Mr. Reeves' lawyer," said the judge.

"I understand," said Jack. "But for purposes of this hearing, I still urge the court to treat Sashi's frequent runaways as newly discovered evidence. I didn't even see this evidence the first time I went through the trial record. I heard about it from the Burgettes' neighbor. Then I went back and sifted through about a thousand pages of scholarly journals, notes, medical records, and other materials that Dr. Pollard claims to have reviewed before he testified."

"The fact that Mr. Reeves' trial counsel failed to dig out that evidence, or simply made a strategy decision not to present it to the jury, is not the state of Florida's fault," said Carmichael.

"Let's not go round and round on this," said the judge, and then he turned to face the witness. "I'll allow a simple 'yes or no' question: Dr. Pollard, based on your review of the medical records, are you aware of the fact that Sashi Burgette ran away from home on multiple occasions prior to her disappearance?"

"Yes," said the witness.

"Fine," said the judge. "Continue, Mr. Swyteck."

That one word—*yes*—was a huge victory. Jack needed more: he needed to convince the judge that she would run away and *stay away* for three years.

"Dr. Pollard, as the expert witness in this case, can you tell us whether a RAD child would likely feel any remorse about running away from home?"

"The brain of a RAD child is not really programmed to feel remorse."

"And if she did run away, would she find herself pining away for Mom and Dad?"

He shook his head. "Not likely."

"Would she be capable of manipulating strangers to give her money or provide other needs?"

"RAD children can be quite manipulative."

"In fact, it's common for adolescents to seem charming and helpless to outsiders, while being quite the opposite at home. Isn't that true, Doctor?"

"That is very true."

"RAD children are also known to be effective liars, are they not?"

"They can be. I've had parents tell me that the only time their child looks them in the eye is when she is lying."

"They steal?"

"Some will."

"They cheat?"

"Again, some will."

"And they will do these things without a second thought—as you said, without remorse."

"Yes."

"Their conscience doesn't work the way yours or mine works, does it?"

"No, it does not."

"Doing things that might shock the average person makes them feel in control. Right, Doctor?"

"Yes, and it's very frustrating for parents. For many, it's overwhelming."

Jack paused to check his notes, then continued. "Dr. Pollard, I'm going to ask you for your expert opinion. Based on your knowledge and experience, and based on your review of Sashi Burgette's medical records, is Sashi more or less likely to run away from home than a child without RAD?"

"Definitely more likely."

"Compared to a child without RAD, is Sashi more or less likely to derive a comforting sense of control from the fact that people are searching but can't find her?"

"Again, more likely. RAD children are in a constant battle to control a situation."

"Last question. Compared to someone without RAD, is Sashi more or less likely to care if Dylan Reeves dies by lethal injection for a murder he didn't commit?"

"Objection, Your Honor."

"This isn't a jury trial, Ms. Carmichael. Let's keep our hands off the hyper-objection button and get through this hearing expeditiously. The witness may answer."

"I would have to say less likely."

"Thank you, Doctor. No further questions." Jack returned to his seat.

"Any cross-examination?" the judge asked.

"Briefly," said the prosecutor. She rose but didn't step away from her table. "Doctor, in response to Mr. Swyteck's questions, you acknowledged that RAD children need to 'control' a situation."

"Yes."

"For example, isn't it true that many adolescents with RAD will chat incessantly in order to control a conversation?"

"Yes, some will. From the moment they wake up until their head hits the pillow. Outsiders will often see these children as precocious. It becomes far less endearing when they reach school age and attempt to control an entire classroom with their chatter."

"Doctor, given Sashi Burgette's diagnosis, what is the likelihood that she could make a phone call to her mother and say absolutely nothing for up to two minutes?"

"Honestly, I would say that's highly unlikely."

"Nothing further," said the prosecutor.

The judge dismissed the witness, and as the doctor stepped down, Hannah leaned closer to Jack and whispered, "I call it a tie."

"You're too generous," said Jack. "It all comes down to Debra."

CHAPTER 17

For the first time in a week, Andie was in the FBI field office in North Miami Beach. Getting back to work was the right medicine—much better than lying in bed and reading preeclampsia horror stories on the Internet. Her ob-gyn had given her the green light on one condition: "Avoid people who make your blood pressure rise." The doctor was only half kidding.

Andie checked in with the assistant special agent in charge. ASAC Guy Schwartz was glad to see her back, but he wanted her to know that if her return was out of concern that a complicated pregnancy might put her over the thirteen-day limit on paid sick leave, she need not worry: five of her colleagues had stepped up to transfer unused personal time to her. FBI recruiters talked a lot about being like a "family," and something like this made it feel true, even if, at times, the "family" did seem a bit dysfunctional.

Schwartz put her to work on a proposed budget for a planned investigation into south Florida "pill mills," pain-management clinics that were essentially drug dealers with prescription pads, dispensing oxycodone and other Schedule II narcotics like expensive candy. Budgeting wasn't Andie's favorite line of work, but she was in no condition to chase down bad guys on foot, and the payoff was that if headquarters approved her numbers, there was an undercover role for her in the investigation.

Around ten she went to the kitchen for a mid-morning smoothie. She needed to keep her calories up, and eating smaller portions more often worked better for her than three full meals a day. She walked back to her office, but numbers were not foremost in her mind.

Andie couldn't stop thinking about her talk with Debra Burgette. The very idea of Chechen parents still looking for their stolen daughter after all these years was beyond disturbing. The chance of their ever finding her on the other side of the world seemed remote. The notion that they would then steal her back—something that Debra had never suggested but that had nonetheless popped onto Andie's "anything is possible" list—seemed even more far-fetched.

Or was it?

Andie minimized the proposed budget that was on her computer screen. The Internet beckoned. Talking with Debra had made her curious about Chechnya in the years between Sashi's birth and adoption. The Chechen heritage of the Boston Marathon bombers had made her only generally aware of the long-running separatist conflicts. She tried a few searches, and grim headlines came rolling in. *Death Toll for Two Wars Estimated at 160,000 . . . Grozny Devastated by Russian Bombardment . . . Thousands of Civilians Killed.*

Andie refined her search, and a chilling image appeared on her screen.

It was a black-and-white photograph from a U.K. news organization. A half dozen children were huddled alongside a gravel road. They had the sad and hopeless look of refugees. The news story opened with a firsthand account of the British reporter's conversation with a Chechen village:

"Why are those children standing by the road?"

"They are for sale," the woman told me. "Pretty little girls go first. Then handsome boys. The rest, the big ones—they go on the side of the road."

Andie read quickly: "After more than a decade of conflict, a rising number of childless families are willing to pay large sums to adopt a newborn baby and frequently resort to illegal methods to acquire one. The problem is compounded by the fact that Chechen society considers illegitimate birth shameful and there is very little formal adoption . . ."

There was more, but Andie had read enough. She checked her online directory and dialed a colleague at FBI headquarters. Special Agent Steve Hidalgo worked in the Violent Crimes Against Children Unit. Andie had first met him when he traveled to Miami to head Operation Cross Country, a coordinated law-enforcement action that rescues sexually exploited children and takes down their pimps in more than a hundred cities every year. Hidalgo also worked with the VCAC Unit's International Task Force, which made him Andie's go-to guy.

He took her call, and after quick pleasantries he was happy to take her question.

"Fire when ready, Andie."

"Have you ever heard of a case where the biological parents have their child stolen from them and then they steal her back?"

"Hmm. The more common abduction involving biological parents is one parent taking the child away from the other in a divorce and custody battle."

"I'm talking about something very different. The parents had their child snatched away. The child ends up in an orphanage in a foreign country and is adopted legally by U.S. citizens. Then the biological parents track down their daughter and steal her back."

"Off the top of my head, I can think of only one case that is even close to that situation. It was actually a woman in Florida."

"Naturally," said Andie. It was a running joke in the Miami field office, the way every crime that "breaks the mold" seemed to have a Florida connection.

"A woman in her late forties was artificially inseminated and gave birth to twins. She had a complicated pregnancy and, for reasons I don't recall, decided to give up the twins for adoption. But it was open adoption, I believe, where she had visitation rights.

When the twins were about eighteen months old, they visited with the birth mother over the Christmas holiday, and she didn't bring them back. I think she was finally arrested in Canada."

"Did she get to keep her kids?"

"No. She pleaded guilty to kidnapping, and the children were returned to the adoptive parents. The adoption was binding."

"Did she try to go through the court system before resorting to kidnapping?"

"I don't remember. But in the situation you're describing, that would obviously make the most sense. DNA testing could easily prove that they are the biological parents. Then it would be just a matter of convincing a judge that their child was stolen from them. No need to resort to kidnapping."

"Unless they didn't trust the court system. Or if they were afraid that the adoptive couple would claim that the child was never stolen—that the biological parents gave up the child and aren't entitled to change their mind."

"That's a fair point," he said.

"How likely is it that the biological parents could track their daughter from a place like Chechnya?"

"How long has it been since she went missing?"

"At least seven years. Probably more."

"Whoa. Lots of complicating factors there," he said. "In the time frame you're talking about, the trail out of Chechnya would be very murky."

"Impossible, would you say?"

"No," he said, and there was a hint of coyness. "No more impossible than what your husband is trying to prove in court."

"You know about that?"

"Everyone in my unit gets daily updates on child murder cases. Anyway, is there something specific you'd like me to look into, Andie?"

She thought about it. As long as she'd known Jack, she'd never blurred the line between one of his cases and an FBI investigation. If she was going to take this any farther, she needed more than curiosity. She needed solid leads—and the approval of ASAC Schwartz.

"Not yet," she said. "But I may be back in touch. And, hey, thanks."

CHAPTER 18

"T"he petitioner calls Debra Burgette," said Jack.

Judge Frederick had declared a short recess following Dr. Pollard's testimony. Fewer than a dozen spectators had turned out to watch the first witness. Triple that number, plus a strong media contingent, had filed in during the break to watch the victim's mother testify on behalf of her daughter's convicted killer. Jack had not publicized Debra's appearance, and, for her sake, he would have preferred less public attention. But word traveled fast in a courthouse where the media were perpetually poised to capture the arraignment of a federal prosecutor caught biting a stripper, the verdict on a high-priced call girl who claimed that "nymphomania made me do it," or some other "trial of the century," Miami-style.

The bailiff swore the witness and Debra took a seat. As Jack approached, he noted her quick, nervous glance toward the first row of public seating. Her ex-husband was seated on the opposite side of the courtroom, directly behind the prosecutor.

"Good morning," said Jack. "Please introduce yourself for the record."

Debra did so. A few more background questions followed, and even for the preliminaries the spectators watched in rapt silence. Then Jack heard one of the heavy double doors in the back of the courtroom creak open. It wasn't loud enough to be a disturbance, but Debra seemed more than slightly distracted as her daughter entered the courtroom. Out of the corner of his eye, Jack could see and almost feel Aquinnah agonize over which side of the courtroom to sit on, Mom's or Dad's. She remained standing in the very back, centered beneath the clock above the double doors, not the first child of divorce to assume the neutral posture of a Switzerland.

"Ms. Burgette, please tell the court about the phone call you received on Sashi's eighteenth birthday."

Jack and Debra had rehearsed the night before, and the strategy was to tackle the most difficult part of her testimony as quickly as possible: the phone calls. Debra drew a breath, and it was clear that no amount of rehearsal could have made this easy for her.

"I received the call in the morning," she said, her voice quaking.

Jack walked her through it, knowing that even though a trial lawyer was not technically allowed to ask his own witness "leading questions," an objection from the prosecutor would have made her look like a complete bully.

"And the following year," said Jack, "on Sashi's nineteenth birthday. Did you receive a phone call?"

"Yes," Debra said, and Jack again guided her through it. They did the same for the third phone call on Sashi's twentieth birthday. Just as Debra had told Jack in their first meeting, she explained that the calls were untraceable because they were from a disposable cell phone with no service contract, and that the police were of the view that it was all a cruel hoax. Then it was time for her to explain why she thought the caller was Sashi. At this point, even with Debra clutching a tissue moist with tears, Jack knew that the prosecutor would have to get tough.

"Ms. Burgette, do you know who these calls were from?" asked Jack.

"Yes. All are from—"

"Objection," said Carmichael. "Judge, I've tried to keep my objections to a minimum, but this does go to the heart of the matter. The witness doesn't *know* who these calls were from. Clearly she *believes* they were from her daughter. But that's pure speculation."

"The objection is sustained," said the judge. "I understand that the purpose of this hearing is to convince the court that Sashi Burgette was still alive after Mr. Reeves was convicted of murder. I'll give Mr. Swyteck a little latitude to establish a factual basis for the inference that these calls are from Sashi Burgette. But we're not going to delve into speculation."

A little latitude was all Jack needed.

"Thank you, Judge. Ms. Burgette, keeping the judge's comments in mind, let me ask you a few questions about your daughter. When did you first meet Sashi?"

"Not until my husband—now my ex-husband—and I were well into the adoption process. An agency accredited by the Russian government helped us put together a dossier, which took about three months. Once the dossier was filed in Russia, we waited another six months to get a referral from an orphanage. That's when Gavin and I traveled to Moscow."

"To meet Sashi?"

"Actually, to meet Alexander. Our request was for a boy. We immediately fell in love with Alexander and wanted to accept the referral. That's when we found out that Alexander had an older sister. Sashi."

"You didn't know that before you made the trip?"

"No. Basically all we knew at the time of the referral was Alexander's age and sex. It was a bit of a leap of faith to get on the airplane."

"Did you meet with Sashi on that first visit?"

"Yes."

"How did that go?"

Debra hesitated. "Not very well."

"How do you mean?"

"We tried talking to her, but we got no response."

"Because she didn't speak English?"

"No, we used a Russian translator. But Sashi just sat there. No response."

"How would you describe her at that meeting?"

"Alert. Watchful. But . . . frozen. That's actually the term for it: 'Frozen watchfulness,' the way a child acts when trying to be alert for the next blow. But we didn't know that at the time. We just had a child who wouldn't talk to us. We thought it might be the translator, so we brought in another one."

"Did that make a difference?"

"No. Again, we would ask questions. Sashi gave us silence."

"What did you do?"

"We asked to see her medical records."

"Did the records explain her behavior?"

"There was nothing specific."

"Anything general?"

"There's a—disclaimer, I guess you'd call it. Families are made to understand that many of the infants and children available for adoption may have developmental delays and may also suffer from malnutrition as well as other effects of being institutionalized."

"Were you satisfied with that explanation?"

"Not entirely. Gavin, not at all."

"But at some point you obviously agreed to adopt both Sashi and Alexander, correct?"

She glanced in her ex-husband's direction, and Jack caught a glimpse of what surely was a longer story. "Yes," Debra said. "After some . . . discussion, let's call it, the final decision was to adopt both children."

"When was the next time you saw Sashi?"

"About three months later. It took that long to get a court date in Russia. We stayed in Moscow another two weeks for the post-finalization waiting period."

"Were you able to talk with Sashi then?"

"It would be more accurate to say we talked *to* her."

"Was she any more responsive than she was in your first visit?"

"Again, she seemed alert. Vigilant, you might say. But there was nothing more."

"You got only silence?"

"Yes."

"Like the phone calls you received on her eighteenth, nineteenth, and twentieth birthdays?"

The prosecutor rose. "Objection, Judge."

"Sustained. I get your point, Mr. Swyteck, but that's just not a proper question. And be advised that I intend to finish this hearing before lunch. How much longer do you plan to go with this witness?"

"Just a few more questions," said Jack. "Ms. Burgette, did there come a time when Sashi did speak to you?"

"When we came back to Miami, we found a psychiatrist, Dr. Wurster, who is fluent in Russian. It took months of therapy, but we finally broke the silence."

"Sashi started speaking?"

"Yes. More and more as her English improved."

"Was it continuous improvement?"

"No. There were setbacks along the way. Times when Sashi would shut down and go silent again. Retreat into that frozen watchfulness."

"Was there anything in particular that triggered those periods of silence?"

"I'd say when she was frightened."

"Do you recall anything specific?"

"There was a lot of tension in our house, even before Sashi disappeared. Most of it related to Sashi. But it wasn't her fault."

The judge interjected gently. "Ms. Burgette, the question is how do you know that Sashi's silence was triggered by fear, as opposed to sadness, anger, stress, or whatever? Did you, personally, observe situations in which she regressed into silence in response to fear?"

"Yes, I did."

Jack followed up. "Can you give the judge an example of such an instance, Ms. Burgette?"

She lowered her eyes and answered in a soft voice. "Whenever Gavin would yell."

"Yell at Sashi?"

"Sometimes. But not necessarily. Just the yelling," she said, her voice drifting away. "All that yelling."

Judge Frederick rose. "Hold that thought, Ms. Burgette. Counsel—in my chambers. Now."

Jack glanced at Hannah, wondering if she knew what the problem was, but she seemed equally confused. The lawyers followed Judge Frederick to the paneled door behind the bench and proceeded, single file, into his chambers. The judge took a seat behind his desk, and the lawyers remained standing. Jack was in front of the floor-to-ceiling bookshelves. The prosecutor positioned herself beside the draped American flag.

"Exactly what do you think you're doing out there, Mr. Swyteck?" the judge asked.

The judge's harsh tone took him aback. "Our evidence is that these phone calls are from Sashi Burgette, and that the silence on the line is consistent with Sashi's psychological disorder."

"Really?" he said harshly. "It looks to me like you're leading an emotionally distraught woman down the path of painting her ex-husband as an abusive father and, quite possibly, a murderer."

"*What?* No, Judge. That's not at all what this is about. The medical records of Dr. Wurster show—and, in response to Your Honor's 'yes or no' question, the state's expert psychiatrist confirmed—that Sashi Burgette ran away from home on numerous occasions. The *new* evidence presented at this hearing is that Sashi made three phone calls to her mother after my client was sentenced to death for her murder. We don't know what kind of emotional trauma Sashi has endured since she last ran away from home, but whatever it is, she has slipped back into a pattern of silence that is triggered by fear."

"You're saying that she's incapable of screaming? Incapable of grunting? If you are, I'm not buying it."

"Ideally I would bring in Dr. Wurster, the psychiatrist who actually treated Sashi. But he has refused to testify on the grounds that if Sashi is alive, his communications with her are protected by the doctor-patient privilege and only Sashi can decide to waive the privilege."

"That's an interesting position," said the judge.

"I thought so, too," said Jack. "I believe he has taken that position at the encouragement of Sashi's father."

"There he goes again, Judge," said Carmichael. "Bashing the father."

The judge raised his arms like a boxing referee. "Enough. Mr. Swyteck, I told you at the outset that we are not going to try this case all over again. The purpose of this hearing is not to suggest that someone else murdered Sashi. The question is whether Sashi is dead or alive. Period. If she's deceased, your client's conviction stands. If she's not, you had better hope that she comes walking through that door right now. Because the evidence you've presented is nowhere near sufficient for me to disturb the jury's verdict of guilty."

"Is Your Honor denying the petitioner's request for relief?" asked the prosecutor.

"I'm rejecting any and all arguments that the victim is still alive."

Jack jumped in. "Judge, there are other arguments in our brief, including very serious challenges to Mr. Reeves' so-called confession."

The brief was on the judge's desk. He quickly thumbed through the table of contents. "I don't need an evidentiary hearing to decide those arguments. I will adjourn this hearing. You will have my ruling on the remaining issues no later than tomorrow. Is that clear?"

Painfully, thought Jack. "Yes, Your Honor."

CHAPTER 19

Jack worked late into the evening in Neil's old "conference room." The refrigerator behind him burped and gurgled like a dinosaur with indigestion. Jack hardly noticed.

There was little doubt how Judge Frederick intended to rule. The entire Freedom team was scrambling to find a new winning argument before Dylan Reeves' entire petition was booted out of court and the stay of execution was lifted. Every half hour or so, Hannah, Eve, or Brian would appear in the open doorway, eyes wide with excitement while pitching another "surefire winner." Jack would pick it apart in seconds, and it would be back to the drawing board. It amazed Jack how the team sustained the energy all these years. They were like his dearly departed golden retriever, who would sit happily and hopefully by the stove each morning, his tail wagging with optimism, absolutely convinced: *This is it, today is the day, Jack is gonna make me pancakes!*

Hannah walked in and put a bag of popcorn into the microwave. "Working in the kitchen again, eh, Jack?"

"Yeah. It's cooler in here."

"No, it's not. It's actually the hottest room in the house."

It was an old house, and Hannah's father had never called it "the office." The microwave beeped. Hannah got her popcorn and pulled up a chair at the table.

"You realize that you're paying us rent to use my dad's old room."

She tore open the bag and offered some popcorn. Jack took a steamy handful. "Yes, I realize that."

"You haven't gone in there since you moved in."

"That's not true."

"It is true."

Jack reached for the saltshaker. "Okay. So I haven't."

"Why not?"

"It's complicated."

"It's a room in a hundred-year-old house, Jack. The biggest room. The nicest room. But just a room."

Jack closed his laptop. "It's not just a room, Hannah. It's four years of memories. Some great. Some horrible."

" 'It was the best of dark and stormy nights; it was the worst of dark and stormy nights.' Is that it?"

Jack smiled. "Your literary references could use a little polish."

"Sorry, boss. I'm part of the gadget generation." She tossed a kernel into the air and caught it in her teeth. "Seriously. What are you afraid of? You think Eve and I might padlock you in there and never let you out?"

"You might," said Jack.

Eve appeared in the doorway. "I got it," said Eve, and her excitement practically knocked Jack and Hannah off their chairs.

"Okay. Let's hear it," said Jack.

She came to the table to make her pitch. "Trial counsel for Dylan Reeves stipulated that Sashi suffered from the 'inhibited' form of RAD. That was a huge mistake. He should have hired his own expert to review Sashi's medical records. That expert might have come to the conclusion that Sashi had the 'disinhibited' form of RAD."

"Where does that take us?"

"The terms are what they imply. A teen with inhibited behavior avoids relationships and attachments with almost everyone. Disinhibited RAD is characterized by indiscriminate sociability, such as excessive familiarity with relative strangers. That's according to the American Psychiatric Association. *And* get this: they are more prone to sexually acting out."

"We're not going to make that argument," said Jack.

"Don't you see, Jack? An effective lawyer at trial would have argued that Sashi had the disinhibited form of RAD. The semen on her panties could have resulted from *consensual* sex with Dylan Reeves."

"Except that it didn't happen that way."

"Jack, this is reasonable doubt on the sexual assault, which, in turn, casts doubt on both the murder conviction and the aggravating circumstances that supported the sentence of death."

"Dylan Reeves admitted to me that he overpowered Sashi with a knife. He says she got away. I have my doubts. I put the odds at fifty-fifty that he raped her that night, murdered her, kept her panties as a 'trophy,' and then jerked off onto them Saturday night before he was arrested."

"I hear what you're saying. Just let me write up a quick draft of the argument and see what you think."

"No. We're not making that argument," said Jack.

"It's our best shot to prove ineffective assistance of counsel in violation of the Sixth Amendment."

"Then we drop the ineffective assistance argument. Sashi Burgette did not consent to having sex with Dylan Reeves. As long as I'm in charge here, we're not going to play fast and loose with the facts to assassinate the victim."

"Ooo-kay," said Eve, rising. She turned and went back to her office.

"Glad to see you're 'in charge,'" Hannah said with a tight smile.

Jack took a breath. "I meant on this case."

His cell rang, and he checked the number.

"It's Debra again," he said to Hannah. "She calls every half hour asking for some good news."

"What are you going to tell her?"

"I don't know," he said, and then he answered.

"Jack! Jack!" She sounded completely out of breath.

"Slow down, Debra. What is it?"

"Sashi called!"

CHAPTER 20

Andie was alone at home when her cell rang. It was Jack. He didn't always love the fact that his wife was an FBI agent. That night, she suspected he did.

Andie wrote fast on a notepad as he relayed everything Debra had told him about the phone call. "Meet me at the field office," she said. "I'll have a tech agent access the call data record for her cell."

"The service provider can't give it to you without a warrant," said Jack.

"Yes, it can."

"No, it can't."

Yet another difference of opinion in the marriage of lawyer and law enforcement. "Tell Debra to call her provider right now and let them know that she consents to the FBI accessing her data."

"That'll work," said Jack.

Andie grabbed her keys and hurried out the door. She checked in with ASAC Schwartz by cell while speeding up the express lane on I-95, making sure he understood that the suspected caller was the victim—*alleged victim?*—in Jack's case.

"Be careful here, Andie," he told her. "You don't want to end up before an ethics review on a possible conflict of interest."

"We gotta move fast if this girl could still be alive. I know the background on this. I'll limit my personal involvement to interface with the tech unit till we sort this out."

"I'm good with that," he said, and Andie was good with it, too.

She didn't often use the police beacon in her unmarked car, but the flashing light helped her make it from Key Biscayne to the field office in record time. She went straight to the tech unit. Special Agent Kevin Kusak was seated in front of the computer terminal, already at work on the information she'd forwarded from her car. Kusak was a member of the FBI's Cellular Analysis and Surveillance Team (CAST), which specialized in cellular records and analysis of cell location evidence. Andie pulled up a chair and sat beside him. The LCD before them was aglow with columns of raw data.

"The call detail record for Debra Burgette's phone confirms that she did have an incoming call from the number you gave me," said Kusak. "It was at nine-eleven p.m. and lasted two minutes."

"Can you attach a name to the incoming number?"

"It's a burner," he said, meaning a prepaid cell phone. "Probably purchased for cash by a guy who walked into the local fly-by-night electronics store dressed up like a cast member from *Duck Dynasty*. No service contract, no way to know who owns it."

"Just like the three other calls Debra received on Sashi's birthdays," said Andie. "Do you have anything on location?"

"Cell tower connection data is coming up now," he said, staring at the screen. "I had to push to get this without a warrant. Ms. Burgette's consent to allow us to access data for her cell has nothing to do with data for the prepaid phone."

"Glad you were able to get it."

"Keep in mind that it won't tell you where the prepaid cell phone is right now. This is not a real-time search. It's historical."

"I understand," said Andie.

"Good," he said. "Some agents come in here expecting too much. Usually it's the old guys who just last week figured out how to use the HOLD button on their landline. They think that because calls on prepaid cells are transmitted over existing networks, I can give them a street address for each call. It doesn't work that way. You don't get the location of the phone. All this tells you is the location of the first cell tower that the call connected to in the network."

"Which probably is the tower that was closest to the cell phone, but not necessarily."

"You've done this before, then?"

Andie let it slide, but her bet was that Kusak had laid eyes on her protruding belly and assumed that she'd been barefoot and pregnant since the dawn of the cellular age. "Yes. I've done this before," said Andie.

Kusak tightened his focus on the screen, then hit the ENTER button. "Got it," he said. "The phone was within two-point-eight miles of BellSouth Mobility cell tower number J-62."

"Where is that?" asked Andie.

"Let me see," he said, switching screens with a click of his mouse. A map of south Florida appeared with cell towers superimposed. "Unfortunately, it's a very densely populated area. Anywhere from Sunny Isles Beach in Miami-Dade County almost all the way up to Hallandale Beach in Broward."

Andie stared at the map, and then it hit her. "Little Moscow," she said.

"What?"

"When I transferred here from Seattle, the first investigation I worked on was the Lufthansa heist at the airport."

"I remember it," said Kusak. "Biggest cash heist ever in Florida."

"The kingpin in the heist owned a Russian-style restaurant right in the Sunny Isles–Hallandale Beach district. Huge Russian-speaking population there. Everyone from Anna Kournikova and NHL stars to ballet teachers and *Mafiya* goons. And it's not just Russians. You have Ukrainians, Belorussians, Lithuanians, Latvians, Moldavians, Uzbeks, Chechens, and on and on."

"I didn't know that."

"You need to get out more."

"Yeah, no kidding. So, does a possible Russian connection help your investigation?"

"The missing girl—the girl who may have made this phone call—was adopted from an orphanage in Moscow. Her biological parents were possibly from Chechnya."

"Glad to be of help," said Kusak.

Andie was about to dial Jack's number, then stopped. Instead she dialed Special Agent Steve Hidalgo at the Violent Crimes Against Children Unit in Washington. The work never ended in that unit, and her hunch that he'd still be at his desk at ten o'clock at night proved correct.

"Steve, hi. It's Andie Henning. Sorry it's late, but you said to call if I had anything for you to follow up on."

"You have something?"

"I need to conference in my ASAC to keep this kosher. I may even have to drop off the call and let you run with this if Schwartz doesn't want me involved. But the answer to your question is yes," she said, glancing again at the map. "I do have something."

CHAPTER 21

Jack was back in court at eight on Friday morning. Based on the emergency motion filed by the Freedom Institute late Thursday night, Judge Frederick reopened the evidentiary hearing for additional testimony from Debra Burgette on the possible whereabouts of her daughter.

Jack rose and walked to the podium. The courtroom was less than half-full, but the media had returned in full force. Gavin Burgette was again in the front row of public seating, directly behind the prosecutor. Jack saw no sign of Aquinnah. Debra wrung her hands, waiting for the first question. She appeared no less nervous than she had in her first trip to the witness stand, but she definitely looked more tired. It had been a late night for her and the entire Freedom team.

The prosecutor spoke before Jack could begin. "Judge, I think it would be appropriate to remind the witness that she is still under oath."

"Are you not awake yet, Ms. Carmichael? That has already been done."

"Oh, my mistake," she said.

Jack knew it was anything but a mistake. It was the prosecutor's calculated reinforcement of an earlier warning that had prompted Debra to tell Jack that she needed her own lawyer: the state attorney prosecutes perjury.

"Ms. Burgette," said Jack, "yesterday you testified about three telephone calls you received on your cell phone, the last of which came on your daughter Sashi's twentieth birthday. Have you received any similar calls since then?"

"Yes, I got one last night."

"Do you recall the incoming number?"

"Yes," she said, and she repeated it.

"Judge, before proceeding further, I wanted to inform the court that as soon as Ms. Burgette called me, I immediately notified the state attorney's office and Miami-Dade Police, as well as the FBI. At this time, I would like to offer into evidence a call-data record that the FBI obtained from Ms. Burgette's service provider which confirms that at nine-eleven p.m. she received a call from the number in question, and it lasted for two minutes."

The judge took a copy from Jack and inspected it. "Any objection from the state?"

"None," said Carmichael. "The FBI provided the same report to us last night."

"The exhibit is admitted. Continue, please, Mr. Swyteck."

"Ms. Burgette, have you ever received a call from that number before?"

"Yes. One time."

"When?"

"The call I received on Sashi's twentieth birthday was from this same number."

"Exactly when was that?"

"Twenty-eight days ago."

"Hold on one minute," the judge said. "You're saying that even though this is a so-called disposable phone, Ms. Burgette received calls from this same number twenty-eight days apart?"

"Yes, Your Honor. Disposable phones aren't exactly like disposable razors. People can keep the same burner for weeks or even months."

"Okay, where is the incoming call on this exhibit?" the judge asked.

"It's highlighted in yellow on page two of the exhibit."

"Yes, I see it now. Has law enforcement been able to identify the owner of that incoming phone number?"

Jack explained the problem of prepaid cell phones, cash buyers, and no service contract. The judge had presided over enough trials of drug dealers to understand.

"Ms. Burgette, tell the court what you heard in the call last night."

"Nothing," she said in a soft voice. "It was silence for two minutes. Just like the last three calls."

"Did you say anything?"

"Yes, of course. I kept encouraging her to say something. I said, 'Sashi, talk to me! Please!'"

"There was no reply?"

Debra shook her head. "No."

"Thank you. No further questions." Jack returned to his seat beside Hannah.

The prosecutor rose. "Judge, I would like a sidebar before cross-examination of this witness."

The judge waved counsel forward. Four lawyers, two from each side, huddled with the judge alongside the bench, their conversation out of earshot of the witness and spectators. The prosecutor spoke first.

"Judge, this witness is the mother of a murder victim. For the reasons I discussed in chambers yesterday, I prefer not to put her through cross-examination and treat her as an adverse witness if the court is still inclined to deny Dylan Reeves' petition and lift the stay of execution."

"The landscape has changed considerably since I spoke in chambers yesterday," the judge said. "In fact, my inclination is to extend the stay of execution as long as the FBI is actively investigating whether Sashi Burgette is still alive."

"No one said the FBI is investigating anything," said the prosecutor.

"I inferred otherwise from Mr. Swyteck's remarks."

"No," she said. "That might be what Mr. Swyteck tried to talk his wife into doing after they went to bed last night, but I know of no FBI investigation."

"That was way out of line," said Jack.

"Yes, it was," the judge said sternly.

"I apologize. But if the court's ruling will be influenced by whether or not the FBI has opened an investigation, then I would like a short recess to get the facts straight."

"Maybe Mr. Swyteck already has that information."

"I do not," said Jack. "That's an internal matter at the Bureau."

"All right," said the judge. "We'll reconvene this afternoon at two p.m. And in case you're worried, Ms. Carmichael, yes, I *will* remind the witness that she remains under oath."

"Thank you, Your Honor," said Jack, and he didn't feel the need to say anything more.

For now.

CHAPTER 22

Andie spent the first part of her morning revising the operational budget for Operation Pill Mill, and the irony was not lost on her when she took a break to head downstairs to the infirmary. Nurse Rebecca was on site in the Miami field office to assist agents and staff with everything from a case of the sniffles to necessary immunizations for travel to the Brazilian rain forest. Andie just wanted her blood pressure checked.

"Your systolic is up a bit from yesterday," said the nurse, as she removed the Velcro cuff from Andie's arm. "Have you been givin' yourself enough lookin'-out-the-winder time?"

Andie assumed that "looking-out-the-window time" was another one of those great expressions that Rebecca had borrowed from her grandma in Birmingham. "Probably not."

"You need breaks, Andie. Breathin' exercises are good. And avoid stress."

Avoid stress. Had Rebecca suddenly forgotten than they worked in the same building? It was "like tellin' the flame to avoid the fire"—another good one from Rebecca's grandma.

"I'll try."

Andie went back upstairs to finish working on her budget. The phone rang as she entered her office. It was Agent Hidalgo from the Violent Crimes Against Children Unit, which came as a surprise. ASAC Schwartz had pulled her off the investigation because of the Jack connection and possible conflict of interest.

"I've spoken with my unit chief," said Hidalgo.

"Steve, before you say anything more, you should know that I'm walled off from this investigation."

"I know. But that's the point of my call. There is no investigation, and I thought you had a right to know."

Andie lowered herself into her chair. "That sure didn't take long."

"Let me put it this way: it would be unprecedented for the FBI to reopen a missing-person investigation where the victim's killer has been convicted and sentenced to death, and he's literally a cell door away from the execution chamber."

Andie couldn't get comfortable. It wasn't Hidalgo. Her baby had picked a most inopportune time to press on her bladder. She lifted herself up from her desk chair and stood at the window. "I wasn't expecting you to issue an Amber alert. But I wasn't expecting to run into a wall so soon, either."

"I understand. But the facts as proven in a court of law are the facts. Miami-Dade Police investigated each of those phone calls that Debra Burgette received on her daughter's birthday. The firm conclusion is that this is a hoax."

"I don't agree with that conclusion."

There was a slight hesitation on Hidalgo's end of the line. "You think Sashi is alive?"

"I don't think this is a pervert getting his jollies by messing with Sashi's mother."

"Are you circling back to the idea that Sashi was stolen back by her biological parents?"

"Let me just say that when Schwartz told me to hand this case off to you, I was hoping someone would at least be open to the possibility that it could have been them. Or maybe a friend, a neighbor, a relative—anyone who, in line with long-standing Chechen tradition, believed it was his or her right and responsibility to raise Sashi after her parents were killed in the war if she hadn't been stolen from her extended family, her community, her village. Or maybe it's someone who doesn't know Sashi or her family at all. Maybe it's someone connected to a completely different Chechen family who thinks their stolen child was sold to the highest American bidder, so they steal Sashi from these rich Americans."

"But if any of those things happened, where has Sashi been for three years?"

"Co-opted. Brainwashed. Locked in a basement, God forbid. Remember, we are dealing with a teenager—now an adult—who has reactive attachment disorder. I'm hamstrung here because this is my husband's case and I can't be involved. But I have to say I'm not comfortable with the door slamming on all these possibilities in less than twenty-four hours. Especially now that we know this latest call originated from the area in south Florida we call Little Moscow."

"Wow. You make a stronger case for Sashi being alive than your husband does. Maybe you should join his legal team."

Andie was about to laugh right along with him, but she didn't hear any laughter coming from the Washington end of the line. *Is that what the pushback from Washington is about, Steve? The mommy-to-be agent helping her husband?*

"Jack doesn't need a cheerleader," she said.

"That's good. Because here's something that might change your view. I asked one of the tech agents to look at the same cell tower data that Agent Kusak examined in your office."

"Did your guy interpret it differently?"

"He understands how Kusak reached his conclusion. The data showed that the call was routed to a cell tower in what you say is Little Moscow. Based on that, Kusak concluded that the prepaid cell phone was located in that same area."

"Right."

"But a call from a cell doesn't always get picked up by the nearest tower. If that tower is overloaded, the call will reroute to another tower. Of course, this is all happening in split seconds."

"Right. So?"

"I don't want to get too deep into tech-speak, but here's the gist. My tech guy looked into the routing patterns in south Florida. The cell tower closest to Debra Burgette's house is—well, let's call it Cell Tower A. If someone makes a call to Debra's house and Cell Tower A is overloaded, the usual pattern would be for that call to reroute to the cell tower in Little Moscow."

"So even though the caller isn't actually in the Little Moscow area, the cell-phone records would suggest—at first glance, anyway—that the call was initiated from Little Moscow."

"Exactly. This is a very congested network. Calls are rerouted every second from overloaded towers. My techie believes that this two-minute call to Debra from the prepaid cell was rerouted."

"So, in his view, Debra and the caller were actually closer to each other than the cell tower records would indicate."

"Right."

"Which in your mind means what?"

"It could mean several things."

"What do you *think* it means?"

"I'm speculating, I admit. But it's at least possible that when Debra Burgette received this phone call, she had her cell phone in her left hand and a burner in her right hand."

Andie hesitated, staring out the window as she followed his implication through to its disturbing conclusion. "Debra called herself?"

"Yeah. And she knew that her cell-phone records would show yet another two-minute phone call from a prepaid cell, which can't be traced back to anyone. The cell tower analysis doesn't rule out that possibility."

"Why would Debra do that?"

"Desperation. She sincerely believes that her daughter is alive. She believes even more strongly that Sashi can be found *only* if she can somehow get law enforcement to reopen the missing-person investigation."

"I see your point. But I also see a gaping hole in it."

"Which is what?"

"If that were Debra's motivation, why did she tell us that she heard only silence on the line? There's no recording of these phone conversations. No data is preserved, other than the length of the call. There's no way for us to know what was said or if anything was said at all. If Debra has been buying prepaid cell phones, making these calls to her own cell, and claiming that Sashi's on the line—a premeditated plan to convince the police that they should reopen the investigation because Sashi is alive— why wouldn't she take her lie to the next step?"

"What next step?"

"If she's making this up, she could just as easily say, 'Sashi called. She talked to me. She wants to come home. Help me bring her home.' Why stop at saying that Sashi called me and won't say anything?"

Hidalgo didn't have an answer. "I see your point, too."

"Good. Where does that get us?"

He breathed out again. "I'm afraid it doesn't get the missing-person file reopened. That much I know."

"Okay," said Andie. "But I'm going to keep my eyes and ears open. And I've got your number on speed dial when I have something."

He seemed to take notice that she'd said "when," not "if."

"I'll be right here," he said. "Anything else I can do for ya?"

Andie was still bothered by Hidalgo's insinuation that she had followed this lead to help her husband. "Yeah, there's one thing. You should call Barbara Carmichael about the cell tower analysis. And share your theory about Debra calling herself as well."

"It's more speculation than theory. I don't think that part is even worth sharing."

"It's important to me that you do," said Andie. "Anything

we do in connection with this case, we need to let the chips fall where they may."

"All right."

"So you'll call her?"

"Yeah. If you want me to."

"Thank you," said Andie. "I want you to."

CHAPTER 23

The hearing in Judge Frederick's courtroom resumed at two p.m.

Jack had nothing to report. If the FBI was planning to reopen the Sashi Burgette investigation, they weren't telling the lawyer for her accused killer. Jack hadn't bothered to call Andie directly and put the question to her. Crossing that line would have been an egregious violation of the unwritten rules that kept them happily married.

The prosecutor delivered the news in open court. "Judge, the bottom line is that the FBI's National Crime Information Center's missing-person file on Sashi Burgette remains closed."

"And that's not going to change?" asked the judge.

"I don't have that information."

Jack believed her. It wouldn't have been the first time that a local state attorney had been left off the FBI's need-to-know list.

"Very well," the judge said. "Shall we bring in the witness?"

"Yes," said the prosecutor. "At this time the state of Florida would like to proceed with the cross-examination of Debra Burgette."

The courtroom deputy brought the witness forward. Debra took her place, and the judge reminded her that she was still under oath. She nodded with so much apprehension that Jack thought she might ask for a blindfold and cigarette.

God, I hope this was the right decision, he thought.

The prosecutor approached and stood before her. It wasn't a threatening posture, but it was clear who was in control. "Good afternoon, Ms. Burgette. I'm sorry we have to see each other again under these circumstances."

Debra nodded again, then cut her eyes toward the gallery. It was only a split second, but Jack followed her gaze, and it led straight to her ex-husband.

"Do you remember the first time we met?" asked the prosecutor.

"Yes," Debra said softly.

"You'll have to speak up a little bit," the judge said.

"Yes," she said, her voice not much louder. "I do."

"That was a horrible period in your life, and I hate to take you back there. But we talked about Sashi at our first meeting. Didn't we?"

"We did."

"You told me that you loved Sashi and that, in her own way, you believed that Sashi loved you. Do you remember that?"

"I do."

"But it was a difficult relationship. You told me that in the four years Sashi lived with you, she'd run away from home several times."

"Yes."

"At least six or seven times, you told me. Maybe as many as ten. Correct?"

"Around that number. But those were nothing like what we're talking about here. Sashi would get angry and run out of the house, and we wouldn't know where she was. And it was awful, and stressful. But she was never gone overnight."

"And part of the reason it was so awful was that you felt guilty."

Jack rose. "Objection," he said, but he used a gentle tone, so as not to jar the witness. "It's just improper to make an insinuation like that in this setting."

"Sustained." It may or may not have been the proper ruling in the legal sense, but Jack had pushed the right button.

"I'll rephrase," said the prosecutor. She returned to the podium and retrieved a notepad. "Let me try to recall your words as precisely as I can," she said, checking her pad. "You told me: 'Every time Sashi ran away from home, I felt like I was to blame. Whenever she ran, it was because I'd missed something. It was her cry for help.' Did you tell me that, Ms. Burgette?"

Jack could feel Debra struggling. The prosecution had fought to keep out all evidence of Sashi's runaways, and now that Jack had managed to get it before the court, Carmichael was using it against the defense—and Debra.

"Ms. Burgette, did you say that to me? Or words to that effect?"

"I think I did."

"You *think* you did? Or you did?"

She swallowed hard. "I'm sure I did."

The prosecutor paused, as if ready to switch topics. "Again, I apologize for having to take you back to the worst day of any parent's life. But I have to ask you a few questions about the day Sashi disappeared."

"I understand."

"You testified at trial that the last time you saw Sashi was on a Friday morning, when you dropped her off near her school."

Debra drew a breath. "Yes."

"Now, you also mentioned that you and Sashi had an argument during that ride to school. Isn't that correct?"

"Unfortunately, yes," she said softly.

"The argument was one of the reasons Sashi got out of the car before you actually reached the drop-off at campus. Isn't that a fact, Ms. Burgette?"

She stared blankly at Jack, as if fully aware that she'd told him a slightly different version. "Traffic was bad, too. She was afraid she was going to be late."

"Ms. Burgette," the prosecutor said, her tone tightening. "Sashi ran from the car, didn't she?"

She swallowed hard, her expression almost numb. "She was in a hurry."

"At trial, you testified that you didn't remember what that argument was about."

"That's correct."

"Do you recall now?"

Debra did a double take, as if the question surprised her. "No."

"That's understandable. Let me see if I can refresh your recollection." The prosecutor went back to her table and retrieved a one-page document from a file. "Your Honor, I have here a copy of Ms. Burgette's cell-phone billing record for the one-month period of time before Sashi's disappearance. May I show it to the witness?"

"If you think it will help her remember, you may."

The prosecutor provided a copy to Jack and to the judge. Then she approached the witness and handed the document to her. "Ms. Burgette, I focus your attention specifically to the lines that are highlighted in yellow. Please review them carefully, and let me know when you have finished."

Jack read the same lines. Phone numbers. None that Jack recognized. He looked up in time to see Debra's copy shaking in her hand.

"This is . . ." said Debra, her voice fading. "I know what this is."

"Does it refresh your recollection as to what you and Sashi were arguing about?"

Debra nodded, and yet her body language indicated that she had needed no reminder—that she had never really forgotten the cause of their argument. Until this moment, however, no one had ever forced the issue.

"We argued about things Sashi was doing on the Internet," said Debra.

"What, specifically?"

Debra breathed so heavily that her shoulders heaved, then slumped. "Sashi was making contact with . . . strangers."

"Men?"

"Yes."

"She was sending pictures of herself to these men, was she not?"

"Yes."

"Some were provocative, shall we say?"

"Yes."

"How did you find out about this behavior?"

Debra's eyes closed, then opened, as if she were summoning some inner strength to speak. "Some of the men called."

"The men Sashi had contacted called *you*, correct?"

"Yes," said Debra.

"Because Sashi was giving these men *your* phone number, correct?"

"That's correct."

"Some of the men that Sashi contacted were what you might call 'undesirables,' am I right?"

"That's an accurate statement."

"At least one of men who called you was a registered sex offender. True?"

"That turned out to be the case."

The prosecutor retrieved the document, holding it up for Debra to see. "In fact, these phone calls—the ones highlighted on this bill—were the reason you and Sashi had an argument on the day in question. Correct?"

Debra drew a breath, then another. "Yes."

"You were angry with Sashi, weren't you?"

"I was."

"You were furious."

"I suppose."

"You were fed up."

"I don't know."

"You said some things you regret."

Debra was tightening up, fighting back tears. "Yes."

The prosecutor checked her notes again, as if to warn the witness that there was no wiggling out of this. "You told her that you were going to send her back to Russia, didn't you?"

Debra's body shook. The dam burst. A tear rolled down her cheek. "Yes."

The prosecutor paused. The courtroom fell silent, save for the sound of Debra's sobbing.

"You didn't mean what you said, did you?"

"No. No, I didn't. I didn't mean a word of it."

"You wish you could take it back?"

"Yes."

"You'd like to have a second chance."

"Of course."

"This week, you went so far as to reopen the 'Find Sashi' command center at a local motel. Am I right?"

"For a time."

"It's closed now?"

"Yes. Acquinnah and I shut it down. The motel was nice enough to give us our money back."

"Nobody came to help find Sashi?"

"Well, Mr. Swyteck came."

Debra was looking right at Jack, as if begging for some show of support. Jack could only watch.

"Anyone else?" asked the prosecutor.

"A couple of my friends stopped by. But not to help find Sashi. They told me I needed to find closure."

"Ms. Burgette, so long as the official police investigation into Sashi's disappearance remains closed, no one is going to help you search for Sashi. You know that's true, right?"

"I don't know."

"Ms. Burgette, I can't say that anyone in this courtroom would blame you, but if it would keep the investigation open, you would lie to the police, wouldn't you?"

"Objection!" said Hannah, rising.

Jack and the judge exchanged glances, since it was technically Jack's role to pose objections, not Hannah's.

"Grounds?" asked the judge.

Hannah paused, struggling. "She's . . . she's just being mean."

The judge leaned back in his leather chair, pondering it. "Well, I can't say I've ever heard that one before. But, you know what? I'm actually going to sustain the objection. Ms. Carmichael, really. Isn't there a more humane way to make the point you're trying to make?"

"I'll wrap it up, Your Honor." She moved closer to the witness, tightening her virtual grasp. "Ms. Burgette, you received phone calls from no fewer than ten different strangers, each of whom had received your cell number from Sashi over the Internet. Isn't that true?"

"It could have been that many. It had gotten out of control."

"You rebuffed every single one of those men, did you not?"

"Of course."

"And be honest now, because I'm sure this has crossed your mind: Couldn't any one of those men have made those phone calls to you in which you heard only silence, after Sashi's disappearance?"

"Objection," said Jack.

The judge considered it. "If the witness can answer, I'll allow it."

Debra leaned closer to the microphone to answer, then hesitated, as if not sure what to say. "I really don't know."

"No," said the prosecutor. "None of us really know, do we?"

"Objection."

"Sustained."

"I have nothing further, Your Honor." The prosecutor took the long way back to her seat, and as she walked past the petitioner's table, she spoke under her breath, so only Jack could hear.

"I can't believe you forced me to do that," she hissed.

The prosecutor returned to her table. Debra remained seated

on the witness stand, seemingly numb from the experience. Jack watched from his seat, crushed by the weight of her stare—her silent cry for help.

"Mr. Swyteck," the judge said. "You may have a few minutes of redirect, if you wish."

"Thank you, Judge," he said, rising. "I'll be very brief. In fact, I have just one question for the witness.

"Ms. Burgette, have you *ever* knowingly provided false information to *anyone* in law enforcement regarding the disappearance or whereabouts of your daughter Sashi?"

She didn't move. Her mixed expression was one of fear and confusion as Judge Frederick prodded her again.

"Ms. Burgette?"

Debra wobbled to her feet.

"Ms. Burgette, there's a question pending," said the judge.

She settled back into her seat. "I'm sorry. Could you repeat it, please?"

Jack did so. It was a simple question, one that any lawyer would ask to rehabilitate his witness on the stand. And yet there was hesitation from Debra.

Finally, she answered. "No, I never lied."

Jack would have liked a more forceful response. He wasn't sure if Debra was so beaten down by the prosecutor's cross-examination that her heart was no longer in the fight, or if there was more to it. But the examination of his own witness was no time to explore the unknown. He decided that he'd get to the bottom of it after the hearing—*immediately* after the hearing—straight from Debra.

"No further questions," said Jack.

"Ms. Burgette, you are excused," said the judge.

Debra rose and stepped down from the witness stand.

Hannah leaned closer to Jack. "What the heck's up with Debra?" she whispered.

Jack wondered as well. Without question, the prosecutor had

siphoned off much of Jack's enthusiasm for representing Dylan Reeves. Maybe she'd drained the last bit of Debra's strength, too. But Dylan Reeves was still Jack's client, and Jack was duty bound to exploit every opportunity—and the prosecutor was far less clever than she thought she was.

"I don't know," he whispered back, "but Barbara Carmichael may have just handed us a new trial."

"Say what?"

"Mr. Swyteck, is that the end of your case in chief?" asked the judge.

Jack rose. "No, Your Honor. There's one more witness I would like to call."

CHAPTER 24

Mr. Swyteck, I need a name," said Judge Frederick. "That's all I'm asking: What is the name of your next—and, hopefully, final—witness?"

"I don't have a specific name," said Jack.

"That sounds like a rather serious problem for you," the judge said.

Jack stepped away from his table, positioning himself more in the center of the room. "Judge, here's the situation. During cross-examination, Ms. Carmichael showed Debra Burgette a phone record that listed at least ten 'undesirables,' including one convicted sex offender, who had called her cell. Less than a month before her disappearance, Sashi Burgette had online communications with each of these men, sent them 'provocative' photographs, and gave them her mother's cell number. In the prosecutor's own words, 'any one of those men' could have made the phone calls that Ms. Burgette now believes were from Sashi." Jack paused for effect, then delivered his punch:

"Well, Judge, it's equally true that any one of those men could be responsible for the disappearance of Sashi Burgette."

The prosecutor rose. "Judge, it's also possible that the bogeyman did it. It's time for this to end."

"Let Mr. Swyteck finish," said the judge.

Jack continued. "Mr. Reeves should have been given the opportunity to explore those leads—especially in this case, where a body was never recovered. But the prosecution never told Mr. Reeves or his trial lawyer about any of this. The failure to turn over the names of other potential suspects is grounds for reversal of Mr. Reeves' conviction and for a new trial."

"This information is *Brady* material, is that your argument, Mr. Swyteck?"

"Yes," said Jack, pleased that the judge got it. *Brady v. Maryland* was the landmark Supreme Court holding that the Constitution requires the prosecution to hand over before trial all material evidence that is favorable to the accused.

"If I understand correctly," the judge said, "you want this court to order the state of Florida to bring forward a witness from the Miami-Dade Police Department or the office of the state attorney to explain why this information was withheld from Mr. Reeves before trial. Do I have that right?"

"Yes," said Jack. "I believe the examination of that witness will demonstrate my client's right to a new trial."

Judge Frederick's gaze drifted to the other side of the courtroom. "What is the state's position?"

"First of all, this hearing was supposed to be limited to one question: Is Sashi Burgette still alive? Clearly Mr. Swyteck has lost that argument. So what does he do? He attacks the police and the prosecutor with allegations of misconduct. This is insulting and offensive."

"Your indignation is noted," said the judge. "Did the government turn over this evidence to the defense before trial or not?"

"No, we did not."

"Why not?"

"There are many good and compelling reasons, Judge."

"Wonderful. I'm eager to hear them. You have thirty minutes to produce a witness who can explain those reasons to the court."

"But—"

"Ms. Carmichael, the alternative is to put *you* on the stand and let *you* explain. I suggest you find a witness."

There was silence, and Jack was certain that silence was far more uncomfortable on the prosecutor's side of the courtroom.

"The state of Florida will produce a witness," she said.

"Good call," said the judge. "We'll reconvene in thirty minutes."

P lease state your name for the record," Jack said to the witness.

The thirty-minute recess had passed in the blink of an eye. Jack had done his best to prepare, but this would be no ordinary cross-examination. The cardinal rule was never to ask a question on cross if you didn't already know the answer: knowledge and preparation were the trial lawyer's instruments of control when dealing with an adverse witness. Jack would be traveling on deduction and instinct to frame his questions. It was enough to get even a seasoned criminal defense lawyer's heart pounding.

"My name is Emilio Hernandez," said the witness. "I'm a detective with the Miami-Dade Police Department."

It took Jack less than a minute to elicit the necessary background, and two minutes more to confirm that Detective Hernandez was indeed *the* person who could explain the handling of evidence gathered from Sashi Burgette's computer, as well as the phone records from Debra's cell that connected her and Sashi to the "strangers"—or, as Jack called them, the potential murder suspects.

"Detective Hernandez, I'm now handing you Exhibit 11, which has previously been identified as the call detail report for Debra Burgette's cell phone for the month prior to her daughter's disappearance. Have you seen this before?"

"Yes. I was the one who obtained that information from Ms. Burgette's service provider."

Jack hesitated. Of all the questions *not* to ask on cross-examination, none ranked higher than the dreaded open-ended "why" question. But Jack was in no position to do otherwise. "Why did you get it?"

"Standard practice in a homicide investigation. We requested cell-phone records from the victim and everyone else in her family."

Jack breathed a sigh of relief. A "why" question that an MDPD detective failed to grab with both hands and shove right down the defense lawyer's throat. *Oh, happy day.* "This report lists many, many incoming phone calls to Debra Burgette's cell. Ten of these entries are highlighted in yellow. Do you see that?"

"Yes."

"We were told earlier that one of these highlighted numbers belongs to a convicted sex offender. Can you tell which one?"

"Yes," he said, referencing the list. "Moving down from the top, it is the third highlighted phone number."

Jack checked his copy. "I notice that there is no account-holder name associated with the incoming call. Just a phone number."

The detective said nothing. He was a well-coached witness: don't start running your mouth every time a defense lawyer pauses; wait for a question. Jack continued, but he wasn't ready to ask another "why" question. He went with his instincts: "Is that because this number was connected to a prepaid cell phone with no registered account holder?"

"Yes, that's correct."

It was the answer Jack wanted, and it provided the assurance he needed to ask the next open-ended question. "Then how did you determine that the person making the call was a convicted sex offender?"

"The physical phone itself was found in the possession of Mr. Carlos Mendoza. And Mr. Mendoza is a convicted sex offender."

A younger lawyer might have jumped up and kicked his heels, giddy with excitement. A quick glance over his shoulder confirmed that Hannah was not far from liftoff. Jack kept it cool.

"Back up a second, please, Detective. When was the prepaid

cell phone found in Mr. Mendoza's possession? Before or after Sashi Burgette disappeared?"

"About six months after."

"How did it happen that MDPD found the phone on Mr. Mendoza's person?"

"He was arrested."

Another score. Jack forged ahead. "On what charges?"

The witness hesitated, as if wishing the lawyer hadn't asked. "Human trafficking."

Holy shit. "Where is Mr. Mendoza these days?"

An even longer pause from the witness, then he replied. "Mr. Mendoza is currently serving a ten-year sentence in Florida State Prison."

Holier than holy shit. "You said earlier that he was arrested six months after Sashi's disappearance. Was he released on bail?"

"No."

"So, he has been incarcerated continuously since his arrest, is that right?"

"Yes."

"Then you would have to agree with me that Mr. Mendoza has not been making phone calls to Debra Burgette on a prepaid cell phone over the past two and half years."

"Objection," said the prosecutor. "Calls for speculation."

"Overruled. The witness may answer."

"Yes. I would agree with that," said the detective.

I could kiss this guy. "It is also a fact that the murder trial against Dylan Reeves began seven months after the disappearance of Sashi Burgette, am I right?"

"That sounds right."

"So Mr. Mendoza was arrested and the prepaid cell phone was recovered roughly *four months* before trial began."

"Roughly, yes."

Jack could feel the momentum, and he was ready to go in for the kill. "In other words, four months before Dylan Reeves' trial,

MDPD knew that Debra Burgette had received a phone call on a prepaid cell from a man who had been charged with the crime of human trafficking. Isn't that right, sir?"

"No, that's dead wrong," he said.

He looked straight at Jack, as if daring the lawyer to ask the dangerous follow-up question—to ask a seasoned detective to explain his answer. Jack knew better, but the witness turned to the judge. "I can explain why, if Your Honor would like to know."

"Yes, the court would like to know."

Just like that, Jack had lost control. *Very smart witness.*

"Your Honor, the counselor's question assumes that MDPD had connected all the dots before the start of Mr. Reeves' trial. The truth is, we didn't immediately *know* that the phone number for the prepaid cell found in Mr. Mendoza's possession matched one of the incoming numbers that appeared on Debra Burgette's call record. There's no MDPD database that magically makes that connection."

Jack wanted his witness back, but the judge was on a roll, firing off another question from the bench.

"When did MDPD first become aware that Mr. Mendoza was one of the callers?"

"Yesterday," said the detective.

"*Yesterday?*" asked the judge, incredulous. "How did you come to find this out just yesterday?"

"It was pointed out to us by Gavin Burgette. Debra Burgette's ex-husband."

"No one mentioned this to you before yesterday?"

"No, Your Honor."

The judge removed his reading glasses, as if that might make things clearer. "How is it that Mr. Burgette comes forward with that information three years after the fact?"

Detective Hernandez seemed more than happy to step into the mind of Sashi's father and answer the question. "Mr. Burgette accepts the tragic fact that the jury got it right: his daughter was murdered by Dylan Reeves. He further believes that one of these men is responsible for the so-called birthday calls to Ms. Burgette."

Jack needed to wrest control back from the judge, albeit respectfully. "Judge, I think the only person who can answer your question is Mr. Burgette. I'd like the opportunity to question him under oath."

The prosecutor jumped in. "I believe this hearing is over," she said. "None of this has anything to do with the question of whether Sashi Burgette is still alive."

Judge Frederick rocked back in his chair again, this time even farther than usual, as if counting the tiles in the ceiling. "It concerns me that the defense was never told that Sashi Burgette was contacting strangers via the Internet in the month prior to her disappearance."

"The defense could have subpoenaed Sashi's computer records," said the prosecutor. "That's all they were entitled to receive."

"It's not that easy," Judge Frederick said. "It seems to me that the government should have handed over Debra Burgette's phone records if you knew that Sashi had given her mother's cell number to strange men she was meeting on the Internet."

"That's exactly right," said Jack. "And at that point, the defense might very well have discovered what MDPD claims it didn't know until yesterday: that one of these callers on Debra Burgette's call report was Carlos Mendoza, who is now serving time for human trafficking."

The prosecutor shook her head. "Judge, if MDPD didn't connect the phone number on the call report to the physical burn phone that was in Carlos Mendoza's possession at the time of his arrest, it seems highly improbable that the defense could have made the connection."

"Then how did Mr. Burgette make the connection," the judge asked, "even if it was just yesterday?"

The prosecutor was silent. So was the witness. No one had an answer. The judge had hurt Jack with some of his questions to the witness, but this one, by contrast, was beyond helpful. It was a home run.

"Judge, again," said Jack, "I'd like the chance to question Mr. Burgette under oath."

"I hear you, Mr. Swyteck. Counsel, please take your seats."

The prosecutor returned to her table, and Jack to his. Hannah looked ready to hug him. The judge addressed them in a solemn tone.

"Let me say that I'm deeply troubled by this development. It does seem to me that more facts need to be fleshed out on this issue. You'll have a scheduling order from me by tomorrow morning, if not sooner. The stay of execution will remain in effect until further order of this court. The witness is excused but shall remain under oath. For now, we're adjourned."

With the crack of a gavel and at the bailiff's command, lawyers and spectators snapped to their feet. As Judge Frederick stepped down from the bench and walked to his chambers, Jack discreetly scanned the courtroom. The crowd had thinned since the conclusion of Debra's testimony, but one empty seat, in particular, caught Jack's attention. It was in the first row of the public gallery, just on the other side of the rail, directly behind the prosecutor's table.

For the first time since the start of the hearing, Gavin Burgette was nowhere to be seen.

CHAPTER 25

Jack drove straight from the courthouse to the Freedom Institute. Hannah was in the car behind him. Even his cell phone was leaving him alone. It was like another era, when driving was actually downtime, his posttrial therapy.

Jack crossed the drawbridge and continued on North River Drive, toward an old neighborhood along the river. Once exclusively residential, the area had evolved into a haven for small business. Many historic houses remained, preserving some sense of the old neighborhood, but they were now home to Pilates studios, computer-repair shops, and everything in between. So much had changed since his days alongside Neil Goderich. Jack, too, had changed. Still, he managed a nostalgic smile as he turned onto Northwest Ninth Court.

Court. Jack suspected that Neil had felt a little karma when, as a young and idealistic lawyer, he'd made that same turn off North River Drive and fallen in love with the perfect place that wasn't located on a street, avenue, boulevard, terrace, lane, or road. When he wasn't *in* court, Neil was *on* court. That was his life.

The Freedom Institute was their life, Hannah. Andie and I are in agreement about this.

Jack parked in the driveway and reached Andie on his cell as he crossed the lawn. "How are you feeling, honey?" he asked.

"I'm fine. Can I call you right back? You caught me right in the middle of something."

"Sure."

He put away his cell. Hannah had parked on the street, and Jack waited for her before heading inside. "Hannah, I want you to get me everything you can on Carlos Mendoza."

"Eve's on it already," she said as they headed up the sidewalk. "The bad news is he refuses to talk with us."

"You checked with the warden?"

"No. Mendoza has himself a high-priced lawyer on retainer. She called here before we could even pick up the phone and dial FSP. She made it crystal clear that Carlos Mendoza is represented by counsel and that he's not talking to anyone."

"I'm sure. Except the prosecutor."

"What?"

"Think about it. Why would a guy who's already serving time need a high-priced lawyer?"

The deduction came quickly. "To get his sentence reduced?"

"Correct, grasshopper. So who does his lawyer talk to?"

Another quick deduction. "You think Mendoza is cutting a deal to testify against Dylan Reeves?"

"It only makes sense. We've asked for a new trial. If I were the prosecutor, I'd be thinking ahead and talking to every single one of those 'strangers' on Debra Burgette's call record. Maybe one of them has a connection to Dylan Reeves. Maybe it's Mendoza."

"But if there was a connection, wouldn't it have come out in the first trial?"

"If there was *no* connection, why would Mendoza be all law-yered up? Situations change. Maybe Mendoza was in no mood to deal the first time around."

"Sounds like another talk with our client is in order," said Hannah.

Jack's cell rang. It was Andie calling back. Jack told Hannah that he'd catch up, and she went inside. Jack stayed on the front steps, beneath the sprawling limbs of a gigantic live oak.

"Sorry about that," she said.

"It's okay. I was just checking in."

"I'm glad you did. I didn't want to bother you in court, but this is my 'Andie the FBI agent' phone call."

"I've been expecting it. The answer is yes, the status of the FBI investigation into Sashi Burgette's disappearance *is* an issue in my case."

"Yeah, and that's only about the tenth time I've heard that today. So I have to give you my speech. Here goes."

Jack listened, but he could practically recite it from memory. Whenever one of his criminal cases had a connection to the FBI, Andie was required to certify to the special agent in charge of the Miami field office that appropriate "information barriers" were in place to prevent any possible compromise of the Bureau's integrity.

"Have you given that speech to our baby yet?" asked Jack. "Or does FBI protocol not extend to future criminal defense lawyers?"

"That's hilarious," she said drily.

"Seriously, though—I can't even work on the case at home while you're there?"

"Technically, that's what the protocol requires."

"But things have hit the proverbial fan here. It's going to be a late night."

"Work at the office. I'll be fine."

Jack hesitated. He'd known Andie to run down drug dealers in a dark alley at midnight. He'd seen the cuts and bruises on her body after an undercover assignment that she couldn't tell him anything about. It seemed silly to say he was worried about her being home alone for a few hours, but the E-word, *eclampsia*, was on his mind.

"I should've been a real estate lawyer."

"Dirt on your hands? Definitely not your thing, Jack."

He laughed. "I'll try to be home by midnight."

"I'll be asleep long before then. So, good night."

"Good night, sweetheart."

He tucked away his cell, started inside, and then stopped.

Dirt on your hands.

It had been an innocent joke, and Andie couldn't possibly have known where Jack's thoughts would take him; but as he stood on the steps of the Freedom Institute, it had triggered his darkest memory: the trial of Eddie Goss, a confessed sexual predator who stood accused of savaging a teenage girl. After the verdict of not guilty, protesters had pelted him with exploding baggies of animal blood on the courthouse steps, no subtlety in the "blood is on your hands" symbolism. Memories like Goss—his last trial for the Institute—kept him from walking into Neil's old room and taking over.

Her blood is on you, Swyteck!

The front door opened, and Hannah peeked her head out. "You coming, Jack? I really think we should set up a phone call with Dylan Reeves."

"Yeah, I'll be right there."

Jack continued up the stairs, went inside, and walked right past Neil's old office, straight to the kitchen.

A ndie tucked her cell into her purse as her ob-gyn entered the examination room.

"It's a close call," Dr. Starkey said with a sigh.

Andie's afternoon blood-pressure check at the field office infirmary had shown more than a "normal" increase since the morning, and Nurse Rebecca had insisted that she see her doctor. The call from Jack had come while Andie was alone in the room, seated on the examination table and waiting for Dr. Starkey. Andie had chosen not to mention any of it, not wanting to worry Jack over nothing.

If it was nothing.

"How close a call is it?" asked Andie.

"If you were a few points higher on the systolic, I would definitely want to induce now."

"But we're still only twenty-eight weeks."

"That's the problem. But if your pressure spikes like this again, and we can't get it under control, we have to be ready."

"But the baby has to be ready, too."

"Before thirty-two weeks, these are never easy decisions. I tell ya what. Let's do another ultrasound and see exactly how big she is."

"She?"

The doctor froze, catching herself too late. "Andie, I am so sorry. I completely forgot that you and Jack didn't want to know."

Andie wasn't angry. She placed her hands gently on her belly and smiled. "My baby girl. Everything's gonna be okay. Dr. Starkey and I are gonna take good care of you."

The doctor smiled, but it was a serious smile. "Yes, we will."

D inner for Jack and the rest of the Freedom team was cold pizza peeled from the top of a cardboard box. One would think that if the delivery boy was going to sit on the pie, he could have at least kept it warm. The foursome was seated around the kitchen table, the speakerphone in the dead center of the table beside a stack of napkins. Dylan Reeves was on the line.

"It was a good day," said Jack. "Your stay of execution is still in effect."

"A 'good day'? Really? I'm on death watch. How good do you think *my* fucking day was?"

"I get it," said Jack.

"No, you don't," Reeves snapped back. "Nobody does, till you're here. I heard the Supreme Court denied Elmer's petition this afternoon."

Elmer Hudson was the other FSP inmate on death watch. He was in the cell ahead of Dylan Reeves.

"That's true. They did," said Jack

"They got a guard sitting outside his cell twenty-four/seven now, watching everything he does, so he doesn't spoil the party and kill himself before they can kill *him*. He goes on Monday afternoon."

"Monday morning, actually," said Hannah.

Jack gave her the "cut" sign, as if to say, "*Not helpful.*"

"Great. Monday fucking morning. And when he's gone, they move me into his cell. Hardly nobody gets out of that cell alive. I'm next in line. Me and Elmer, we're the lucky Lotto winners: four hundred fuckheads on death row, only three signed death warrants. Elmer's number one, and I'm number two. Once Elmer's gone, there's nobody between me and the needle. If Judge Frederick says no more stay of execution, I'm dead."

Eve reached over the speaker to peel off another slice of cold pizza, pulling as much of the congealed mozzarella from the delivery box top as possible. "Jack's *abuela* is praying for you, Dylan," said Eve.

Jack did a double take. Abuela was a devout Catholic, but he was quite certain that the only prisoners she'd ever prayed for were political ones in Cuban jails.

"God bless her," said Reeves.

He wasn't the first death-row inmate to find religion. Indeed, Reeves' police interrogators had used scripture against this prodigal son of a preacher: "*Therefore, confess your sins to one another and pray for one another, that you may be healed.*"

"Dylan, I need to ask you a question," said Jack. "And I need a completely truthful answer."

"Ask it, then."

"Do you know a man named Carlos Mendoza?"

There was silence on the speaker. Jack wasn't sure if his client was taking a little extra time to search every corner of his memory for any connection to a man by that name, or if the name had immediately registered and Reeves was simply crafting his response.

"Never heard of him," said Reeves. "Why?"

Jack gave him the thirty-second version of the courtroom exchange, Mendoza's conviction and prison sentence for human trafficking, and his connection to the prepaid cell number that appeared on Debra's call record.

"And the police never told my lawyer about this guy Mendoza?" asked Reeves.

"They should have. That's one of our arguments," said Jack.

"Sounds like a good one," said Reeves.

"There's a weak link in it," said Jack. "There are ten strange men in total whose phone numbers appear on Debra Burgette's call record. Nine of them we know for sure that Sashi had communications with over the Internet. We have actual printed e-mails of Sashi sending nine different men her photograph along with her mother's cell-phone number. But Carlos Mendoza is different. His phone number is on Debra's phone record, but there's no evidence from Sashi's computer records that she ever had any contact with Mendoza."

"Maybe Sashi talked to him on the phone."

"There would have been a record of that," said Jack.

"Maybe they met in person. Just like I met her in person in the park."

Met her, thought Jack. Another death-row euphemism. "Maybe. But it won't be easy to prove. Mendoza won't talk to us. We can subpoena him, but he could invoke the Fifth Amendment. Or he could just lie."

"I think you gotta do whatever it takes!" said Reeves. "I'm running out of time here."

Jack looked around the table, tired eyes all around from one long night after another. "Yeah, we know," said Jack. "Time is short."

Jack left the Freedom Institute before midnight. Saturday was just a few minutes old when he got home—technically speaking, one day closer to his client's execution.

He parked in the driveway and walked quietly to the front door, trying not to make any noise that might wake Andie on the inside. The porch light was burning, and he was aiming his key at the lock on the front door when he heard a car door slam across the street. Someone had been waiting in one of the cars parked at the curb. A man started walking up Jack's driveway, his heels clicking on the pavers, his face obscured by a shroud of cloud-filtered moonlight. Jack waited at the door. The man continued up the sidewalk at a deliberate pace, no hurry at all, and then stopped before the steps to the front porch. He was just within reach of the porch light's glow.

It was Gavin Burgette.

Jack readied himself, recalling Gavin's threat the first time they'd met.

"Don't do anything stupid, Gavin."

"I'm not here to kick anybody's ass," he said.

"How long were you waiting in your car?"

"Not long. Half an hour."

"You could have called me. I have a phone, you know."

"The wait did me good. I honestly didn't decide for sure to say anything until I reached for the door handle and got out of the car. I needed time alone to sort out my thoughts."

"About what?"

He took another step forward, closer to the bottom step. "I had a talk with Debra tonight."

"Does she know you came here?"

"It was her idea."

"Her idea?"

"Debra and I haven't agreed on much lately, but one thing I can't argue with: if a man is going to be executed, you shouldn't have any doubts about his guilt."

"Are you having doubts?"

He didn't answer right way. "I'm not as sure about this as Debra is. But it's possible."

"What's possible?"

He looked away for a moment, then back. "That we don't have the right man."

Jack was speechless, but he forced a reply. "Is there something you want to tell me?"

"At the very least, I guess I owe you an apology."

Jack stepped down from the porch, and the two men looked at one another, eye-to-eye. "You want to go for a little walk, Gavin?"

"That would be good."

Jack started, then stopped. "But let's be clear about one thing."

"What?"

"You don't owe me anything," said Jack. "Least of all an apology."

CHAPTER 26

It was eleven o'clock Saturday morning, and even though Jack had captioned his request to present additional testimony as an "emergency," he hadn't expected to be summoned into court on the weekend. He was wrong.

"Mr. Swyteck, call your witness," said Judge Frederick. "And I mean it: there will be no further time allotted to this hearing. I'm starting a five-week jury trial Monday morning with eighteen defendants. You have one hour."

Jack intended to make the most of every minute. "The petitioner calls Gavin Burgette."

It felt strange: to call such an important witness in a proceeding that meant the difference between life or death, and yet the courtroom was nearly empty. Saturday at the courthouse could be like midnight at the crypt. Hallways were silent. The media were absent. All but Judge Frederick's courtroom were tombs of darkness behind locked doors. The emergency hearing had drawn just two spectators, Debra Burgette and her daughter Aquinnah. Both were seated in the front row behind Jack and Hannah, on the petitioner's side of the courtroom. The "rule of sequestration" normally prevents witnesses from being in the courtroom when another witness is testifying, but the rule does not apply to a homicide victim's immediate family. If Debra wanted to be present for her ex-husband's testimony, no one could deny her that right. By the same token, Gavin was free to take the stand even though he'd sat through his ex-wife's testimony from the front row behind the prosecutor.

Sashi's father swore the oath and took a seat. His attire was casual smart, a blue blazer with a red necktie, but his demeanor was anything but casual. A witness stand could be an unsettling place for the most powerful of business people, even when the stakes were utterly meaningless when compared to the loss of a child.

Jack approached slowly, respectfully. "Good morning, sir."

"Morning."

"Mr. Burgette, you testified at the sentencing phase of Mr. Reeves' trial, did you not?"

"I did."

"And you asked the jury to recommend the death penalty for Mr. Reeves. Is that correct?"

"That's correct."

"And you supported the trial judge's decision to follow that recommendation."

"Yes."

"In fact, less than a week ago, you were of the firm view that Mr. Reeves' sentence of death by lethal injection should be carried out as set forth in his signed death warrant. A fair statement?"

"Yes. I'd say as of two days ago I was of that firm view."

"Has your view changed?"

"Objection," said the prosecutor. "The witness's personal views are completely irrelevant."

The judge hesitated, and lawyers on both sides of the courtroom seemed to experience the same intellectual disconnect: the objection was technically correct, but to hear the prosecutor blurt it out in open court—that the views of the victim's father were completely irrelevant—just didn't sound right.

The judge cleared his throat. "Sustained."

Jack retrieved an exhibit from a table near the stenographer. "Sir, I'm handing you Exhibit 11, which was previously identified as the call record for the cell phone of Debra Burgette. It's for the thirty-day period prior to Sashi's disappearance. Have you seen this before?"

The witness inspected it. "Yes. Two days ago. Detective Hernandez of MDPD showed it to me."

"How did that come about?"

"Detective Hernandez told me that he had done a comparison of Debra's cell-phone call report to my call report from the same time period."

Jack retrieved another exhibit, which the witness identified as his call report. "What did the comparison of those two call reports show?"

"Both Debra and I received phone calls from a number that the police were unable to identify. It was from a prepaid cell phone."

"Which number was that?"

"On Debra's report, it's the third one down from the top. On my report, it is the fifth one up from the bottom."

"Were you able to identify the caller?"

"Not at first. I told Detective Hernandez that the number looked vaguely familiar, but it wasn't listed in my cell contacts. I then checked my SIM card for numbers that I had blocked during this time period. And there it was. I then remembered that this call was from a man named Carlos Mendoza."

"When you say you blocked Mr. Mendoza's number, was that before or after the incoming phone calls listed on your call report."

"After. Obviously."

"So you did speak to him?"

"Yes."

"Did you know that Mr. Mendoza was a convicted felon?"

"I had no idea until Mr. Hernandez told me two days ago."

"Do you recall what this phone call from Mr. Mendoza was about?"

"Yes. It was about Sashi."

Jack paused. He was sure he had the judge's attention, but a subtle change of pace would ensure that the judge wasn't thinking about the Saturday-morning fishing trip he was missing.

"Mr. Burgette, tell the judge a little bit about what was going on with Sashi in your home during this time period."

He shifted in his chair, speaking more directly to the judge. "Sashi was becoming a huge problem at home. Debra told you how she would run away, not tell us where she was. You heard about the things that she was doing online with strangers. That's just the tip of the iceberg."

"Where were you during this difficult time period?"

He looked away, regretful. "I was home when I could be. But of course during the day I was at the office. I travel a lot for my work. The two months before Sashi disappeared were especially busy for me. I had one company that was about to do a public offering. I was in a bidding war with two other private equity firms to make another acquisition. I was mostly out of town. Sometimes out of the country for a week or more at a time."

"Where was Debra?"

"Debra was a work-at-home mom. Aquinnah was a high school junior. Alexander was still in elementary school. And there was Sashi. Not easy. Aquinnah and Alexander had all the normal bumps in the road, but even those little things become big things when Mom is giving every ounce of energy to a seventeen-year-old girl with special needs. Debra was on the front line, holding things together twenty-four/seven."

"Did you have hired help?"

"We burned through them like dry timber. I think the longest anyone lasted was two weeks. If Sashi didn't want you around, trust me, she could get you out of her life. And I don't mean harmless pranks from *The Sound of Music*—frogs in the nanny's bed, that sort of thing."

"What are you talking about?"

"Horrible accusations. For example, Debra was devoting so much of her time to Sashi that she had no time to help Alexander with his homework. So we hired a tutor. That guy lasted one day. Sashi went on Facebook and accused him of sexually molesting Alexander."

"Was it true?"

"*No*. But we hired quality people who make their livelihood based on their reputations. It was the same thing with Aquinnah's friends. They couldn't come over without being accused of stealing Sashi's purse or snooping in her bedroom. Eventually the word on the street was to steer clear of the Burgette family. Debra . . . poor Debra was at the end of her rope."

"Did you get professional help for Sashi?"

"Sashi was seeing a psychiatrist. Dr. Wurster. He told us that the misbehavior we were seeing in Sashi was typical of children with RAD—reactive attachment disorder."

"How often was she seeing a psychiatrist?"

"Three times a week at four hundred dollars per session, none of it covered by insurance. We were spending a hundred thousand dollars a year on treatments and meds."

"Did you consider other options?"

He struggled, then answered. "I don't remember how, exactly, but we heard about rehoming."

The judge perked up. "About what?"

"Rehoming," said the witness.

The judge wrote it down. "That's not a term I'm familiar with. At least not in this context. I thought rehoming is what you did with a pet that you'd become allergic to."

"I'll walk the witness through it," said Jack. "Mr. Burgette, what is your understanding of 'rehoming'?"

"It's an option available to adoptive parents. You hire a broker who 'rehomes' the child with a new family."

The judge laid his pen aside. "You *sell* your child?"

"No, Your Honor," said Gavin. "That would be illegal. You place the child with a new family that is better able to provide for her."

"You *give her away*," the judge said sharply. "Is that what you're telling me?"

Gavin lowered his eyes, then glanced in the direction of his ex-wife. "It's called rehoming," he said softly.

It was clearly a point of discomfort. Their walk around Jack's neighborhood eleven hours earlier had gone smoothly until this point. Then it was agony. Jack gave him a moment, then continued. "How did you hear about this option?"

"From Debra."

"How did Debra find out?"

"Debra was part of an online support group, I guess you'd call it, for families who had adopted a RAD child from a foreign country."

"Was Debra's group sponsored by any organization?"

"Not that I know of. My understanding is that it was informal. Just well-meaning families who adopted orphans, usually older kids, from a foreign country, and wanted to give them a better life. Some of these kids have experienced terrible things. War. Starvation. Emotional trauma. The adoptive parents aren't always told about the child's past, or at least not the full extent of the child's issues. For some families it's way more than they can handle."

"Was Sashi more than the Burgette family could handle?"

"There were times when we thought so. One time, I was on business in Mexico City. Debra called me. She had just reached the breaking point. That's when she told me about rehoming."

"When was that?"

"I'd say a couple months before Sashi disappeared."

"What was your reaction?"

"About what you'd expect. I said absolutely not. Sashi isn't a shirt. We can't take her back to Nordstrom for an exchange or our money back."

"Was that the end of the matter?"

"I thought it was."

"What happened next?"

"About two weeks later I got a phone call. From *this* guy," he said, holding up his call record. "Carlos Mendoza."

"Were you expecting this call?"

"No."

"What did you and Mr. Mendoza talk about?"

"He said he had met with Debra. That he had found an adoptive family who would accept Sashi. That all the paperwork was in order, except for one thing. He needed an executed power of attorney from me, authorizing the new family to take Sashi."

"What did you tell him?"

"I said, 'Look, pal, I don't know who you are or what the hell'—sorry, Your Honor."

"It's okay. Continue."

"I said I don't know what you're talking about, but you're not getting a power of attorney from me so you can hand over my daughter to somebody else. And I hung up."

"Then what?"

"I spoke to Debra."

"How did that go?"

"Not well. I don't feel the need to get into every little detail of what was said. If you wanted to point to the beginning of the end of our marriage . . . I guess this was it."

"And after—"

"But I want to say something about this."

The judge sat up. "There's no question pending, Mr. Burgette."

Jack could have moved on. He tried to make eye contact with the witness, tried to divine what he wanted to say, but Gavin was looking past the lawyers, to the first row of public seating. He was looking at his ex-wife. Jack gave him an opening.

"What did you want to add, Mr. Burgette?"

It wasn't really a proper question, but the judge and the prosecutor let it go.

"I wanted to say that nobody can understand the kind of pressure that Debra was under. I didn't even understand it, and I was living in the same house. She got desperate, she called this guy Mendoza, he pretended to be someone he wasn't, she trusted him, he ran with it, and—"

"Judge, I'm sorry," said the prosecutor, rising. "But I have to object. This is just a narrative."

"Sustained. Mr. Swyteck, return to question-and-answer format, please."

"Did Mr. Mendoza ever meet Sashi?" asked Jack.

"Not to my knowledge."

"Did you have any further dealings with Mr. Mendoza?"

"Yes. A few days later, he called me again."

"What did he want?"

"Again he told me everything was set. I just had to sign the papers. It would all be legal and completely discreet. No court hearing was required. Just a power of attorney from each parent is all it takes."

"What did you tell him?"

"The same thing I told him the first time. Only I used a few more choice words, and that's when things escalated."

"Escalated how?"

"He was really angry. He said that he had gone to all this work, that a deal is a deal, and that we were jerking him around. He even threatened to sue me."

"Did you have any further dealings with Mr. Mendoza?"

"He called one more time. I recognized the number, so I didn't answer. That's when I put a block on that number. And that's why his number stuck in my mind when Detective Hernandez showed it to me two days ago."

"So, as of the time you broke things off with Mr. Mendoza, he was angry?"

"Very angry."

"He wanted Sashi?"

"Objection."

"Overruled. The witness can testify as to his impression."

"It was my impression that Mr. Mendoza wanted Sashi very badly."

Jack walked back to the table and skimmed his notes.

The judge checked the wall clock. "How much more do you have, Mr. Swyteck?"

"I'm ready to wrap up. Mr. Burgette, when Sashi went missing, you didn't tell the police about Mr. Mendoza, did you?"

"No. We didn't."

"Why not?"

"Well, like I said, Mr. Mendoza and I had some harsh words, but the most he ever threatened to do was to sue me. I thought he was a legitimate businessman. I had no idea he was a criminal."

"So you and your wife, at the time of Sashi's disappearance, decided to keep that information to yourselves?"

"Look, I know that sounds horrible. But we loved Sashi. We really did. This brief look at the rehoming option was our low point. If we had thought there was any chance that Mr. Mendoza had abducted Sashi, then of course we would have said something. But Sashi's panties were found in the back of Dylan Reeves' car. His semen was on them. He acted guilty. For God's sake, man, the police *told us* he did it. They said Dylan Reeves was our guy! We didn't see any point in telling the whole world that Debra had been thinking about rehoming a child she loved and devoted herself to. That's it. That's the bottom line. Okay? Thank God this is a Saturday and the courtroom is empty when the truth comes out. How would you like a story like that about your family on the front page of Sunday's paper?"

The question hung in the silence, and a part of Jack was glad he wasn't required to answer it. As he stepped away, a shuffling noise in the gallery caught his attention, which was followed by the clicking of heels on marble tiles.

Debra hurried up the center aisle to the courtroom's rear exit, pulled open the heavy mahogany door, and disappeared into the hallway. Jack said nothing, and the courtroom remained still as the sound of her footfalls reverberated down the long, empty corridor and echoed all the way back to Judge Frederick's courtroom. The echoes came faster as her walk became a run, and then they faded into silence as Jack imagined her running as fast and as far away as possible from the courtroom, the courthouse—her demons.

Jack took a breath and squared his shoulders to the bench. "I have no further questions, Your Honor."

CHAPTER 27

A girl. Andie spent Saturday morning at the house, smiling at the thought. But there was a tinge of sadness.

Andie had been convinced that her first pregnancy was a girl. At six weeks, she'd even picked out a name, Viola. Girl-friends had warned her to stay away from baby stores until the third month, that anything could happen early in a pregnancy, and that it was wise to be patient and not open the door to added heartbreak. She'd heeded that advice, until the seventh week, when she'd ventured into a baby store and loaded up on pink. In week eight, she'd miscarried.

This pregnancy had been cause for joy—and guarded optimism. The week-eight ultrasound was a milestone. "Do you want to know the sex?" the technician had asked. Jack squeezed her hand. Their eyes met, and it was clear that he was leaving it up to her. Did she want to go out on that emotional limb again—knowing the sex, naming the baby, decorating a nursery? "No," said Andie, and Jack had seemed to understand the decision.

Twenty weeks later, she'd thought she was in the homestretch. She still was. "Look at it this way," her doctor had told her. "The finish line is closer." The unspoken concern was whether she and Jacqueline would sprint through the tape or stumble trying to get there.

Jacqueline? Nope. Not gonna do Jack and Jackie.

A friend picked her up at noon for lunch in the Brickell area.

She and Nancy Galardi caught up with small talk in the car ride
across the causeway to Perricone's Marketplace and Café, a slice
of old Miami by way of New England. Like so much of Miami's
history, the house that originally sat on the property was destroyed. In lemons-to-lemonade fashion, a visionary restaurateur
bought himself an eighteenth-century barn in Vermont; moved
the hand-hewn beams, walls, and floor planks to Miami; and
then, piece by piece, rebuilt the homey atmosphere of a long-lost
My-amma. It had been one of Jack and Andie's favorites when
they were dating.

There was a wait for their table, so they found a seat at the
bar. Nancy ordered a glass of wine, which drew nasty glares from
two women at a nearby table. They were the overfit type, fake
boobs on a stick wrapped in spandex, and they'd apparently taken
one look at Andie and jumped to the conclusion that Nancy was
pregnant, too, not just a little overweight. Andie took sparkling
water and, just to make the self-appointed mommy police crazy,
a twist of lemon in a cocktail glass. *Voilà*: a pregnant woman and
her faux vodka tonic.

"So what was the burning question you wanted to ask me?"
asked Nancy.

Lunch wasn't totally a social visit. Nancy was a social worker
from the Florida Department of Children and Family Services,
the Florida agency in charge of placing neglected or abandoned
children.

"I'm curious about something called private rehoming," said
Andie.

"Why? Are you doing an investigation into this?"

"It came up in one of Jack's cases. He was telling me about it
last night."

"Ah, so you two *do* talk shop in between making babies. I
wondered how that whole criminal-lawyer-married-to-the-FBI
thing worked."

"He wasn't breaching any confidentiality. It was just something he thought I would find interesting. Maybe it's because I'm pregnant. Or because I'm adopted. I don't know."

"There must be someone in the FBI who knows more than I do."

"But I can't pick someone's brain at the Bureau about an issue in one of Jack's cases. That's where the marriage gets complicated. It's called avoiding even the appearance of impropriety. So I thought of you. Ever come across it?"

Nancy swallowed her wine. "Yes, actually. It's miles away from what I do through foster care. The parents I work with have so many hurdles to clear. Criminal background checks. Home inspections. Dozens of hours of training. Post-placement follow-up by social workers."

"That's not part of private rehoming?"

"Not at all. It's basically a do-it-yourself way for parents to end adoptions quickly and quietly. Usually an international adoption gone sour."

"But the parents who end the adoption have to report back every year to the country they adopted their child from. Don't they?"

"In theory. But if the child is from a country that isn't a signatory to the Hague Adoption Convention, it would be hard to enforce any reporting requirements. And even signatories have different rules. Some require annual reports until the child turns eighteen. Some have only a year of follow-up."

"There must be horror stories."

"I've heard a few. A convicted sex offender who forged his recommendations and took three or four kids. A fourteen-year-old girl from Liberia who spent her first night in her new home sleeping naked with her new parents. It happens."

The bartender refilled Andie's glass with sparkling water, then stepped away.

"I did some searching on the Internet," said Andie. "Is that the way it's done? Online?"

"Mostly. Parents advertise on message-board forums. 'Nine-year-old Indian boy, eager to please.' Whatever. 'Respite-

Rehoming' was a big one that Yahoo shut down. 'Way Stations of Love' was on Facebook."

"And this is legal?"

"Well, I know from my own experience that state agencies are supposed to sign off when custody is transferred across state lines. But people find loopholes. And when they do, the only people vetting the new parents are the parents who are fed up and trying to get rid of the kid."

"Unbelievable."

"Not really," said Nancy. "As long as there are families at the end of their rope, there is going to be rehoming. A lot of people just don't understand that doing something like this over the Internet can be no different than dropping your kid off in a back alley with someone like . . . who knows? You fill in the blank."

Carlos Mendoza.

"Yeah," said Andie. "I definitely see what you mean."

"Anything else you'd like to know, inquisitive one?"

Andie looked away, thinking, and then her gaze returned to Nancy. "You said it would be easier to rehome a child from a country that hasn't signed that convention."

"The Hague Convention. Anybody who's come within a million miles of a foreign adoption knows about it."

"Is Chechnya a signatory?"

"No clue," she said, as she reached for her phone. "Lemme Google it."

"I could have done that myself," said Andie.

"Here it is," said Nancy. " 'Chechnya. See Russian Federation.' "

"Russia is what I should have asked about, anyway. The girl in Jack's case was born in Chechnya but was adopted from an orphanage in Moscow."

"I thought you said this was just your idle curiosity."

"It totally is," said Andie.

"Here we go: the Russian Federation is a signatory but has not ratified the convention."

"So, a child from Russia could be rehomed and the American parents wouldn't have to worry about annual reporting back to Moscow?"

Nancy scratched her head, confused. "That doesn't sound right to me. I know families who have adopted from Russia, and they have reporting requirements."

"But we Googled it," said Andie. "It must be right."

Nancy joined in the sarcasm with a roll of her eyes, then laid her cell on the bar. "Have I been helpful, madam?"

"Very," said Andie.

"So you're buying lunch?"

Andie smiled thinly. "I don't know. Google it."

CHAPTER 28

Jack watched from his seat at the petitioner's table as the prosecutor approached the witness. He'd felt good about Gavin Burgette's direct testimony. He hoped it would hold up on cross-examination.

"Mr. Burgette, as I told your ex-wife, I know this must be painful, so I will be brief," said the prosecutor.

"Thank you."

"I listened carefully to your testimony, and I apologize for having to ask what might seem like pointed questions. But, sir, you can't offer one piece of evidence that your daughter is still alive, can you?"

He bristled, and from Jack's perspective, it was almost like watching one of those Internet videos of a guy taking a bullet at close range to prove how well Kevlar worked.

"I guess you weren't kidding about the 'pointed questions,'" said Gavin.

The judge peered down from the bench. "Sir, please refrain from commenting on the questions. Your job is to answer them."

"Sorry," said Gavin. "The answer to the question is no. I don't have that specific evidence."

"You've received no phone calls from your daughter Sashi since the arrest of Dylan Reeves. Have you?"

"No."

"You've received no phone calls that you suspected were from her?"

"No."

"And you can't offer one piece of evidence that your daughter ever had any contact, in person or on the Internet, with Carlos Mendoza?"

He thought for a moment, but of course there was only one answer. "No."

"One last question," she said as she took a step closer to the witness, her gaze tightening. "You can't offer one piece of evidence that your daughter was murdered by anyone but Dylan Reeves, can you?"

"Objection," said Jack.

"Grounds?"

"Debra Burgette's testimony established that there is insufficient evidence that Sashi was murdered, let alone murdered by Dylan Reeves. Mr. Burgette's testimony has clearly established that if the prosecution had complied with the law and informed the trial team about Carlos Mendoza and rehoming, there would at the very least have been reasonable doubt as to whether Mr. Reeves committed a homicide."

"That's a legal argument for your brief, not an objection. Overruled. The witness may answer."

Gavin glanced in Jack's direction, seeming to take the lawyer's cue. "I think my testimony suggests that it could have been Mr. Mendoza."

"I'm not asking about your theories," said the prosecutor. "I'm asking about *evidence*. Here's my question again, sir: You can't offer a single piece of evidence that your daughter was murdered by anyone but Dylan Reeves, can you?"

He hesitated. "Nothing more than I've already offered."

"Which is nothing."

"Objection."

"Overruled."

The witness considered his response. "It is what it is," he said.

"That'll do," said the prosecutor. "No further questions." She returned to her seat at the table beside counsel from the Florida attorney general's office.

Judge Frederick excused the witness. Gavin Burgette made no eye contact with any of the lawyers as he crossed the courtroom and took a seat beside his daughter in the first row of the gallery. They said something to each other. Jack couldn't hear what was said, but they held hands, which was sign enough that neither the tragedy nor the divorce had broken their bond.

"Will counsel please rise?" said the judge, pausing long enough for the lawyers to comply. "Mr. Swyteck, I presume that concludes your presentation of evidence."

Jack considered his response. Pop psychology was not his area of expertise, but Jack was reading the judge's body language loud and clear. With a five-week jury trial starting on Monday, Judge Frederick was ready to shove this case out the door.

"There is one more witness we would like to call. Unfortunately, he is unavailable to us."

"I presume you mean Mr. Carlos Mendoza?"

"Yes. Since he is not available to come to the courtroom, we'd like permission to take his deposition at Florida State Prison and make the transcript part of our record."

"Judge, the state of Florida objects to discovery in aid of this petition," said the prosecutor.

"Of course you do," said the judge. "Let me take that under advisement for a moment. Ms. Carmichael, assuming that I deny the request to depose Mr. Mendoza, does the state have anything to present?"

"No, Your Honor. We believe the petitioner has failed to carry his burden of proof."

"Very well. The court is prepared to issue its ruling."

Jack and Hannah exchanged a glance as they rose. They tried not to look too surprised, but Jack had expected closing arguments to be followed by a written order by Monday, not an immediate oral ruling from the bench.

The judge removed his eyeglasses to address counsel, speaking extemporaneously, no script to read. "Ladies and gentlemen, it is an extraordinary proceeding indeed when the parents of the victim in a homicide case testify on behalf of the man convicted of murdering their daughter, and where the mother genuinely believes that her daughter is still alive. It should go without saying that convicting a man of murder and sentencing him to death where no murder has been committed would be a violation of his constitutional rights."

So far, so good, thought Jack.

"However . . ."

That dread transitional word, which hit Jack like a punch to the chest.

" . . . overturning a jury verdict is not something this court can do lightly. The petitioner is required by law to present clear and convincing evidence. With respect to the challenge to the sufficiency of the evidence of Sashi Burgette's death, the prisoner's petition for writ of habeas corpus is denied."

The judge paused, and at that moment, Jack was relieved that Debra Burgette had left the courtroom.

"However . . ."

That wonderful transitional word, which lifted Jack's spirits.

" . . . this court continues to have serious concerns about the failure of the police and the prosecutor to inform the defense that Mrs. Burgette contacted and provided information to Carlos Mendoza about rehoming her daughter less than thirty days prior to Sashi Burgette's disappearance; that both Debra and Gavin Burgette received phone calls from Mr. Mendoza; and that Mr. Mendoza was later arrested and convicted on charges of sex trafficking."

"Judge, pardon the interruption," said the prosecutor, "but it's important to note that Mr. Mendoza was not even arrested on sex-trafficking charges until *after* Sashi Burgette disappeared."

"But it was *before* the trial against Mr. Reeves commenced. I'm not ruling against the state of Florida—*yet*—but an argument could be made that you should have told the defense about Mr. Mendoza before trial. Therefore, it is the ruling of this court that good cause has been shown to allow Mr. Swyteck to depose Carlos Mendoza. The request for this limited discovery in aid of this petition for habeas corpus is therefore granted. The stay of execution shall remain in effect until further order of this court."

With a bang of the gavel it was over.

"All rise," said the bailiff, which brought Gavin Burgette and his daughter Aquinnah to their feet, the only people in the courtroom who weren't already standing. The judge stepped down from the bench, a deputy opened the paneled door at the side exit, and the judge disappeared into his chambers.

Jack turned. Gavin Burgette and his daughter were standing at the rail. Aquinnah looked confused.

"What exactly does this mean?" she asked.

"We're still alive," said Jack. "The stay of execution remains in effect."

"That part I understand. And you'll have to forgive me, but I don't know whether to be happy or sad about that."

"Aquinnah, please," her father said.

"It's okay," said Jack. "I understand the ambivalence."

"Anyway, I wasn't really asking what this means for your client. I don't know when my mother is going to feel ready to talk about this, but the first question she's going to ask me is what does this mean for the missing-person investigation. Is Sashi's file closed for good now?"

"We have to be honest with her," said Jack. "This hearing was our best shot at getting it reopened. It didn't happen."

"We can take it up to the federal court of appeals in Atlanta," said Hannah.

Jack nodded, but it was without conviction. "Like I said: this was our *best* shot. An appellate court is not likely to disagree with Judge Frederick on this issue."

Aquinnah took a half step back from the rail.

Her father put his arms around her. "I think it's best if you tell your mother," he said.

She nodded. "It's a good thing, Daddy," she said in a gentle voice. "In the bigger scheme of things, this is all a good thing."

CHAPTER 29

J ack arrived as the hearse was leaving. It was 8:06 a.m., Monday morning.

Sixty-six minutes past the scheduled execution of Elmer Hudson, Florida State Prison Time.

Jack knew the drill. As Hudson's body left the prison yard feet first, corrections officers would gather up Dylan Reeves' personal belongings and move him and the last of his worldly possessions into death-watch Cell No. 1. It was far from the first time that Jack had represented a man so close to a date with death, but it was one of the few in which Jack had solid questions about his client's guilt. Jack couldn't say that he felt any personal affection for Dylan Reeves. He did feel a deep sense of responsibility, however, which dated back to the law according to Neil: "Don't ever represent a man who's fighting for his life, Jack, if you're not all-in for the fight."

Jack checked in at visitor reception. He was alone, having made this trip without Hannah, mindful of the limits on compensation to court-appointed counsel in capital cases. A corrections officer was seated on the other side of the three-quarter-inch glass. "I'm here for the deposition of Carlos Mendoza," Jack said.

Mendoza was one of over a thousand inmates at FSP who weren't on death row, though being part of the general population at FSP was no picnic. Florida prisons had the highest rate of "suspicious deaths" and "force incidents resulting in death" in the country.

"Carlos Bad Boy, huh?" the guard said. "Whole buncha suits here to see him today."

Jack had read the indictment, and apparently the name—Carlos Mendoza, aka "Carlos Bad Boy"—had followed him through the court system and into prison.

The guard led Jack through a set of secure doors to the attorney visitation room. Visits with attorneys and clerics were among the limited exceptions to the no-contact visitation rule, but the prisoner had not yet arrived. There was a rectangular table in the center of the windowless room. A stenographer was set up with her machine and seated beside the empty chair for the witness. Barbara Carmichael and an attorney from the Florida office of the attorney general rose from the government's side of the table, and the lawyers shook hands.

"Mendoza is meeting with his attorney," said Carmichael.

A witness has a right to be represented by counsel, and Jack knew from his failed attempts to interview Mendoza that he'd hired a crackerjack criminal defense lawyer. Maddie Vargas was a pit bull who had parlayed years of experience in the public defender's office into a successful private practice. Mendoza was typical of her clientele: men who were facing or serving long prison sentences for violent crimes and who could afford to pay her nonrefundable retainer upfront. Vargas wouldn't be paid in Criminal Justice Act vouchers for her representation of Carlos Bad Boy.

The metal door on the opposite side of the room opened. A corrections officer entered first, followed by the shackled prisoner in the company of another two guards. Mendoza was an imposing figure even in his prison jumpsuit, several inches taller than Jack, and built like Jack's friend Theo.

Entering last was Maddie Vargas, a middle-aged woman who wore too much makeup and not just one but two heavy gold bracelets on each wrist. Her auburn-colored hair was cropped a little too severely, not much longer than her client's prison cut.

"Nice to meet you," Jack said.

"We actually met years ago," said Vargas. "At a fund-raiser for your father's second campaign for governor. A thousand bucks a plate for a rubber-chicken dinner. But at least your old man was nice enough to appoint me to the Florida Bar Grievance Committee. Here's my card, in case you're ever facing disbarment. It's one of my subspecialties."

"Thanks," said Jack. He put her business card away without reading it. Encounters like this one reminded him that Harry Swyteck, like all politicians, would cash checks from just about anyone.

The chains rattled as Mendoza took his seat at the end of the table, next to the stenographer. Vargas sat at his side. Jack noted the lovely tattoos on his knuckles: BAD on the right; BOY on the left, both of which looked to be either self-inflicted or the rushed work of a very drunk artist. The guards assumed their posts on opposite sides of the room, one at the door to the cell block, two at the door to freedom. The stenographer swore the witness. Jack was ready to begin.

"Mr. Mendoza, you were convicted on charges of human trafficking, correct?"

He glanced at his attorney before answering. "Yes."

"The victim was a thirteen-year-old girl, correct?"

"*Alleged* victim," said Vargas.

"He's been convicted," said Jack.

"Wrongfully."

"At his sentencing hearing Mr. Mendoza admitted to the crime, apologized to the victim, and expressed his remorse to the court."

The prosecutor spoke up. "Mr. Swyteck seems to make a fair point."

"Fine," said Vargas. "Restate the question."

Jack noted the unusual level of cooperation between Vargas and the prosecutor. Then he asked his question. "The victim was a thirteen-year-old girl who had run away from home, correct?"

"Right," said Mendoza.

"She lived with you in your apartment for two months, right?"

"Yes."

"And in order to live in your apartment, you required her to dance nude at Club Mariah, a strip club on Miami Beach. Correct?"

"That was the arrangement."

"And you also required her to have sex with adult men for money, right?"

He glanced uneasily at his attorney, but she interposed no objection.

"Sometimes," he said.

"Now, Mr. Mendoza. Have any other girls under the age of eighteen ever resided with you?"

"Objection," said Vargas. "Don't answer that."

"Unless Mr. Mendoza is asserting his Fifth Amendment rights, I want an answer," said Jack.

The witness exchanged glances with his attorney, then looked at Jack. "I refuse to answer on grounds that I might incriminate myself."

"Have you arranged for any other girls under the age of eighteen to have sex with adult men?"

"I refuse to answer on grounds that I might incriminate myself."

"Have you ever communicated in any way with a girl named Sashi Burgette?"

"I refuse to answer on grounds that I might incriminate myself."

"Have you ever communicated in any way with Debra Burgette?"

"I refuse to answer on grounds that I might incriminate myself."

"Debra Burgette's ex-husband testified that you did have communications with Debra. Are you denying it?"

"Same response."

"Have you ever communicated in any way with Gavin Burgette?"

"Same response."

Jack paused. Mendoza's assertion of his Fifth Amendment rights, as opposed to a flat denial of Jack's accusations, was a curious move. That, coupled with his lawyer's apparent coordination with the prosecutor on Jack's objections, made Jack seriously suspicious. It begged for deeper exploration. As a matter of tactics, however, a change of subject was in order before circling back for another run at the witness. "Mr. Mendoza, as of now you have served twenty-six months on a sentence of ten years. Is that right?"

"Two years, two months, and five days."

"You count?"

"Absolutely. Working on early release for good behavior."

Vargas tugged at his arm. "Answer only the question you are asked, and then wait for the next question," she said in a tone that not many people could get away with.

Jack continued. "Are you working on any other strategies for early release from prison?"

"Objection. Vague." There was no judge to rule on objections, which was normal in any deposition. Vargas was merely making a record.

"Let me be more specific," said Jack. "Have you or your attorney spoken to anyone at the state attorney's office about testifying in a possible retrial of Dylan Reeves on charges of murdering Sashi Burgette?"

"Objection." This time, it was Vargas and the prosecutor in unison.

"You can answer the question," Jack told the witness.

"No, don't answer that question," said Vargas.

"I'm entitled to an answer," said Jack.

"It's an improper question," said Vargas. "Don't answer it."

Jack retrieved Vargas' business card from his pocket and returned it to her. "Ms. Vargas, unless you'd like to represent yourself in a disbarment proceeding, I suggest you withdraw your instruction to the witness. There's no basis for it."

"Are you threatening me?"

"Let's take a break," said the prosecutor.

"Not when there's a question pending," said Jack.

"We're taking a break," the prosecutor said sternly. She and Vargas huddled in the corner, whispering back and forth. A moment later, they returned to the table. It was the prosecutor who spoke for the record, the stenographer taking it all down.

"The state of Florida joins in the witness's objection to any questions about ongoing discussions between Mr. Mendoza and the state attorney's office in connection with the case against Dylan Reeves. We are therefore terminating this deposition and will file an immediate motion for a protective order with the court."

"You made me travel all the way up here to tell me that the state of Florida is shutting down the deposition? Really?"

"I've stated my position," said the prosecutor.

"So am I to infer that the state attorney is cutting a deal with Mr. Mendoza in exchange for future testimony against Mr. Reeves?" asked Jack.

The prosecutor gathered her notepad and pencils. "I'm not the witness. And I don't have to answer your questions. We're leaving now."

Vargas rose, following the lead of the government attorneys. "My client and I are leaving as well," Vargas said. "Please return Mr. Mendoza to his cell."

A pair of corrections officers approached the prisoner, the door opened, and the guards escorted Mendoza to the cell block. The attorneys exited through the other door, but Jack stopped for a word with the stenographer.

"I'll need that transcript on an expedited basis," he said.

"That will cost extra," she said. "Another dollar per page."

"Well worth it," said Jack.

Jack headed over to Q-Wing before leaving FSP. It seemed even quieter than usual on death watch, and not just because there was one less inmate at noon than there had been at sunup. Even the corrections officers seemed somber when Jack arrived. There was no small talk on an execution day; no "Give my regards to Harry Swyteck."

A visit with Dylan Reeves wasn't the point of Jack's trip to Raiford, and Jack couldn't actually say that he needed to see him. He just felt like he should go, driven perhaps by a morbid sense of obligation that arose from the sobering awareness that this could be the last time he would see Dylan Reeves alive.

They sat alone in the attorney visitation room. Jack had given his client a rundown of how the deposition of Carlos Mendoza had blown up, but Jack could tell that he wasn't really listening.

"You want to hear something funny, Swyteck?"

Jack stopped talking. His client's flat and even tone belied the promise of "something funny."

"What?"

"The guards wake us up every morning here at five a.m. to feed us. And every morning, you know what I get with my food?"

"Coffee?"

"A daily vitamin," he said, laughing without heart. "So, there I am, alone in my cell with my breakfast. Elmer Hudson is already in the killing room, counting down the minutes. I'm three hours away from moving into his cell, the next guy on the gurney. And they got me taking a multivitamin. How fucked up is that?"

Jack said nothing.

Reeves' mirthless chuckle faded and his expression turned very serious. "Elmer paced all night. I could hear his feet shuffling across the floor. Pacing, pacing, pacing. Hell, I was up every half hour myself, and it wasn't even my turn."

"Hard to shut off your mind, I'm sure," said Jack.

"Yeah. I heard the guard walk up to Elmer's cell and tell him it was time. You know what I was thinking?"

Jack shook his head. "I really don't."

"I was thinking that we always want what we can't have. You know what I mean?"

"In general, I do. Though I'm not sure I take your meaning here."

"It's like this, Swyteck. Elmer's up all night pacing because he's number one on death watch, and he don't want to die. Last month, ten feet right above us, some guy who's not on death row hangs himself in his cell."

"I heard about that," said Jack.

"Yeah. Don't you see what I'm saying? You're fighting to keep me alive, and this guy just wraps a cord around his neck and checks out. That's what this place does to you. It's all fucked up."

Jack allowed him another minute to vent. Or was he actually philosophizing—venturing for the first time in his life into the cell block of irony? That was another weird thing about death row: it could turn a Dylan Reeves into an Albert Camus.

Reeves fell quiet. Jack turned the conversation. "The judge rejected our argument that Sashi Burgette is alive," he said.

His client showed no reaction.

"We can appeal that ruling," said Jack.

"Okay. So appeal it."

"There's a downside," said Jack. "If we take an appeal, it will only encourage Sashi's mother to keep clinging to the hope that her daughter is alive."

Reeves' expression slowly changed. He seemed annoyed. "What do you want from me, Swyteck?"

Jack leveled his gaze. "You know what I want," he said. "I

don't give you false hope. I don't want to give anyone else false hope, either."

Reeves leaned forward, laid his hands atop the table, and looked Jack straight in the eye. "I can't tell you Sashi Burgette is alive," he said in a detached voice. "All I can tell you is what I told you the last time: *I* didn't kill her."

CHAPTER 30

J ack was back in Miami just ahead of the late-afternoon rush hour. He avoided the expressway out of the airport, and a twenty-minute drive down LeJeune Road took him straight to Ingraham Park.

Jack had phoned Debra several times since Saturday's court hearing. She'd returned none of his calls—until Monday afternoon, when Jack's cell rang as he boarded the plane in Jacksonville. It was important that Jack understand why she ran from the courtroom, she'd said, and she wanted him to meet her at Ingraham Park to talk about it. The meeting place was no random choice. It was where Sashi had gone missing.

Jack parked at Cartagena Circle, crossed the arched pedestrians-only bridge over the canal, and entered the park. Ingraham was one of the Miami-Dade Park Service's success stories. The fountain at the center of this beautifully rebuilt green space was surrounded by monoliths of coral rock that were arranged Stonehenge fashion and connected by trellises to create a welcoming semicircle for visitors and joggers. The lush landscaping and manicured lawns were in sharp contrast to Merrie Christmas Park, just down the road, which was closed indefinitely after it was discovered that only a thin layer of sod separated playful children from the toxic residue of a towering trash incinerator. "Old Smokey" had belched clouds of ash all over the West Grove neighborhoods—Theo's old haunts—for forty-five years before its closing in 1970, and it was still linked to an alarming occurrence of pancreatic cancer among nearby residents. Jack and a University of Miami law professor had filed the lawsuit to clean up the park and avert another generation of cancer victims. No one gave him any grief about saving those lives.

Jack found Debra sitting on a bench near the fountain. She was watching young children at play on the monkey bars. Teenagers were exercising on the outdoor weight-lifting equipment. A couple of college students tossed a Frisbee over their sunbathing girlfriends on the lawn. Each was a little reminder that, before Sashi's disappearance, crime in this upscale park was generally on the order of pranksters dumping laundry detergent in the churning fountain.

Jack apologized for being a few minutes late and then took a seat on the bench with her.

"That's my Alexander," she said. "The boy on the top bar."

Jack spotted him. He was laughing and happily holding his position against an onslaught of other would-be kings of the mountain. "Great-looking kid," said Jack.

"Yes. Beautiful. Both he and Sashi. Just beautiful to look at."

Her gaze drifted toward the waterway and the stretch of grass behind the stand of banyan trees where Dylan Reeves claimed to have "met" Sashi.

"You know why I asked you to come here, right?" she asked.

"Why don't you tell me?"

She turned her head and looked him in the eye. "Because this is a place where I would never lie about what happened to Sashi. And I want you to know that I am *not* lying to you."

"I've never accused you of lying."

She looked skeptical. "I'm sure Gavin has put a few questions in your mind."

"Not really. He's actually very understanding and forgiving."

"Forgiving," she said, scoffing. "*He's* forgiving?"

Debra fell silent. Jack's gaze again drifted toward Alexander, then back. "What are you telling me, Debra?"

A breeze rustled the palm fronds above them. She brushed a wisp of hair from her face and said, "Gavin lied."

Jack took a moment to absorb it. "On Saturday, you mean?"

"Yes, on the witness stand. That's why I ran from the courtroom." She spoke in an even tone, but the bitterness came through. "He lied to you, he lied to the judge, and he lied under oath."

"That's a big accusation."

"It's a fact."

"All right. Let's break this down. What specifically was Gavin lying about?"

"First of all," she said, and Jack could see her anger rising, "*he's* the one who found out about rehoming. And he's the one who found Carlos Mendoza. Not me."

"How did Gavin find him?"

"I have no idea. This was not presented to me as a choice. It was a done deal. Gavin said he found a broker who would help us find another family who could give Sashi a new home."

"Did he tell you the broker's name?"

"Yes. Carlos Mendoza. Gavin said that Mendoza had already introduced him to the new family, and they were perfect for Sashi. A couple in Tampa."

The list of potential witnesses seemed to grow longer every time he spoke to Debra. He decided not to challenge her on that yet.

"What are their names?"

"I never found out. I was so opposed to it that names didn't matter."

"Is that what you told Gavin?"

"Yes. This was the part of Gavin's testimony on Saturday that put me over the edge. He made himself sound like a saint: that whole bit about how Sashi is not a shirt and we can't just take her back to the department store. That's what *I* told *him*."

"The cell-phone records do show that Carlos Mendoza made more calls to you than to Gavin."

"Of course they do. Gavin was meeting with Mendoza in person. I wasn't. Mendoza wanted Sashi, and I wouldn't give Sashi to him."

"You mean you refused to sign the power of attorney?"

"No, I mean I physically wouldn't deliver my daughter to him and this family from Tampa."

"But did you or didn't you sign the power of attorney?"

She averted her eyes, a hint of shame in her tone. "Yes. I did sign. Gavin didn't give me any choice about that."

"That can mean a lot of things," said Jack. "I'm guessing it doesn't mean he put a gun to your head."

"No. But he made it clear that if Sashi didn't leave, he would. He said he trusted Mendoza, and that the couple from Tampa sounded like a perfect fit. If I didn't sign the power of attorney, our marriage was over. He would divorce me and leave me with nothing. So I signed."

"So, both you and Gavin signed a power of attorney?"

"Both of us, yes."

"Did Gavin give the signed document to Mendoza?"

"*Yes.* That's why Mendoza was so mad when he called me. I wouldn't go through with it. I finally told Gavin, 'If you want a divorce, fine, divorce me. But if you rehome Sashi, I'll go to the police and have you arrested for kidnapping.' "

"Did you mean that?"

Debra paused, as if she'd never even asked herself that question. "I don't know. But I refused to budge."

"Let me make sure I understand this. You're saying that at the time Mendoza was making phone calls to you on his prepaid cell—right before Sashi disappeared—he had everything he needed to rehome Sashi? Legal documents. New parents. Approval from Gavin. Everything."

"Yes," she said. "Everything except Sashi."

"Except Sashi," said Jack.

The breeze kicked up again, strong enough to stir the silence and carry some of the fountain's mist over them.

"This is the truth," said Debra, breaking the silence. "I swear it is, Jack. I *swear* to it."

"That's good," said Jack. "Because you're gonna have to."

CHAPTER 31

Over the dinner hour, Jack put Debra's words into a sworn affidavit. Debra signed it and it was notarized at the Freedom Institute. Hannah—the notary public—was seated at the kitchen table with them.

"What happens next?" asked Debra, as she laid her pen aside.

"We file your affidavit with the court," said Hannah.

"Not yet," said Jack. "First, I want to sit down with Gavin, go over each of these assertions, and get his reaction."

"His reaction will be to punch you in the nose," said Debra. "Why can't you just let him see it after you file it, like everyone else? He's already had his say in court, and he completely lied about me."

"That's the problem," said Jack. "I'm the one who put him on the witness stand. I can't just file an affidavit from you and pretend like your ex-husband never testified. I'm discrediting my own witness."

"He should be discredited."

"Maybe. But before I do that, he deserves a chance to explain himself. Doesn't that sound like the fair thing to do?"

Debra considered it, then nodded weakly. "I suppose."

"Apart from your concern about rhinoplasty in my immediate future, is there any other reason I shouldn't share this with Gavin before filing it with the court?"

"No. Not if you feel like you need to."

"I need to," said Jack.

"Okay," she said. "Then do it."

Jack drove to the south end of prestigious Brickell Avenue, where a breathtaking stretch of waterfront high-rises stood like a mile-long line of forty-story dominoes. Jack was probably the only guy in Miami who could visit Brickell and be reminded of the Anne Frank House, but there was a parallel. Like the old Amsterdam flats along the canals, the massive Brickell condo buildings had a sideways feel to them: the short sides of the rect-angle faced the street in the front and the water in back; the much longer sides stretched for what seemed like the length of a soccer pitch.

Jack valeted his car and took the elevator to the twenty-third floor, where Gavin had been leasing a two-bedroom unit since his divorce from Debra. Dressed in tennis whites, Gavin was still cooling down from a rooftop match when he greeted Jack at the door. He offered Jack a cocktail, but Jack declined, preferring to get in and out quickly. Gavin fixed a gin and tonic for himself, garnished it with a refreshing slice of cucumber, and then led Jack out to the wraparound balcony, where they settled into a pair of patio chairs. Jack took in the view, and the bay glistened in the moonlight as Gavin read his ex-wife's affidavit.

Finally, Gavin laid the document atop the glass-top table and looked at Jack.

"You bought it hook, line, and sinker, didn't you, Swyteck?" It wasn't the punch in the nose that Debra had predicted. It was a sardonic smile.

"Bought what?" asked Jack.

"That's the same bullshit that Debra accused me of in the di-vorce. It's all a rehash of the 'horrible dad' allegations she made to try and keep me from seeing Alexander."

"If you want to point out any inaccuracies, now's the time."

"No," he said, shaking his head. "I'm not going to play her game, and I'm definitely not going to stoop to her level and trade insults and accusations in a courtroom. She can say all of these things if she wants—paint me as the bad parent who led the charge to rehome Sashi. But it's a breach of the confidentiality agreement we signed as part of our divorce settlement. It's going to cost her."

"I don't know anything about that," said Jack.

"You will, if you file this affidavit," said Gavin. "I strongly recommend that you speak to my attorney before you take Debra's word at face value and make this a publicly filed document."

"That's a fair suggestion," said Jack. "How do I reach your attorney?"

Gavin rose, opened the sliding glass door, and called into the condo. "Nicole, can you come here a minute?"

An attractive brunette came out of the kitchen and joined them. She held a glass of white wine in one hand and laid the other affectionately on Gavin's shoulder.

"What's up, babe?" she asked.

She wasn't the typical bimbo that Jack would have expected a financial hotshot to hook up with on the rebound. She looked more like someone Andie might have counted among her friends.

"Nicole, say hello to Jack Swyteck," said Gavin. "Jack, meet my lawyer."

CHAPTER 32

Gavin Burgette stood at the floor-to-ceiling window and soaked in the view of sparkling Biscayne Bay, the Port of Miami, and sun-bathed South Beach beyond. It wasn't yet nine a.m., Eastern Time, and he'd already finished two important calls, one with a sovereign-wealth-fund manager in London, and the other with a financial analyst in Berlin.

The south Florida office of Garner Investments was a lavishly appointed penthouse in Miami's Financial District. Not bad for a kid from West Miami who'd started out selling luxury automobiles. A keen eye for big spenders ready to part with their money was his gift. A little car knowledge and a lot of smooth talking had paid his way through business school at the University of Miami, where he'd graduated in the middle of the pack, nowhere near good enough to land a job at a top Wall Street firm. But Gavin was a hustler, and it wasn't beneath him to pop in and visit all those satisfied customers who'd purchased Porsches, Audis, and BMWs from him over the years. In most cases, he didn't get past the receptionist. A few came out to the lobby, shook his hand, and said they'd call him when the lease was up on their Lexus. One guy—an old Cuban-American who'd come to Miami on a raft made out of plastic bottles, and who'd started out selling cars in Hialeah—found an idle hundred thousand in his portfolio that Gavin could "play with." Gavin turned it into half a mil. In five years, he was turning away clients. In ten, he'd built a book of business that had the blue chip firms courting *him*.

"There's a client here to see you, Mr. Burgette."

Gavin turned away from the window to see his assistant standing in the open doorway. "Do I have a nine o'clock appointment?"

"It's not on your calendar. He says his mother asked him to drop in and say hello to you. Ellen Ferguson. His name is Jeffrey."

The Ferguson family was old Palm Beach money. Two weeks had passed since Gavin had introduced himself to eighty-six-year-old Ellen at the annual gala for the Everglades Foundation, and he'd really turned on the charm. He'd even managed to work his way into a photograph with Ellen that the foundation had posted on its website and that the *Palm Beach Post* had run in its weekend society section. He'd followed up with a personal letter but heard nothing back. Until now.

"Tell Jeffrey I'll be right out."

Gavin straightened his necktie, popped a couple of "curiously strong" mints into his mouth to kill the coffee breath, and then headed down the hall to the lobby. A slender dark-haired man rose from the couch as Gavin entered.

"Mr. Burgette?" he said, as he approached.

"Jeffrey, I presume?"

He offered an envelope. "This is for you," he said. "From my mother."

Gavin smiled and took it.

"Nice picture of you and Ellen on the Web, by the way," said "Jeffrey," his voice laden with sarcasm.

And then he took off.

Gavin closed his eyes slowly, then opened them, realizing what had just happened. This guy was no relative of Ellen Ferguson, and this staged encounter had nothing to do with the Ferguson family. Gavin had always regarded the pushy custom-tailored-suit salesmen as the undisputed pros at finagling their way into a penthouse office under false pretenses. They had nothing on process servers. He removed the summons from the envelope. A quick glance at the case caption confirmed that it related to the habeas petition of Dylan Reeves before Judge Frederick. The rest spoke for itself: YOU ARE HEREBY COMMANDED TO APPEAR IN COURT-ROOM 3, THE UNITED STATES DISTRICT COURT . . .

"Shit," he said as he reached for his cell phone. He quickly returned to his office, closed the door, and dialed his lawyer, which at this hour meant dialing his own landline at the Brickell condo.

Gavin and Nicole had maintained a professional relationship throughout his divorce proceeding, and twenty years of nuptial-ending nuclear warfare had made her into a consummate trial lawyer. The Burgettes' divorce wasn't even close to "ugly" by Nicole's standards, but Gavin had still paid his lawyer plenty—enough for her to have taken his call immediately, even if they weren't sharing a bed every night that Alexander spent at his mother's house.

He quickly filled her in, then gave his order. "Nicole, you just gotta make this go away."

"Scan it and shoot it over to me," she said.

"I will. Frankly, I'm shocked by this. I thought Swyteck had gotten the message loud and clear last night that he needs to think twice before filing Debra's affidavit. And now he's slapping me with a subpoena? It doesn't make sense."

"Are you sure the court issued it at Swyteck's request?"

"I just assumed," said Gavin.

"Look at the signature line. Could be on the second page."

Gavin flipped ahead and found it. "Barbara fucking Carmichael," he said. "Why would the prosecutor subpoena me?"

"My guess is that the state is planning to put on live testimony in opposition to Dylan Reeves' petition. And at least some of that testimony is coming from *you*."

"I've said all I need to say to this judge. What more do they want from me?"

"I dunno. Let me call Carmichael and find out."

Gavin raised the mini-blinds behind his desk. From the north window of his corner office he had a clear view across the Miami River and all the way to the federal courthouse.

"Better call her quick. This says I have to be there at noon—*today.*"

CHAPTER 33

A ndie reached St. Hugh's Cemetery just as the wrought-iron gates swung open at nine a.m. She'd driven alone. It was something she needed to do for herself, by herself.

She parked near the main mausoleum and walked to the office entrance. An elderly couple was in the waiting room. They were speaking Spanish, but Andie understood enough to know that they had come to purchase side-by-side plots. They were holding hands like teenagers, making the sad task seem not so sad—even romantic.

"Can I help you?" the saleswoman asked as she approached.

"I'm here to visit, but I don't know exactly where the gravesite is," Andie said. "Do you have a directory by name?"

She escorted Andie to the computer terminal on the other side of the waiting area. Andie typed in the information, and the location appeared on the screen: Section H, Plot 11. She jotted the coordinates on a printed map of the grounds and set out on her mission.

The journey started on a wide path of pea gravel. Andie passed countless tombs, many adorned with angels, griffins, or cherubs. A few graves were brightened by fresh-cut flowers, but the most impressive splashes of pink, orange, and other flaming colors came from bougainvillea vines and hibiscus bushes that had been planted many years earlier, probably by mourners who had since found permanent rest here. Andie continued along a shaded path until she came to a small clearing where several paths intersected like the spokes of a wheel. She checked her map, but it wasn't very helpful. She wasn't sure which way to go.

"Lost?" a man asked.

Andie looked up. He was an older man, dressed in coveralls and a baseball cap. A thick mustache made it difficult to see his mouth, and crescents of sweat extended from the underarms of his T-shirt. From the dirt on the man's knees Andie assumed that he was part of grounds maintenance.

"Yes, I am," said Andie. She gave him the coordinates.

"I can take you there." He led her down a path that stretched beneath the sprawling limbs of strong oaks. The stone markers were gradually becoming less impressive. They were newer than the ones Andie passed at the beginning of her journey, but they were hardly new. Most of the departed here had died before Andie was born.

"Here it is," said the groundskeeper.

Andie stopped and looked down at the plain white headstone. It was about the size of a child's pillow, with simple cherub carvings on either end. The engraved name told her that she had come to the right place:

Ana Maria Fuentes-Swyteck.

It was a sobering moment. Slowly, almost without thinking about it, she lowered herself down onto her knees. The coolness of green grass pressed through the hem of her maternity dress. She leaned forward and ran her finger along the grooves on the headstone, tracing the name and the dates.

"Hello, Ana Maria," she whispered.

Andie tried to conjure up an image of Jack's mother—she'd seen photographs—but nothing was in mental focus. She was powerless to envision this special person who had left Cuba as a teenager, left her own mother behind in Bejucál, come to Miami as a refugee, fallen in love with a cop who had big dreams, and given birth to a baby boy. Instead, complex feelings about her own child and condition consumed her, and at that particular moment there simply wasn't room in her heart for anything or anyone else. In a moment of confused empathy, she imagined her own baby fully grown and coming someday to visit the grave of a mother she had never known. She wondered how Jack must have felt whenever he came here, seeing his date of birth carved into stone as his mother's date of death.

Perhaps Andie knew Ana Maria better for having visited this place. She knew Jack a little better, too. But she didn't feel any better. She felt . . . scared.

Andie climbed to her feet, but she didn't step away from the gravesite. She dug her phone from her purse and dialed Jack. She was relieved to hear him answer, and she dispensed with the meaningless "Hi, how are you, honey?"

"I need to hear you say it again," she said into her phone.

"Say what?" asked Jack.

"That everything is going to be okay."

He hesitated, and Andie could almost hear him wondering what had brought this on. She was relieved that he didn't go down that route and, instead, simply gave her the comfort she needed. "Everything's going to be okay," he said. "Perfect, in fact."

"You promise?"

"Yes, love. I promise."

She forced a little smile—a sad one nonetheless. "I believe you," she said. Her gaze remained fixed on the headstone, and she rested her free hand atop her belly. "We all believe you."

Jack was in the office by nine thirty. He'd been awake since five, preparing at home for a mediation conference in a nice and bland breach-of-contract case in which his client was highly unlikely to die. Then it was back to the daily diet of the Freedom Institute and the world of Dylan Reeves.

"Oh, Jack!" his secretary called out. Bonnie was known as

"the Roadrunner," and with her trademark burst of speed, she'd nearly raced right past him on his way into the kitchen for coffee. "This just came in by e-mail. You have a hearing before Judge Frederick at noon."

"Seriously?"

She handed him the papers, which she'd printed for him. There were three: the notice of hearing at noon; a copy of a subpoena served on Gavin Burgette; and a notice of filing the affidavit of Debra Burgette. Each was signed by Barbara Carmichael.

"Hannah?" Jack said in a loud voice. In three quick steps he was inside her office.

She looked up from her desk. "What's cookin', good-lookin'?"

Another phrase she'd borrowed from her father. Under the circumstances, Jack wasn't amused. "We agreed last night that we were not going to file the affidavit of Debra Burgette until I sorted out the conflict between her testimony and her ex-husband's."

"Right. So?"

"Barbara Carmichael just filed a copy of Debra's affidavit with the court, and there's a hearing at noon. How did the prosecutor get hold of an affidavit that *we* drafted if *we* didn't file it?"

Hannah was suddenly pale. She checked her e-mail program, and she almost seemed to melt into her chair. "Oh, shit," she said.

Jack took another step inside and closed the door. "What happened?"

"Oh, God," she said.

"Hannah, talk to me."

She looked up, and the worried expression on her face was unlike any he'd seen from her before. "After Debra signed her affidavit, I scheduled an automatic e-mail to serve a copy of it to Barbara Carmichael at eight a.m."

"Why did you do that?"

"Because I thought we were going to file it with the court this morning."

"I told you we weren't going to file it."

Hannah grimaced, as if in pain. "I know. You told me after I scheduled the automatic service." She swallowed the lump in her throat. "I forgot to cancel it."

"Oh, boy."

"Jack, I'm so sorry. We've been busting Carmichael's chops because the prosecution withheld crucial evidence from Dylan Reeves' trial counsel. The last thing I thought we needed was to have her accuse us of sitting on crucial evidence as well. So I set up the automatic e-mail to make sure it was served as soon as we filed it. I am so sorry."

Jack drew a breath, trying not to be too obvious about the headache he could feel coming on. "It's all right," he said.

"No, it's not. I can't believe I did that. Shit! I'm such an idiot!"

"You made a mistake."

"Mistakes get people killed around here. That's what my dad always said."

Jack paused, and as bad as this seemed, it made him realize what had been missing from his years as a sole practitioner: there was no being mentored; no chance to be a mentor. "No, that's not what your dad *always* said, Hannah."

"What?"

"Remind me to tell you the story of when Neil sent me all the way to Tallahassee to cover a hearing for him—and I went to the wrong courthouse."

She managed a semblance of a smile. "Thanks," she said.

"No problem," said Jack, as he opened the door. "We'll deal with it."

CHAPTER 34

Jack was in Courtroom 3 at noon. Jury selection in Judge Frederick's five-week conspiracy trial had entered its second day, and the lunch hour was the judge's only window to accommodate the prosecutor's request to call Gavin Burgette back to the witness stand.

"Exactly what is the issue?" the judge asked.

The courtroom was quiet. Dozens of prospective jurors had vacated the public seating area to hit the nearest fast-food joint and return before one o'clock. Judge Frederick was on the bench, but no way was he going to skip lunch, his gavel in one hand and a ham sandwich in the other.

Jack spoke first. "Judge, last night Debra Burgette signed an affidavit describing how Carlos Mendoza had means, motive, and opportunity to abduct Sashi Burgette. The prosecution's failure to disclose this evidence to Mr. Reeves before his trial is a violation of his constitutional rights and requires a new trial."

"Then why was the affidavit filed by the prosecution?" the judge asked.

Jack was about to explain Hannah's mistake, but the prosecutor beat him to the punch.

"The state of Florida is taking the bull by the horns," said Carmichael, "with an emphasis on *bull*. Debra Burgette's affidavit is replete with falsehoods, including accusations against her ex-husband. We would like the opportunity to put Mr. Burgette back on the witness stand. His testimony will demonstrate that the petitioner has no real evidence to support his request for a new trial. At most, this is a he said/she said battle of conflicting testimony that belongs in divorce court."

"Permission granted to file a counter-affidavit from Gavin Burgette," the judge said.

"We prefer to present live testimony. We have subpoenaed Mr. Burgette for that purpose."

Gavin's lawyer stepped up to the rail in the first row of public seating behind Jack. "Excuse me, Your Honor," said Nicole.

"Who are you?" asked the judge.

"Nicole Thompson, with the law firm of Thompson and Tuttle, Your Honor. I represented Mr. Burgette in his divorce, and I am his counsel here today. We oppose the subpoena."

"On what basis?"

"Judge, Mr. Burgette took the high road in his divorce. Debra Burgette's affidavit revisits wild accusations that my client chose to resolve privately in a confidential divorce settlement. My client has no interest in trading insults and accusations with his wife in open court."

"His testimony is crucial," said the prosecutor. "It will show that Debra Burgette is not a credible witness. Your Honor should completely disregard *all* of her testimony and deny the petitioner's request for relief."

"I object," said Jack.

"*You* object? I'm in day two of jury selection in my biggest trial of the year, and I barely have time to grab a sandwich for lunch. But the state is entitled to present evidence in opposition to the petition. Right now is the only availability on my calendar. Mr. Burgette, I'm sorry if you feel like this is an unnecessary intrusion into your privacy, but another man's life is at stake. I'll give you twenty minutes, Ms. Carmichael. Call your witness."

She did, and Jack watched as Gavin Burgette walked to the witness stand and swore the oath. Jack also noticed that neither

Debra nor her daughter Aquinnah was anywhere in the empty courtroom.

The prosecutor handed the judge and the witness a copy of Debra's affidavit, and her questioning began. In staccato fashion, the prosecutor's questions and the witness's rapid-fire answers refuted Debra's written testimony as lies.

"At paragraph two, Debra Burgette stated under oath that it was your idea to rehome Sashi. Is that a true statement?"

"Not true."

"Paragraph three. She stated that you were the one who initially contacted Carlos Mendoza. Is that a true statement?"

"Not true."

"Paragraph four states that you threatened to divorce her if she did not sign the necessary legal documents to rehome your daughter. True?"

"Not true."

"Paragraph five: that you delivered the power of attorney to Mr. Mendoza."

"Not true."

"Six: that Mr. Mendoza made arrangements for you to meet a couple from Tampa who were willing to rehome Sashi."

"Not true."

The same question-and-answer format continued for several minutes. Finally, the prosecutor laid Debra Burgette's sworn affidavit aside, the witness having refuted his wife's every factual assertion.

"No further questions," said Carmichael, and she returned to a seat at her table.

"Mr. Swyteck, you have ten minutes for cross-examination," the judge said.

"Thank you, Your Honor," he said as he approached the witness.

Jack didn't know if the judge would believe Gavin or Debra, but the prosecutor had been right in one respect: a battle of he said/she said was not Dylan Reeves' ticket to a new trial. Jack would have to push through the conflict and score in a big way if he was going to leave Judge Frederick's courtroom with any hope of finding the truth—and of keeping his client alive. He had his doubts about Debra, but she wasn't even in the courtroom, much less on the witness stand. If he was going to cut through this logjam, it would have to be through Gavin.

"Mr. Burgette, you testified at Dylan Reeves' trial, correct?"

"Yes."

Even his one-word response hissed with anger. Gavin seemed to recognize that this was Jack's last shot, and that Jack would be coming after him.

"And you attended each day of the trial?" asked Jack.

"Didn't miss a single one."

"Your testimony was that on the day Sashi disappeared, you were out of town on a business trip."

"That's right."

"You arrived home after dark, around eight o'clock?"

"Yes."

"By that time, your wife was already concerned about Sashi. Isn't that right?"

"That was my testimony, yes."

"She had called you three times?"

"I don't recall the exact number. More than once."

"When you got home, you tried to calm her down."

"I tried."

Jack opened the trial transcript to the pertinent page. "You testified as follows: 'Debra and I searched the house for anything that might tell us where Sashi had gone.' Is that still your recollection?"

"It is."

"You, personally, looked in Sashi's bedroom, correct?"

"Yes."

"You found nothing helpful."

"Nothing."

Jack paused, then continued. "At trial, you heard your wife testify that it was very unusual for Sashi to leave the house without her cell phone."

"Yes."

Jack had the relevant portion of the trial transcript in hand. "And you also testified that Sashi, quote, 'never left the house without her cell.' Correct?"

"Yes, I did."

Jack laid the transcript aside, stepped closer to the witness, and faced him squarely. "Around ten o'clock, your wife went back upstairs to check Sashi's room again. Isn't that right?"

"Yes."

"Only then did she find Sashi's phone?"

"Right."

"That's when Debra called the police. Because she knew it was very strange that Sashi would be without her cell for almost an entire day."

"That's correct."

"So, when you got home and went upstairs to check your daughter's room, you didn't see Sashi's cell?"

"Obviously, I didn't."

"*Is* it obvious?" Jack asked, his tone more assertive than inquisitive. "Or did you put it there?"

The prosecutor sprang from her chair. "Objection. That's an accusation, not a question, and it's completely baseless."

"Overruled," said the judge. "Mr. Swyteck, I assume that you will establish some basis for this line of questioning. And let me also remind you that you have all of five minutes left. The witness may answer."

"No," said Gavin, scoffing. "I didn't plant Sashi's cell phone in her room, if that's what you're asking. That's preposterous."

Jack retrieved Gavin's call detail report, which was already in evidence as an exhibit. "Mr. Burgette, your call record shows that, on the day Sashi disappeared, at eleven-oh-seven a.m., you called Carlos Mendoza. You don't deny making that call, do you?"

"I made it."

"You also admit that you spoke to Mr. Mendoza. Am I right?"

"Yes."

"You made a deal with Mr. Mendoza, didn't you?"

"Objection, Your Honor."

"The witness can handle himself here," said the judge. "Overruled."

"I did exactly the opposite," said Gavin. "My recollection is that Mr. Mendoza had contacted Debra the day before. I called to tell him to stop bothering my wife."

"That's all you told him?"

"That's all I recall."

Jack checked the call report, then handed it to the witness. "It took you six minutes to tell him that?"

He checked the exhibit. "Apparently. That's what the call report says."

"Are you aware that the entire Gettysburg Address was delivered in less than two minutes?"

"Objection," said Carmichael, groaning.

"Sustained. But your point is noted, Mr. Swyteck."

Jack retrieved Debra's call report, which also was already in evidence. "Your wife's call report shows that the final incoming call from Carlos Mendoza was three days before Sashi disappeared. Do you read it any differently?" he asked, as he handed the witness the exhibit.

Gavin checked the report. "It appears that your reading is correct."

"So it took you three days to get around to calling Mr. Mendoza to tell him to stop harassing your wife? Do I have that right?"

"Objection."

"Overruled. I'd like to hear the answer to that."

"As I mentioned before, this was a very busy time for me."

Jack continued in an assertive tone, but not too accusatory, mindful of the fact that he was questioning the victim's father. "Mr. Burgette, on the day Sashi disappeared, you weren't on a business trip, were you?"

"I think I've already answered that."

"The truth is that you were with Sashi. Isn't that right, sir?"

"No, that's not right."

"Sashi had her cell phone with her on that day, like she always did. Isn't that so?"

"I don't know. Like I said, I wasn't with her."

"You took Sashi's phone from her when you delivered her to Mr. Mendoza. Isn't that what really happened?"

His eyes narrowed, and Jack was beginning to see the angry side of Gavin that he hadn't seen since their first meeting in Neil's kitchen. "No," he said, in a low, threatening tone. "That's *not* what happened."

"When Sashi had run away from home in the past, both you and your wife had used the GPS tracking chip in her cell phone to find her. Isn't that a fact, Mr. Burgette?"

"Yes," he said, his anger continuing to build. "We did. It didn't always work, because sometimes Sashi would turn the power off or the battery would run out."

"So if Sashi had kept her cell phone with her, and if the power was on, you or your wife could have located her on the day she disappeared. Correct?"

"I suppose that's possible."

"That's why you took Sashi's cell phone away from her."

Gavin Burgette glanced at that judge, then glared at Jack. "I categorically deny that I did any such thing."

"It was you who put Sashi's cell in her bedroom when you got home around eight o'clock that night."

"No."

"That's why Debra didn't see it earlier when she checked Sashi's bedroom."

"I don't know why Debra didn't see it."

"You let Debra report to the police that Sashi had run away from home."

"I . . . yes. I didn't stop her."

"Because a false police report was better than telling her what you had really done."

"Objection," said Carmichael. "Judge, this is bordering on harassment."

"Sustained. You have one minute, Mr. Swyteck."

Jack took another step closer. He wasn't surprised that the judge had sustained the objection. However, instinct told him that Gavin was hiding something, and as unpleasant as it was to go after him as a witness, Jack knew that he was going to have to take one more shot to get to the truth.

"Mr. Burgette, you made a deal with Carlos Mendoza. You rehomed your daughter. And you took her phone so that Debra couldn't figure out what you had done or where you had taken Sashi. Isn't that the truth, sir?"

"Objection," said the prosecutor. "Judge, really . . ."

"Yes," the judge said. "Your questions assume too much, Mr. Swyteck. It has yet to be established or even alleged that the Burgettes did anything more than *consider* rehoming their daughter."

"Debra did," said the witness.

Jack froze, as did everyone else in the courtroom. It was suddenly quiet enough to hear the inrush of cool air from the AC vents.

The judge peered down from the bench, his gaze locking on the witness. "Debra did *what*, sir?"

The witness drew a breath, then spoke like a man who'd held a secret too long, his voice filled with more regret than accusation. "Debra rehomed Sashi."

Judge Frederick glanced at the lawyers, as if to acknowledge that this was a game changer, and then he continued with the witness. "With or without your consent, sir?"

"I . . . I considered it, okay? Our family was falling apart. Torn apart, really. Sashi was . . . *her illness* was killing us. It got to the point that both Debra and I did sign a power of attorney. But I changed my mind. We agreed that it was wrong. That was how we'd left it. Then something must have happened when I was gone."

"When did you find out that your wife had actually rehomed Sashi?" the judge asked.

He was gazing at the floor, a beaten man. "The school called and told me that Sashi was absent again—which, frankly, was nothing out of the ordinary. Sashi was always cutting school. Debra would drop her off, and three or four hours later we'd find her at Starbucks or the movie theater. I was away on business, so I called Debra to tell her to handle it. Right away, I got the sense that something was very wrong. She told me that she and Sashi had a terrible argument on the way to school. In fact they never made it to the school. At first, she gave me the story that traffic was bad and Sashi got out to walk the rest of the way. But that was just a story. It took a while, but finally Debra confessed to me. She'd reached the breaking point: she rehomed Sashi."

"Rehomed her with whom?"

His voice shook as he answered. "Carlos Mendoza. That six-minute phone call on Friday morning, the one that you pointed out was longer than the Gettysburg Address—that was me trying to *undo* what Debra had done. I was trying to get my daughter back home. Not *rehomed*."

Gavin's lawyer rose from her seat in the public gallery. "Judge, may I please confer with my client? There may be Fifth Amendment rights that should be asserted here."

"It's the truth," the witness said in a hollow voice, barely audible. "I swear it is. I swear."

"Mr. Burgette, there is no question pending," the judge said, "and I strongly encourage you to confer with counsel before you speak another word."

Then the judge's glare fixed on the prosecutor. "As soon as my jury selection concludes this afternoon, I intend to read the transcript of Mr. Swyteck's deposition of Carlos Mendoza—as far as it went, anyway, before it was shut down. And I want everyone in my chambers at six p.m. this evening, including the counsel for Mr. Mendoza, whom I will have my law clerk notify immediately. The witness is ordered to remain within Miami–Dade County. We are adjourned," he said with a crack of his gavel.

"All rise!"

The judge grabbed what remained of his sandwich, stepped down from the bench, and walked briskly toward the side door to his chambers.

Jack watched in silence. His mind was awhirl, but his thoughts settled on those last few words that Gavin Burgette had uttered— seemingly to no one. Jack was struck by their similarity to words he'd heard from Debra.

"This is the truth. I swear it is, Jack. I swear to it."

The paneled door closed with a thud, and the judge was gone. The prosecutor gathered her briefcase, pushed through the gate without a word to Jack, and hurried to the rear exit. Gavin Burgette stepped down from the witness stand and huddled with his lawyer in private on the opposite side of the courtroom, near the empty jury box.

Jack packed up his laptop and stepped away from the table, wondering if he was even beginning to hear "the truth."

CHAPTER 35

Andie had a visitor at the Miami field office. It was mid-afternoon, and she'd just finished a phone conference with an assistant United States attorney over a request for a wiretap when the receptionist buzzed her on the intercom.

"There's a Debra Burgette here to see you."

Given the fact that Debra was a key witness in Jack's case, Andie could have simply said that she was unavailable. But the fact that Andie couldn't be involved didn't mean she had to be rude. She'd spent too many hours with victims and their families to opt for the total brush-off.

"I'll come out," she told the receptionist.

The shortcut from Andie's office to the lobby was through the narcotics unit, and she wasn't surprised to see that somebody had finally made them take down the *So Many Colombians, So Little Time* bumper sticker that had been pushpinned onto the bulletin board. By the time she reached the secured door at the end of the hallway and buzzed herself through to the lobby, she'd formulated several polite ways to tell Debra that she couldn't meet with her.

Debra rose from the couch in the waiting area, and Andie greeted her cordially. The receptionist was seated behind bullet-proof glass in protected space that resembled a ticket booth. Andie and Debra were alone but near the elevators, and Debra seemed concerned about a possible interruption by random passersby.

"Can we go back to your office?" she asked. "Someplace more private to talk?"

"I'm sorry, but I shouldn't really be talking to you," said Andie. "The Bureau has me walled off from this case. It has to be that way, with Jack representing Dylan Reeves."

"Oh, I see. But there is something I want you to know."

"If it has anything to do with Jack's case, I can't discuss—"

"I didn't rehome Sashi," she said.

"Confidential matters like that are between you and Jack."

"There's nothing confidential about it. Gavin accused me of rehoming Sashi in court today. I wasn't there. I just knew he was going to start saying horrible things about me, and it made me physically ill. I couldn't even drive, let alone sit through another court hearing. But I heard about it afterward from Barbara Carmichael."

"I don't get updates from the prosecutor," said Andie.

"Well, if your husband doesn't tell you, I'm sure you'll see it on the news. That's why I came here. I wanted you to hear this from me: it isn't true."

"Okay. I heard it."

"Do you believe me?"

"It doesn't matter if I believe you."

"It matters to *me*," said Debra.

"We really shouldn't be talking about this."

Debra took a seat on the couch. "Come," she said. "Sit with me for two minutes. Just listen to what I say. You don't have to say anything. Just sit. You must want to sit. It's been a long time, but I remember what it's like to be that pregnant."

Andie hesitated, then took a seat. "Okay. Two minutes."

Debra scooted to the edge of the couch and turned to face Andie more squarely. "Barbara Carmichael never believed that those phone calls I got on Sashi's birthday were from my daughter. Now, with this last call I testified about, it's gotten even worse: she thinks I called myself."

Andie simply listened, offering no response.

Debra continued. "She thinks I bought a prepaid cell phone and called my own number."

"Did that also come out in court today?" asked Andie.

"No. Barbara Carmichael talked to me afterward. She said that it's not clear where this hearing is headed. But if I let Jack put me on the witness stand again, she is going to present evidence that I fabricated the whole thing by purchasing a prepaid cell and dialing my own number. She said the evidence came from the FBI."

Andie didn't respond. Agent Hidalgo had promised to pass along his theory/speculation to the prosecutor, and he'd obviously followed through.

"Do you know anything about that, Andie?"

"I'm not at liberty to discuss this, Debra."

"I really wish you would."

"I can't. In fact, we've already talked much more than we should. It's best if you leave now."

Andie rose from the couch and started toward the elevator, but Debra didn't follow.

"I offered to take a lie detector test."

The way she'd just blurted it out had caught Andie off guard. Debra was still seated on the couch, her gaze aimed at the floor. Andie walked toward her. "When?"

She looked up at Andie. "Today, when Ms. Carmichael told me about the FBI analysis of the cell-phone towers. I told her that I would take a polygraph examination."

"What did she say about that?"

"She wasn't interested. Actually, it was worse than not being interested. It's as if she doesn't want me to pass."

"That wouldn't make sense," said Andie. "She probably thinks you're under too much stress to get an accurate result."

Debra paused, and then an idea seemed to come to her. "I'll take one now, if it would help. You must have someone here who can do it, right?"

"Debra, I don't think that would help anything."

"Ask me anything you want. Ask me if I rehomed Sashi. Ask me if I'm making up these phone calls."

"I can't do that. Please, you really should go."

Andie stepped away, and this time Debra followed her to the elevators. Andie pushed the call button, and they stood in silence as the floor numbers flashed above the elevator. They were standing side by side, their reflections in the polished metal doors looking back at them.

"I got slaughtered in my divorce, Andie. I almost lost custody of Alexander. I didn't even get half the house. Gavin owns it. When Alexander turns eighteen, I'm on the street."

"That's really none of my business," said Andie.

"My point is that those two—Gavin and his lawyer—they are vicious. There's a reason they're together now. They will say anything and do anything to win."

Jack had told her about his meeting with Gavin and his live-in lawyer at Gavin's condo.

"This isn't about winning," said Andie.

"Oh, that's where you're wrong. Trust me: for Gavin, it's always about winning."

The elevator doors parted. Debra stepped inside but held the door open. "There are things I know about Gavin—things that, for Aquinnah's sake, I have never told anyone. Things I can't ever say, thanks to this confidentiality agreement he made me sign in our divorce."

"I don't know what to tell you, Debra."

"I don't want you to tell *me* anything. Tell it to your husband. After what Gavin said in court today, Jack has to be losing trust in me. He's probably starting to see Gavin and me as two sides of the same coin. That's wrong. Tell Jack that he can trust me."

"I'm sorry. That's a conversation I can't have with Jack."

"Yes, you *can*," said Debra as the doors started to close. "And while you're at it, tell him to ask my ex if *he'd* take a lie detector test."

The doors closed, and Andie was alone in the lobby.

CHAPTER 36

The six o'clock status conference was held in Judge Frederick's chambers. Two of his law clerks were at a conference table outside the door to the judge's office, drafting bench memos while sharing a pizza for dinner. Barbara Carmichael and her colleague from the Florida attorney general's office had again managed to snag the spot to the judge's left, beside the draped American flag. Jack and Hannah were to the judge's right, exactly where Jack had nearly melted through the floor during a tongue-lashing from Judge Frederick for "bashing the father." Five days had passed since then. Five days closer to "the big day" for him and Andie.

And for Dylan Reeves.

Shit, Jack. Why do you even make an association like that?

It was the sound of Andie's voice in his head, which was quickly displaced by the judge's baritone.

"Where is counsel for Carlos Mendoza?" Judge Frederick asked.

"Here I am!" said Maddie Vargas as she hurried into the judge's office. "Sorry I'm late. Traffic in downtown Miami is fucking crazy."

Jack noticed that she smelled like a cigarette as she blew past him on her way to the prosecutor's side of the room.

"Glad you could make it, Ms. Vargas," the judge said. "Let's all clean up our language and get started, shall we?"

Vargas leaned closer to the prosecutor. "Did I say a bad word?"

she whispered, but it was loud enough for everyone to hear. Vargas was one of those lawyers who dropped the f-bomb so often outside the courthouse that she didn't even notice her own slip of the tongue in front of a judge. Or in church. Or at the playground. *"Tommy, get the fuck down from there!"*

The judge reached for the deposition transcript on his desk. "I've read Mr. Mendoza's deposition. Let me start by following up on the question that Mr. Swyteck asked and that brought the deposition to a halt: Has the state of Florida cut a deal with Mr. Mendoza in exchange for testimony against Dylan Reeves?"

"I can answer that now," said the prosecutor.

"Good," said the judge. "Because I'm ordering you to answer it. Oh, and I'm also ordering you to reimburse Mr. Swyteck for the cost of traveling to FSP because you had no business shutting down this deposition."

"Yes, Your Honor."

"'Yes,' you'll pay the fine?" asked the judge, "or, 'Yes,' there's a deal?"

"Both," said the prosecutor.

"Now we're getting somewhere," the judge said. "What are the terms of the deal?"

"We have yet to dot every 'i' and cross every 't' in a formal immunity agreement. But that's in the works."

"Give me the gist of it," the judge said.

The prosecutor checked her notes to make sure she got it right. "Mr. Mendoza has agreed to testify fully and truthfully about each of his communications with Debra and Gavin Burgette about the rehoming of their daughter Sashi."

"And in exchange for that, Mr. Mendoza gets what?" asked the judge.

Vargas spoke up. "My client will not be prosecuted for any of his dealings with the Burgette family, and the state attorney will recommend additional credit for good behavior to be applied to his existing sentence. Right, Barbara?"

"That's correct," said the prosecutor.

"Just to clarify," said Jack. "Is the witness going to testify that Debra rehomed Sashi, that Gavin rehomed Sashi, or that no one rehomed Sashi?"

"We're still working on the details of his testimony," said Carmichael.

"Those are hardly 'details,' " said Jack. "This goes to the heart of the matter."

"As I said, when we finalize the deal, we will submit Mr. Mendoza's testimony to the court by written affidavit."

Jack shook his head. "Judge, I have a huge problem with the most important testimony in this proceeding coming before the court in an affidavit that's drafted by lawyers. I need to finish my deposition. I have a right to cross-examine this witness."

The judge leaned back in his chair, thinking. "I agree that this is very important testimony. If Sashi Burgette was rehomed, it means that when her parents reported to the police that she ran away from home, it was a complete fabrication—which is itself a crime. Right, Ms. Carmichael?"

"That's correct, Your Honor."

"More important," the judge continued, "it raises serious questions as to whether Dylan Reeves was, in fact, the last person to see Sashi alive."

"I think it also raises the possibility that she is still alive," said Jack.

"I've already ruled against you on that issue," said the judge. "I'm not making any judgments in the lay sense of the word about a mother who continues to search for her missing daughter. From a legal standpoint, however, your only remaining argument is that someone other than Dylan Reeves murdered Sashi Burgette."

"I understand," said Jack.

"So here's what we're going to do," the judge said. "Given the importance of this witness, I hereby order the Department of Corrections to bring Mr. Mendoza into my courtroom, where he will be subject to cross-examination, and where I can evaluate his credibility as a witness, live and in person."

"Carlos will be thrilled," said Vargas. "A trip to Miami, all expenses paid."

"I hate to burst anyone's bubble," the judge said, "but the last time I checked, our holding cell didn't rate anywhere near five stars on Hotel-dot-com. In any event, Ms. Carmichael, I will leave it to you and your colleague from the attorney general's office to coordinate with the warden at FSP and report back to the court on the timing of Mr. Mendoza's appearance."

"Yes, Judge." It was the lawyer from the AG's office who spoke this time, and it occurred to Jack that those two words were the first he'd heard from her since the filing of the petition.

"It behooves the state to move as quickly as possible on this," the judge said. "The stay of execution will remain in effect until after I have heard Mr. Mendoza's testimony and issued a final ruling. Mr. Swyteck, how many days are we from the scheduled execution?"

"Twenty-one," said Jack. "Dylan Reeves' death warrant expires at midnight, October twentieth."

"The execution is set for seven a.m. on the nineteenth," said the prosecutor.

"My wife's due date," said Jack, and he immediately heard Andie's voice in his head again. *Shit, Jack. Why do you even . . .*

"We'll have Mr. Mendoza here long before that," said the prosecutor.

"Very good," said the judge. "And if the state keeps that promise, I promise you, Mr. Swyteck, that I will issue a ruling soon enough for you to be at your wife's side for the birth of your child."

Jack could have kicked himself. Delay was a death-row inmate's last line of defense: even with the syringe loaded and the prisoner on the gurney, there was always the hope that the state legislature might abrogate the death penalty before the executioner could find a vein. Jack had just given the judge the impression that he'd be doing the petitioner a favor by moving things along quickly. *Shit, Jack. Why do you . . .*

"Thank you, Judge," said the prosecutor.

"Yes," said Jack. "Thank you."

The judge dismissed them, and the lawyers filed out of his chambers and into the main corridor of the old courthouse. Jack asked for a moment alone with the prosecutor before they parted ways. They found a quiet spot near the marble staircase.

"That was an interesting point that Judge Frederick made about the false police report," said Jack.

"Yeah, I made a note of that."

"You seem to be in a wheeling-and-dealing mind-set," said Jack. "Got anyone on your hit list besides Mendoza?"

"Nope," she said.

"That's what I wanted to hear," said Jack. "Things are going to get ugly if certain witnesses recant their testimony in order to avoid criminal charges for filing a false police report."

"Jack, really. You know me better than that. After all this family has been through, it would be a terrible overreaction to threaten Debra and Gavin Burgette with a pissant charge like filing a false police report. Don't you think?"

"All that matters is what you think, Barbara."

"It would be overreaching. That's my view."

"I'm glad to hear that."

"Unless you win a new trial for Dylan Reeves."

Jack was taken aback, which made the prosecutor smile. "That was a joke, Jack. You really don't get my sense of humor, do you?"

"I have to be honest, Barbara. I really don't."

"Say hello to Andie for me. Tell her I *guarantee* Daddy will be there for the delivery."

"You're all heart," said Jack, as he watched her walk away.

CHAPTER 37

It was approaching seven o'clock, and Debra Burgette was exactly where she could be found on any given Tuesday evening: on Collins Avenue in Little Moscow.

Potapova Ballet Academy was in Sunny Isles Beach, and for many south Floridians it epitomized the growing Russian influence in a barrier-island stretch to the north of Miami Beach. Its founder was trained at the prestigious Vaganova Academy, and after a successful professional career in St. Petersburg, Madame Potapova brought her talents to a much warmer clime. The academy had grown steadily over the years, to the point where more than two hundred students learned the Russian style on a year-round basis in a little one-story studio that sat in an upscale strip mall between the Atlantic Ocean, to the east, and the Intracoastal Waterway to the west. Most of Potapova's students were girls, but Madame Potapova was equally proud of her boys.

Alexander Burgette was one of her favorites.

Debra had wanted both Sashi and Alexander to retain important elements of their heritage, and ballet was part of the Russian soul. She didn't force it on them, and the results were mixed. Sashi had lasted all of three weeks; Alexander had flourished. It made him nervous and even a little self-conscious whenever Debra watched him in class, so Debra found a seat in one of the metal folding chairs in the hallway outside the closed doors of Studio B. The mother of twin girls—two promising ballerinas—was in the chair next to her.

"Is class running on time tonight?" asked Debra, just making small talk.

The woman looked up from her phone, got up without a word, and walked away. Debra wasn't sure what to make of it, so she let it go and retreated into her own phone. She could play the "my cell is more interesting that you" game as well as anyone.

A handful of dance moms were gathered at the other end of the hall, right outside the closed door to the studio. Each was taking a turn at the diamond-shaped window to steal a glance of her child in the hands of a master.

"She's giving Alexander another correction," said the dance mom at the window.

Debra smiled to herself. In the world of ballet, "corrections" were a good thing. It might mean a loving touch from the instructor that raised the pupil's chin a quarter of an inch; a strong verbal command to tuck the buttocks; or even a blunt reminder that the dancer is an artist, not a weight lifter, and that the face must convey grace and effortlessness, not a hernia or a bowel movement. A correction in any form meant that the dancer had been noticed and was no longer an anonymous wannabe. Students craved them. Dance moms kept score with them.

"That's his third one tonight," said another mom.

Another one glanced down the hallway in Debra's direction. "Madame Potapova probably feels sorry for the poor boy."

The words hit Debra like a slap in the face. She'd experienced awkward nights at the academy before, all related to Sashi. This evening, however, was unlike any before. Not one of the mothers had said a word to her since she'd walked through the door, and the one-two punch of that snide remark after the other mom had gotten up and left was a death sentence in a dance academy. Debra felt utterly shunned; she was officially an outcast.

News of her ex-husband's testimony—that evil Debra had rehomed their daughter—had gone viral on the dance-mom grapevine.

Live piano music floated from behind the studio door and soothed Debra's ears. Every so often the strong Russian voice of Madame Potapova herself could be heard. An eight-count in English. A dance combination in French. A word of praise in Russian. Debra focused on the music. Tchaikovsky. She was no aficionado of classical music, but after four years at the academy she recognized most of the pieces. This one by Tchaikovsky she would never forget. It was the same music that had played in the background on a Tuesday long ago, when Sashi was just fifteen—when Madame Potapova had pulled Debra into her office to talk in private about her daughter.

S ashi has the natural facility," said Madame Potapova in her heavy Russian accent. "Legs are beauteous. Hands, exquisite. Those feet—her arches—are a gift from the ballet gods."

"Thank you, Madame Potapova," Debra said respectfully.

Potapova had such an elegant nature that, even when seated behind a desk, her posture and positioning exhibited the lines of a classic ballerina. But she rarely smiled. She definitely wasn't smiling at this meeting.

"But Sashi cannot stay in my academy."

Debra's heart sank. She knew what Madame Potapova's response would be, but she had to ask the same question that she'd asked so many times before, whether speaking to the administration at Sashi's third high school or to the headmistress of a dance academy.

"Can Sashi have just one more chance? Please?"

She shook her head. "I've been more than fair. She comes to class, and she's always the last to get her pointe shoes on. When I give the girls a combination, she either stands there, defiant, re-fusing to dance, or she makes up her own combinations and does whatever she wants. And then there's the talking and distracting the other girls. If I reprimand her, she sasses me. I can't have that in my class."

"Could we possibly do a few private lessons?"

"That's not possible. My time is very limited. Not even my most talented students are able to get the private time they deserve."

"Please. I can pay more than the going rate."

"It's not about that," said Potapova. "There are issues here that I do not feel I am equipped to resolve."

Join the club.

The headmistress's expression turned even more serious than usual. "Today Sashi threatened to kill herself."

Debra froze. "When?"

"Fifteen minutes after you dropped her off."

"In front of the whole class?" asked Debra.

"No. She was acting up during barre and bothering the girls around her. I gave her three warnings, but she ignored me. I finally pulled her out of the studio, left Ms. Alvarez in charge of the class, and took Sashi down to my office. I told her 'That's it. No more, Sashi. Don't come back to the academy until you can behave yourself.' That was when she totally broke down."

"You mean crying?"

"I mean bawling. She went on and on about how her life is more tragic than Anna Karenina's, how nobody understands what's going on at home. Finally, she said she just wants to kill herself."

"I have never heard her say that before," said Debra.

"I don't know if she is being dramatic, or if she is serious. But this is something I don't think you should ignore."

"No, you're absolutely correct. Thank you for telling me."

Potapova hesitated, then continued. "There's something else she said. It's about your husband."

A wave of trepidation washed over Debra, and she was afraid to ask. "What about him?"

Potapova looked her in the eye and said, "Sashi says that he makes her feel uncomfortable."

"Well, Gavin can lose his temper."

"It's not his anger that bothers her. Sashi says it's the way he looks at her. The way he touches her when no one else is around."

Debra caught her breath. "Madame Potapova, I can assure you that Gavin has never done—"

"I'm telling you what Sashi told me."

"I appreciate that," said Debra. "We're getting Sashi the best help we can afford, but what you're describing is very typical of a fifteen-year-old girl who is attachment-challenged."

"Attachment-challenged?"

"Yes. All of the misbehavior you're seeing isn't really her fault."

"Surely it's not *my* fault."

"Oh, no. I wasn't suggesting that it was anything you did. But when you threw her out of ballet class, Sashi did the one thing her brain is programmed to do whenever something bad happens. She has to make it better *right now*. Over the years she has learned that anytime she gets in trouble, the one thing that never fails to fix the situation is to tell stories that will make people feel sorry for her. It's really that basic: Sashi's brain says, 'I feel lousy right this second, and all I have to do now is manipulate this person into feeling sorry for me and coddling me by telling this sad tale that my parents abuse me.' All she is looking for is someone gullible enough to buy her story, right there in that second."

"Ms. Burgette, do *I* come across as gullible to you?"

"No, not at all. But Sashi thinks she can manipulate anyone."

"If that's the case, I absolutely don't want her coming back to my academy. Alexander is more than welcome to stay. But Sashi, no."

It was a familiar verdict. "I wish you would reconsider."

"No, that's my final decision."

Debra chose not to push the issue. Maybe it was because she knew that Madame Potapova was not one to change her mind. Or maybe she'd just lost too many battles in the never-ending fight to find someplace—anyplace—for Sashi to fit in.

"Thank you for letting Alexander stay," said Debra. She rose and started toward the door.

"Ms. Burgette. There's one other thing."

"Yes?"

"I know you say these stories that Sashi tells are made up. But I have almost two hundred girls here between the ages of six and seventeen. I can't take chances. I don't want your husband coming here."

"That's really unnecessary, Madame Potapova. My husband is an honorable man."

"Your husband is lucky I'm not passing this along to the Department of Children and Family Services."

"Please don't do that," said Debra. "*Please*, don't."

Potapova narrowed her eyes, turning on her powers of interrogation. "Are you absolutely certain that Sashi is making this up?"

"Yes, I'm a hundred percent certain."

Their eyes locked, and they held it for a period of time that seemed much longer to Debra than it actually was. Debra hoped that she was getting through to her, because she didn't know how she could tell Gavin that he'd been banned from the academy like a sexual predator.

Finally Madame Potapova spoke.

"I'm less than a hundred percent," she said. "I'm sorry."

I'm ready, Mom. Let's go," said Alexander.

He was standing before her in the hallway, dressed in Potapova Academy black sweatpants and a white T-shirt. Flip-flops had replaced his ballet shoes, and a nylon gym bag was slung over his shoulder. Debra rose from the folding chair and gave him a quick hug. Together they walked down the hall and left the academy through the main door.

"How was class?" she asked as they started down the sidewalk.

"Good. Where'd you park?"

It wasn't an idle question, and she knew the answer would please him. "Right in front of Matryoshka Deli Food."

"Awesome! Can I get *ptichye moloko?*"

Debra had only a rudimentary grasp of Russian, but she'd heard those two words often enough to know about the bird's milk cake, a dessert made famous by the pastry chef at Praga, one of Moscow's most famous restaurants. It was a thick slice of French marshmallow covered in chocolate, and Russians had been crazy about it for decades. "Bird's milk" didn't sound either biologically possible or particularly appetizing to Debra, so she could only assume that something was lost in translation.

"Of course you can," she said.

Darkness had fallen, and Potapova Academy and Matryoshka Deli were at opposite ends of a safe and well-lit strip mall, but Debra was enjoying the walk with her son on this warm night. They passed a Ukrainian restaurant, a Latvian bakery, a law office that displayed the flag of either Belarus or Moldova in the window—they looked nothing alike, but Debra always mixed them up—and a host of other small businesses that catered to a Russian-speaking clientele that wasn't strictly "Russian." As they continued down the sidewalk, Debra noticed a man standing beside his car in the parking lot, the dome of his shaven head shining in the yellowish glow of a streetlamp. He seemed to be staring at them. Debra tried not to be obvious about it, but as they passed beneath a storefront overhang and walked in the shadows, she cast her gaze in his direction for a better look. He didn't move. He kept looking at her. Watching her. Watching Alexander.

Debra walked faster, quickly changing direction, holding Alexander a little closer to her than she might otherwise have held him.

"Mom, what are you doing?"

"We're going to the car," she said in a calm but assertive tone.

"But what about my cake?"

"Not tonight."

They were just a few steps away from the car, but Alexander was gently pulling toward the entrance to Matryoshka Deli. Debra pulled much harder in the opposite direction.

"Mom, you promised!"

She unlocked the door with her keyless remote and opened the door for him. "Get in, Alexander."

"Why?"

"I don't like the way that man was looking at us."

"What man?"

"Just get in!"

Alexander did as he was told and closed the door. Debra hurried around to the driver's side and noticed that the man was still standing beneath the streetlamp, still watching. She climbed behind the wheel, quickly started the engine, and backed out of her parking spot as fast as she could.

"Who was looking at us, Mom?"

"Nobody."

"Then why are you acting like this? Did I do something wrong?"

"No," she said, glancing in her rearview mirror as she drove away. The man in the parking lot was gone, she noticed. "None of this is your fault, Alexander."

CHAPTER 38

J ack drove from the federal courthouse to the Freedom Institute. Andie had called and told him to meet her there. She and Theo were in the reception area, formerly known as the living room, when Jack opened the front door.

"Watch out for the cable," said Andie. She was standing beside a cluttered desk in the center of the room.

"What cable?" he asked, but his foot found it. He stumbled to the floor and landed on hands and knees, which put him at eye level with Theo, who was under the desk, working on a tangle of more computer wires.

"You okay, bro?" asked Theo.

Jack had to think about it. Andie hurried over and asked the same question, minus the "bro."

"I'm fine," he said as he climbed to his feet. "What are you doing?"

"Installing a microcell," Theo said from under the desk.

"A what?"

Andie explained. "Parts of this old house are cellular dead zones. You can't be stuck here with zero bars on your cell when the baby says it's time and I'm headed to the hospital, trying to call you. The microcell fixes that. We just have to figure out how to run the network cable without turning the room into an obstacle course."

Theo popped up from under the desk. "I got an idea," he said, and then he left the room.

Jack stepped closer to his wife and spoke softly, so as not to be overheard. "Are you sure he knows what he's doing?"

"Nope," said Andie. "But he works for free." Andie ran her finger along the desktop. The dust was so thick that she could have written her name in it. "Free is the upper limit of your budget, I'm guessing."

Andie settled into the desk chair, which squeaked as she swiveled to look around the room. It was the kind of place that real estate agents would have described as "charming" with "good bones" and "lots of potential." The floors were Dade County pine, which hadn't been used in south Florida construction for at least seventy-five years, and the finish was original. Chunks—not chips—of plaster had fallen from the walls, which needed much more than a coat of paint. The crack in the ceiling was the Miami version of the San Andreas Fault.

"Can we really swing this, Jack?"

"Swing what?" he asked.

"You, working here. Can we swing it financially?"

"I told you before: I don't work for the Institute."

"Really? In the last week, what have you worked on besides the Dylan Reeves hearing?"

"I have my regular caseload. But a death case naturally puts other things on hold."

"Will you actually get paid for all your time?"

"At some point. I submit my time and expenses to the court, and, if it's 'reasonable,' I get paid under the Criminal Justice Act. It will be the government rate, not my normal hourly. But I get paid."

"What will you do when Hannah comes to you and says the Freedom Institute can't pay its light bill, its property taxes, or whatever else they're in arrears on? Are you gonna tell her 'too bad, so sad' and keep your check from Uncle Sam?"

He shrugged. "We'll cross that bridge when we come to it."

"That's what I thought you'd say," she said, and her expression turned serious. "I've been thinking. We're a two-income family.

Each of us should be able to follow a career path that makes us happy—within reason, of course."

"Andie, you don't have to worry. I'm not going to drop my practice to do death penalty work."

"But if that's what you want, you should be able to. Even if, you know, it was just you and the baby. For some reason."

"What—what are you saying?"

She paused, then finished her thought. "We've never talked about this, but my benefits from the Bureau include life insurance. It's not a lot, but I thought you should know about it."

Jack's confusion was turning to concern. "Did the doctor tell you something that you're not telling me?"

"No. It's nothing like that."

"Are you sure?"

"Yes. Jack, listen to me. You knocked up a girl and got married. You're just one step away from being a grown-up, so let's get this life insurance conversation out of the way."

Humor—the oldest trick in the book for hiding bad news. "You promise you're not holding something back from me?"

"I'm fine. If I weren't, I would tell you."

"Okay, good."

She smiled coyly. "Actually, the doctor did tell me one thing—a happy thing—that I haven't told you."

"What?"

"You sure you want to know?"

"I do now."

Another sly smile. "How do you feel about the name Riley Suzanne?"

Jack did a double take. "It's a girl?"

She nodded. "Dr. Starkey slipped and told me. I hope you're not mad."

He smiled, hurried around to her side of the desk, and hugged her in the chair. "I'm not mad. I love Riley. And I love that we're having a girl."

"Me, too," she said.

"In fact, as soon as Theo finishes with this microcell, I'm going to call my accountant and set up her college fund. Hannah tells me she has a connection at Barnyard. But it's very expensive, you know."

"You mean Barnard?"

The inside joke was funnier when Hannah had told it. "Yeah, Barnard."

Jack's cell rang. Five bars. Whatever gadget Theo had tweaked on the other side of the house had done the trick. The microcell was working.

Judge Frederick's law clerk was on the line when Jack answered.

"Mr. Swyteck, I just sent an e-mail notification, but the judge asked that I speak directly to all counsel to advise that Mr. Mendoza will be transported to Miami tomorrow morning. The evidentiary hearing will reconvene at six p.m. tomorrow in Judge Frederick's courtroom. You should come prepared to examine the witness. No continuances will be granted."

"I'll be there." Jack thanked her and hung up. Then he shared the news with Andie, who understood the immediate ramifications.

"Theo can take me home," she said.

"You sure?"

"Yeah. It's gonna be a late night, right?"

Jack thought of the work ahead of him, the hours of preparation it would take to control a witness like Carlos Mendoza and expose him for what Jack already knew he was: a man for whom an oath meant nothing, and who would say anything for his own benefit.

"Really late," said Jack.

Andie gave him a kiss, then called out for her driver—"Theo?"—but she got no answer. "Where'd he go?"

"I'll get him," said Jack. He started down a dark hallway that led to what used to be the Florida room, which was still the largest room in the old house. It was the space covered by Jack's lease. It used to be Neil's office.

Jack stopped in the open doorway. Theo was inside. Jack knocked on the doorframe, but Theo didn't stir. His gaze was locked onto the far wall. Jack hesitated before entering, recalling Hannah's words on the night she'd pointed out that he had yet to enter Neil's space:

"It's a room in a hundred-year-old house, Jack. The biggest room. The nicest room. But just a room . . . What are you afraid of?"

Jack drew a breath and stepped inside, the floorboards creaking beneath each footfall. He walked past Neil's old desk. On it, in the glow of a brass lamp, where a nameplate might have sat, was an engraved desk plaque that bore one of Neil's favorite sayings: "An Eye for an Eye Makes the World Blind."

Jack continued toward Theo, his gaze slowly sweeping the room. Countless plaques, awards, and framed newspaper clippings covered the walls. It had been years since he'd read some of the older articles. While the newsprint had yellowed with age, the clippings still told quite a story, from Neil's roots in civil rights litigation in the South—*"Volunteer Lawyers Jailed in Mississippi"*—to his role as gadfly in local politics: *"Freedom Institute Lawsuit Against Miami Mayor Sparks Grand Jury Indictment."* All were impressive. But Theo was transfixed by the framed article near the window with the eye-catching headline "Groundbreaking DNA Evidence Proves Death Row Inmate Innocent."

Jack stepped closer and stopped, reading a story he could have recited in his sleep:

After four years in Florida State Prison for a murder he did not commit, twenty-year-old Theo Knight—once the youngest inmate on Florida's death row—is coming home to Miami today . . .

The two men, once lawyer and client, stood side by side, staring at the words on Neil's wall.

"Seems like another lifetime, doesn't it?" asked Theo.

"Or maybe even somebody else's life."

There was more silence, and Jack could only wonder what was going through Theo's head. The anger. The memories. The time they'd met, when he'd told Jack to take his Yale law degree and his "save the black man" complex and go fuck himself. The time they'd said their goodbyes, after the prison barber had shaved Theo's head and ankles to attach the electrodes, only to find out that it wasn't going to happen after all, that Jack had pulled off a miracle and won what Neil would call the cruelest of "cruel and unusual" punishments—an unexpected stay of execution from a federal appellate judge as Theo was a mere eight steps away from the electric chair.

"You think Dylan Reeves is innocent?" asked Theo.

Jack thought about it—really thought about it. "I don't know."

"Did you think I was innocent?" Theo turned his head, looking right at Jack. "At the beginning, I mean."

Jack shook his head. "Nope."

"When did you come around?"

"Honestly? After the DNA test came back. Hell, even then I had to sleep on it."

That drew a little smile. "Fuckhead. It's cuz I'm black, ain't it?" he asked, tongue in cheek.

"Uh-uh. Cuz you're a Yankees fan."

Theo chuckled, then it faded. "Seriously, what took you so long?"

"Shit, Theo. What do you think? When the average Joe turns on the local news at night and sees a guy getting stuffed into the back of a squad car, does he point to the TV and say, 'Hey, lookey there, honey. They're hauling another innocent man off to jail.'"

"Probably not."

"*Probably?* Are you kidding me? Your first thought is: *He did it.* Or you might think: *Well, even if he didn't do what they say he did, he had to be doing something.* Or better yet: *Maybe he wasn't doing anything this time, but he's done a whole lotta other things in his lifetime, and that's why he's being arrested.* The last thing anyone thinks is that the cops got the wrong man, this guy is innocent, and praise the Lord, I sure hope this poor slob can afford a clever lawyer who will clear his name. The human mind doesn't go there. It sure as hell doesn't go anywhere *near* there when your client is already convicted and sitting on death row."

"So for four fucking years you thought I was guilty?"

"I didn't say that. Just because I wasn't convinced you were innocent doesn't mean I thought you were guilty. I was in that twilight zone of capital cases, where a lawyer really starts losing sleep at night, thinking things like: *Wow, what if I fuck up? What if this guy is innocent?*"

"You having those thoughts about Dylan Reeves?"

Jack didn't answer right away. "I'll let you know."

"When?"

"Tomorrow," said Jack. "After I cross-examine Carlos Bad Boy."

CHAPTER 39

Gavin picked at his Mexican food through dinner. The waiter noticed.

"Was your meal not to your satisfaction, sir?"

The night was too warm to dine outside, so Gavin and Nicole were seated at an indoor table. Rosa Mexicano was a short walk from his Brickell condominium and one of their regular week-night haunts, even if its multiple locations did push dangerously close to "chain" status. A dollop of Rosa's famous guacamole could make cardboard edible. So could a couple of their grog-sized margaritas, but Gavin wasn't drinking, either.

"Everything was fine," said Gavin. "I just wasn't hungry to-night. You can bring the check."

The waiter took their plates and stepped away. Nicole reached across the table and took his hand. "Are you afraid of what Carlos Mendoza is going to say tomorrow?"

"No. What scares me is having *no idea* what he's going to say."

The waiter brought them a plate of complimentary sweets with the bill. "No rush. Whenever you're ready," he said as he backed way.

Nicole unwrapped one of the hard candies. Gavin waited until the waiter was out of earshot, then continued. "Let me ask you a legal question."

"Great. Another tax-deductible meal."

He took Nicole's humor as pure irony; with his tax shelters, it had been almost ten years since Gavin had actually owed the IRS money.

"I think there's a real possibility that Swyteck will get a new trial for Dylan Reeves."

"From what I know, I see it as a remote possibility. But, okay—for purposes of the question, I'll accept your premise."

"Forget the retrial. The issue I'm worried about could come up even in this hearing before Judge Frederick."

"Tomorrow?"

"No, not tomorrow. But soon enough. Every time somebody new testifies at this hearing, it seems to open the door to another witness."

"Is there a potential witness you're concerned about?"

He breathed in and out, then looked away.

"Gavin?"

An elderly couple at a nearby booth seemed more interested in what Gavin was saying than in what they could possibly say to each other after forty years of marriage. Maybe Gavin was paranoid, but he would have bet good money that the woman was adjusting her hearing aid to pick up his conversation with Nicole.

"Let's talk about this later," said Gavin. "In private."

"All right. Lemme run to the little girls' room, and then we can go."

Nicole pushed away from the table. Gavin glanced at the bill as she walked away. He laid down his credit card and sat alone at the table, drifting deeper into thought.

Surely she knew which witness was of concern to him. Nicole was a smart woman and a sharp lawyer. More to the point, it was the same potential witness that had worried Gavin in the divorce—the one that Nicole had figured out how to silence.

The problem—and the solution—had come up in the very first meeting between lawyer and client at Nicole's office in Coconut Grove.

W hatever we do, we can't let Dr. Wurster testify," said Gavin. He was seated in an armchair that faced Nicole's granite-

and-glass-top desk. Her office had that efficient, modern décor that looked smart but wasn't particularly comfortable.

She listened from her leather-and-chrome desk chair. "Who is Dr. Wurster?"

"Sashi's psychiatrist."

"And why are you so concerned about him?"

The designer chair may have won awards, but it was killing his back. He leaned forward, edging close enough to rest his forearms atop her desk. "Sashi was a fucking mess, okay?"

"I understand."

"At the homicide trial, the prosecutor did a masterful job of keeping the jury from hearing many details about her problems. Every time Dylan Reeves even made reference to Sashi's attachment disorder, Barbara Carmichael jumped to her feet and objected, indignant as hell, calling Reeves' lawyer a victim basher."

"That's a tough spot for a defense lawyer when the victim is a seventeen-year-old girl."

"Even tougher when the lawyer is a fuck-up, which Dylan Reeves' lawyer was."

"Your wife's divorce lawyer is no dummy."

"I know. I'm sure Debra will try to hand me the bill for it, too. Anyway, Sashi's psychiatrist—Dr. Wurster—never had to testify at trial. The only psychiatrist who testified was Dr. Emmitt Pollard."

"And who is Pollard?" she asked, as she jotted the name on her pad.

"He's just an expert that Barbara Carmichael retained for the trial. Pollard never met Sashi. He knew a lot about RAD, and he was able to give an expert opinion on how children and young adults with an attachment disorder act toward strangers. He was pretty effective in convincing the jury that Sashi would not have engaged in consensual sex with Dylan Reeves. But he couldn't say anything specific about therapy sessions with Sashi because he never had any. Which was perfect."

"Perfect in what way?"

"The last thing I wanted then—and the last thing I want now—is Sashi's psychiatrist on the witness stand testifying hour after hour about every crazy thing she ever said to him in a therapy session."

"Why is that 'the *last thing*' you want?" she asked, making air quotes.

"Because she made things up, Nicole. That's what kids with RAD do. Sashi accused Aquinnah's friends of stealing. She accused Alexander's tutor of being a pedophile. She accused a teacher at Grove Academy of hitting her, even though ten witnesses said she hit *him*. She just made things up. Horrible things."

"Did she make things up about you?"

He hesitated, then answered. "I don't know. But I sure as hell don't want to find out when Dr. Wurster gets on the witness stand. Debra and I are fighting over who gets custody of Alexander. For all I know, Sashi told her therapist that I beat her every night before she went to sleep."

"Or worse," said Nicole.

"Yes," said Gavin, and then he swallowed hard. "Or worse."

Nicole thought for a moment. "I see your concern. So the legal question is: How do we find out what Dr. Wurster is going to say before he testifies?"

"No. My question is: How do we keep Dr. Wurster from *ever* being a witness?"

Nicole was silent, but Gavin could almost see the wheels turning in her head. She swiveled her chair to face the computer screen, and then she studied what she'd pulled up.

"What are you checking?" asked Gavin.

She didn't answer right away. In a minute, however, it was clear from the expression on her face that a major brainstorm was in progress. "Patient-psychotherapist privilege," she said.

"I've heard of it. Sadly, however, the patient here is dead."

"It doesn't matter. The privilege survives the death of the patient. But put that aside. I have something much more bulletproof in mind. You told me that your wife still thinks Sashi is alive, right?"

"Yeah. Debra got a phone call on Sashi's birthday. It was an un-traceable number from a disposable phone. The caller said nothing. There was just silence on the line. But Debra is sure it was Sashi."

"And the police said it was a hoax," she said, checking her notepad again. "Do I have that right?"

"Yes. I sided with the police. That's one of the major triggers that spelled the beginning of the end for our marriage. I couldn't stand hearing it anymore. '*Gavin, how can you give up? Gavin, this is your daughter. Gavin, Gavin, Gavin.*'"

"I understand. We can use this to our advantage. All I have to do is lock Debra in at her deposition—get her to commit to her belief that Sashi is still alive."

"What does that do for us?"

"If Sashi is alive, she'd be over the age of eighteen now, right?"

"Yes. In fact, that prepaid cell-phone call I mentioned came on her eighteenth birthday."

"Perfect. If Sashi is alive, she's the only one who can waive the privilege. Unless a judge orders otherwise, she's the only person on the planet who can say, 'Dr. Wurster, you can speak freely about anything and everything you and I talked about in any of my therapy sessions.'"

Gavin thought about it. "That's clever."

"Thank you. But we should take Debra's deposition sooner, rather than later—before she has a chance to change her po-sition and come around to your view that Sashi is, indeed, deceased."

"So if she changes her view, you're saying . . ."

"If you're concerned about what Dr. Wurster might say, it's important that your wife continue to believe that Sashi is alive. I hate to sound so cold and callous about it, but this is divorce, and we're asking a judge to grant custody of Alexander to you instead of his mother. That's an uphill battle in any case. It's an impossible battle if you think Sashi said horrible things about you to her psychotherapist and then the psychotherapist shares those things with the judge. You understand my point, Gavin?"

He thought about it, his gaze drifting off to the middle distance. "Yeah," he said. "I understand completely."

Ready?" asked Nicole. She was standing beside their table, having returned from the ladies' room. The sound of her voice drew Gavin from his memories. He rose, and they walked together toward the restaurant exit.

"Why don't we sit at the bar and get a drink?"

"I'm really not in the mood."

"Come on," she said.

A waiter opened the door for them, and they stepped out into the night. "Sorry," he said, as they started down the sidewalk. "I'm just really worried about this."

"About what?"

"Debra and me," he said.

"That's over, Gavin."

His gaze drifted toward the rising drawbridge on the river, just ahead of them. "No, it's not," he said. "I think it's gonna get ugly."

"That's what you said about the divorce. We rolled over her."

"That's because both sides had enough sense to leave Carlos Mendoza out of the divorce. Now the horse is out of the stable. If Debra turns this thing around and accuses me of rehoming Sashi, I have clients who will no longer do business with me. I have a son who may never talk to me again."

Nicole took his hand and walked closely at his side. "Good news," she said.

"What?"

They stopped at Gavin's car. She squeezed his hand firmly, put her lips to his ear, and whispered, "I never lose."

CHAPTER 40

Hump Day. Andie was in her office, doing back bends for sciatica, when the inspiration for the world's most ridiculous Halloween costume came to her. All she needed was one of those old Joe Camel masks. She'd pull it over her head backwards, arch her back until her belly pointed up at the ceiling, and then shuffle through the office asking, "Hey, hey, hey—what day is it?"

But we're not gonna wait till Halloween, are we, baby?

Her back cracked as she straightened up, and that pain down the back of her leg suddenly seemed not so bad.

There was a quick knock, the door opened, and ASAC Schwartz poked his head into her office. "Got a minute, Henning?"

He turned and started down the hall before she could even think about saying no. Andie caught up and followed him to his office. Schwartz went straight to the leather chair behind his desk. "Have a seat, Henning."

It sounded more like an order than an offer. As she lowered herself into the armchair, taking care not to trigger that sciatica again, Schwartz pushed a large manila envelope across his desktop until it was within her reach.

"This just came by courier," he said. "It's from Debra Burgette, addressed to me. You know anything about it?"

"No. What is it?"

He took the envelope, which was already opened, and removed a thin report with a spiral binding. "She hired a private examiner and sat for a polygraph," he said.

"When?"

He doubled-checked. "Yesterday, according to the examiner. Three o'clock."

"That was right after she came here to see me."

"I heard. That's why you're here. Look, Henning. It made sense for you to follow up with the tech unit when that phone call came in and Debra Burgette claimed it was from her daughter. That was a potential emergency. But as far as any additional follow-up is concerned, you're walled off from anything to do with the Burgette family so long as your husband represents Dylan Reeves."

"That's exactly what I told her."

"It's going to be a black eye for both of us if Jack Swyteck or one of his co-conspirators at the Freedom Institute calls his wife to the witness stand."

"You mean one of his colleagues."

"That's what I said."

"No. You said one of his co-conspirators."

He paused, and they both seemed to appreciate the Freudian nature of that slip.

"My point is that you can't have anything to do with Debra Burgette."

"I understand," said Andie. "Debra came to see me on her own. My take is that her friends, neighbors, the press, and possibly even the two children she has left—they've all turned against her since her ex-husband testified that Debra rehomed their daughter. She wants somebody in law enforcement to believe she didn't do it. She started with me."

"Because you're Jack Swyteck's wife."

"Probably. But the fact is, she didn't get past the lobby."

"What made her run out the door and take a polygraph examination?"

"She didn't run," said Andie. "She walked like a normal human being and pushed the elevator button."

"You know what I'm saying. The sequence here is that she saw you and then she went to take a lie detector test."

"Maybe she had it lined up before she even came to see me. I don't know."

"Did you ask her to take a polygraph?"

"No. Debra offered. I told her that it probably wouldn't help, and that she needed to leave."

"Really? If she took a polygraph examination, that would be very helpful to your husband's case, wouldn't it?"

"Not at all. It's not admissible in evidence."

"I'm not talking about legal niceties. Barbara Carmichael is no sleazebag prosecutor. Do you think she would completely disregard a polygraph examination in shaping her theory of the case?"

"She might. Who's the examiner?"

"Jorge Delgado. Twenty-five years with MDPD before he opened a private testing service."

"Debra picked a reputable guy."

"Yes, she did. I know you don't like my implication, but I need to do my job, and I need a straight answer: Did you recommend him to her?"

"No. I did not."

"Did you even mention casually, 'Hey, Jack, Debra Burgette told me she's willing to sit for a polygraph. Maybe you should follow up on that?'"

"No. I would never have that conversation with Jack."

"Even if it could make the difference in his case?"

"Especially if it would make a difference in his case. And, by the way, it's not even clear to me that a polygraph examination would help Jack. It depends on the questions."

"I can tell you exactly what they were," he said as he flipped the next page, then read aloud: "Question one: 'Did you rehome your daughter Sashi with Carlos Mendoza?' Answer: 'No.' Examiner's conclusion: 'No signs of deception.' Question two: 'Did you enter into any kind of arrangement with Carlos Mendoza to rehome your daughter Sashi?' Answer: 'No.' Examiner's conclusion: 'No signs of deception.'"

Andie hesitated. "That actually would hurt Jack's case. Jack wants Judge Frederick to believe that after Dylan Reeves tried to rape Sashi and she got away, she had nowhere to run but back into the hands of Carlos Mendoza."

"Unless his theory is that *Gavin* Burgette rehomed Sashi."

"You don't understand the case. This is a habeas petition. Jack has to show that Dylan Reeves deserves a new trial because the first time around the prosecutor failed to turn over evidence that Sashi had been rehomed and was living with Carlos Mendoza—one very bad actor. If it's a lock that Debra didn't rehome her daughter, Jack's chances of winning just went down by fifty percent."

Schwartz took a minute, and that knitted brow above his graying eyebrows told her that he was working hard to grasp the legal theory. "I follow you," he said finally. "But now I'm even more concerned."

"Why?"

He leaned forward, and Andie suddenly felt his interrogation mode tighten. "You just explained Jack's case like a constitutional law professor. And you're telling me that you are abiding one hundred percent by the information barriers imposed on you, and that the two of you don't talk about his case?"

"No, sir. We don't. And, by the way, even though I didn't stick around long enough to get a law degree, I did get an A in constitutional law as a first-year law student at U.C. Santa Barbara."

He laid the report on his desk, then rose. Andie pushed herself up from the armchair. "Are we finished?" she asked.

"For now."

Andie thanked him and started toward the door.

"Henning," he said.

She stopped. "Yes?"

"You're very highly regarded here. Don't screw it up over a guy like Dylan Reeves."

She could have told him that it was about Sashi Burgette, not Dylan Reeves, but it probably wouldn't have helped. "I'll take that to heart," she said.

"See that you do," he said.

She let herself out, taking a few deep breaths on the walk back to her office.

CHAPTER 41

Jack was seated at Neil's desk, reviewing the "Final Report of Jorge Delgado: Polygraph Examination of Debra Burgette." Hannah was standing over his left shoulder, silently reading along as Jack turned the pages. Debra watched from the other side of the desk, her whole body a clenched fist of anxiety.

Jack had taken her call after lunch. "I passed a lie detector test," she'd said, and they agreed to meet at the Freedom Institute. The clock was ticking. The hearing before Judge Frederick, and Jack's cross-examination of Carlos Mendoza, was just a few hours away.

Jack looked up from the report. Hannah indicated that she had finished as well. She walked around the desk and took the chair next to Debra's.

"Who else has seen this report?" asked Jack.

"Well, I have no way of knowing if he's actually seen it yet, but I sent it by courier this morning to your wife's boss. The assistant special agent in charge."

"Guy Schwartz?"

"Yes."

"Anyone else?"

She shrugged. "Whoever Mr. Schwartz may have shown it to."

The name Andie Henning came to mind, but Jack didn't mention it. Nor did anyone else. "Are you planning to show it to Barbara Carmichael?"

Debra took a breath. "She hasn't been my best friend lately, has she? I was thinking I might let her read about it in the *Miami Tribune*."

There was more than a hint of bitterness in her tone. "Is that your plan?" asked Jack. "To send this to the media?"

"You ask that like there's something wrong with it."

"It's just a question."

She looked at Hannah, then back at Jack. "Do you have any idea what the words Gavin spoke in that courtroom have done to me?" she asked, her voice shaking with anger.

He didn't answer. Neither did Hannah.

"I don't have a single friend in this town who will return my phone calls. The women at Alexander's dance academy treat me like a leper. I've told Aquinnah that it's not true—I didn't rehome her sister. But what a horrible spot she's in: either her father's a malicious liar or her mother is the worst parent on the planet. All I can hope for is that the truth will come out before Alexander hears about any of this."

"I'm doing my best to make sure it does," said Jack.

"I appreciate that. But you need to understand that this is getting beyond stressful. It's to the point that I'm starting to fear for my own safety."

"Are you getting threats?"

"Not really. This case isn't on CNN every night, but it's getting enough local coverage for complete strangers to form an opinion and hate me."

"I'm not saying you're paranoid," said Jack, "but the feeling that people hate you is probably more in your head than reality."

"You think so, huh? Last night I picked up Alexander from his dance studio, and I swear some man was looking at me like he was ready to take Alexander away from me."

"Where?"

"Little Moscow. Right at the shopping mall where Alexander takes lessons."

"Who was the guy?"

"I have no idea. But there are plenty of newspapers in Little Moscow, and dozens of bloggers who follow local events, all in Russian. Who knows what they're saying about the horrible American mother who rehomed her Russian daughter?"

Jack looked at Hannah. "That might be worth looking into," she said.

"Put it at the top of our list of things to do that we have neither the time nor the money to get done," said Jack.

"You're missing my point," said Debra. "I'm trying to hold my family together and save what's left of my reputation. It may not serve your purposes for me to take it to the media, but I'm sorry: I'm going to use that polygraph any way I can to prove that I am not the terrible person that my ex-husband says I am."

Jack glanced again at the report. "Jorge Delgado is probably the most reputable private examiner in Miami."

"He wasn't cheap."

"How'd you link up with him?"

"I Googled 'Miami polygraph examiners.' The list of clients on his website is like a who's who of corporate Miami."

"I'm not surprised," said Jack. "Corporate investigation into employee theft is a private polygrapher's bread and butter. Who drafted the questions for your examination?"

"Mr. Delgado did. Why do you ask?"

"Sitting for a polygraph examination is risky—especially if you don't have your own lawyer to help shape the questions."

"I don't have a lawyer."

"You may want to rethink that going forward. Your ex-husband is using his divorce lawyer. Probably wouldn't hurt to give yours a call."

"I still owe him thirty thousand dollars. Don't think he'd take my call."

"I can recommend someone."

"I don't need one."

"Hopefully not. Barbara Carmichael did tell me that she's not looking to make life miserable for you or your ex-husband. But even Judge Frederick mentioned that lodging a false missing-person report with the police is a crime."

"It *wasn't* a false report. Sashi—went—missing," she said, halting between each word to emphasize the point.

"I got it," said Jack. "You should still hire a lawyer."

"Is that what we're going to make this meeting about? How I need to hire a lawyer?"

Jack paused, giving her a moment to cool off. "What would you like it to be about, Debra?"

"I'd like to know what you're going to do with Carlos Mendoza."

He glanced at Hannah, then back at Debra. "That's between my client and me."

Debra moved forward in her chair, almost to the edge. "I know it helps Dylan Reeves if you can convince the judge that I rehomed Sashi. That would be something that his lawyer should have told him about before the trial. I get that. But Sashi wasn't rehomed . . . unless Gavin did it."

"Interesting," said Jack, as he reached again for the report. "You weren't asked that question in your polygraph examination—whether Gavin rehomed Sashi."

"Because the answer is 'I don't know.' The last time I saw Sashi was when I dropped her off at school on Friday morning. Gavin was away on his 'business trip,'" she said, making air quotes. "Or so he says. Nobody ever really questioned that story until you went after him on the witness stand."

"Honestly, I was simply following my instincts. I had no factual basis to question that he was on a business trip."

"Nor did I," said Debra. "But when you backed him into a corner, what did he do? He blamed me. 'Debra did it.' That's his story now."

Jack looked at Hannah again.

"Should I add that to our no-time-or-money-to-get-it-done list?" she asked.

"Keep it simple," said Jack. "Ask Nicole Thompson to provide travel records that will show where her client was that day."

"Will do."

"But let's stay focused on Carlos Mendoza," Jack said, his gaze shifing back to Debra. "So, tonight, when I cross-examine Mendoza, you want me to reverse the tide—is that it? You want me to turn 'Debra did it' into 'Gavin did it'?"

"Yes. No." She closed her eyes, her face filled with anguish. "I don't know."

"You can only pick one," said Jack.

She was shaking, and in her eyes Jack could almost see the roiling emotions inside her. "I still believe Sashi is alive," she said. "I don't think Dylan Reeves should die for a murder that never happened. But . . ."

"But what?"

Her hands tightened into a fist to stop them from shaking. "I'm not willing to let you, or anyone else, create the impression that I rehomed my daughter. I know this is terrible to say . . . but I would rather Dylan Reeves die on the gurney for a murder he didn't commit than have my children—Aquinnah and Alexander—think that I would do such a thing to their sister. I'm sorry," she said, sniffing back a tear, "but that's how I feel. I may never get Sashi back. I can't lose two more. Can you understand that?"

The question was simple enough, but the preface was layered with complexity; and Jack thought of all the times he'd put the screws to a witness in similar fashion, and then demanded "a yes or no answer." Nothing in this case was that black and white.

"I think you've made your position clear enough," said Jack.

She took a tissue from her purse and dabbed her eye. "You're judging me."

"Only your credibility. It's not my job to make value judgments."

"You don't believe me. Even with the polygraph exam, do you?"

"I think most of this will sort itself out after I cross-examine Carlos Mendoza."

"I agree. I just . . . I just hope you will keep in mind the results of my lie detector test before you let him get away with accusing me of something I didn't do."

"It will be a vigorous cross-examination, Debra. I can promise you that much." Jack rose. "Thank you for coming," he said as he walked around to the other side of the desk.

Debra rose and shook his hand. "I plan to be there tonight," she said.

"There's likely to be media coverage. If I were your lawyer, I'd tell you not to comment."

"If you were *my* lawyer, you'd tell me to release the polygraph exam, wouldn't you?"

It was a stronger comeback than Jack had expected. Jack treated it as rhetorical and let the meeting end on that note. "I'll see you this evening, Debra."

She thanked the lawyers, and then Hannah escorted her out of the office and to the front door. Jack returned to his desk. He was seated in his chair, taking one more look at the polygrapher's report, when Hannah returned.

"Can I ask you a question, Jack?"

He laid the report aside. "Sure."

She took the chair that Debra had vacated. "My dad had pretty strong views on polygraph examinations. Do you put much stock in them?"

"My opinion: put a seasoned detective in a room with a suspect for thirty minutes, ask him if he thinks the suspect is lying or telling the truth, and his instincts are likely to be more accurate than any reading you'll get from a polygraph examiner. Er, excuse me: 'forensic credibility examiner.'"

"Dad felt the same way. But Jorge Delgado is kind of a legend in law enforcement, isn't he? If anyone is going to get an accurate reading, it would be him."

Jack's gaze drifted across the room to the framed newspaper clipping on the wall—the one about Theo Knight's release from death row. "Delgado polygraphed Theo," said Jack, "when he was with MDPD."

"Are you shittin' me?"

"Nope. The cops picked up Theo for killing a convenience-store clerk. Theo's story was consistent from the beginning. He went into a convenience store. The place was empty. Theo figured the clerk was in the bathroom or maybe in the stockroom, sleeping on the job. So he helped himself to the cash drawer. On his way out, he found the clerk on the floor in a pool of blood. Theo denied he was the killer, but no one believed him. This was before the days when mom-and-pop convenience stores like this one had security cameras that could have proved him innocent. He agreed to sit for a polygraph, thinking that would put an end to it."

"But he failed?" asked Hannah.

"According to Delgado, he failed. Theo's answers showed 'significant signs of deception.'"

"I guess I'm not the first defense lawyer to say it," said Hannah, "but just because someone flunks a polygraph doesn't mean he's guilty."

"And just because Debra passed doesn't mean she's telling the truth."

Hannah nodded. "I'll let you get back to work."

"Thanks."

She started out, then stopped in the doorway. "By the way, I like your new digs. And Dad's desk looks good on you."

Jack offered a little smile, which she returned, along with a thumbs-up sign. Then she left him alone, and Jack went to work on his cross-examination outline.

A few last-minute changes were in order.

CHAPTER 42

D ebra parked in the parent lot at Grove Academy and followed the walkway to the main courtyard. Alexander par-
ticipated in team robotics every Wednesday till four, so this
was Debra's weekly reprieve from the stress of the three p.m.
pickup line.

"Good afternoon, Ms. Burgette," said the security guard at
the gate.

Security didn't know every GA parent by name; for better or
worse, the parents of Sashi Burgette were known by all.

"Hello, Wilfredo," she said as she passed.

Despite Sashi's expulsion, the GA campus could still have a
calming, almost enchanting, effect on Debra. The sheer beauty
of the grounds was part of it. New England had its ivy-clad halls,
but it was hard to beat century-old vines of bougainvillea ablaze
with blossoms of orange, pink, and purple. More than anything,
however, she loved the way Alexander had thrived there. She
walked upstairs to the new STEM lab and peered through the
window. The robotics coaches were supervising a dozen boys and
girls—future engineers at work on the design and construction of
electronic gadgets and gizmos born of a child's imagination, from
robotic arms to miniature all-terrain vehicles of the future.

Debra didn't see her son.

She knocked on the door, and the coach answered. "Where's
Alexander?" Debra asked.

The coach stepped out of the lab and closed the door, which sent Debra's heart racing. "Is everything okay?" she asked.

"Yes," he said. "I just don't want the other children to hear."

"Hear *what*?" she asked with urgency.

"Alexander is in Mr. McDermott's office."

Debra hated to assume the worst, but she hadn't visited the headmaster's office since Sashi's expulsion. "Alexander?" she asked in disbelief. "Did he do something wrong?"

"Not that I know of."

"Then why isn't he here with his team?"

"Department of Children and Family Services sent a social worker to the school today. They've been interviewing all of Alexander's teachers."

Debra's mouth fell open, but the words were on a couple-second delay. "What's this about?"

"All I was told is that your son is not to participate in after-school activities until the investigation is concluded."

"Investigiation into *what*?"

"I don't know. And even if I did know, I probably couldn't tell you."

"Did DCFS talk to you?"

"My interview is scheduled for tomorrow. Administration asked me to send you down to Mr. McDermott's office when you came by to pick up Alexander. So that's where you should go."

Debra just looked at the coach a moment longer, still not quite comprehending. "All right," she said finally. "Then that's where I'll go."

The walk downstairs from the STEM lab was decidedly without any of the calm and enchantment she'd felt on the way up. Alexander was a good boy. A *very* good boy. She knew better than to think for one second that the DCFS investigation had anything to do with his conduct. Unless the GA campus had become like the Potapova Ballet Academy, where bitchy mothers seemed to find sport in openly disparaging her. Perhaps one of the older GA students had picked up the dirt on Debra at home and had said something to Alexander. Maybe her son had come to her defense. Maybe he'd gone too far. It broke Debra's heart to think it; in a way, however, it also made her a tiny bit proud of him.

Debra entered the administration suite and announced herself to the receptionist, who asked her to wait. A minute later she returned and led Debra back to the headmaster's office. The assistant head of school was also there. It was déjà vu, shades of Sashi's expulsion, except that this time she was on her own, without Gavin.

"Where's my son?" asked Debra.

"He's with the school nurse," said McDermott.

"Why? Is he hurt?"

"No," said McDermott. "Sit down, Ms. Burgette. Please."

She moved warily toward the chair and took a seat, though her posture sent a message that she was anything but relaxed. "What is going on?" she asked.

"I'll be happy to tell you what we know," said McDermott.

He had his "game face" on, Debra noted, the pleasant but plastic half smile that people of power and position wore whenever an attorney advised them to be "firm but polite."

"A social worker from DCFS came here today to interview Alexander's teachers."

"That much I know," said Debra. "What are they investigating?"

"The allegation, we were told, is negligent endangerment of a child."

"What? By whom?"

"You."

It was as if he'd run his sword between her ribs. "Mr. McDermott, I have never put Alexander in *any* kind of danger."

"That may well be. But here's the school's posture on this. DCFS has the right to interview Alexander's teachers. The social worker also asked to interview Alexander—alone."

"No, absolutely not," said Debra. "I'm sorry if I sound defensive, but I know from my experience with Sashi that when you've done nothing wrong, the stupidest thing you can do is put your child alone in a room with a social worker who thinks he's seen it all and heard it all before."

"Well, now you understand the school's problem. Honestly, we don't know if we are legally obligated to comply with the DCFS request, or if we must follow your wishes. We have a call in to our attorney for his guidance. Until then, we have placed Alexander with the school nurse."

Debra heard what he was saying, but her mind was racing, and she was at least three steps ahead of him. "They're here to take him, aren't they?" she asked.

"Excuse me?"

"The social worker came here to take my son away."

"Nobody has told us that."

"This is about the crazy stuff my ex-husband said in court. He accused me of rehoming Sashi. Now DCFS wants to step in and take her brother away before I can rehome him."

"Ms. Burgette, I'll be honest. Of course we heard about the rehoming allegations, but we don't know anything more than what has been reported in the media. At this point, Grove Academy is simply trying to comply with its legal obligations—not just to DCFS, but also to Alexander, and to you as a parent."

Debra rose quickly. "I want my son."

"Ms. Burgette, please sit down."

"Give me my son!"

"There's no reason to raise your voice. It's best if we all calm down and wait until the school's attorney calls back with his guidance."

She checked her anger and adopted a more even tone. "I'm here to pick up Alexander. You have no right to keep him here. If you don't hand him over right now, you and your lawyer will have kidnapping charges to add to your list of concerns."

The administrators exchanged glances, but neither the head nor the assistant seemed to have an answer to Debra's threat. "I'd much prefer to wait until we hear back from our attorney," said McDermott.

"No," she said firmly, and she wasn't quite sure what inner source she'd tapped into to find such resolve. But it felt right. "I'm not waiting for you to hear back from anyone. I want my son. *Now.*"

McDermott rose, seemingly resigned to the fact that he needed to make a decision. "Fine. Take him," he said. "Be sure to sign out at the nurse's office."

"Thank you."

"Please," he said, almost scoffing. "Don't thank me."

She was eager to leave, but not on that note. "This will be sorted out soon. You'll see. I've done nothing wrong, and my son is not in any danger."

"Let's hope so," said McDermott. "For Alexander's sake."

She would have liked to say more—even drop an extra copy of the results of her polygraph examination on McDermott's desk. But turning the headmaster's opinion was not a priority at that moment. Not even the six o'clock court hearing was a priority.

She left McDermott's office and hurried down the hall to get Alexander—before DCFS beat her to it.

CHAPTER 43

I t was six p.m. in Judge Frederick's courtroom, and Jack was on deck. Barbara Carmichael would have first crack at the star witness for the prosecution.

"The state of Florida calls Carlos Mendoza," said the prosecutor.

A side door opened, and a pair of deputies escorted the prisoner to the witness stand. Carlos Mendoza had traded in his FSP uniform for the orange prison jumpsuit of Federal Corrections. He'd paid a visit to the prison barber as well, his clean-shaven credibility undoubtedly part of his deal with the prosecution.

Jack's gaze quickly swept the courtroom as the witness swore his oath. Media attention had grown slightly, though no cameras were allowed in federal court. A sketch artist was at work in the front row, reaching for her prison-orange shade of chalk. Mendoza's attorney sat directly behind the prosecutor, on the public side of the rail. Both Debra and Gavin Burgette were in attendance. Debra was alone, seated on the petitioner's side of the courtroom. Gavin was with his lawyer on the opposite side, probably more to separate them from Debra than to show support for the prosecution. Aquinnah, Jack presumed, was home watching Alexander.

"Mr. Mendoza," the prosecutor began, "the state has reached an agreement with you regarding your testimony today, correct?"

"Yes, ma'am."

Yes, ma'am. Jack almost rolled his eyes. One lawyer was as guilty as the next when it came to cleaning up scumbags for a courtroom appearance, but a "Yes, ma'am" from Carlos Mendoza was along the lines of "Pip-pip, cheerio" from Theo.

"In brief, could you please tell the judge your understanding of the agreement?"

Mendoza recited the essential terms, but the purpose of Carmichael's question was to emphasize that the government wasn't cutting a deal with a convicted felon in exchange for testimony; it was in exchange for his *truthful* testimony.

"Mr. Mendoza, do you understand that by testifying here today you are waiving any rights against self-incrimination that you may have under the United States Constitution?"

"Yup."

The prosecutor shot him a subtle but reproving look, which got him back in line.

"Yes, ma'am. I understand."

"Have you conferred with an attorney about the waiver of your rights?"

"I have."

The prosecutor stepped back from the podium, signaling a transition. "Mr. Mendoza, prior to the disappearance of Sashi Burgette, did you have any communication with her mother, Debra Burgette?"

"Uh-huh. I mean, yes, I did."

"Did you have any communications with her father, Gavin Burgette?"

"Yes, ma'am."

"In general, what was the purpose of the communications you had with Mr. and Mrs. Burgette?"

The witness leaned closer to the microphone and said, "The rehoming of their adopted daughter, Sashi."

Jack glanced again at Debra. He wasn't sure, but she seemed a whiter shade of pale.

"Mr. Mendoza, we know that Sashi Burgette went missing on a Friday, the fourteenth of September. When did you have your first communication with anyone from the Burgette family about Sashi?"

"About five weeks before that. Early August."

"Was that communication with Gavin or with Debra Burgette?"

"Debra Burgette."

Jack wasn't alone in his reaction, and he noticed that even the judge's gaze had suddenly shifted to the first row of public seating—specifically, to Debra Burgette. Had there been an escape hatch beneath her seat, Jack guessed that she would have used it.

"What was the nature of that communication?" asked the prosecutor.

"Debra was a member of one of those online support groups. It was for Americans who did an international adoption and ended up with . . . uh, damaged goods, I guess you'd call it."

The prosecutor winced, clearly unhappy with his choice of words. She moved on quickly. "What was the name of that online group?"

"Way Stations of Love."

"Were you also a member?"

"Yeah."

"Were you the parent of an adopted child?"

"No, ma'am."

"Why did you join the Way Stations of Love support group?"

"Business reasons."

"Could you explain that answer, please?"

The witness drew a breath, but Jack detected no signs of nervousness. Mendoza simply appeared to be tired of talking.

"I was getting into the broker business for rehoming."

"The judge has heard plenty of testimony about rehoming. But can you explain what you mean by 'broker business'?"

"I would be a middleman. The guy who matches up parents

who want to get rid of—I mean, give up—the child, and the parents who want to adopt. A support group like Way Stations of Love is filled with parents who adopted and then got buyer's remorse, you might call it. It seemed like a good place to troll for business."

"Just to be clear: your first communication about rehoming Sashi Burgette was with Debra Burgette, through the online support group. Is that accurate?"

"No, I wouldn't say that exactly. Debra and me never talked about rehoming online."

The prosecutor did a double take, as if the witness had veered off course from their agreed-upon script. "Are you sure about that?" she asked pointedly.

Way off course, thought Jack.

"Yeah, I'm sure. The reason I went on the Internet was just to meet people—to make connections with burnt-out parents like Debra Burgette. But I never brought up rehoming online."

"Did you bring it up later?"

"Yeah. Around Labor Day weekend, I called Debra Burgette on her cell."

"Did she give you her cell-phone number?"

"No."

"How did you get it?"

"Easy. People are stupid, all right? They join these online support forums and think that because they make up a screen name it's all anonymous. They post things about themselves, their family. I click 'like' on everything. They like being liked. It makes them feel good. So they keep posting. I ask them for advice, and suddenly they think they're the next Dr. Phil. Before you know it, we're best virtual buddies. When I put all these bits and scraps together, I know who they are, where they live, what their husband does for a living, what color underwear they like, and on and on. One piece of personal information leads to another. That's how I got Debra Burgette's number."

The prosecutor stepped away from the podium, retrieved an exhibit, and approached the witness. "Mr. Mendoza, I'm handing you a call report from a cell phone issued to Debra Burgette. Do you recognize the phone number for the incoming call at line eleven of this report?"

He checked it, then answered. "Yeah. That was the number for a prepaid cell I was using."

"You spoke to Debra on that day—September fifth?"

"Yeah."

"Tell us what you said in that conversation, please."

"I told her that I was a former social worker with the Department of Children and Family Services. I said I was a volunteer who helped families like hers—good people who had gone through an international adoption and ended up with more than they could handle."

"Excuse me for interrupting, but were any of those credentials true?"

He smiled thinly, as if proud of himself. "No. It was all a lie. But it broke the ice."

"Go on. What else did you say?"

"I told her that someone from Sashi's school—a teacher with a good heart who preferred to remain anonymous—had passed along Debra's name and number to me."

"Was that true?"

"No. But at this point the ice was more than broken. It was pretty much melted."

"What else did you say to Ms. Burgette?"

"I kept it light," he said. "No pressure. I described the services I could offer to her and asked if I could help her in any way."

"Did you mention rehoming, specifically?"

"Yeah. That was the whole point of the call."

"What was Ms. Burgette's response?"

"Objection," said Jack, rising. He didn't have to tell the judge that it was hearsay for Carlos Mendoza to repeat what Debra Burgette had said in their phone conversation.

"Sustained."

The prosecutor paused to rethink her question. "Did you reach an agreement with Debra Burgette about rehoming Sashi?"

"No. Not with Debra."

"What did you do next?"

"A few days later, I called her husband."

The prosecutor presented the next exhibit, the cell-phone record for Gavin Burgette, and focused his attention on the call from Mendoza's prepaid cell. "Please look at the incoming call on September eighth. Was that from you?"

He checked the exhibit quickly. "Yeah. That's my prepaid cell again."

"What did you and Mr. Burgette talk about?"

"Rehoming Sashi."

"Specifically, what did you tell him?"

"I told him that me and his wife spoke and that I knew all about their problems with Sashi. I told him that it's normal for parents to feel guilty about rehoming, and his wife was definitely feeling some of that. But I said my read of Debra was that she would, you know, go along with it—if he took the lead."

Jack glanced at Debra. It was almost imperceptible, but she was shaking her head, silently denying it.

"What did you do next?" asked the prosecutor.

"I used my lawyer to draw up a power of attorney for Debra and Gavin Burgette."

That got Judge Frederick's attention. "Excuse me, Mr. Mendoza. When you say 'my lawyer,' do you mean Ms. Vargas?"

He smiled a little, as if the question were almost funny. "No, Judge. It's a software called 'My Lawyer.' It comes with, like, five thousand forms."

The judge seemed satisfied. The prosecutor continued. "Why did you create a power of attorney?"

"I needed the Burgettes to sign it to rehome their daughter."

"That's all it takes—a power of attorney?"

"You can make it more complicated, if you want. But I keep things simple. All the new parents really need is something that says they now have the authority to make all the decisions the old parents would make."

"So, did this power of attorney identify the new parents?"

"No. Normally it would. But the Sashi deal was being done a little different. The Burgettes were supposed to give the power of attorney to me, and then I would take care of whatever legal stuff was needed to get Sashi with the new family."

"Did the Burgettes sign the power of attorney?"

"I had some follow-up conversations with Gavin, and he kept telling me the documents were signed, but I never got them. So I don't know if they signed or not."

"What happened next?"

"I called off the deal."

"Why?"

"I had a married couple in Tampa who were interested. But after I sent all the information to them about Sashi, they backed out."

"What was the name of the couple in Tampa?"

"Honestly, I don't remember. This was more than three years ago. I only met them online. After they backed out, I pretty much flushed it."

"When was your last conversation with Debra Burgette?"

He checked her call report again. "I see here it was September eleventh."

"Three days before Sashi disappeared," said the prosecutor, reminding Judge Frederick of the timeline. "What did you talk about?"

"Honestly, I don't remember anything about that call. It says here on the report that it lasted one minute, but I doubt it was even that long."

"Okay. What about Gavin Burgette? When was your last conversation with him?"

Mendoza checked the call report. "We spoke on Thursday, September thirteenth. The day before Sashi disappeared."

"That's the six-minute call referenced in Mr. Burgette's report, correct?"

"Yeah."

"Do you remember anything about that conversation?"

"Yeah, I remember it. I said my clients backed out and the deal for Sashi was off."

"Was that the end of the matter?"

"No. We kept on talking a couple minutes. Then, we, uh . . . we started negotiating a price."

"A price for what?"

"Sashi."

Gavin Burgette didn't jump to his feet, and there was no Perry Mason–style outburst from the gallery. But he was seated in the first row just on the other side of the rail, and his reaction was loud enough for Jack to hear it from his seat: "That's a *damn lie.*"

The judge responded with a crack of his gavel; he'd obviously heard it, too. "Mr. Burgette, one more word from you and I'll have you removed from the courtroom."

The prosecutor resumed her questioning. "What exactly did you and Mr. Burgette negotiate?"

"Okay, so this is where we were: Sashi was damaged goods, all right? I mean, all these rehoming kids have problems, but this girl had *problems.* My clients didn't want her. The Burgettes still wanted me to take her. So we were negotiating what it would cost them for me to . . . you know, take her off their hands."

Jack heard something between a groan and a deep sigh from behind him. It could have been anger, or disbelief, or both—but this time, Gavin's reaction wasn't enough to draw the judge's ire.

"Did you reach an agreement with Mr. Burgette?" asked the prosecutor.

"Uh-uh. We were talking about something like a hundred grand, but it never went solid."

"Why not?"

The witness shrugged, as if the answer were obvious. "Sashi went missing. Nothing left to talk about."

The prosecutor returned to her table, quietly conferred with co-counsel, and made one final check of her notes. "Thank you, Mr. Mendoza. Your Honor, I have nothing further."

Jack had expected the testimony to end on a strong note, but not necessarily with a bombshell.

"Mr. Swyteck," said the judge, "I'm sure you're prepared to cross-examine, but I've been going since eight a.m. and I'm exhausted. I hate to hold this prisoner in Miami another day, but I'm only human. Let's reconvene tomorrow at six p.m. We'll go for one hour. The witness shall remain under oath, and there shall be no third-party communication with him overnight. We're adjourned," he said with a crack of the gavel.

All rose on the bailiff's command, and when the judge disappeared into his chambers, the courtroom deputies escorted the prisoner to the side exit, where elevators would transport him to the holding cells. Mendoza's lawyer stepped up to the rail to confer with the prosecution team, all seemingly satisfied with a good day's work.

"What now?" asked Hannah as she packed up their trial bags.

Jack was watching Gavin Burgette and his lawyer walk toward the rear exit. A handful of reporters followed them, and a few were firing off questions, even if they were being ignored. Jack would have expected Debra to remain behind at her seat until Gavin and the new woman in his life were long gone. Not this time.

Debra Burgette headed up the center aisle with purpose, in hot pursuit of her ex.

CHAPTER 44

I need to talk to you right now," said Debra.

Gavin and Nicole were five steps ahead of her, hurrying across the plaza outside the courthouse. Debra had managed to hold her tongue for the five minutes it had taken to ride the elevator down and follow them out of the building.

Gavin stopped and turned. "Really? Here?"

They were at the curb, standing in the glow of a streetlamp. The downtown rush hour was over, and the only people on the sidewalks were a handful of homeless guys and a couple of German-speaking tourists who obviously had no idea that not a single shop or restaurant in the courthouse district remained open after dark.

"I know what you did," said Debra.

Nicole tugged at his arm. "Let's go, Gavin."

He didn't move. "What *I* did?"

"You called DCFS, you bastard. Didn't you?"

"What?" he said, incredulous.

"A social worker showed up at Alexander's school today. They interviewed his teachers. Now they want to interview *him*. This is all because you accused me of rehoming Sashi. Now DCFS thinks Alexander is in danger."

Nicole edged her way forward. "Do you deny you rehomed her?"

"What kind of question is that, Nicole?"

"The kind of question a lot of people are asking—especially the ones who wonder why you're so sure she's alive?"

Debra was about to spit fire, and then it hit her: "*You* called DCFS. Didn't you?"

"I don't know what you're talking about," said Nicole.

"This won't stick," she said, glaring at her ex. "You know I didn't rehome Sashi."

"It took you long enough to deny it."

"No, what took a while was to figure out what kind of scheme you were up to. I denied it in no time. I passed a lie detector test. I showed the report to Jack Swyteck, and I sent it to the FBI. I'm going to send it to DCFS, too."

"I can get a hamster to pass a polygraph," said Nicole.

"Just shut up," said Debra. "You took everything, Gavin. I can't even afford to hire a lawyer. But you are not going to take Alexander from me."

"I'm not trying to take Alexander," he said.

"Yes, you are. I couldn't understand why you would lie on the witness stand like that. I even started to wonder if Swyteck had put the idea in your head, since it would help his client if I rehomed Sashi. He did the same thing to me, you know. He had me thinking that maybe you rehomed her. But you didn't see me haul off and make a wild accusation against you in a courtroom."

Nicole tugged at his arm again. "Let's go, Gavin."

"Yes, please. Go, Gavin. I can't stand to look at either one of you. But you want to know the worst of it? For a little while there, I thought you genuinely believed that Sashi might be alive. At the very least, I thought maybe you were finally willing to put the bullshit aside and find out, once and for all, what really happened to our daughter."

Gavin breathed in and out. "Sashi was murdered by Dylan Reeves. And, yes, you did have everyone doubting that for a couple days—maybe even the judge. But you see what happens when you keep reopening this old wound? People get hurt. This is your fault, Debra. Not mine. Blame yourself for what happens. Not me. And not Nicole."

Gavin turned, Nicole took his arm, and together they walked away. Debra stood at the corner and watched as they crossed the street and entered the parking lot.

Debra's car was parked on the street around the corner, two blocks from the courthouse. She followed the sidewalk, passing one dark storefront after another. Most shops were secured for the night with roll-down shutters or burglar bars. A rush of warm wind from the alley lifted a fast-food wrapper from the asphalt and sent it swirling over Debra's head. It was nothing to worry about, but it somehow made her feel more alone on a street that was a long, long way from Cocoplum. She walked faster, but then she stopped and glanced over her shoulder. She thought she'd heard footsteps.

She saw nothing but the fast-food wrapper blowing like tumbleweed across the empty street. She turned and continued toward her car, walking in the shadow of a dark office tower. It was completely vacant for renovation, not a single light burning in its twenty stories of black windows. The block-long construction zone, idle for the night, lay between Debra and her car. She would have to walk through one of those temporary pedestrian tunnels that kept workers from dropping tools and debris on passersby below. She opted to cut across the street to the open sidewalk, which made her feel safer—for a moment. Then she heard footsteps again. She glanced quickly over her shoulder, but she saw nothing.

Definitely heard footsteps.

Her heart was pounding, her mind was racing, and without even thinking about it she covered the last twenty yards to her car in an all-out sprint. She dug the key from her purse, unlocked the door, jumped behind the wheel, and started the engine. The tires squealed and the engine roared as the car leaped away from the curb. Her hands were shaking as she gripped the wheel and sped down the street.

I know I heard something.

The traffic light was red, but she blew through the intersection, steered onto the entrance ramp to I-95, and merged into traffic at seventy miles per hour.

Then she dialed Aquinnah on her cell—someone to talk her home, calm her nerves, and tell her it was time to stop living in the rearview mirror.

CHAPTER 45

Jack checked his cell as he exited the federal courthouse. He had a voice-mail message from a number he didn't recognize. The voice was unfamiliar, too.

"Mr. Swyteck," the recording began, "this is Herb Graner, the lawyer for Dylan Reeves."

Jack stopped at the street corner. Graner had represented Reeves at trial, and Jack had been eager to hear from him. Graner apologized for not returning the phone calls sooner, but he'd spent the last thirty days in residence at the Hazelden Betty Ford Foundation for treatment of alcohol and drug addiction. Jack pressed the phone harder against his ear to drown out the street noises and hear better.

"Today's my first day back at work," he said. "I'll be in the office late tonight catching up. Call or come by if you like. Thanks."

Jack called right back. True to his word, Graner was still in the office and willing to meet. The law office of Herb Graner, P.A., was downtown, in the Alfred I. duPont Building, just a few blocks from the federal courthouse. Jack headed straight over, and in fifteen minutes he was seated across the conference table from the lawyer who, ironically, had been entrusted with the job of saving Dylan Reeves' life while drinking himself to death.

Graner's appearance was reminiscent of Jack's late mentor, Neil Goderich, right down to the braided gray ponytail and the casual, open-collared shirt. The difference, of course, was that Neil had learned to "just say no" even before it became a public service announcement. Graner had never really caught on to the concept.

Beads of sweat glistened on his brow. "Sorry about the AC," said Graner. "Shit always breaks when you're out of the office."

Jack removed his suit coat and loosened his tie, but the room was still a sauna. "No worries. I'm used to it. It comes with the turf in historic buildings, I guess."

Miami's duPont Building was a notable survivor in a city that cleared away history for new high-rises on a weekly basis. Built in 1939, in the Moderne style, the city's second skyscraper still bore the name of Alfred I. duPont, who'd invested well in the Florida banking business. His first fortune, however, had come as a young man in the gunpowder business, and nineteenth-century history would record him as "one of the nation's top powder men." From the razor cuts on the conference room tabletop—Jack guessed that hundreds of lines of coke had been cut there—it appeared that Herb Graner was quite the "powder man" himself.

"Let me see if I can put my hands on the Reeves working file," he said, as he pushed away from the table. "I've got some notes in there, I'm sure."

The prospect of attorney notes piqued Jack's interest, but he didn't hold out much hope. Every available surface was covered with expandable files, loose notepads, and law books. There were filing cabinets, but they were almost completely hidden behind floor-to-ceiling stacks of dusty Bankers Boxes, some of which effectively bricked over the room's only window. Many were yellowed with age.

"I'm sure that file is here somewhere," said Graner. "It's only three years old. I usually wait at least five years before sending anything to deep storage."

Jack would have guessed it was more like *twenty*-five. "I can help look, if you can narrow down the boxes."

Graner planted his hands on his hips, breathing out. "I don't have a clue. I'll call my secretary. Not sure how she does it, but she knows where everything is."

Graner scanned the room for a telephone, as if he knew it had to be somewhere in all the mess of files and papers. He gave up and dialed on his cell. It was a short conversation, punctuated by a few grunts from Graner's end, followed by an "I'm truly sorry, Colleen." He tucked the phone away, then spoke to Jack.

"Colleen and I have been together forever, and it's always the same routine. Bitches me out for bothering her at home; then she calls back in five minutes with the answer. We'll just have to cool our heels for a while. Which gives you and me a chance to talk about the elephant in the room."

Jack knew what he meant. It was always a bit awkward to be the posttrial counsel in a death case who was arguing to the court that the trial lawyer was *so bad* that the client was effectively deprived of his right to counsel under the Sixth Amendment to the Constitution. "You read the brief we submitted to Judge Frederick, I take it?" asked Jack.

"Oh, yeah," he said, his tone a bit less congenial. "Let me get this off my chest right now. You pissed me off, Swyteck. I read it while I was in residence. It made me so mad that they made me shut down anything related to law, or they were gonna kick me out of the program."

"I understand."

"Do you? I was sober for eight years before I took on Dylan Reeves' case. This is the case that pushed me off the wagon."

"I'm sorry to hear that."

"Dylan's daddy was a preacher. I was a member of his church. The family doesn't have a lot of money to throw away on the prodigal son. Mr. Reeves asked me to take the case for ten thousand dollars, including costs. That was the cap. Not a penny more. I said I'd do it."

"That was generous of you."

"Yeah, it was. So that's problem number one I have with people who second-guess and say, 'Why didn't Dylan Reeves' lawyer follow up on this lead?' Or, 'Why didn't the lawyer hire this expert?' It's like hiring a roofer, and then when the job is done you ask him, 'Why didn't you paint the house?' Because you didn't fucking pay me to paint the house, asshole!"

"I get that," said Jack. "To a point."

"Let me give you an example. I considered hiring a psychiatrist to testify about RAD. It's not easy to find one who's qualified to testify about RAD and who's *willing* to essentially attack a murder victim in a courtroom. But I found one. You know how much she wanted? A five-thousand-dollar retainer, plus two hundred dollars an hour for court time."

"That's a lot of money."

"That's over half the pot! Even at ten thousand dollars, when all was said and done, I made maybe fifteen dollars an hour on this case."

"In hindsight, he might have been better off with a public defender."

"Yeah. Everybody's a genius in hindsight."

The phone rang. As predicted, it was Herb's secretary. Herb rose and followed her directions, speaking into the phone: "Uh, uh, uh-huh. Got it, sweetie. Thank you."

He put the phone down, his gaze locking onto a Bankers Box at the top of a teetering stack on the other side of the room. "Colleen to the rescue," he said, smiling. "There it is."

Jack helped him pull it down, careful not to knock over the entire stack, and they placed it on the razor-scarred tabletop. Graner removed the cardboard box top eagerly, as if opening a time capsule. From Jack's vantage point, the contents didn't appear to be well organized. It looked as if someone had scooped up a mess of fallen papers from the floor and simply shoved them into a box.

"My interview notes gotta be here somewhere," he said. "That's what I think you'd find most helpful."

Jack spotted a black three-ring binder that was still atop the stack. It had been beneath the working file, but with the box gone, Jack could see that it was marked *State of Florida v. Dylan Reeves*. Jack laid it on the table and started through it.

"What is this, Herb?"

He stopped shuffling through the box and took a look. At first, his expression showed no recognition. Then it came to him. "That came from the state attorney before trial. It was part of the *Brady* production."

The prosecutor's compliance with *Brady v. Maryland*—the government's obligation to turn over potentially exculpatory evidence to the defense before trial—was a major point in Dylan Reeves' petition.

"I've never seen this before," said Jack.

"I didn't use it at trial. Neither did the prosecution."

Jack opened the binder. Inside there were section dividers with tabs. The pages that followed each tab were printed copies of online chats. Jack read the first one, an exchange between "Manly Man" and "Cherry," written in sexting shorthand.

what do u like
u know what
u want me to sing u love songs
no
u want me to recite poetry
nope
u want me to suck your big cock
Ahhhhhhhh.
is it out now
yep
i want it all the way out

Jack flipped ahead. Each tab contained a different online conversation between Sashi and the strangers that she'd met in the virtual world. It also held copies of the photographs they'd exchanged, just as Debra Burgette had testified at the hearing.

"Why didn't you use this at trial?"

"Why?" he asked, suddenly defensive again. "First of all, I had no budget for a private detective, let alone a cybersex expert. And I did talk to a tech guy. As best he could tell, 'Manly Man' lived in Romania. What would that have proved in a murder case in Florida?"

"There are at least ten others here," Jack said, flipping through them. "'TooCool,' 'Supersized,' 'Pleaser'—one of these guys could have lived *next door* to Sashi."

"If I had to do it again, maybe I'd do it different. But I made a decision. It made no sense to attack a teenage victim as an online slut if I couldn't afford an expert witness to explain what reactive attachment disorder is. With the jury I had, victim bashing was a sure way to lose."

Jack was suddenly thinking ahead seventeen years, trying to imagine the mistakes his own daughter was going to make. Hopefully none as bad as Sashi's, but who was to judge?

"You have to remember, Jack: this was a case with no witnesses, and the police never recovered a body. 'No body' should equal 'no conviction.' My strategy was to make the prosecution prove its case, not to shift the burden to us to prove that Dylan didn't do it."

"Like you say, hindsight is twenty-twenty."

"No. I'm going to stand my ground on this. It was the right strategy, and I'd do it again. If I could just find my notes here . . ."

Jack watched as Graner flipped through the pages one by one. Every so often he would pause, as if he'd found something interesting, then shake his head and move on. With equal frequency he'd remove a stray item—an empty french fry container or an electric bill he'd forgotten to pay—and toss it aside.

Then he hit pay dirt.

"Here we go," he said, as he handed his notes to Jack. They

were still part of the original yellow legal pad that had never been pulled apart.

Jack laid the pad on the table, took a seat, and started reading. Graner watched over his shoulder, mostly in silence, with only an occasional interruption.

"Amazing, isn't it?" asked Graner.

"What?"

"How hard it can be to read your own handwriting."

"I thought it was just me," said Jack. He kept slogging through it. The handwritten words at the bottom of page five caught his attention. He read them to himself, then aloud, for Graner's benefit, in case he couldn't make it out: "'Scumbag,'" said Jack, quoting verbatim, "'but could be innocent.' You're talking about Dylan Reeves there?"

"Yeah," said Graner. "That's what I wrote."

"Why?"

Graner retrieved his notes from Jack and took a couple of minutes to scan ahead. His eyes narrowed, his lips puckered, and his face went through a half dozen other contortions in an effort to shake something loose from a foggy memory. "Damned if I remember. A lot of booze since then. Maybe it was just my impression."

"Were you drunk when you interviewed him?"

"I told you I was sober for eight years before this case."

"That's not what I asked," said Jack.

He looked at his notes—chicken scratch—and shook his head. "Yeah, I was probably drunk."

He seemed to be soul-searching, struggling to say more. Jack gave him a moment.

"You know, this was my first capital case," said Graner. "You handle a couple of robbery cases, some DUIs, and you think you're a criminal lawyer. You lose at trial, maybe your client does a little jail time. I found out quick when I took on this case: not every lawyer is cut out to do death work."

"Believe me, I know."

"But let me be clear about this," said Herb. "I might not have a perfect memory—or any memory—of what was said in an interview three years ago. But I pulled myself together in that courtroom."

"Dylan said he smelled scotch on your breath."

"I took *one* shot in the morning, okay? Just to calm my nerves. I was *not* ineffective."

Jack hadn't come to argue that point. "Take another look at the notes, Herb. See if you can make out anything that would have made you write 'might be innocent.'"

He groaned—not because he didn't want to help, Jack sensed, but only out of self-loathing and regret over the lawyer he'd become. He took a minute. Then another. Finally, there was a glimmer in his eye.

"FU."

Jack recoiled. "Fuck you, too."

"No. It's here in the notes. FU. That means 'follow up.' These are possible witnesses I was supposed to follow up with and interview. Two of them."

"Can you make out the names?"

He held the paper closer to his eyes. "Michael, is the first name. Last name," he said, squinting, "Volkov. Not Michael. Now I remember. It was a Russian name. Mikhail Volkov."

Jack wrote it down. "Second name?"

"Just two capital letters. Maybe somebody's initials," he said, showing Jack the scribble on the yellow notepad page.

"BB," said Jack, reading it. "What does that mean?"

There was another spark in Graner's eye. "Bad Boy!" he said. "That's it: Bad Boy."

"As in *Carlos* Bad Boy?" asked Jack, his adrenaline pumping. "In your first interview, Dylan Reeves told you about Carlos *Bad Boy* Mendoza?"

"I'm pretty sure all I got out of Dylan was 'Bad Boy.' I seem to recall that Dylan didn't know his real name."

Jack looked at the notes again, shaking his head with disbelief. "Okay. Really, really think hard. Tell me anything you can remember that Dylan Reeves told you about this 'Bad Boy.'"

Graner shook his head, grimacing. "I really don't remember. Maybe nothing. You should ask Dylan."

"I already asked him six different ways if he knew anything about Carlos Mendoza. I got nothing."

"Show him my notes. Ask him again."

"I will. But right now, let's drill down on what you remember."

Graner fell back in his chair and ran his fingers through his hair, exasperated. "I don't remember shit, okay?"

"Try."

"I *am* trying," he said, suddenly more annoyed than exasperated. "Fuck it. You know what? If Dylan Reeves won't talk to you about Bad Boy to save himself, don't make me feel like the bad guy for not remembering. It isn't my fault."

It was a pretty lame rationalization from a lawyer who was charged with the responsibility of defending a capital case—but in a way, he had a point.

Why wouldn't Dylan Reeves have told me?

"If I were you, Jack, you know what I'd do?"

"I couldn't even begin to guess," said Jack.

He leaned into the table and stabbed the other name on the notepad with his index finger. "I'd find this Mikhail Volkov. And I'd talk to him."

Jack considered it, nodding slowly. "Not a bad idea. That's exactly what I'll do."

Graner gathered up his notes. "Let me make a copy of this for you. I think the machine still works." He started toward the door, then stopped.

"You'll keep me in the loop, right?" he asked.

Jack assumed he was talking about the ineffective-assistance argument. "Sure."

"I told you this was the case that made me relapse—that not all lawyers are cut out for death work. That goes double when you think maybe your client didn't do it. You know what I'm saying?"

"I do, Herb."

Their gaze held for a moment longer, and Jack could feel the pull of Graner's unspoken wish—his need for Jack to say that he'd done a good job for Dylan Reeves, or, at the very least, that he hadn't let his client down.

"I'll make those copies."

"Thanks," said Jack, and then he added what he could. "You've been a big help."

CHAPTER 46

Jack left the duPont Building with a photocopy of Herb Graner's interview notes. In fifteen minutes he was at Cy's Place in Coconut Grove.

Cy's Place was Theo's second successful establishment, a true jazz club that he'd named after his great-uncle Cy. It was special in Jack's book. The grand opening had proved to be the night when everything clicked for Jack and Andie. They'd talked and laughed till two a.m. as Uncle Cy on the saxophone gave them the flavor of the old Overtown Village and its long-gone heyday as Miami's "Little Harlem." Six months later, at the second anniversary of his thirty-ninth birthday, Jack had taken a knee on the dance floor and popped the question in front of all of his friends, Neil Goderich among them. It was one of the last times he'd see Neil.

"My buddy says he'll get back to us in five minutes," said Theo. He was on the working side of the bar. Jack was on a stool that probably should have had his name inscribed on it.

"Sounds good," said Jack.

It was a short list of people who could find a missing witness with a Russian surname and possible underworld connections—especially considering Jack's time constraints. He couldn't just ask Andie to run a background check through the FBI database, not unless she wanted to lose her job. That left Theo as his best option. Theo had connections on both sides of the law. Jack didn't ask which side he was using to track down Mikhail Volkov.

"You two guys sound like a couple of hockey players," Theo said, and then he broke into the voice of a play-by-play announcer: "Volkov with the kick-save; Swyteck on the rebound—and he *scooores!*"

"Seriously? What do you know about hockey?"

"Why wouldn't I like hockey?"

Jack tugged at the soggy label on his longneck bottle. "I'm gonna leave that one alone."

Theo stepped away to tend to another customer—one who actually paid.

Free beers. There'd been so many of them. Happy times, mostly. But it made him think of some lonely nights, too, from the end of his first marriage to the end of the road with Renée or Valerie or so many other flavors of the month who turned out not to be "the one." After one too many shots of Theo's "tequila with no training wheels"—no salt and no lime—he'd call himself a cab, put himself to bed, and, in between wishing that the bed would stop spinning and that his head would stop pounding, he'd wonder if someone like Andie might ever come along. Actually, his mind had never conjured up "someone like Andie."

He reached for his cell and dialed her number. It went to voice mail, so he left a message. "Hey, honey. Another late night. Call me when you get this message. Love you."

"Aww. Love you, too," said Theo in his mushy voice.

"Go away."

"Uh-uh. My buddy got back to us." He laid the printed report on the bar top. Jack took it and held it up to the neon beer sign for easier reading.

"Two prior convictions," said Jack, summarizing. "Three years probation for violation of Florida Statutes, Title Sixteen, Chapter Eight Hundred."

"What's that?"

"Lewd and lascivious conduct. Everything from child molestation to indecent exposure. If Volkov got no jail time, my guess is that his offense involved some kind of exhibition and not anything physical."

"Like jerking off in public?"

"Could be."

Theo leaned on the bar, resting on his forearms in a way that made the muscles in his arms seem even more intimidating. "We need to pay jerko a visit. I can leave Manny in charge and go right now."

"Just show up at his door? That's your plan?"

"What do *you* want to do? Skype? Face time?"

"No. But that's a long drive. He lives in South Broward. We could get there and he might not even be home."

"Jack, read the conditions of probation. Dude has a nine p.m. house-arrest curfew."

Jack checked. He'd missed it in the dim bar lighting. I still want to think this through."

"What's there to think through? We got a name. We got an address. He's gotta be home. And you got no time to hire an astrophysicist to write you a decision-making algorithm."

"Huh? How do you know about algorithms?"

"I learned it playing hockey. What the fuck, Jack? You think I wipe down the bar all night long and don't learn a thing? I know enough about algorithms to know that technology is overrated."

"Really?"

"Yeah. Really. Some things get done right the first time. You leave that shit alone. There's no improving it."

"Like what?"

"Like . . . great music. I mean, does it work for you if Joe Cocker skips the fast train and buys a ticket for an aeroplane because"—he paused for effect, then broke into song—"*My baby, she sent me an e-mail*"?

Jack thought about it. "I see your point."

"How could you miss it?"

"So, getting evidence from a witness is like great music?"

"Ain't nothin' like the real thing, baby."

Jack folded up the report and tucked it into his coat pocket. "All right," he said. "Let's go see Mr. Volkov."

CHAPTER 47

On the way home from the courthouse, Debra stopped by Aquinnah's house to pick up Alexander. He'd spent the evening with his older sister while Mom and Dad sat on opposite sides of Judge Frederick's courtroom.

Aquinnah lived in a nicely updated duplex on a quiet street in Miami Shores, not far from Barry University. Gavin owned it "as an investment," renting out one side and letting Aquinnah live in the other so that she wouldn't have to stay in student housing. It was much more space than Aquinnah needed, and sometimes Debra wondered if he'd bought it just so Aquinnah wouldn't feel the need to escape the dorm and visit her mother.

Alexander was ready to go and had his school backpack over his shoulder when Debra arrived. It was another thirty minutes from Aquinnah's place to Cocoplum. As always, Alexander made efficient use of the time. He was in the backseat, doing his homework in the glow of the reading lamp. There had been no argument about it. No temper tantrum. No need to threaten or bribe him. Debra hadn't even asked if he'd finished his homework while at his sister's house. He'd just cracked his textbook and done it.

My good boy.

Raindrops started to fall as she pulled into the driveway.

"Let's run for it," she said.

They jumped out of the car and hurried up the walkway to the front door. The leafy canopy of an oak had shielded them from most of the downpour, and they were mostly dry when they got inside.

"Go up to your room, put on some dry clothes, and finish your homework," she said.

"I finished my homework in the car."

More resistance than usual, but he was nine, after all. "Then check it."

"Mom, it was so easy."

"Check it anyway."

"I did check it."

"Go up and *recheck it*," she said.

Alexander took a step back, confused by a tone he rarely heard from his mother. "Okay. I'll check it."

"I'm sorry, honey. I didn't mean to yell at you."

He slung his backpack over his shoulder and went upstairs. Debra stood in the foyer and watched until he got all the way up and she heard his bedroom door close. Then she walked briskly down the hallway to the study.

The study had once been Gavin's home office. Overnight, it had transformed into the at-home storage and control center for the "Find Sashi" campaign. Bankers boxes lined the floor. The closets and bookshelves were stuffed with flyers, ribbons, banners, posters, reward notices, and everything else that had been part of the "Find Sashi" effort. The most important materials were in a locked cabinet behind the cluttered desk. Debra dug the key from the desk drawer and unlocked the cabinet.

There were six shelves from floor to ceiling. Each shelf held a tightly packed row of three-ring binders that were arranged like library books, spine out. Each notebook contained something that Debra thought might be relevant to Sashi's disappearance, or to the trial of Dylan Reeves—everything from copies of newspaper coverage to a transcript of her call to 911 to report Sashi missing. Debra's notion of "might be relevant" was beyond broad. Or so the police had told her when she'd carted a set of notebooks into the Miami-Dade police station for the detectives on the case. Debra had created an index, but it was strictly for the benefit of law enforcement. She'd been through these notebooks so many times that she didn't need an index. She went straight to binder no. 44 and pulled it off the shelf.

It popped when she cracked it open; the binders were squeezed so tightly together on the shelf that the laser-jet ink had bonded several printed pages together. She peeled the sticky ones apart, taking care not to rip any.

Debra was still thinking about the sound of those footsteps that had followed her from the courthouse to her car. She'd seen no one, but she had heard *something*. One thought had led to another, and the chills she'd felt tonight harked back to Tuesday's trip to the dance academy—to that man staring at her and Alexander on their way to Matryoshka Deli Food. Could those have been *his* footsteps that she'd heard tonight? Or was she truly paranoid? The encounter in Sunny Isles had happened well after sunset, but the lighting in the strip mall was more than adequate, and she'd gotten a pretty good look at him.

And now that she'd had time to reflect, it was starting to come clear that perhaps she'd seen that man's face before.

Too anxious to sit, she stood at the desk and flipped through the first few pages eagerly. There were tabs in the notebook. The pages that followed each tab were printed copies of e-mails and other online communications. Each tab contained a different online conversation between Sashi and the strangers that she'd met in the virtual world. It also held copies of the photographs they'd exchanged.

Debra gasped as she flipped past Tab D: a color photo of a potbellied man and his Viagra-inspired manhood. It was enough to make a mother vomit, and the mere sight of it triggered a memory so painful that Debra had to pause and collect her breath. That photo had been the last straw—the one that had prompted her threat to send Sashi back to Russia.

Debra refocused and continued on through the notebook. It was like watching a horror movie, only real. Men of all ages, races, and backgrounds had been snared in Sashi's web. Her m.o. had been consistent. She would tantalize her targets with a series of communications and tease them with increasingly provocative selfies, which had undoubtedly translated into hours of self-gratification for the pathetic recipients. Each was deluded into thinking that he could have his way with a beautiful, sex-starved seventeen-year-old girl. All he had to do was dial the number that Sashi provided in the final e-mail.

Little did he know that the frantic voice on the line would be that of Sashi's mother.

Debra turned to the next tab and froze. Shielding her eyes from the pasty-white naked male's body, she focused on the lines of the man's face, his piercing dark eyes, the contours of his clean-shaven head. The challenge was to compare the photograph in the notebook to a mere memory, although the image was burned in her mind. The face on the page; the man at the strip mall. The face; the man. Back and forth she went, several more times than necessary—because she wanted to be certain.

She sank into the chair, still staring at the photograph.

"You again," she said to no one but herself.

CHAPTER 48

The drive from Cy's Place to Hallandale Beach Boulevard was forty minutes, most of it straight up I-95. Jack rode shotgun and used the time to prepare his cross-examination of Carlos Mendoza. Theo drove, breaking the boredom every so often with a soft but distracting relapse into the new and technologically improved version of "The E-mail."

"My baby, she sent me an e-mail. / Said she—"

"Theo, stop," Jack said as he looked up from his laptop. "I'm in my cross-exam zone here."

"My bad. Sorry."

In silence, they drove east toward the northern tip of Little Moscow.

For over seventy-five years, Gulfstream Park has been one of the premier Thoroughbred racing venues in the world, but its surrounding neighborhoods are a mixed bag. Condos, marinas, pricey shopping destinations, and other signs of gentrification stretch toward the ocean to the east. West of the racetrack was a middle-to-lower-middle-class area that, depending on the specific address, was either on the rebound or in serious decline. The streets were paved and quiet, but there were no sidewalks, and the only streetlamps were at major intersections. Houses were relics of the 1950s, one- and two-bedroom shoe boxes, some with the original metal awnings and jalousie windows. There were a few vacant lots, most of which marked the final resting place of a mobile home that was built long before anyone had ever heard the term "manufactured housing" and that had seen one too many hurricanes. The residents of the area were mostly immigrants from the former Soviet Union who preferred to keep to themselves, not the jet-setters who were personal friends of Vladimir Putin and quick to let you know it.

It was dark between the lone streetlights at intersections, and Theo flipped on the high beams so that Jack could check the address on a mailbox. They were getting close. An old ranch-style house on the corner looked to be the right place, though in the darkness Jack couldn't make out the street number at the front door.

"That has to be it," said Jack.

Theo pulled up to the curb, directly across the street. The house had no garage, and there was no car in the driveway. The windows were dark. Not even the porch light was burning.

"Looks like Mr. Volkov might be in violation of his curfew," said Theo.

"Or his driver's license is suspended and he doesn't have a car. Let's check."

They got out of the car, crossed the street, and walked up the short paved way to the front door. Jack knocked, and they waited. The windows remained dark. Jack put his ear to the door: not a sound emerged—no footsteps, no TV, no pet. Jack was about to knock again, but Theo beat him to it—with authority.

"Do you have to make it sound like a drug bust?" asked Jack.

"We ain't here to sell him Thin Mints and Shortbread cookies," said Theo.

No one came to the door.

"Is it possible he doesn't live here anymore?" asked Jack. "How current is the info from your friend?"

"It's the same database that Volkov's parole officer would use. He lives here. I guarantee it."

A quick double-check of the house number confirmed that they were in the right place.

"Maybe the court dropped the curfew from the terms and conditions of his probation."

"Well, it's just nine-twenty," said Theo. "He could be running a little late. Let's wait in the car a few and see if he shows up."

They stepped down from the porch and went to the car. Jack was about to power up his laptop and get back to work when a pair of headlights shone at the street corner. A two-door Mazda came toward them. The driver was visible only in silhouette, but it appeared that he was alone. The car turned into the driveway, the driver's door opened, and a man who was built more like Jack than Theo stepped out and started toward the front door.

"There's our boy," said Theo.

They got out of the car, and Theo took the lead, which was fine with Jack. Theo was to the streets what Jack was to the courtroom.

"Hey, Volkov," Theo called out.

The man stopped midway between the driveway and his front door. He shot a quick but suspicious look at the two who were crossing the street and coming toward him.

"We need to talk—"

He turned and ran in the opposite direction, stopping Theo in mid-sentence. It suddenly occurred to Jack that they probably looked like a couple of parole officers out to bust Volkov for a curfew violation, but Theo was in hot pursuit before Jack could question what he was thinking. Jack followed as Theo gave chase around the house and into the backyard. A chain-link fence ran the length of the property line, and the alley on the other side was well lit by a streetlamp. Theo quickly closed the gap, and when the man stopped for an instant to open the gate, Theo caught up and slammed the gate shut. Theo never laid a hand on him, but the man fell to the ground in a defensive posture, breathing heavily from the short run.

"Stop," the man said, but his voice sounded strange—like a burp.

"Relax, dude. We just want to talk," said Theo, as Jack reached them.

The man answered in fragmented sentences, and it wasn't because the sprint had left him breathless. It was his way of talking—more burping. "Leave. Me. Alone."

Theo made a face, confused. "What the fuck?"

In the glow of the streetlamp, Jack noticed a deep, thick scar that ran all the way across the man's throat.

"Go. Away," he belched.

Jack understood. One of his father's closest friends had smoked for forty years and lost his vocal cords to cancer. Esophageal speech was a learned method of swallowing air and gradually expelling it, as in a belch, to produce a sound.

"I have to ask you about Carlos Mendoza," said Jack.

He swallowed more air, then expelled it firmly: "No."

"I'm the lawyer for Dylan Reeves. You know Dylan, right?"

Volkov didn't answer.

"I need you to tell me what you know about Sashi Burgette."

"I. Know. Nothing."

"Mr. Volkov, you're Dylan's last shot."

"Nothing!" he said in his loudest belch yet, punctuating it with a slashing motion across his throat.

Jack understood perfectly. Volkov's loss of his voice was not from disease or accident, and the hideous scar across his neck was not from surgery. Talking about Carlos Mendoza was how Volkov had ended up with his throat slashed and his vocal cords severed.

"You want me to give him some encouragement?" asked Theo.

Volkov's eyes widened at the suggestion, but Jack didn't even start down that road.

"We're going to do this by the book, and Mr. Volkov is going to do the right thing."

"Say what?" asked Theo.

Jack looked straight at Volkov, his glare tightening. "It's obvious why you didn't talk when you made those phone calls," said Jack. "But I want to know *why*, Mr. Volkov. Why did you call Debra Burgette every year on Sashi's birthday?"

He didn't answer. But there was no denial.

"What do you know about Sashi Burgette?" asked Jack.

Volkov glanced at Theo and then back at Jack before forcing out his one-word response: "Things."

"What kinds of things?"

He swallowed and answered in his halting cadence. "Things. I wish. I didn't."

"Did Dylan Reeves kill Sashi Burgette?"

They locked eyes for a moment, perhaps a few seconds. It seemed much longer than that to Jack. Finally, Volkov swallowed more air.

"Dylan," he belched. Then he took another gulp and released it with the rest of his answer: "Should. Have."

CHAPTER 49

No flights were available, so Jack slept in the passenger seat while Theo drove the six hours to Florida State Prison. Theo didn't want to go inside. He waited in the car. Who could have blamed him?

Jack checked in at Q-Wing and was escorted to death row. Five to six a.m. was the breakfast hour for all condemned inmates, but Jack's guess was that Dylan Reeves would skip it. It wasn't an exact science, but by Jack's calculation, Reeves had entered the up-all-night-and-pacing phase of death watch. Three meals a day were delivered like clockwork, but in death-watch Cell No. 1, food went untouched until repeated trips from one end of the twelve-by-seven cell to the other left the inmate so starving and exhausted that he had to sit and eat.

Around five-thirty the guards brought Reeves to the attorney-visitation room and left the two men alone. Jack took stock of his client. He wasn't doing well, even by death-watch standards. Just the few days since their last visit had left him noticeably thinner. His glassy, sunken eyes signaled lack of sleep. Jack's guess about pacing had been spot-on. Even with the correction officer's assistance, Reeves had practically fallen into the chair on the other side of the table.

"My feet are fucking killing me," he said, groaning.

Jack had seen death-row inmates walk them raw. "We can get a doctor to look at them."

That drew a sardonic smile. "Yeah. Don't want to make a bad impression when they carry me outta here feetfirst."

Sometimes, a little sarcasm from a death-row inmate could be a good sign; a sense of humor meant he still had hope. Other times, it was simply bitterness—a sign that he'd given up. It all depended on the delivery. Jack didn't detect much hope in his client's demeanor. He shifted gears. "Last night I spoke with Mikhail Volkov."

Reeves snapped out of his self-pity for a moment. "Poor bastard. What did he burp to you?"

"Not much. He's still afraid to talk."

"Wouldn't you be?"

Jack leveled his gaze, looking for a straight answer. "Is that why you didn't tell me about Carlos Mendoza?"

"Did you get a good look at what Bad Boy done to Volkov? That was what he got for telling the cops that Bad Boy was living with a thirteen-year-old prostitute."

It wasn't the explanation Jack had been expecting. "I thought it was to make sure Volkov kept his mouth shut about Sashi Burgette."

"It's both."

"Let's break this down," said Jack, "because I need to understand. Volkov was the tipster who got Bad Boy convicted for sex trafficking. Is that what you're telling me?"

"Yeah. Not that Mikhail was completely innocent. He was the night manager at the motel."

"So Volkov knew what was going on?"

"More than *knew*. He even referred a few clients to Bad Boy, who wanted a turn with a teenager. Somebody from MDPD got wind of what was going on and put the squeeze on Mikhail, and he cut a deal. He got probation, Bad Boy got jail time—and then Bad Boy got even."

"Okay. So the last thing Bad Boy needs is to add a murder conviction to his rap sheet. And I understand that you don't want to end up like Mikhail. But this doesn't end well for you if we lose this petition."

Reeves shook his head, telling Jack that he most definitely did *not* understand. "You only seen half of what they done to Mikhail. He pisses in a plastic bag strapped to his leg. You know what I'm sayin'? If you win this petition, I get off death row, but I don't leave Raiford. I go back into gen-pop. That's where Carlos Mendoza is right now. He'll be my fucking neighbor. How long you think I'd last in there if I save my ass by pointing the finger at Bad Boy?"

"We can try to get you moved to another facility."

"Bad Boy has friends everywhere. No offense, Swyteck, but look at the high-priced lawyer he hired. He's got enough money on the outside to make bad things happen inside, no matter where I go."

"We'll deal with that problem when we have to. First, we have to get you off death watch."

"Look, it's this simple: I'd rather go to sleep on a gurney than have my throat slashed and my dick cut off. Okay? You need to figure out a way to win without sticking your finger in Bad Boy's eye."

Jack sat back, folded his arms, and shrugged. "Then we lose."

"What?"

"No Carlos Mendoza, no way we win."

"Look, man. I wasn't saying Bad Boy has a better lawyer than I do, okay?"

"This isn't about my ego. I'm talking legal reality. Let me explain how this works, Dylan. This isn't a trial. This isn't even a *retrial.* This is a habeas petition. I can't conjure up new theories and throw new evidence against the wall and see what sticks. The law limits what I can do."

"Just put me on the stand. I'll tell the judge I didn't do it."

"No, you're not listening. I can't call you as a witness to testify about something you could have testified to at trial. That's not how the system works. You can't choose to remain silent at trial and then years later, on the eve of your execution, run to a federal judge and say, 'Hold everything, I changed my mind. Now I want to testify.'"

"Okay. I get that."

"We're onto something here with Carlos Mendoza. Talk to me, Dylan. What does Mikhail Volkov know about Sashi?"

He didn't answer.

Jack tried again, starting with something simple. "How did you and Mikhail know each other?"

"From the motel. Like I said, he was the manager. It's one of those places where you can rent a room for an hour or for a month. Whatever you need. I stayed there sometimes."

"Did you and Volkov ever talk about Sashi?"

"Yeah. Sure."

"Tell me about the first time Sashi came up."

Reeves drew a deep breath, then let it out. "First time was when Mikhail showed me some pictures."

"Pictures of Sashi?"

"Yeah. He told me he had an online thing going with a hot seventeen-year-old. I said bullshit, but then he showed me the pictures and the e-mails. This girl could write the dirtiest fucking e-mails you ever read. Mikhail said he was 'this close' to setting up a meeting with her when the ol' lady stepped in and screwed everything up."

"By 'old lady' you mean Debra Burgette?"

"He didn't say her name. But, yeah, I assume it was her."

"Then what?"

"We showed the pictures to Bad Boy. Showed him what she wrote in her e-mails, too. He took one look and decided he had to have her."

"Did he say how he planned to get her?"

"Not right away. I didn't hear nothin' about it for at least a month."

Jack was working a timeline in his head. "A month" was about how long Carlos Mendoza had spent trying to get the Burgettes to rehome Sashi. "So after the month, you and Mendoza had another talk about Sashi?"

"Yeah. We talked. He wanted me to bring her to him."

"Kidnap her?"

The word made him squirm. "He just wanted me to bring her to him alive. He didn't say nothin' about a ransom like a kidnapping."

"Is that when you followed Sashi to Ingraham Park?"

"No. It's like I told you before: I watched her for a time. Then I went to the park."

"To abduct her?"

Another grimace at Jack's word choice. "To make the pickup," said Reeves.

"Did you make it?"

"No. Come on, man. Now you're just bein' stupid, Swyteck. You know what happened. I told you and Miss Hannah, or whatever her name is. I fucked it up. I wasn't supposed to, you know, come on to her."

"You mean rape her?"

"What I'm sayin' is that she got away. I didn't rape her. I didn't kidnap her. If you want to be legal about it, I stole her panties. That's it."

"If that's the truth, then what happened to Sashi?"

He sat forward in his chair, leaning onto the table, his dark and tired eyes meeting Jack's stare. "I have no idea. I'm guessing Mikhail knows, and that's why he has no voice and no dick. But I'd be makin' shit up if I told you what happened to Sashi after she ran away from me in that park. All I know is I didn't kill her."

Jack took a minute to organize his thoughts, jotting a few of them down on his notepad. Then he looked at his client. "In twelve hours, I'll be in Judge Frederick's courtroom, and Carlos Mendoza will be on the witness stand. I have enough pieces to put together a good-faith theory of what happened."

"Okay."

"The problem is, how to present it to the judge. I'm not sure he'd let me call yet another witness. And even if I subpoena Mikhail Volkov, he won't tell the truth. He won't say a word about Carlos Mendoza, especially in a courtroom."

"I don't blame him."

"So, here's where we are. You *can't* testify. Volkov *won't* testify. The only way I can prove my theory is to go after Carlos Mendoza on the witness stand tonight and see if I can break him."

"Then do it."

"No. First I need you to understand fully what I'm going to do, and I need your permission to do it. Because this isn't going to leave you smelling like a rose. You may think all you did is steal Sashi's panties, but attempted sexual assault of a minor involving the use of a deadly weapon—your knife—is a felony of the first degree. My strategy won't get you out of prison. But it might save your life."

There was silence. Somehow, during all those hours wrapped up in his thoughts in Cell No. 1, Reeves had apparently managed to blot out that knife again. He pushed away from the table and started to pace, walking lightly on his overworked feet. Finally, he stopped and looked at Jack.

"You got any other bright ideas on how to keep me off the gurney? I mean anything at all?"

"We have an argument for ineffective assistance of counsel. Your trial lawyer was an alcoholic. He failed to follow up on important leads."

"What's the chance of winning on that?"

"The problem is that if you read the transcript, Herb doesn't come across as ineffective. He's a high-functioning alcoholic, at least in the courtroom. No one would fault him for advising you not to testify. That was a strategy call—and, frankly, it was probably the right one. I would have given you the same advice. I give ineffective assistance maybe a five percent shot. Probably less."

"Shit. Anything else?"

"Nothing I have any degree of confidence in."

He looked away, then back. "Okay. Then there's your answer, Swyteck."

"And the answer is . . ."

He swallowed hard, and in what surely was a reflex, he brought his hand to his throat and stroked it exactly where Volkov had been slashed. "I got no choice. Go for it."

"Good decision."

"Just one thing, Swyteck."

"What's that?"

"Don't fuck it up, man. Please. Don't fuck this up."

CHAPTER 50

Courtroom tension. Jack had felt it many times before. Often it came with a dose of self-doubt and second-guessing. *Should I have stricken juror number five? Should my client have testified in his own defense? Should we have taken a plea?* On that Wednesday morning, the tension was laden with doubts of a different stripe—and perhaps a touch of cynicism: *Is there anyone in this courtroom who is telling the truth?*

The trip to and from FSP had left him stiff and exhausted, but the adrenaline was pumping—and Jack was determined to get an answer.

"Mr. Swyteck, please proceed with your cross-examination," said Judge Frederick.

It was just after six, and the judge had allotted exactly one hour for Carlos Mendoza. Jack had that much time to pick the witness apart. He rose, buttoned his suit coat, and stepped forward.

"Thank you, Your Honor."

Jack understood the size of his task. It would have been hard enough to raise questions in the minds of jurors—to simply make them wonder if Mendoza had been involved in the disappearance and murder of Sashi Burgette. Herb Graner had missed that opportunity at the trial three years earlier. At this stage, Jack couldn't simply stir things up and hope that, in the confusion, a jury would find "reasonable doubt" and vote for acquittal. At the habeas stage—even with his client's life on the line—Jack had to convince a federal judge that Carlos Mendoza was such an important witness that the prosecutor's failure to point the defense in Mendoza's direction was a violation of Dylan Reeves' constitutional rights.

Jack approached and stopped just a few feet away from the witness. He faced Mendoza squarely, planted his feet firmly, and looked his target straight in the eye. It was the "I'm in control" body language that made for effective cross-examination.

"Mr. Mendoza," he began in a firm voice, "you don't deny that—"

"Excuse me, could I have a glass of water, please?" asked Mendoza.

Jack stared at the witness for a moment, then glanced over his shoulder into the public seating. Mendoza's lawyer was watching from the first row, and she seemed pleased. Like any good lawyer, Maddie Vargas assumed that Jack had worked long and hard on his first question—the wording, the delivery, the cadence. The interruption was calculated to throw him off: it was the courtroom version of "icing the kicker"—a football coach calling a time-out just as the opposing team's place kicker was about to kick the winning field goal.

"Surely," said the judge. "Some water for the witness, please."

A courtroom deputy filled a plastic cup and brought it to the witness. Mendoza drank slowly, seeming to enjoy the fact that all eyes were upon him. Or perhaps he was taking one more look around the courtroom to see who had come to watch the show. Debra and Gavin Burgette were seated at opposite ends of row one in the public gallery, as far away from each other as possible. Several reporters had shown up, though the media seemed far less interested in the fate of Dylan Reeves when someone other than Sashi's parents was on the stand.

"I'm finished," the witness announced.

"Wonderful," said the judge, but he was looking straight at Mendoza's attorney. "Ms. Vargas, there will be no more of this sort of nonsense, please," he said, completely onto her tricks. "Mr. Swyteck, proceed."

Jack went straight to it. Hannah had prepared a PowerPoint of photos and exhibits that Jack needed. He brought up the first photo on the screen: a mug shot.

"You recognize this man, don't you?"

"Yeah. That's Mikhail Volkov."

"Mr. Volkov managed the Bali Hai Motel, correct?"

"Yes."

"He testified before the grand jury against you, correct?"

"He did."

"You subsequently entered a plea of guilty to charges of sex trafficking, correct?"

"Right."

Jack brought up the next photo on the screen—one that Theo had snapped on his cell phone the night before. "This is also Mr. Volkov, right?"

"It looks like him."

"You see the scar on his neck?"

It was clearly visible, but Mendoza flashed a puzzled expression and shook his head. "I don't see any scar."

The judge leaned over and gave him a stern look. "It's as thick as a rope, Mr. Mendoza. Witnesses do not play games in my courtroom. Now, take another look and answer the question."

His gaze shifted toward the screen. "Oh, that scar. Yeah, I see it."

"That scar wasn't there before Mr. Volkov testified against you, was it?"

"I have no idea."

"Mr. Volkov managed the motel where you lived, right?"

"Yeah, that's what I said."

"You lived there for six months."

"About that."

"You saw him every day."

"Almost."

Jack was satisfied: the judge knew that Mendoza was a liar who would lie about everything. It was time to move into the substance.

Jack returned to his table and took the notebook from Hannah. "Your Honor, the court has heard testimony from Debra Burgette that in the six-week period prior to her daughter's disappearance, Sashi had some sexually explicit communications with strangers over the Internet. I want to question this witness about some of them, but I prefer to use this notebook rather than flash the images bigger than life on the screen."

"Any objection from the State of Florida?"

"Yes, we strongly object," said Carmichael, rising. "This hearing started out as a limited inquiry into whether or not Sashi Burgette is still alive. Mr. Swyteck has kept pushing and pushing to the point that we are now essentially retrying the case. This notebook was made available to the defense before Mr. Reeves' trial but his lawyer never offered it into evidence."

"Mr. Graner would have offered it," said Jack, "had the prosecution lived up to its obligations and disclosed the fact that Debra and Gavin Burgette were in rehoming negotiations with a human trafficker before Sashi disappeared."

"That's a cheap shot," said the prosecutor. "Mr. Swyteck knows that at the time of those communications, neither Debra nor Gavin Burgette knew that Carlos Mendoza was a criminal."

"I wasn't taking a shot at the Burgette family, Your Honor. Before the trial began, the police had Mr. Mendoza in custody and they had in their possession the disposable cell phone that he'd used to call the Burgettes. All I'm saying is that the police and prosecutor should have connected the dots, realized that Carlos Mendoza might have had a connection to the disappearance of Sashi Burgette, and complied with their disclosure obligations under the United States Constitution and the Supreme Court's decision in *Brady v. Maryland*."

"Save the legal arguments for your briefs," the judge said. "The objection is overruled. But I'm not giving you carte blanche, Mr. Swyteck. For the tenth time: this is not a retrial."

"I understand, Judge." Jack turned to the witness and handed him the notebook, which was opened to the appropriate page. "You've seen this photograph before, haven't you?"

"Nope. Never."

"You recognize the face in that photograph as Sashi Burgette, don't you?"

He looked again. "Yeah. Very pretty girl. A shame what happened to her."

The judge leaned over again. "Just answer the questions, Mr. Mendoza."

"Yes, Judge."

Jack retrieved the notebook and handed him another exhibit. "Mr. Mendoza, yesterday you testified that your first communication with Debra Burgette was through a message board called Way Stations of Love. Do you recognize this exhibit as a printout of those online communications?"

He checked it and nodded once. "Yes."

"What's the date of your first message-board communication?"

He checked again. "August tenth."

Jack stepped away, holding the printout in one hand and the notebook in the other. "So it's your testimony that the naked selfies that Sashi Burgette sent to Mikhail Volkov on August third were completely unrelated to the communications you initiated with Debra Burgette on August tenth."

He thought for a moment, seeming to make sure he wasn't stepping into a trap. "Yeah. That's what I'm telling you."

"The one had nothing to do with the other?"

"That's right."

"A total coincidence, you say?"

"Objection. Asked and answered for the third time."

"Sustained. Point taken, Mr. Swyteck. Move on."

Jack went to the table and put the exhibits aside. Then he returned to his place before the witness. "Mr. Mendoza, you testified yesterday that you spoke to both Debra and Gavin Burgette about rehoming their daughter Sashi. Is that right?"

"Yes."

"You found a couple in Tampa who were interested in taking Sashi. Correct?"

"That's right."

"And at some point they changed their mind; that Tampa couple were no longer interested in Sashi. Do I have that right?"

"Yeah. Uh-huh."

"You believed that the Burgettes were serious about rehoming Sashi."

"Right."

"You thought you had a deal with them, correct?"

"More or less."

"You were angry when the Burgettes backed out."

The prosecutor was on her feet again. "Objection. That wasn't the testimony of the witness. The Burgettes did not back out. Mr. Mendoza testified that he called off the deal."

"Sustained."

Jack moved on. "You're not in the business of rehoming adopted children, are you, sir?"

"No. This was my first attempt."

"The only business you were in was the trafficking of minors in the sex trade. Isn't that right?"

"I never did that, except that one time. The one I was convicted for. I'm sorry I did it, and I'm paying my debt to society now."

Jack almost expected Maddie Vargas to stand up in the gallery and applaud her client's speech. "When the rehoming deal with the Burgettes fell apart, you still wanted Sashi, didn't you."

"I wouldn't say that."

"You created the power of attorney that was needed to rehome Sashi. That was your testimony yesterday, right?"

"Yes."

"You drafted it so that the power of attorney was granted to you, correct?"

The witness hesitated.

"I have a copy of yesterday's transcript if you need it," said Jack, and it did the trick.

"Yeah," said Mendoza. "I made it out to me."

"You did it that way because you never intended to rehome Sashi with anyone in Tampa."

"That's not right."

"You intended to keep Sashi, didn't you, Mr. Mendoza?"

"No. The deal fell apart. End of story."

"But you can't remember the name of the couple in Tampa."

"No, I forgot it."

"Let's be honest, Mr. Mendoza. That couple never existed. Did they, sir?"

"Objection."

"Overruled."

"That's completely false," said Mendoza.

Jack took a step closer to the witness—as close as he could get without the judge telling him to back away. "Now, Mr. Mendoza, were you aware that Dylan Reeves had been watching Sashi Burgette for several days before she disappeared?"

"Objection, Your Honor. Once again, that evidence is not in the record."

Judge Frederick scratched his head. "Ms. Carmichael, I've been at this since nine o'clock this morning, and even with my brain half fried, I would know enough not to object to that question if I were the prosecutor."

She took the hint: Jack's point did seem helpful to the prosecution. "I'll withdraw the objection."

Mendoza answered. "Uh, no, I didn't know that. But I'm not surprised."

"You're not surprised because you *asked him* to watch Sashi, didn't you?"

"No."

"So this is huge coincidence number two—is that it?"

"Objection. Vague."

"I'll clarify," said Jack. "Mr. Mendoza, your testimony is that you—a sex trafficker—tried to convince the Burgettes to rehome their daughter. You drafted a power of attorney granting all parental authority to yourself. And it was a complete coincidence that Sashi was simultaneously being watched by Dylan Reeves. Do I have that right?"

"Stranger things have happened."

"Yes, stranger things *did* happen, didn't they, Mr. Mendoza? Isn't it a fact that you thought Sashi Burgette would be a perfect fit for your sex-trafficking business?"

"I didn't give it any thought."

"That's why you tried to convince the Burgettes to rehome her, isn't it?"

"No."

"That's why you gave yourself power of attorney."

"No again."

"You were angry when the rehoming deal fell apart."

"I—not really."

"You spent six minutes on the telephone with Mr. Burgette trying to persuade him to reconsider."

"No, he offered to pay me a hundred grand to take her."

"Really? And was that going to be Visa, MasterCard, or American Express?"

"Objection."

"Sustained."

Jack stayed with it, sensing that Mendoza was beginning to boil. "When the rehoming deal fell apart and you couldn't put Humpty Dumpty back together again, you came up with a new plan."

"I have no idea what you're talking about."

"You asked Dylan Reeves to bring Sashi to you."

"I didn't ask him to do anything."

"Dylan Reeves failed you, and that's when you took matters into your own hands."

Mendoza narrowed his eyes, and Jack could see that he was getting under his skin. He hoped the judge could, too.

"I still don't know what you're talking about."

Jack took another step closer. "You took Sashi Burgette."

"That's a lie," he said, his voice rising.

"You took her, and within hours, if not minutes, you found out why the Burgettes considered rehoming her. Sashi Burgette was way more than you could handle."

"Not true."

"You bit off more than you could chew. You had to get rid of her, and you killed her."

"No, sir."

"You killed her, and only you know where her body is."

"Objection, Your Honor. Mr. Swyteck has crafted a very interesting story, but there's not a single fact to back it up."

The judge hesitated. He clearly had his doubts about Mendoza, and he knew Mendoza was a sex trafficker and a liar. Jack seemed to have his judicial mind engaged. But the prosecutor was right.

"Sustained. Mr. Swyteck, I need to reel you in here."

"My apologies, Your Honor."

"No need to apologize. But we do need to move this along. If we finish on schedule, the prisoner can be transferred back to FSP tonight."

"Just one more question," said Jack, as he turned to face the witness. "Mr. Mendoza, Mikhail Volkov knows what you did to Sashi Burgette, doesn't he?"

"You'll have to ask Mr. Volkov what he knows."

It was the answer Jack wanted. "You're right," he said, and then his gaze drifted toward Judge Frederick. "You're absolutely right. We need to ask Mr. Volkov. No further questions, Your Honor—for *this* witness."

Jack returned to his seat at the table beside Hannah. She said nothing, but she seemed to know as well as Jack did that he hadn't hit the home run they needed. Jack's hope was that the judge would bite at his suggestion and let him call one more witness.

"Any redirect examination?" asked the judge.

"No, Your Honor," said the prosecutor.

"Then that concludes this evidentiary hearing."

Jack popped to his feet. Subtlety was not the solution. "Judge, Mr. Mendoza testified at some length about a man named Mikhail Volkov. The petitioner would request the opportunity to call—"

"Judge, really?" said the prosecutor, interrupting. "When is this going to end?"

"It's going to end *now*," said the judge, turning toward the defense team. "Mr. Swyteck. Ms. Goldsmith. You've done admirable work, and your commitment to your client has been nothing short of exceptional."

Oh, God, thought jack. *Compliments to the defense lawyers: the judicial kiss of death.*

"This court has reviewed the extensive record in this case. The court has allowed post-trial discovery and conducted a post-trial evidentiary hearing that went well beyond the scope of relief ordered by the court of appeals. The petitioner has had the opportunity to present and cross-examine new witnesses. I have weighed the credibility of witnesses, considered the substance of their testimony, and reviewed hundreds of pages of new exhibits. Based on all of this, it is the court's determination that Mr. Reeves was afforded a fair trial. The state of Florida probably could have been more diligent in complying with its pretrial disclosure obligations to the defense, particularly with respect to communications between the Burgette family and Carlos Mendoza. However, any and all errors alleged by the petitioner had no impact on the verdict of guilty or the sentence of death by lethal injection. Any such errors were what the law regards as 'harmless error.'

"The petition for writ of habeas corpus is therefore denied.

The stay of execution is lifted. The court's written order shall be lodged with the clerk immediately. I will have a memorandum of decision for you in the morning. The witness is dismissed and is to be remanded to custody. We are adjourned."

The crack of the gavel hit Jack like ice water.

"All rise!"

"Harmless error?" Hannah whispered. "Is he serious?"

It was a bitter pill for a condemned man and his lawyers to swallow, the judicial equivalent of *"You're absolutely right, but it doesn't make a dime's worth of difference."*

As the judge stepped down from the bench, Jack glanced at the prosecutor, who seemed more than pleased, and then at Carlos Mendoza's attorney, who was downright smug.

"It isn't over," he said in a voice barely loud enough for Hannah to hear. "Not yet."

CHAPTER 51

The entire team convened around the kitchen table. Jack had Dylan Reeves on the speakerphone. Hannah, Eve, and Brian listened as Jack delivered the news. The mood was somber, but their client was taking it better than expected.

"What now?" asked Reeves.

"Judge Frederick slammed us by lifting the stay of execution," said Jack. "He should have at least left it in effect until we took our appeal. So first thing tomorrow morning we file an emergency motion with the court of appeals in Atlanta. If we get it, then the court can schedule oral argument before a panel of three judges, who will give full consideration to all of the arguments that Judge Frederick rejected."

"But what if we don't get a stay?"

"We take a shot at the U.S. Supreme Court."

"What if that doesn't work?"

A volley of uneasy glances worked their way around the table. "Then you'll want to make your preparations," said Jack. "Phone calls. Letters. Time with clergy. Any personal items you may want someone special to have."

"It's time to say my goodbyes. That's what you mean?"

Jack hesitated. It wasn't the first time he'd had this conversation with a client, but having to tell people how much time they had left on this planet was one reason he'd decided against med school. "Yes."

Reeves sighed so deeply that it crackled over the speaker. "When will we know?"

"Tomorrow's Friday, so . . . no later than Monday, I would expect. But it could be anytime before your execution date. I can't say exactly."

"So this is probably my last weekend, huh?"

Probably. "We'll know more by Monday," said Jack.

"Is there anything you need from me?"

"No. Now it's up to your lawyers to convince the court of appeals."

"Okay, then. It's in your hands."

"It is."

"You'll let me know as soon as you hear?"

"Of course."

All eyes were on the speakerphone, which was silent. Jack would let his client decide when it was time to end this call.

"All right," said Reeves. "I'm gonna hang up now. But . . . thank you. Okay? That's all."

There was a clunk before the click on the line, the sound of an unsteady hand returning the phone to its cradle. The dial tone hummed, and Jack silenced it with a press of a button.

"You're welcome," said Jack.

Hannah pushed away from the table. "I'll start on the emergency motion."

"Brian and I will get going on the brief," said Eve.

"What are you gonna do, Jack?" asked Hannah.

Jack rose slowly, sliding his hands into his pants pockets. "I want to pay one last visit to Debra Burgette."

CHAPTER 52

Jack reached Debra on her cell phone as she was driving back from Aquinnah's place. Alexander had stayed with his sister for the hearing, and Debra didn't want to talk on the cell while he was in her backseat. She was passing downtown on her way to Cocoplum, and she offered to stop by the Freedom Institute.

"I have a little something for you," she said.

Her car pulled into the driveway just after eight. Jack greeted her at the door. Alexander was with her. "Introduce yourself to Mr. Swyteck," she told him.

He did, and they shook hands. "I've heard a lot of good things about you, Alexander."

"I've heard good things about you, too," he said.

Jack glanced appreciatively at his mother, but the moment still felt awkward, if not bizarre, on the heels of Jack's conversation with the man convicted of murdering her daughter.

"May I use your restroom?" she asked.

Jack showed her the way, which left him alone in the reception area with the younger brother that Sashi had led from a war zone in Chechnya to an orphanage in Moscow, only to leave him behind in Coral Gables. *Beyond bizarre.*

"Wow!" said Alexander. "That is so cool!"

He was staring at the motorcycle. "It belonged to my old boss," said Jack.

"Why do you park it here in front of the stairs? Do you ride it up to the second floor?"

"No, no," said Jack, smiling. "No one goes up there anymore."

"Why not?"

It had been closed off ever since the termite inspector came crashing through the ceiling and landed in the dining room. Jack gave a simpler explanation. "It's just really old up there. Do you want to sit on the bike?"

"Seriously?"

Jack smiled. "Come on."

They walked over, and Alexander climbed into the leather saddle. He could barely reach over the gas tank and grab the throttle, but that didn't seem to dampen the thrill.

"How fast does this thing go?"

"Honestly, I don't know. No one has ridden it in a while. This is what you'd call a classic. It's a BSA, made in England around 1950."

"I like it. How much you want for it?"

Neil had thought about selling it many times, whenever money was tight, but he'd always managed to hang on to it. "Sorry, not for sale."

Debra returned, and Jack suggested that Alexander wait in the back room and watch TV while he and Debra talked.

"Mom doesn't let me watch TV or play video games on school nights. She says I do enough of that at my dad's house."

"Moms are usually right," said Jack.

"Yeah. That's pretty much all I do when I'm there. He's got a girlfriend."

That struck Jack as odd, given all of Gavin's legal and other maneuvering to get primary custody.

"We'll make an exception tonight," said Debra.

Jack took him to the TV room, found something he liked, and then led Debra back to Neil's old office. Jack went to the sitting area rather than his desk, and they sat across from each other at the chessboard on the coffee table.

Debra handed him an envelope, and for a moment Jack thought it might contain a check, until he opened it. Inside was a wallet-sized photograph of a seventeen-year-old Sashi.

"I didn't want your last impression of her to be those photographs you saw in the notebook," said Debra. "This is how I remember her."

Jack studied it. She had a pleasant expression, even if she wasn't smiling. *I wonder if she ever smiled?*

"Thank you," said Jack. "I hate to dwell on the notebook, but I did want to talk about one of the men in there. The name that came out in court tonight."

"Mikhail Volkov?"

"Yes. He hasn't admitted it, and unless we find the disposable phone that was used to make those phone calls to you on Sashi's birthday we can't ever prove it. But I believe he's our guy. I'm sorry to have to tell you that, because you came to me hoping that it was Sashi, and that she was still alive. But I feel like I have to tell you this. It wasn't Sashi. I do believe it was Volkov."

If Dylan Reeves had taken his news well, Jack sensed that Debra was on the other end of the spectrum. But she was keeping it inside.

"Why are you so sure?" she asked.

"For one, it makes geographic sense: the cell tower analysis indicated that the last call you received was placed from Little Moscow."

"The FBI told the state attorney it came from my house."

"They said it was possible it came from your neighborhood. I obviously think that's a bogus theory—that you made the call to yourself."

"Which is my point. Does anybody *really* know where the call came from? It all seems like technical mumbo jumbo and guess-work to me."

"It's not just the cell towers," said Jack. Volkov also had motive to strike back at you. Sashi toyed with him. She led him on. It would have been one thing if he'd simply been burned by a teen-ager. But look at how this turned out for him. He's been muti-lated. In his mind, that never would have happened if it weren't for Sashi."

"So he takes it out on me? Calls me on my daughter's birth-day?"

"Who else is he going to take it out on? He thought he was on his way to a rendezvous with a teenage girl. It all blew up when he dialed the cell number Sashi gave him and you answered."

"That might explain why he called me on her birthday. But why did he call me during the hearing? And why has he been fol-lowing me and Alexander?"

"Following you? Are you talking about the man who was watching you and Alexander outside that deli in Little Moscow—the one you told me about the last time you were here?"

"Yes."

"You didn't say that was Volkov. You said it was just a random person who saw your picture in a Russian-language newspaper and was sneering at you for rehoming Sashi."

"That's what I thought initially. Even though I got a pretty good look at him outside the deli, it wasn't until last night that I made the connection in my mind between the man at the deli and those men Sashi was contacting on the Internet. So I double-checked the notebook. I was ninety-nine percent sure I had a match. And after this evening's hearing, when you put up those pictures on the screen in the courtroom, I was absolutely certain."

"Debra, I made a point of letting you know that the Institute has limited time and even more limited resources. We can't in-vestigate every lead. But if you had told me that you were being watched by one of those strangers that Sashi had contacted on the Internet, I would have been all over it."

"But I didn't make that connection till last night."

"Then you should have called me last night."

She lowered her eyes. "I'm sorry. You're right. But it's not like

I withheld information that would have helped your client. As you said, if I was being harassed by someone from Little Moscow, it means Sashi probably didn't make those phone calls to me. And if Sashi wasn't making those phone calls . . ." She still couldn't say it, and Jack didn't fill in the blank for her. He was trying to understand her reluctance to follow up on Mikhail Volkov. To Jack, Volkov was a solid lead to the truth; to Debra, he was a clear path to a conclusion she couldn't accept.

"You need to report this to the police," Jack said. "It would be difficult to convict Volkov on stalking charges based solely on anonymous calls from a prepaid cell that can't be linked to him with any certainty. But if you can identify him as the man who was watching you and Alexander, the state attorney could make a case against him."

"Calling the police is one option," she said.

"There's no better option when you're dealing with a stalker," said Jack.

"But . . . I think maybe he wants to tell me something."

"What?"

"You're going to think I'm crazy, just like everyone else does. But after all this courtroom drama, we still don't know what happened to Sashi. I think Volkov is afraid to say what he knows after the horrible things that Carlos Mendoza did to him. I think he's trying to 'tell me' without telling me that Sashi is still alive."

Jack considered it, but only for an instant. Debra might never let go. "If you're sure that the man watching you and your son was Mikhail Volkov, my strong advice is that you report it to the police."

She seemed to be waiting for him to say more—perhaps a validation of her theory that Sashi could still be alive. It didn't come. "Well, I need to get Alexander home and to bed," she said, rising.

Jack walked her out of the office, and she stopped him in the hallway before reaching Alexander. "I'm going to either find Sashi, or find out what happened to her. You know that, right?"

Families didn't always find answers, but Jack saw no point in saying it again. "I hope you do," he said. "But please be careful. And promise me that you will tell the police about Mikhail Volkov."

She didn't answer as quickly as Jack would have liked. "I will," she said, and Jack walked with her as she started down the hall toward her son.

CHAPTER 53

A ndie took Uber to Abuela's town house, and Jack met her there. They wanted his grandmother to be the first to know that Baby Swyteck was no Junior, and her name was Riley. Jack had to get back to the Freedom Institute, so they blocked out half an hour, which was barely long enough for Abuela to stop shedding tears of joy.

"*La niña preciosa!*" she said as she caressed Andie's belly.

"Precious little girl," said Andie, translating for Jack.

"I know what it means," he said.

Abuela fired back in Spanish: "*Yes, Siri told him.*"

It was a running joke that Andie's Spanish was better than Jack's, but it had nearly sent Abuela into cardiac arrest to catch him pulling out his iPhone at last year's *Noche Buena* celebration to ask, "*Siri, how do you say 'pig roast' in Spanish?*" His Anglo father and stepmother spoke only English in the home he grew up in. It took three decades after his mother's death for Abuela to find a way to leave Cuba for Miami, and she'd made it her sole mission in life to give her gringo grandson a crash course in the Spanish language and all things Cuban. Jack's hope was that the gift of a granddaughter might finally bump his grade up from a C minus.

Jack got a call from Hannah on his cell, and he stepped out the back door to take it on the patio, leaving Andie and Abuela alone at the kitchen table.

"Rah-lee," she said. "*Que linda.*"

"*Ry-ley*," said Andie. They'd been over this five times. It hadn't occurred to her how hard it would be for Abuela to pronounce it. "Like the old Mexican song," she said, then sang it: "*Ay, ay, ay, ay, canto y no llores.*"

"Ah! *Ry-lee!*"

They smiled and shared a little laugh, but eventually Andie steered the conversation to a more serious matter. Her Spanish wasn't perfect, and she wanted no misunderstanding in her word choice, so she reverted to English.

"I visited St. Hugh's Cemetery this week," she said.

Abuela knew exactly what she was saying. "I go every week."

They hadn't told her about Andie's preeclampsia, or how the fact that Jack's mother had developed the same condition made them feel. Andie wasn't exactly sure why she'd brought it up. She just wanted to know more than Jack seemed willing to tell her. Abuela didn't need much prodding.

"I in Bejucál when Ana writes me," she said, using the easier present tense, as she often did when speaking English. "The letter say, '*Abuela Querida . . .*'"

Dear Grandmother. The way her face was beaming made Andie smile.

"I press it to my heart. I say, *Gracias a Dios! Gracias a La Milagrosa!*"

Andie had to think about those last few words for a moment, but she was pretty sure that they translated to the Miraculous One. "Who is *La Milagrosa?*"

"Young woman. It makes many years now—nineteen-oh-one. She dies giving birth to a baby. Baby die too."

"How sad."

"*Sí.* Now she lies—lays?"

Andie couldn't keep it straight either. "She's buried?"

"*Sí.* In *Habana, el cementerio de Colón.* With baby at her feet," she said, pointing at her own. "Many years pass. They open the . . ."

"Tomb?"

"Tomb. *Sí*. The baby is . . ."

Andie watched as she demonstrated. For a moment, the old woman was a young mother with her baby cradled in her arms, rocking gently back and forth.

Andie wasn't one to buy into miracles along the line of the Jesus Nebula or the Virgin's apparition on a piece of burnt toast, but Abuela's story gave her chills, if only for the way she told it.

"Today still, women in Cuba who pray for baby go to La Milagrosa. They give flowers. *I* go there. *I* pray. *I* give flowers. Ana Maria have baby," she said, smiling, but the smile turned sad.

Andie knew how the story ended, and she didn't want Abuela to feel that she had to finish if she didn't want to.

"Now I have Jack," said Abuela.

"*We* have Jack," said Andie.

The smile returned. Abuela rose, went to Andie, and embraced her. "And we have Riley," she whispered.

Jack was in the moonlight on Abuela's patio, seated in a white wooden rocking chair, his phone pressed to his ear.

The call had come from Gavin Burgette. His exact whereabouts on the day of Sashi's disappearance had been an issue ever since Jack, on cross-examination, had raised the specter that Gavin was away from home on something other than a "business trip." That was the reason for this call.

"Nicole says that your partner has been asking for travel records to document my business trip," said Gavin.

"Yeah. I asked Hannah to handle it."

"Well, she's handing it, all right. She's being a fucking pest."

Jack smiled to himself. *You go, Hannah.* "When can we expect to see the records?" asked Jack.

"Never."

"It's a simple request," said Jack. "A little documentation would put an end to the question of whether you were on a business trip, whether you were meeting Carlos Mendoza to rehome Sashi, or whether you were somewhere else."

"The answer is somewhere else."

Jack rose from the chair, surprised by the answer. "Where?"

Gavin breathed out, almost groaning over the line. "I was with another woman, okay? You happy now?"

Jack wasn't shocked. "Should I be?"

"I would think so," he said, more than a little sarcastic. "You've been on a mission to destroy what's left of this family. In fact, why don't you conference in Debra right now? Take away what little self-esteem she's got. Then bring in Aquinnah and Alexander— just to make sure they hate their old man. Go ahead, Swyteck. Let's make sure that every corner of the globe is covered in your scorched-earth crusade against the Burgette family."

"This isn't personal, Gavin. I'm just trying to get at the truth."

"And now you have it."

"I don't hear a name."

"You're not getting a name. I'm not dragging her into this. This has gone far enough. I wasn't out of town rehoming Sashi. So tell Hannah the eager beaver to back off and stop asking Nicole for documentation of my business trip. It's not going to help your client. Just *drop it*."

The call ended, and if it hadn't been a cell, Jack was certain that he would have heard the sound of Gavin slamming down the phone in his ear.

Jack tucked his iPhone into his pocket and stood on the patio for a moment, his gaze drifting toward the low-hanging moon. Then he turned toward the back door. Through the glass, he saw Andie and his grandmother in the kitchen, locked in a tight embrace. He opened the door and went inside.

"What's going on?" he asked.

They didn't answer. Andie's eyes were closed, he noticed, and a tear was running down her cheek.

"Hey," said Jack, trying to get their attention. "What's the big idea? You did a group hug without me?"

Andie didn't seem to take his meaning at first, but as their embace ended, Abuela pointed to her pregnant belly, and all three smiled at the suggestion that the "group" included Riley. Abuela crossed the kitchen, kissed her grandson on the cheek, then gave him the knowing eye.

"Get use to it," she said.

CHAPTER 54

On Friday morning, Debra dropped off Alexander at Grove Academy, stopped for coffee at a drive-thru, and then headed home. She was waiting at the red light near Ingraham Park, thinking of Sashi, when a radio commercial grabbed her attention. It was for eSpark.com, an online dating service.

The dating game hadn't been her focus since the divorce. Time was only part of the problem; finding someone worth the effort was an even bigger challenge. Online services had their appeal, but the Sashi experience had made her gun-shy about meeting people through the Internet. To be sure, it hadn't been Sashi's original intent to show her mother just how dangerous the Internet could be. A month before Sashi had started trolling the dark side of the World Wide Web, she'd created an eSpark account in Debra's name. When the first "spark" reached out to Debra, it didn't go well at all between mother and daughter.

Sashi! Did you give my cell-phone number to this man?"

They were standing on opposite sides of the kitchen counter, and Debra was showing her the "Recent Call" displayed on her cell. It was a 954 area code.

"Oh, that's Tom."

"Yes, I know his name is Tom. He told me. And he seems to think we've been talking to each other on eSpark for the past two weeks."

"Well, you have. Kind of. I was for you."

Debra gasped. *"What?"*

He's a nice guy, Mom. An accountant in Fort Lauderdale. And he's cute. Look at his picture," she said as she pulled up the website on her cell.

"I don't want to see his picture! Sashi, I'm a married woman!"

"A married woman who hasn't been happy for a long time."

"That's not true."

"It's so true. I know it. I hear you and Dad arguing all the time."

"Yes. Usually about you."

"Oh, so this is the thanks I get? Please, just *talk* to Tom. He's perfect."

"I'm not going to talk to him!"

"Come on. I won't tell Dad. It'll be our secret."

"Sashi, just because you and your father aren't getting along doesn't mean I need to start looking for a new husband."

"You should be."

"How dare you say that."

"How dare you pretend you haven't thought about it."

"That's it! No Internet for a week."

"Don't make me laugh."

"Now it's two weeks."

"You are such an ungrateful bitch! I try to do something nice for you and—"

"Something *nice*? Put aside the fact that I love your father. For all we know, you've hooked up with some online pervert."

Sashi glared, her voice taking on a cold, threatening edge. "You want to see an Internet pervert, Mom? Okay. Ask and you shall receive. I'll show you an Internet pervert."

The traffic light changed to green, but Debra didn't notice. She was trapped for another moment in her memory of that tipping point in her life with Sashi. The car behind her honked, which startled her. She proceeded through the intersection, followed the traffic circle into Cocoplum, and continued past the guardhouse toward her tree-lined street.

A nondescript white sedan was waiting at the curb in front of her house. Debra parked in her driveway, and as she climbed out of her car, both the driver and the passenger got out of the waiting vehicle. Debra walked to the front step and waited as the middle-aged man and woman approached. They introduced themselves as Tony Jacobs and Melissa Gomez, and they flashed their credentials.

"We're with the Department of Children and Family Services," said Jacobs.

Debra's heart sank, and she couldn't help sounding defensive. "What do you want?"

"May we come inside?"

"No."

"It will just be a minute."

"Then let's do it right here. It's a beautiful morning, isn't it?"

Jacobs checked out the blue sky, his eyes hidden behind dark sunglasses, his intentions less well hidden behind a plastic smile. "Yes. A Miami Chamber of Commerce day, I'd say."

Debra tried to be more pleasant. "I don't mean to be rude, but if I don't get started on my to-do list soon, I'll never get through it. What is that I can help you with?"

"Well, a couple of things," said Jacobs. "We understand that you objected to the department's request to interview your son, Alexander."

"I objected to them interviewing him at school without his parents present."

"Understood," said Jacobs. "We have completed our interviews of Alexander's teachers at Grove Academy," he said, and on cue his colleague handed him a clipboard with a typed report. It looked like interview notes. "One teacher we interviewed—I can't give you a name—said the following: 'One day during the lunch break, Alexander was sitting by himself. He appeared sad. I asked him what was wrong and he said that his mother had threatened to send him back to Russia.'"

"That's not true!"

Jacobs handed the clipboard back to his colleague. "Are you saying your son is a liar?"

"No. That teacher must be mistaken about what he or she thinks Alexander said. I never threatened to send Alexander anywhere."

"But you admitted in court and under oath that you considered rehoming his older sister Sashi?"

"To say I 'considered' it is an overstatement. I was never serious about it."

"You also testified in court and under oath that you threatened to send Alexander's sister back to Russia."

Debra closed her eyes slowly, then opened them. It had been the most painful moment of her testimony. Even the prosecutor had been delicate in questioning her about her regrettable loss of cool right before Sashi's disappearance. And now it was being used against her in the worst way.

"I was never going to *do* it," said Debra. "It was said only out of anger."

"Has anyone ever told you that you have a problem with your anger?" asked Jacobs.

"No one has ever said anything except that I love my children and that I'm a good mother."

The social workers exchanged dubious glances. Then Jacobs continued, handing her a one-page typewritten document. It looked different from the interview notes he'd read to her earlier.

"Ms. Burgette, here is what we propose," said Jacobs.

Debra gave it a quick look. "What is this?"

"It's a safety plan."

"I don't understand."

"The plan would be in effect during the period of time that it takes DCFS to investigate whether Alexander should continue living with his mother."

"His—you mean *me*?"

"Yes. You're his mother."

"An investigation into *what*?"

"I'm afraid I'm not authorized to tell you that."

"That's ridiculous."

"That's the law," said Jacobs.

Debra struggled to find words, but none would come.

Jacobs continued in a businesslike tone. "Under the plan, Alexander would stay with someone other than his mother while the department completes its investigation."

"*What?* No, I'm not going to agree to that."

"That's your right," Jacobs said. "I must tell you, however, that if you do not agree to a safety plan, DCFS may take protective custody of your child for forty-eight hours without asking your permission. It would then be up to a court to approve the safety plan."

"No. Forget it. I'm not agreeing to this. I want to talk to a lawyer."

"You certainly have that right. But it is my strong suggestion that you also create a list of people who could take care of Alexander during the period of the DCFS investigation. Both the department and the court will give due consideration to your recommendations. If you don't create a list, then it's purely up to us to find appropriate placement."

Debra felt as if the ground were starting to shake. "I want you to go. Both of you. *Now*."

"There's no need for that tone," said Jacobs.

"Get off my property, and stay away from my son."

She hurried up the steps, unlocked the door as quickly as possible, and ran inside. She didn't mean to slam the door so hard that the window rattled.

It just happened.

CHAPTER 55

t was just after nine a.m., and if Jack read Hannah's draft of the motion for stay of execution one more time, his head would explode.

"Looks good," he told her. "File it."

Hannah had worked all night. Jack had been revising her draft since sunrise. For better or worse, it was ready to be filed electronically with the court of appeals in Atlanta. There was no way to know which of the eleven federal appellate judges would review it. It was naive to think that it didn't matter, but Jack knew better than to dwell on the "luck of the draw" and other things that he couldn't control. Hannah was another story. She was seated behind her desk, fingers crossed on her left hand, her right index finger poised over the mouse, just a click away from hitting the SEND button.

"Please, please, please let it go to Judge Clark."

The Honorable Thomas A. Clark was a true southern gentleman of a judge whom Jack remembered well from his early days at the Freedom Institute. Back then, Florida and Georgia were executing more death-row inmates than the other forty-eight states combined—Texas included. Jack would regularly file eleventh-hour requests for stays of execution with the federal circuit in Atlanta, most of which were speedily, and quite correctly, denied. But there was always a glimmer of hope if Clark was on the case.

"You know that Judge Clark is deceased, right?"

"Yeah. But he still has more brain power than most of those dimwits."

Jack couldn't argue with the point.

The Friday challenge for the team was not to hang by the phone and check their e-mails every five minutes. "The watched pot never boils," Neil used to say. "The court will rule when the court will rule." Easy enough for the lawyers to say. Try telling that to a client who was pacing his feet raw in death-watch Cell No. 1.

It was mid-afternoon and Jack was at his desk when he got the phone call that he least expected, short of a call from the clerk of the court telling him that their motion for stay of execution had been granted. Debra Burgette was on the line. She told him about her morning conversation with DCFS.

"I told you before," Jack said into the phone, "and now it goes double: you need a lawyer."

"I know. And you said you could refer one."

"I'm happy to do that. Her name is Jenna Collins."

"Thank you," she said, and she repeated it back to him as she wrote it down. "Now I have one more favor to ask."

Jack braced himself, not sure what to expect. "Okay. What?"

"I think it's very important that Ms. Collins meet Alexander as soon as possible, but I don't want to drag him into a lawyer's office. This is already affecting him at school. Do you think you and Ms. Collins could come by the house at six?"

"I'll check with Jenna. But, Debra, I can only refer you to an attorney. Dylan Reeves' case is still active. I can't represent you."

"I understand. I'm not asking you to come to the meeting as my lawyer. But here's the thing. The social workers who ambushed me this morning told me that they interviewed Alexander's teachers. Supposedly, Alexander said some things to one of those teachers that DCFS is now using against me. I'm going to ask Alexander about it when I pick him up at school today, but I'm not sure he'll tell me everything. He seemed really comfortable with you last night when you met him. Could you just come by and talk with him—see what he'll tell you?"

"Debra, I don't know . . ."

"Please, Jack. I want Alexander to talk with someone one-on-one, without Mommy being there, before a DCFS social worker corners him in a room and grills him. I trust you. I trust you with my son."

Jack could have said no, but her request seemed sincere. And something inside him—something that had been swirling in his mind since their talk last night—made him want to follow up with Alexander.

"All right," said Jack. "I'll confirm with Jenna. If you don't hear otherwise from me, we'll be there at six."

"Thank you, Jack. I am so indebted to you."

"You're really not." They said goodbye, and Jack hung up.

Really not.

CHAPTER 56

Jack and Jenna Collins drove separately to Cocoplum, but they reached Debra's house at the same time, a minute or two before six. They'd known each other since law school, and Jenna had since built a reputation as a top-notch specialist in family law who worked at a reasonable price. The sight of Debra's Mercedes-Benz in the driveway, however, might have impacted her new lawyer's definition of "reasonable."

Jack could only imagine what was going through Jenna's mind when the Porsche 911 pulled up.

Jack and Jenna were standing on the front porch, and Debra opened the door, as her ex-husband stepped out of his new toy.

"You didn't tell me that Gavin was going to be here," Jack said.

"He's early. This is Gavin's weekend to have Alexander. Technically he can pick him up at six, but usually he works till at least eight. I swear, it's like he and Nicole have a sixth sense. The one time I need him to be late, he shows up early. Come inside. I'll handle this."

Jack quickly introduced Debra to her new lawyer, with everyone understanding that there was more to come once Debra got rid of her ex. Jack and Jenna showed themselves to the couch in the living room. Debra stayed behind in the foyer, standing at the half-open door. Jack could see and hear her from where he was sitting, but he couldn't see Gavin, who didn't get past the threshold.

"You're early," said Debra.

"Is Alexander ready?"

"No, actually. I wasn't expecting you at six."

"The visitation order says pickup is at six. It's six. I'm here. He needs to be ready."

She glanced in Jack's direction, then back at Gavin. "It's really not convenient right now. Maybe Alexander could stay a couple extra hours at your place on Sunday night if you come back around eight?"

"I can't. I already went online and bought tickets to that new Bradley Cooper movie. It starts at seven."

"Alexander can't see that. It's rated R."

"Nicole and I are going. I hired a babysitter to take him to whatever else is playing. Disney or whatever—something appropriate."

"Alexander doesn't want to sit in a movie theater alone, with a babysitter. Why can't he just stay here, and you can pick him up after you and Nicole see your movie?"

"Because it's my weekend to have him. And now you're five minutes into my time. So, if you please, go upstairs and bring him down to me."

Jack heard nothing for a moment. Even from the living room, however, he could tell that Debra was fuming, and he assumed that glares were shooting like lasers in both directions. Finally, Debra turned and walked toward the stairway, leaving the front door open so that Gavin could hear her apology to her guests, her parting shot at her ex.

"Nice guy, isn't he?" she said angrily. "I'm sorry, but we'll have to do this another time."

Debra continued up the stairs. Jack rose, and Jenna did likewise. "I'm sorry," he said softly.

"No worries," said Jenna. "This is what I do."

They heard footsteps overhead—one set, just Debra's, as she walked down the hall toward Alexander's room. Then there was the sound of a bedroom door opening and closing, followed by footsteps, and then another door opening and then closing.

"Alexander?" Debra's voice was loud enough to carry all the way down the stairwell and into the living room. "Alexander, where are you?"

Jack and Jenna looked at each other.

"Is Alexander downstairs?" Debra shouted from the top of the stairs.

"I don't know," Jack answered. "Where should we look?"

Gavin entered through the open door and stepped into the foyer. "I'll check," he said, as he started down the hall.

Debra came down the stairs quickly, her expression showing concern, if not worry. "Alexander?"

Gavin returned to the living room, and the worry had officially kicked in. "He's not in the kitchen, game room, or the guest room."

"See if his bicycle's in the garage," said Jack.

"Does he have a bike?" asked Gavin.

"*Yes*," said Debra. "It's blue. I'll check the backyard."

Jack followed her through into the kitchen and out the French doors to the patio. Debra broke to the left side of the swimming pool. Jack and Jenna went to the right, around the stone fire pit, the swing set, and a basketball hoop.

"Alexander!"

They saw no sign of him. Jack ran around to the side of the house, and Debra went the other way, each calling out Alexander's name loud enough to be heard by the other. Jack checked the bushes and even behind the pool heater and the air-conditioning unit. Nothing. They reconnected at the front porch. Gavin joined them from the garage.

"His bike is still here," said Gavin.

Debra caught her breath. "Oh, my God!"

Jack waited for one of them to say that he or she was going to call the police, but perhaps they were in shock. "Someone needs to dial 911," said Jack.

"I don't have my phone," said Debra. She looked ready to buckle at the knees anyway.

"Okay, I'll do it," said Jack.

"No, I will," said Gavin as he reached for his cell.

Jack focused on Debra. "When did you see him last?"

"About an hour ago," said Debra, her voice shaking. "He went up to his room. I packed for him, but he's such a little grown-up he always checks to make sure I put everything he needs in the bag. I went downstairs and got on the treadmill."

Jack got a visual in his head: boy upstairs alone; mom downstairs on a noisy treadmill.

"Do you wear headphones when you exercise?"

"Yeah," she said, and then she took his point. "Do you think someone came in the house?"

Jack went with a less scary option. "Or Alexander left and you didn't hear him."

"Yes, that could be it," she said. "Maybe he didn't want to go with his dad this weekend."

Gavin covered his phone, clearly having overheard his ex-wife while on the line with 911. "Debra, I swear, if you are fucking around and sent Alexander somewhere to keep him away from me . . ."

"No! I would never do that!"

Gavin didn't seem totally convinced, but he got back on the line with the 911 operator.

"I'll check the neighborhood," said Jenna. "Can someone text me a recent picture of him?"

"I will," said Debra, and she hurried toward the house for her cell phone. They agreed to split up and walk in opposite directions, but Jack let Jenna go first as he grabbed a moment alone with Debra in the driveway. "After we talked, I told Andie that you thought Mikhail Volkov was watching you and Alexander. Did you tell the police like I asked you to?"

Her face went ashen.

Jack tried not to make her feel worse. "Be sure to tell them when they get here," he said.

He stepped away quickly and caught up with Jenna at the end of the driveway, the first two foot soldiers in the search for Alexander.

CHAPTER 57

A nother Friday night. Another missing Burgette child.

"Unbelievable," said Jack.

He was standing on the street outside Debra's house in Cocoplum, bathed in the glow of police beacons that flashed in the growing darkness. Theo was with him; like dozens of other volunteers, he was drawn to the scene by the need to show up and do *something*.

"Fucking unbelievable is right," said Theo.

The front door to the house was wide open. Police radios crackled all around him, as several squad cars were parked on the grassy swale along the sidewalk, along with a green-and-white van from the Miami-Dade Police crime-scene investigation unit. Jack took it as a positive sign that no ambulance or medical examiner's van had yet arrived. Still, he knew a cadaver-sniffing dog when he saw one, and the canine unit was in the neighborhood. Crime-scene investigators crisscrossed the yard, coming and going under the yellow police tape at the front porch. The first media van appeared around seven, too late for the first evening broadcast but in plenty of time for "breaking news at eleven." Jack recognized the reporter. Two summers earlier, Jack's defense of a young mother accused of murdering her two-year-old daughter had garnered major media interest, and Susan Brown had covered the trial. She checked her makeup in the van's side mirror and then called the cameraman over as she approached Jack.

"Hey, Swyteck. Can I get you in a thirty-second spot?"

Jack took a step back. "Both parents are here, Susan. I'm sure they'd welcome help from the media. A personal plea from them would be a better way to motivate the community."

"Good thought. Can you point them out for me?"

Gavin was standing in the driveway, beside his Porsche, along with two MDPD officers. The doors and trunk were open. Jack knew that in any missing-child case, especially one involving divorced parents, search of the parents' vehicles was standard.

"I'll take you to him."

Jack led Susan Brown up the sidewalk and made the introductions. Gavin didn't seem to warm to the idea immediately. "Can I talk to you a second, Swyteck?"

The two men stepped to the other side of the driveway, away from the police and the camera crew. "I don't want to go on television if this isn't real," said Gavin.

"What do you mean, not 'real'?"

"Apparently Debra had a really bad meeting with DCFS this morning."

"I know," said Jack.

"She has a crazy idea in her head that Nicole and I are behind these social workers' push to take Alexander away from her. But she's wrong, and her thinking makes no sense. The department knows that both of us looked into rehoming Sashi. It came out at the hearing. DCFS is going after Debra *and me*."

"So you think Debra is staging Alexander's disappearance to get back at you?"

"I don't know. Look, I told you I was with another woman when Sashi disappeared."

"I didn't pass that on to Debra."

It took a moment, but Gavin seemed to believe him. "Okay. Good. And for what it's worth, that's not who I am."

"What's not?" asked Jack.

"I'm not a cheater."

If it walks like a duck . . .

"Okay, I cheated," he said, shaking his head in confusion. "But I am not a cheater. I hated myself for it. I hated what our family was becoming. I hate what we've *become*. This is so completely fucked up. All I can tell you is that I married Debra Kincaid, woman of my dreams. I divorced Debra Burgette, fucking nut job. Is she playing a game here with Alexander? I honestly can't say. I don't put anything past her anymore, no matter how outrageous it might sound."

Jack paused, not wanting to seem too quick to dismiss his concern.

"Do the TV interview, Gavin."

Their eyes locked. Then Gavin broke away and walked toward the camera, but one of the police officers stopped him.

"Excuse me, Mr. Burgette. We need a cheek swab from you."

"A what?"

"DNA sample. It's standard in an investigation like this. Open your mouth, please."

Gavin glared at Jack—as if to say, "*See what I mean?*"—as he submitted to the swab.

Jack's gaze drifted past him, across the driveway and the yard, all the way to the front porch. Debra was standing in the open doorway, beside a detective. She seemed to be searching in the distance for someone, as well as the streetlamps would allow, and then she spotted Jack. She came quickly down the stairs, and Jack met her halfway across the driveway. She was about to say something, but the blast of brightness from the television lights startled her. They were warming up for Gavin's interview.

The cameraman was ready. The reporter fixed her hair for the fifteenth time and smiled.

"Not so toothy," the cameraman said. "The poor guy's kid is missing. And in five, four—"

"Let's step over here," Jack told her. They walked toward the garage, out of the glow of the camera lights.

"Any news?" asked Jack.

"I can't get hold of Aquinnah," she said, and she sounded more than concerned. "I don't know what's going on. Hopefully, she's out for a run or just has her phone off. The police are headed to her duplex now."

"I'm sure it will be okay," Jack said, but he was nowhere near "sure."

"I'm busy with MDPD. They need all kinds of information about Alexander. Could you go over to Aquinnah's place and see what's going on?"

"Of course. I'll go right now."

She jotted down the address for him on the back of one of his business cards. "Thank you so much, Jack."

"You bet."

"I'll put some other volunteers on the neighborhood search with your friend Jenna."

"I'll text her to let her know," said Jack.

Debra turned and walked quickly back toward the house. Jack rounded up Theo and explained the assignment on the way to his car. His cell phone rang as he opened the door. It was Hannah. For a moment, he'd almost forgotten about the Freedom Institute.

"What's up?" he asked as he slid into the driver's seat.

"We just heard from the court of appeals," she said.

Jack froze, but he knew what she was going to say.

"It's a one-line order signed by Judge Isaacs: 'The petitioner's emergency motion for stay of execution is denied.'"

Jack breathed out, suddenly speechless.

"Jack? You there?"

"Yeah. All I can say is that I was wrong to think it."

"To think what?"

He pulled the door closed and started the engine. "That things couldn't possibly get worse."

CHAPTER 58

D ebra was in her kitchen, seated across the table from MDPD Detective Raul Perez and his younger partner. Perez was an unusual combination of Hispanic good looks and a dry "just the facts" demeanor. There was a reason his colleagues called him "José Viernes."

"We picked up Mikhail Volkov," said Perez.

Debra had heeded Jack's advice and told MDPD about him. "Do you think he did it?"

"He denies it. Says he was at work till five. We're checking that out."

"If that man took my child . . ."

"Let's not limit our focus just yet," said Perez. "Here's where things stand in general. Every neighbor in the area is being interviewed. Every emergency room in the county is on alert. National Center for Missing and Exploited Children is already on board. Alexander's photo went out with height, weight, eyes, and hair information, a description of the clothes he was wearing, his shoes—"

"Oh, I just remembered! He has a birthmark about the size of a quarter behind his left knee."

"Good. We'll add that. Now, let me tell you what the team has found here so far. We've swept the house and checked every door, every window, every point of access. There is no sign of forced entry."

"There are other ways to get in besides breaking in," said Debra.

"Agreed," said Perez. "The door to the cabana bath was locked. French doors from the master bedroom to the balcony, also locked. French doors from the kitchen, the front door, and the utility door to the garage—all *un*locked."

"That makes sense. I had just come in through the front door and was talking to Gavin on the porch when this happened. I went out through the kitchen to look for Alexander. Gavin went to the garage."

"Was the kitchen door locked or unlocked when you went out to the patio?"

"Locked. We're fanatics about locking doors and windows in this house. We've . . . been through this before."

"Right. Did Alexander have a key to the house?"

"Yes. I pack one in his overnight bag whenever he goes away for the weekend."

"And you're sure that his bag is gone?"

"Yes. I've triple-checked the whole house. It's not here."

"And you didn't hear a car pull up, a door open, or anything like that?"

"No, I've told you at least twice now: I do an hour on the treadmill every Monday, Wednesday, and Friday afternoon. I wear headphones. I really can't hear anything."

"Sorry for the repetition, ma'am. Just being thorough. Who else has a key to the house? His father?"

"No, Gavin doesn't—at least not that I know of. My daughter Aquinnah has one."

"Anyone else? A friend? A neighbor?"

"No."

Perez massaged between his eyes, thinking. "So we have three possibilities," said Perez. "One, Alexander left by himself. Two—"

"Excuse me," said Debra. "Alexander didn't run away. He would *never* do that. He's the opposite of his sister Sashi."

"All right. For discussion, let's assume that's not what happened. That means Alexander left with—"

"Sorry to interrupt again," she said. "But he didn't just 'leave.' If he went with someone he knew—someone like Aquinnah—either he or Aquinnah would have told me."

"Got it," said Perez. "So Alexander was *abducted* either by a stranger or by someone he knows. Now, seeing as how the abductor locked the door on the way out, we ask ourselves: Which of those two possibilities seems more likely?"

Debra gave it a moment of consideration. "I don't think it cuts either way. If a child abductor doesn't want to arouse suspicion, why wouldn't he lock the door? Especially if there was a house key in Alexander's bag."

"A fair point. But here's what troubles me: we still don't know where Aquinnah is. And her car is missing from her driveway. We ran a vehicle check for her and issued a statewide BOLO—'be on the lookout.' Nothing has turned up yet, but we're on it."

Debra closed her eyes, then opened them slowly, barely able to say what she was thinking. "If that monster took *both* my children . . ."

"We should be able to verify pretty quickly whether or not Volkov was at work till five. His alibi could check out."

"I don't care if he has an alibi. Volkov is a predator who makes friends with dangerous people. Just because he was at work doesn't mean he's clean. He could have an accomplice."

"Another fair point. And it's normal to fear the worst. But there's a less catastrophic possibility. Ms. Burgette, can you think of any reason Aquinnah might have to take her little brother?"

"Aquinnah? No. That makes no sense."

"Sometimes what seems to make no sense actually makes perfect sense if you take the time to think about it."

Debra's head was starting to hurt. She already had too much to think about. "Okay. I will give it some thought."

Perez flipped the page on his notepad, as if the investigation itself were getting a fresh start. "If you don't mind, I'd like to drill down a little more on Aquinnah and Alexander."

"What do mean by 'drill down'?"

"I want to know more about their relationship."

"They're very close," said Debra. "They've always been."

"I don't want your characterization of it," he said, his voice taking on the dry edge that had earned "José Viernes" his nickname. "I want the facts, ma'am."

"That's fine," said Debra. "I'll tell you whatever you want to know."

CHAPTER 59

Rush hour was technically over, but northbound streets leading out of downtown were jammed through sunset. Jack took every available shortcut, but it was well after dark by the time he and Theo pulled up at Aquinnah's place.

"Next time, *I* drive," said Theo as they climbed out of the car.

The scene was eerily like the one they'd left at Cocoplum. Squad cars lined the curb, beacons flashing. Police tape marked off one of the front doors—the entrance to Aquinnah's half of the duplex. Police radios crackled in the night as uniformed officers secured the perimeter. Two crime-scene investigation vans, one from MDPD and one from the FBI, were parked in the driveway. Jack wasn't surprised that the Bureau had gotten involved, but he did a double take when he saw the agent standing beside the van—the woman with the opened blue windbreaker and the pregnant belly. Andie spotted him a second later and walked over.

Andie had worked child-abduction and serial-killer investigations in Seattle before transferring to Miami to do undercover assignments, but Jack was still a bit taken aback to see her. "You're on this case?"

"Yeah," she said. "Half the agents in our office who used to do child abductions have been reassigned to Homeland Security. My ASAC said he needs me."

"Debra Burgette asked me to check things out here for her. Can you fill me in? Or is the conflict-of-interest barrier still in place?"

"I guess we can talk. This doesn't technically deal with Sashi."

"Well, if you have any lingering concerns, the court of appeals turned us down an hour ago. Hannah is taking our last shot at the Supremes tonight."

"I'm sorry—if that's the right thing to say."

Another young woman approached, dressed like a college student. "Are you Jack Swyteck?"

Jack answered, and she introduced herself as Aquinnah's best friend, Charlene Spencer. "Aquinnah's mom called and said you were coming," she said. "I'm sort of the unofficial point person here."

"What can I do to help?"

"We've got social media covered. Maybe you'd be better doing some old-fashioned legwork?"

Jack was twice her age but didn't take the "old-fashioned" thing personally. "Sure."

"Awesome. I made a list of Aquinnah's favorite places: restaurants, coffee shops, fitness center, stores, hangouts. I'm sending volunteers to check every location and to talk with anyone and everyone who might have seen Aquinnah."

"That sounds like a good idea."

"Or you can stay and walk the neighborhood. There's a group going out in about three minutes."

Charlene pointed, and Jack spotted a group of about two dozen volunteers standing at the corner under the streetlamp—mostly women in their twenties who had canceled their Friday-night plans to help. It was like Cy's Place on ladies' night.

"I'm going with that group," said Theo.

"You go right ahead," said Andie. "I need a minute with Jack."

Theo headed off with Charlene. Andie waited until they were out of earshot, then started. "You can join in the hunt for Aquinnah if you want, Jack. But can you keep a secret?"

"Of course."

"I'm not saying it's a hundred percent, but the inside track says Aquinnah took him."

Jack's mind had already gone there, but it wasn't necessarily a happy place. "She took Alexander *with* her? Or took him . . . to hurt him?"

"That's the big question, isn't it?"

Jack nodded slowly. "I first met her at the motel when Debra created the 'Find Sashi' center. She came to court a few times. My impression was that Aquinnah was more 'over it' than overwhelmed by all of this. I don't know of any reason for her to hurt Alexander. But this kind of pressure can do strange things to people."

"Especially during such impressionable years. Aquinnah was an only child and had the perfect life till she was thirteen. Sashi moved in and, by all accounts, tormented her and everyone else for the next four years. For the last three years her mother has been all about 'find Sashi' and, according to Charlene, ignored Aquinnah since she was seventeen. Her parents ended up divorcing. The one bright spot seems to be Alexander, who by all accounts is a great kid."

"He is," said Jack.

"He may be the one person Aquinnah wants to hang on to. And now DCFS is threatening to take him away from the family. She could have snapped and done what she saw her sister do countless times. She ran. And she took her little brother with her."

"With her," said Jack. "That's what we hope."

"Yeah," said Andie. "That's the best case."

"Where do you think she went?"

"That I can't tell you, Jack. Not because of any conflict of interest. That part of the investigation is completely confidential at this point."

"Right, of course. And how about Debra?"

"What about her?"

"Have you told her the Aquinnah theory yet?"

"I haven't, personally. MDPD is nudging her in that direction, trying to see if she'll even consider the possibility that Aquinnah did something like this. The plan is to get her to come up with a list of places where Aquinnah might have taken him."

Jack's gaze drifted toward the police tape at the front door, then back. "I know you asked me to keep 'the secret,' but Debra is probably feeling pretty awful right now. Do you mind if I talk to her about it?"

Andie told him it was okay, smiling with her eyes as she laid her hand on the side of his face. "You're a pretty good guy, Jack Swyteck."

"Thanks."

"For a lawyer."

She gave him a quick kiss goodbye, and he watched as she walked back toward the FBI van. He texted Theo, telling him to grab a ride back to Coconut Grove with one of the volunteers.

Then he went to his car, wondering what he was going to say to Debra, hoping that Aquinnah had indeed taken Alexander—and praying that she'd taken him *with her*.

CHAPTER 60

Debra bummed a cigarette from a girlfriend, found a quiet spot in her neighbor's backyard, and lit up.

Debra had smoked in college but stopped when she got pregnant. She didn't pick it up again until Sashi's disappearance. She'd managed to quit again—it was going on thirteen months—but tonight marked her relapse. Detective "José Viernes" had asked her not to smoke near the crime scene, so she took it next door. Getting away from the commotion was actually doing her good. It was her first moment alone since MDPD's arrival.

Perez had been pushing hard for details about Aquinnah and Alexander. The detectives had done the same thing three years earlier, only that time it was about the two sisters. The focus in both cases was slanted toward the last twenty-four hours. Her recount of the day and the previous night with Alexander was so normal—so unlike the twenty-four hours before Sashi had disappeared.

Debra glanced across the yard toward her own house. Standing in the darkness, she could see clearly through the rear windows into her brightly lit kitchen. She could almost see herself at the stove, with her seventeen-year-old daughters seated at the kitchen counter. Alexander was asleep in bed. Yet again, Gavin was out of town "on business." It was a Thursday evening. The night before Sashi went missing.

A tall pot of homemade minestrone was simmering on the gas burner. Debra was stirring it with a long wooden spoon, standing on the cook's side of the island. Aquinnah and Sashi were seated on bar stools on the other side of the granite counter.

Debra filled the first bowl, placed it in front of Sashi, and started to fill a second.

"Mom, have you called Tom from Fort Lauderdale yet?" asked Sashi.

Debra dropped her stirring spoon into the soup pot. "Sashi!"

"I was just asking."

Debra fished the spoon out of the pot with a ladle, careful not to burn her fingers. Over the previous week, there had been plenty of arguments about the "real Internet pervs" that Sashi had promised to show her mother, but not a word about Tom the accountant from eSpark.com.

"Who's Tom in Fort Lauderdale?" asked Aquinnah.

Debra filled another bowl and placed it in front of Aquinnah. "No one."

"He's the answer to Mom's prayers."

"Sashi, that's enough from you," said Debra. She placed a bowl of grated Parmesan on the counter between the girls. "The soup is better with cheese. Have some."

"Answer to what prayers?" asked Aquinnah.

"Can we drop this, please?" asked Debra.

"Mom needs a new man," said Sashi.

"Sashi, I am warning you," said Debra, pointing with her ladle for emphasis. "Don't push me tonight."

Aquinnah laid her soup spoon aside. "Dad's been out of town a lot lately."

"He's very busy with his work, honey."

"Is everything okay?"

"Yeah. His work is good. He's busy."

"I didn't mean at work," said Aquinnah. "I was wondering . . . you know: Are things okay between you and Dad?"

"Yes, of course, sweetheart."

"Are you sure?"

"*Yes.* Everything is fine."

Sashi coughed. "Fine if you want a husband who cheats on you."

"I said that's *enough*," said Debra.

Aquinnah shot a nasty look at her sister. "Dad doesn't cheat."

Sashi blew on a spoonful of soup. "Wonderful. I live with *two* refugees from planet head-up-Uranus."

"You are so gross," said Aquinnah.

"Gross is the way your father looks at me," said Sashi.

"Oh, *puh-leeze*," Aquinnah said with a roll of the eyes. "Here we go again."

"No, here we *don't* go," said Debra. "Stop it right now, girls."

"What did *I* do?" asked Aquinnah.

"Just stop. Both of you. And, Sashi, stop calling him *Aquinnah's* father. He's your father, too."

"Whatever."

"And take those gloves off at the table."

It was Sashi's latest fashion statement. Nobody in Miami wore black leather gloves, especially not gloves up to the elbow, especially in September. Nobody but Sashi.

"I can wear gloves if I want to."

"I asked you to take them off."

"No."

"Take them *off*," said Aquinnah.

Debra turned around to shut down the burner. "Aquinnah, stay out of this."

"Yeah. Stay out," said Sashi.

"Ow!" Aquinnah shouted. "That was sharp!"

Debra turned. Aquinnah was rubbing her elbow. Sashi was eating her soup, a smug expression on her face.

"Sashi, what's in those gloves?" asked Debra.

"Nothing."

"I'm bleeding!" shouted Aquinnah.

Debra looked more closely at the gloves, but she was still on the other side of the counter. "Sashi, is that a *pin* in your fingertip?"

Sashi didn't answer, but it appeared to Debra that the pointed end of a short pin was protruding from the right index finger of Sashi's glove.

"Mom, I'm bleeding!"

"Give me those gloves," said Debra.

Sashi narrowed her eyes and turned on her other voice—the defiant one. "No."

"Give them to her!" shouted Aquinnah.

"Go to hell," said Sashi.

"You go to hell," said Aquinnah. "But first go kill yourself—like you told Madame Kirova you would."

Debra glared. "Aquinnah, how do you know about that?"

"Dad. He said you told him."

Debra's mouth fell open. "He wasn't supposed to tell *you*."

Sashi's expression changed again, transforming from defiance to contempt. "You don't know what you're talking about, Aquinnah."

"Oh, yes I do. Dad told me."

Sashi threw her spoon across the room, and it clanged against the wall. "I didn't tell Madame Kirova that I was going to kill myself!"

"OMG," said Aquinnah. "Do you ever stop lying?"

Debra crossed the kitchen and picked up the spoon, saying nothing—hoping yet again that this would pass.

"Maybe I *will* kill myself," said Sashi. "Would that make you happy, Aquinnah?"

"Yes, actually. I'd throw a party."

"Stop it!" shouted Debra.

Sashi jabbed her sister with the pin again—this time in the leg. Aquinnah screamed. Sashi screamed louder—a long, bloodcurdling scream that sounded like a mortally wounded animal. Then, with a quick swing of her arm, the bowl of hot soup went flying across the counter. Aquinnah started to cry. Debra tried not to panic, but she feared that this was "the big one"—the kind of meltdown that her virtual friends on the RAD message boards had warned her about.

"You are all such liars!" screamed Sashi.

Debra ran to the cabinet. It was where she kept the scented oils. When the meds didn't seem to work, the psychiatrist recommended aromatherapy. A quick swipe on the neck or wrist at the outset of a rage could make all the difference. The trick was to get Sashi to breathe in and absorb it before the eruption, or else it was as pointless as trying to coax molten lava back into the volcano.

Debra approached gently with the vial. "Sashi—here, honey."

Sashi swatted it away. The vial flew against the wall. The strong scent of lavender suddenly filled the room. Debra hurried to the cabinet for another vial: essence of jasmine, said to fight stress and reduce anxiety. This time she dabbed the oil onto a dish towel.

"Mom, I'm bleeding over here!" said Aquinnah.

Debra's focus remained on Sashi. She spoke softly, lovingly, trying to calm her. "Sashi, just breathe this, okay?"

"Fuck you, Mom!"

"Hel-*lo*, I'm still bleeding over here!"

"Aquinnah—shut up!" said Debra.

"What?"

"Go to your room! Don't you see what you caused here?"

Debra whispered more gentle words of encouragement to Sashi, and out of the corner of her eye, she saw Aquinnah fuming and watching in disbelief.

"Are you kidding me, Mother? Really?"

"Aquinnah, go!" said Debra, and then she continued in her soothing voice with Sashi. "Come on, baby. Breathe."

"She's crazy, Mom! She stabbed me with a pin—twice! And you're blaming *me*?"

"This is *not* Sashi's fault."

"It's never her fault. She gets away with everything. It's always *my* fault!"

"You didn't have to grow up in an orphanage."

"You didn't have to ruin my life!"

Aquinnah stormed out the room, her angry footfalls pounding the hardwood floor.

D ebra's cell phone rang. It was Jack Swyteck. "Debra, hey. I'm in your driveway. Can you come out and talk for a minute?"

She breathed out her last soothing drag. "Any news to report from Aquinnah's house?"

"I'm hearing the same thing you are."

"Oh." It was all she could say.

"I think we should talk about it. Don't you?"

She thought for a moment, then crushed out her cigarette. "Okay. Let's talk."

CHAPTER 61

Aquinnah was seated on the edge of the mattress on a squeaky motel bed, staring in disbelief at the lead story on the ten o'clock news.

"Lightning has struck twice for this south Florida family, piling tragedy on top of tragedy in a parent's worst nightmare. Good evening, I'm Craig Roberts . . ."

Side-by-side photographs of Aquinnah and Alexander flashed on the screen as the anchorman continued:

"A massive search is under way tonight as law enforcement faces the daunting task of finding not one but two children from the same family. Alexander Burgette, age nine, was apparently snatched from his Coral Gables home this afternoon while his mother, Debra Burgette, was exercising on the treadmill."

They'd gotten that part right. Aquinnah knew that her mother would be on the treadmill from four to five on Friday. That had been her routine as long as she could remember. Aquinnah knew she wouldn't hear the car pull up or the front door open and close.

"And Alexander's twenty-year-old sister, Aquinnah, has also been reported missing. Earlier this evening, Action News reporter Susan Brown was at Alexander's home in the upscale Cocoplum community, where his father, Gavin Burgette, had this to say . . ."

The bathroom door opened, and Alexander stepped out wearing his pajamas. "Is that Dad on TV?"

Aquinnah grabbed the remote and switched it off. "Never mind about that," she said.

He sat on the edge of the mattress beside her. "I don't like this."

"I told you: it's only for a little while. And it's only for our own safety."

He shook his head. "I don't know."

She'd told him very little, but she stuck to the story. It was based on what Debra had told her about that night outside the Russian deli. "The man who Mom spotted outside the Matry-oshka Deli is very dangerous, Alexander. If we don't hide, he'll get us both. We only have to hide until the police catch him."

"I hope they catch him soon. Do you think we're safe here?"

Her story was bogus, but his question was valid. The size of the manhunt had her concerned, and she was nervous about the way the motel manager had looked at her. Perhaps he'd seen something on the news and recognized them. Paying in cash so that police couldn't monitor her credit card activity would only add to his suspicions.

"I really want to go home," said Alexander.

"We can't. Not tonight."

"Mom is going to be worried. Can't we call her?"

"No. We can't call anybody until I figure this out."

"Figure what out?"

She couldn't tell him. He was just nine. He couldn't hear the truth. She held him close. "I love you, okay? This isn't something you can possibly understand. But I promise: if you do what I say, this will all work out fine. Okay?"

He didn't seem totally sold. "I'm scared."

"Don't be scared. I've got this under control. But I'm not sure we can stay here tonight."

"Why not?"

"We need a better place to hide."

"From what?"

"From everybody. Only for a little while. You have to trust me, okay?"

"Okay."

"So if you just lie down for a little while and be quiet, I'll think of a place."

She pulled back the covers for him. He climbed into bed and settled his head onto the pillow. "Can I play on your phone for a few minutes?"

She'd left it at home so that police couldn't track her by GPS. "Go to sleep, Alexander."

He lay quiet for a minute. Then his eyes popped open, and his face lit up. "I know where we can hide," he said.

"Please. Try to rest."

"No, I'm serious. It's the perfect place. No one ever goes there," he said with a clever grin.

"No one?"

"Nope. Nobody will ever find us."

She felt chills for a second, thinking about Sashi. "Okay. Tell me."

CHAPTER 62

It was almost midnight when Jack reached the Freedom Institute.

Hannah and the rest of the team had gone home around ten. The emergency motion for stay of execution was in good shape. Hannah had been e-mailing drafts to him throughout the night, but Jack was old school, and he liked to read a printed copy before filing—especially when it was going to the U.S. Supreme Court, and positively when it was a death-row client's last shot at life.

Jack opened the front door and switched on the light. It was quiet as a tomb. He'd insisted that the team not wait for him, but he'd half expected Hannah to hang around until he'd given the official and final blessing on their work. Over the past twelve days, however, they'd put in more than their share of all-nighters, and Jack was on his own.

I know Dylan Reeves is not asleep.

Jack flipped on more lights and went to the kitchen. The inkjet printer was on the counter next to the coffeemaker. It made more noise than a percolating Mr. Coffee as it powered up from sleep mode. Jack sent the draft motion from his laptop to the print queue and crossed his fingers. The old machine inhaled a blank sheet and spit out a crisp page one.

Forty-nine more to go, baby.

Jack's talk with Debra had run longer than planned. So long

and so well, in fact, that MDPD had asked Jack to help her create the list of places that Aquinnah might be hiding with Alexander. Law enforcement was reasonably certain that she wasn't on the road. The BOLO had turned up no sightings, and with no activity on her credit cards, she couldn't have rented a car.

The printer continued to rumble, more pages slid into the bin, and then Jack heard a strange noise that didn't come from the printer. It hadn't even come from the kitchen. The printer was still humming as he stepped into the reception area.

"Hannah? Is that you?"

He heard only the usual printer noises. He checked the front door. No one was there, but he made sure it was locked. Then he went back to the kitchen. Almost half of the brief had printed. He removed the printed pages and straightened them.

Then he heard that noise again.

He hit the PAUSE button and the printer fell silent. Jack listened. Nothing. He laid the pages on the counter and again stepped into the reception area. A palm frond outside the window moved silently in the breeze. Old houses made noises, he reminded himself, and he was standing in one of Miami's oldest. But that sound—whatever it had been—didn't ring like the usual creaks and groans. He gave it another minute, waiting and listening.

Then he heard it again—definitely not the usual old house creaks. It was more like a thump. And it had come from upstairs. Jack stared at the ceiling, as if willing that noise to come again.

There was only silence.

Jack's gaze swept the room, and it came to rest on the motorcycle at the foot of the stairway. Jack suddenly remembered his talk with Alexander about Neil's old BSA.

"Why do you park it here in front of the stairs? Do you ride it up to the second floor?"

"No, no. No one goes up there anymore."

Jack had found the front door locked upon his return. The old house, however, had an outdoor stairway. It led to the screened-in porch off the master bedroom.

"You clever little boy," Jack said quietly.

He was reaching for his cell to dial 911 when he heard a little voice from the top of the stairs.

"Mr. Swyteck? It's me. Alexander."

Jack froze.

"Can we come down, please? It's really dark up here. I'm scared."

Jack was a push of the button away from dialing emergency, but he held steady. "Okay. Sure."

Aquinnah's voice followed. "Don't call the police. Not if you want to know the truth."

The truth. Jack wasn't sure if she meant the truth about her having taken Alexander, or the truth about Sashi. He was willing to put down his cell phone long enough to find out.

"I won't call the police," said Jack.

"All right," said Aquinnah. "We're coming down now."

CHAPTER 63

Alexander started down the stairs first. Aquinnah was right behind him. Jack waited at the landing, on the other side of Neil's antique motorcycle. They moved slowly, tentatively, and were halfway down when Aquinnah told her brother to stop.

"This is far enough," she said.

Alexander sat on the step, half-asleep and leaning against the baluster. His shoes were untied, and he was wearing jeans and a pajama top, as if they'd left their last hiding spot in a hurry. Aquinnah stood on the step behind him.

"How did you get here?" asked Jack.

"Taxi," said Alexander, yawning.

Aquinnah was apparently smart enough to know the police were on the lookout for her car. "You should put a lock on that back staircase," she said.

"Not much here worth stealing," said Jack.

He'd hoped a little levity would help put her at ease, but it didn't seem to have any effect. Jack would have liked more time to break the ice. But even if his client's life weren't at stake, a lot of folks were worried about her and Alexander, and law enforcement was going full tilt. Jack had to push her, get what he could, and then call the cops. "Is there something you want to tell me, Aquinnah?"

"You've heard so many lies."

"So let's clear things up."

Aquinnah checked on Alexander. His eyes were closed, and the frightened expression had given way to the sweet dreams of a nine-year-old.

"I think he's out," said Jack.

Aquinnah joined her brother on the step, sitting close enough to keep him from tumbling down the stairs in his sleep. Even in her big-sister role, however, Aquinnah looked distressed. It was a touchy situation, and Jack worried that she might change her mind about sharing the truth and shut down completely.

"Why did you take your brother?" asked Jack.

She was looking straight ahead, staring over the top of Jack's head, avoiding eye contact. "I don't know," she said in a hollow voice.

"There had to be a reason."

"Because . . . I don't want to lose him."

"Why would you lose him?"

"Because of what happened. That night."

Jack took a half step closer, standing right up against Neil's old motorcycle at the base of the stairs. "You mean the night Sashi disappeared?"

She lowered her eyes until they met Jack's. Then she nodded.

"Tell me what happened, Aquinnah."

She took another moment, then began. "Sashi ran away."

"When?"

"In the morning. After Mom dropped her off for school."

"How did you find out?"

"Mom told me when I came home. I was like, '*Again?*' She did it all the time, you know."

So Jack had heard. "Did you look for her?"

"Mom did. She wanted me to stay home with Alexander in case Sashi came home."

"Where was your dad?"

His questions were coming much more quickly than her answers. "Out of town," she said.

"Did your mom find her?"

Aquinnah shook her head. "She came home."

Jack caught his breath. "When?"

"While Mom was out looking for her. It was getting dark." She swallowed so hard that Jack noticed even from where he was standing. "She said she was raped."

Jack checked his anticipation. They were getting to the heart of Dylan Reeves' case. "By whom?"

"Some man in the park."

If it was Dylan Reeves, he deserved to be in prison—but the wrong man was on death row. Jack had to be careful not to pressure her; he couldn't afford to lose her. "I know for a fact that Sashi didn't call the police to report it," said Jack.

"No. She said no one would believe her."

"You didn't call, either."

"No," she said, and her voice began to quake. "I told her she was right. No one would believe her. *I* didn't believe her."

"You told her that?"

Her eyes welled, and Aquinnah started to tremble. "I said, 'You're a liar, Sashi!'"

Jack could see there was more to come, but Aquinnah was no longer looking at him, and she delivered the rest as if she were in another place, another time. "'You ran away, you know you're in trouble, and you think that making up this story about being raped will make everyone feel sorry for you. But it's not going to work this time. You've used up all your chances. Dad's gonna send you back to Russia!'"

It took a moment for Jack to form the next question. "Was your dad really going to do that?"

"I don't know," she said, sniffling back tears. "But that's what I told her."

"What did Sashi do?"

"She went berserk, like she always did. She was screaming and yelling, and I told her that all the lying was finally catching up with her." Aquinnah lowered her voice and directed her answer toward the empty steps below her. "She said she was going to kill herself."

"Did you believe her?"

"She'd said that before. To her dance instructor. To Mom and me. This time, I . . ."

"You what?"

Another long pause, and a deep sigh followed. "My mother never slept. Never. Mostly because of all the worrying she did about Sashi. The doctor gave her a prescription. So I . . ."

"Go on. You . . ."

"I went to the medicine cabinet. I got the pills. I went back to Sashi's room."

She stopped, as if she couldn't bear to think of it, much less say it.

"Was Sashi there?" asked Jack.

Aquinnah nodded. "She was on her bed. I threw the container of pills at her and said, 'Here! Go ahead. Kill yourself! Do us all a favor!'"

The sudden shouting made Alexander stir. Then he settled back to sleep on the step.

"Did she?" asked Jack.

Aquinnah didn't answer. She leaned closer to her little brother, sobbing.

"Aquinnah, this is important. Did Sashi kill herself?"

Her silence said it all. Jack's heart was pounding, and he was suddenly glad that they had not yet filed that motion—Dylan Reeves' last chance with the courts. "Does your mother know any of this?"

"We never told her."

"We?"

"*I* never told her. I never told either one of my parents."

"But how could they *not* know? What happened to Sashi's body?"

She closed her eyes, then opened them. "The Everglades."

Florida's "river of grass." Over seven hundred square miles of tropical wetlands. Between the man-eating predators and the advanced rate of decomposition, the Everglades were quite possibly the world's most unforgiving repository of missing persons. "By yourself?"

She nodded.

Jack struggled to visualize it. "How did you get her downstairs and into the car? She probably weighed as much as you do."

She didn't answer.

"Aquinnah, did someone help you?"

She still didn't answer, but another possibility came to Jack's mind.

"Or was your sister half out of it from the pills, but still conscious enough to walk to the car with your help?"

Aquinnah hugged her brother so hard that he woke for a moment, and then he fell back asleep. "I think I've said enough," said Aquinnah.

"This is important," said Jack.

"Call the police, Mr. Swyteck. It's time for my brother to go home."

There were questions still unanswered and points that needed clarification. But there were also a worried mother and father who deserved to know that their children were safe.

Jack reached for his cell, then thought better of calling 911. All he needed was a rogue cop to bust down the door, mistake Jack for a child abductor, and pump six slugs into his chest for "resisting arrest"—a needless risk when he had an FBI agent on speed dial.

"I'm dialing," he told Aquinnah. "While we're waiting, I want you to come down here and write down everything you told me. Will you do that?"

Aquinnah didn't answer. Andie's voice was in Jack's ear. "Honey, where are you?"

"Hold on one sec, okay?" He held the phone away from him, looking straight at Aquinnah. "Please. Will you do that for me?"

He could still hear Andie's voice a foot away. "Jack, who are you talking to?"

Aquinnah was staring blankly over Jack's head again, silent.

"Aquinnah, please."

"Jack, are you with Aquinnah? Jack?"

Aquinnah was more vacant than ever.

Jack spoke into the phone. "Andie, I'm at the Freedom Institute with Aquinnah and Alexander. They're both safe. Come right now."

CHAPTER 64

Jack put Debra in his office. Alexander was bundled in her arms as they rocked gently in Neil's old rocking chair.

"I'll need to debrief the boy," said Detective Perez. He was standing in the doorway to Jack's office.

"Give them a minute," said Jack.

The detective glanced in the direction of the mother with her son. "All right. A minute."

MDPD had arrived first on the scene, and, given the responding officer's obvious level of testosterone, Jack was glad that he'd phoned Andie. If Andie hadn't spun things the right way to law enforcement, Jack would have likely ended up facedown on the floor with a boot pressing on his neck. Perez arrived two minutes after the first MDPD squad car, followed by Andie and another FBI agent.

"I'll check on Aquinnah," said Perez.

Jack went with him. Aquinnah was in the kitchen with Andie and FBI Agent Foster. Her father entered through the front door as Jack was crossing the reception area. Nicole Thompson was with him.

"Where's Aquinnah?" Gavin asked, his voice filled with urgency.

Jack pointed. "She's with the FBI. Alexander's in my office with his mother."

Gavin and Nicole went straight to the kitchen. Jack followed.

"I'm her father," Gavin said as he entered.

The conversation stopped cold. Aquinnah was seated on one side of the table; the agents were on the other, nearest the refrigerator. They all looked in Gavin's direction.

"You need to stop whatever it is you're doing with my daughter," said Gavin.

"Your daughter is twenty years old," said Andie.

"I'm still her father."

"She's an adult."

"All the more reason she needs a lawyer. Nicole represents her."

Andie glanced at Aquinnah, and Jack could see from the expression on her face how the mention of "a lawyer" changed the equation. "Aquinnah, is this your lawyer?"

Aquinnah hesitated, as if not sure what to say.

Gavin stepped closer to the table. "Nicole will represent her until she can get her own criminal defense lawyer."

Andie asked again: "Is this your lawyer?"

She looked at Jack, then at her father.

"Aquinnah, just say *yes*," said Gavin.

"Yes."

"No more questions," said Nicole.

"Hold on a second," said Jack. "I have a client who is scheduled to die for a murder he didn't commit. I *need* Aquinnah's help."

"I'm sorry," said Nicole. "I'm here to help Aquinnah help herself."

"She told me that Sashi committed suicide."

"We're not going to get into the substance of anything, and I'm not sure how she would know that anyway."

"Aquinnah gave her the pills. She *told me*."

"Then obviously she needs a lawyer," said Nicole. "You of all people should appreciate that, Mr. Swyteck."

"Don't play this game, Nicole. My client needs her help."

"I'm not saying you won't get help. But it won't be tonight. When is the execution date?"

"Tuesday."

"That's an eternity."

Jack bit back his anger, trying not to snap at her. "You're right, Nicole. At this stage, every *minute* is an eternity."

Gavin gave his daughter a stern look. "Let's go, Aquinnah."

Aquinnah rose, making eye contact with no one as she walked around the table toward her father.

"We'll be in touch," said Nicole.

Jack and Andie exchanged glances, and she didn't have to say a word to him: Jack knew that the FBI had to let her go. Nicole and Aquinnah went straight to the door. Gavin told them that he would meet them in the car and went into Jack's office.

"Let's go, Debra. We all need to leave."

Jack walked up behind Gavin so that he could see Debra, and so that she could see him. "They want to talk to Alexander," said Debra.

"No," said Gavin. "This is something you and I need to talk about and agree on."

Jack tried a more reasonable tone. "Gavin, this is not the time to circle the wagons. I think we all want to know the truth."

"Stay out of this," said Gavin. "Debra, don't be bullied into doing something we'll all regret. Let's go someplace we can talk."

She struggled to get out of the chair. Alexander was almost too big to carry, and he grumbled with sleepiness as she settled him onto his feet.

"Time to go, big boy," she said in a sweet voice.

Debra took him by the hand and led him across the room. Gavin took Alexander's other hand as they approached, speeding him and his mother along to the front door.

"Debra, you have a say in this," said Jack. "We need to talk to Alexander."

Gavin pulled the door open and stopped. "Debra, for the last time: I'm not asking you to do this for *me*. Do what's best for the children. It can wait till the morning."

Debra grimaced, her expression pained. "I'll call you, Jack. I promise."

They hurried out the door, and it closed with an empty thud.

A round one-thirty Jack said good night to Andie and good morning to Hannah. His wife was headed out the door, and his partner was returning. The rest of the Freedom team was on its way.

"We have a lot of work to do," said Jack.

He'd filled her in during the phone call, and Hannah had already divided labor in her head. "I'll get Brian to research newly discovered evidence. Eve and I can rewrite the motion."

"Good. I'll work on an affidavit from Aquinnah."

"Do you think Nicole will let her sign it?"

"The first step is to convince her that throwing a jar of sleeping pills at someone is not a crime, even if Sashi was threatening to commit suicide."

"Are we sure it's *not* a crime? Maybe we should get Brian to research that, too."

"I got a better idea."

Jack went to his office. Hannah followed. Jack didn't know Barbara Carmichael's home phone number, but 411 had it. Never had he heard of the state of Florida joining in a death-row inmate's emergency motion to stay an execution, but under these circumstances it seemed worth a shot. He dialed. On the fifth ring, she answered. She'd obviously been sound asleep.

"Good Lord, Swyteck. This had better be a real emergency."

"It's an emergency, all right," said Jack. "And it doesn't get any more real."

CHAPTER 65

Jack and his team pulled another all-nighter. There was a working shower in the downstairs bathroom, and occasionally the water was even hot. Brian was in it, and Jack was next in line when Barbara Carmichael called. Jack and Hannah had her on the speaker in the kitchen.

"I wanted to let you know that Aquinnah Burgette submitted to a polygraph examination," said the prosecutor.

"When?"

"Just this morning."

"And?"

"She failed."

It was almost as if the floor had fallen out below him. "Back up a step," said Jack. "Aquinnah failed on what?"

"On certain key questions concerning the disappearance of Sashi Burgette."

"Such as?"

"All of them."

Jack knew that there were usually no more than three operative questions in any polygraph examination. "I'd like to know what questions she was asked."

"That's confidential pursuant to an agreement between the state attorney's office and Aquinnah's attorney."

"Do you mean Nicole?"

"Yes."

Jack was starting to feel outgunned. "Let me ask you this: Who chose the examiner?"

"Aquinnah's attorney made a recommendation, and I agreed to it."

"Who was it?"

"Charles Whitehurst."

"*What?* How could you possibly approve him? Whitehurst is a known whore among criminal defense lawyers. He'll give the desired answer to anyone who will write him a check. If his conclusion was that Aquinnah failed, Nicole obviously *wanted* Aquinnah to fail."

"That's your opinion. Another person might conclude that Aquinnah has taken a page out of Sashi's book. She's become quite the storyteller."

"This is not a *story.* I witnessed it. This was a confession. I don't mean to sound sanctimonious, but I need you to work with me a little bit—in the interest of justice."

"The wheels of justice are already on track. There. Now we're both sanctimonious."

"Barbara, come on. An affidavit from Aquinnah would completely exonerate a man who is quickly running out of time."

"After this morning's polygraph examination, it would be my position that any such affidavit is perjury."

"Any affidavit would be based on exactly what she told me."

"Look, the bottom line is that there isn't going to be an affidavit. Aquinnah and her lawyer made that decision after the polygraph. All I can tell you, Swyteck, is to submit an affidavit from yourself on your client's behalf."

"The court will attach no evidentiary weight to that, and you know it."

"But you'll probably still file it, which is fine. It's Saturday, and I'll be checking my e-mail from home. Have a good weekend."

She hung up. Jack and Hannah were alone in the kitchen. The silence lingered until Hannah broke it.

"What do you want to do, Jack?"

He checked the time. Breakfast was over on death row. "Let's call our client."

"What are you going to tell him?"

Jack reached for the phone. Then he paused, looking Hannah in the eye. "That I believe him."

CHAPTER 66

J ack poured himself a mug of coffee as Hannah double-checked the final revisions to their draft motion for stay of execution. It was approaching nine a.m.—the deadline that Jack had set for filing with the Supreme Court. A decision needed to be made.

Hannah turned the final page and pushed the motion to the table's edge. "I think it's good."

Jack went to the refrigerator, but there was no milk for his coffee. "I agree. But 'good' doesn't do it. *Good* gets our client executed."

She voiced no counterargument. "Where does that leave us?"

Jack tasted his coffee. The morning brew he remembered at the Freedom Institute was never good enough to drink black, but this wasn't bad. It was the first thing he'd found better without Neil. "I'm starting to think the Supreme Court isn't the right shot. Maybe we should go back to Atlanta and ask the court of appeals to reconsider."

"Reconsider? Really? You know what my old man used to say about trying to get a federal judge to 'reconsider,' don't you?"

Jack did indeed. "'A judge who has judged loves finality,'" he said, quoting his mentor. "'The death penalty is "finality" with an exclamation point.'"

"Wise words," said Hannah.

"Maybe we'll find a judge who hates exclamation points."

"They *are* kind of cheesy," said Hannah.

"Like laughing at your own joke, some famous writer used to say."

"James Joyce."

"You sure?"

"Yes. I learned it at Barnyard."

"We're officially getting punch-drunk," said Jack. Outsiders found it odd, but it was an occupational hazard of death work.

"Sorry, chief. So what's your thinking behind going back to the court of appeals?"

"We won there before. They ordered Judge Frederick to hold the evidentiary hearing. It might be worth a shot to see if we can get them to send it back to him for further proceedings based on new evidence."

"Nice in theory. The problem is that we don't have new evidence. Not without a sworn affidavit from Aquinnah that says Sashi killed herself."

"Right. That's why I need to make a final run at Nicole. I gotta make this happen."

The front door opened. Theo entered and walked straight to the kitchen. It wasn't the norm for Jack to enlist Theo as an investigator twice in one week. But if Jack's latest hunch was correct, traffic records might just be the key to finding out what really happened to Sashi, and the Department of Motor Vehicles was closed on a Saturday, making Theo his go-to guy by default for this fact-finding mission.

"Whaddaya got for me?" asked Jack.

He dropped the cardboard box on the table. "Doughnuts."

"Doughnuts are good," said Hannah.

"And they're still warm. Try the chocolate crumb cake."

"*Theo*," said Jack. "I meant what did you find out?"

Theo took a seat at the table. "I think we're close to fillin' the hole in the Gavin Burgette doughnut."

"Tell me."

"On the day Sashi Burgette disappeared, Gavin's Porsche passed through the Golden Glades turnpike exit at four forty-six p.m."

"Northbound or southbound?"

"Southbound."

"That makes sense," said Jack. "He was driving back toward Miami from whatever 'business trip' he was on. So on a Friday, if he's passing Golden Glades at four forty-six p.m., that puts him at Cocoplum around . . ."

"Six o'clock," said Theo. "Give or take a few."

Jack was constructing a timeline in his head. "Aquinnah told me that she gave the sleeping pills to Sashi and dumped her body before her father got home. Hannah, what time did Gavin Burgette say he returned from his business trip?"

"Around eight o'clock."

"What time did Debra Burgette say Gavin got home?"

"Debra testified that she was out looking for Sashi until Gavin got back," said Hannah. "She met him at the house at eight o'clock."

"So, two things," said Jack. "One, if Gavin really didn't get home till eight, Sashi's body was already gone. Otherwise, Debra would have seen it."

"Right."

"But if Gavin got home as early as six . . ."

"He would have found Sashi dead from the sleeping pills," said Hannah.

Jack thought for a moment. "Or nearly dead."

Theo swallowed another chocolate crumb doughnut. "Dude, dead is one situation. Nearly dead? That's a whole nother thing."

"You're absolutely right," said Jack, his thoughts churning. "A whole nother thing."

CHAPTER 67

A sliver of morning sun was peeking through the blinds in her bedroom window when Andie woke. It was Saturday, so she hadn't set an alarm. She checked the digital clock on the nightstand. It was 10:06 a.m., and she was still tired. The usual discomforts of the third trimester had kept her awake until four. Whirling thoughts about the Burgette family had only compounded the problem.

She checked Jack's side of the bed, which was empty. She assumed that he'd worked all night at the Institute, but it was possible that he'd come and gone after she'd finally fallen asleep.

Andie scooted to the edge of the mattress. She slid her legs off the edge, let her feet drop toward the floor, and sat upright. Going vertical produced a mild head rush, but nothing worrisome. The standing order from the doctor was to self-check her blood pressure first thing in the morning, and then every three hours. Her digital monitor was on the nightstand, just beyond her fingertips. She leaned toward it with her arm fully outstretched and fingers wiggling as she tried to extend her reach. Just as she had the monitor in hand, the phone rang in the kitchen, which startled her—no one ever called on their landline—and she dropped it.

"Shit," she said, then chided herself.

I wonder if Riley can hear that?

After five rings, the phone went silent. Jack was phasing out the landline, so they had only the phone kitchen, and the ringer was set loud enough to be heard anywhere in the house.

It was ringing again. Somebody really needed to reach her, which only made her groan.

Some people might say that a dropped monitor and a ringing phone were no big deal—that Andie was "hormonal" and "feeling overwhelmed." But at this stage of pregnancy, stooping over to pick up anything and then walking all the way across the house before her first trip to the bathroom was a dicey proposition. She left the monitor on the floor, put on her robe and slippers, and started down the hall. The phone stopped ringing before she could get there. She turned around, and it started ringing again.

Call me on my damn cell, will ya?

She went to the kitchen and answered the phone. It was Debra Burgette.

"Oh, thank God you picked up," said Debra. "I don't have your cell number."

You're forgiven. "Glad you called. I was thinking about you last night."

"And I've been thinking about what Jack said—that I have a say in whether police talk to Alexander."

"He's right," said Andie.

"Well, if someone has to talk to Alexander, I want it to be you."

It was music to Andie's ears. "I can meet you at the field office. You remember where it is?"

"Yes. But we have to do this soon. It's Gavin's weekend, but things got so screwed up, Alexander wanted to stay with me last night. I have to drop him at Gavin's by noon."

"I can meet you in thirty minutes."

"That's fine. I'll see you then."

"See you then," said Andie.

Jack took a quick shower at the Institute, jumped in his car, and rolled down windows to air-dry his hair on the short drive to Jackson Memorial Hospital

Jackson was one of the nation's premier public hospitals. While it made headlines for groundbreaking research in cancer and spinal injury, its other strengths were myriad, and it didn't take long to connect the dots from a friend to a "friend of a friend" and find a renowned expert in just about any medical discipline. Jack didn't need the world's foremost authority. He just needed a quick favor from someone who was willing to explain the basics, and explain them correctly.

The "friend of a friend" method worked beautifully; there were occasionally advantages to sharing a surname with the former governor of Florida. At eleven o'clock he was seated at a table in the hospital cafeteria, having coffee with a sleep-disorder specialist.

"Caffeine is not your friend," said Dr. Trish Hollings. She was drinking bottled water.

Jack covered his cup. "Shhh. You'll hurt his feelings."

The doctor smiled, then checked her watch. "I'm sorry to be so short, but I have a meeting with half a dozen med students in ten minutes."

"That's plenty of time," said Jack. "I just need to pick your brain quickly."

"About what?"

Jack pushed his coffee—his nonfriend—to the side. "Sleeping pills."

Andie met with Alexander in the interrogation room at the Miami field office. She'd enlisted Dr. Paula Cohen, one of the FBI's child psychiatrists, to assist her. The table and chairs had been removed. Andie, Dr. Cohen, and Alexander were on the floor, seated on a blanket. Debra, MDPD Detective Perez, and

ASAC Schwartz were in an adjacent room, listening by speaker and watching from behind the one-way mirror.

The first segment was the easy part: just talk and spend time together to make Alexander feel comfortable. When he seemed ready, Andie shifted gears.

"Alexander, how old were you when your sister Sashi went away?"

"Six."

"Can you remember anything about the day it happened?"

He nodded. It was an assured nod, and Andie had no reason to doubt it. She'd met people who were as young as three or four at the time of the event but retained vivid memories of their mother crying when President Kennedy was shot or their father cursing at the television on 9/11. The day the police had swarmed the Burgette house and Alexander's entire known universe had turned upside down in the frantic search for his sister probably wasn't a day that Alexander had been too young to remember.

"I want you to tell me everything you remember about that day," said Andie. "Can you do that for me?"

He nodded once more.

Andie smiled a little, just enough to let him know that he was doing fine. "Okay. Let's get started."

CHAPTER 68

Jack entered Nicole Thompson's law office with low expectations. His expectations rose considerably when Gavin joined them. A lawyer-to-lawyer meeting would likely have produced little. With Gavin in the room, Jack had a shot—not at getting an affidavit from Aquinnah, but perhaps something more.

What a control freak this guy is.

Nicole was seated behind her granite-and-glass-top desk. Jack and Gavin sat in matching chairs that were straight out of *Modern Living* magazine, made from twisted chrome bars and hard leather straps. Gavin pulled his chair to the side of the desk so that both he and his lawyer were facing Jack. Nicole got things started.

"We've spoken with Aquinnah," she said. "I explained that you had requested an affidavit from her to file on behalf of Dylan Reeves. I'm sorry you drove all the way over here, but I can only confirm what I told you on the telephone: Aquinnah will not provide an affidavit."

"I can file a motion with the court to take her deposition."

"Good luck with that," said Nicole. "Your case is no longer before Judge Frederick, and I'm pretty sure that it's written in Rule One of the Rules of Appellate Procedure that depositions in cases before the court of appeals are allowed only on cold days in hell."

She was right, which was why Jack and Hannah had never even considered it.

"Maybe Dylan Reeves can give us a weather check when he gets there," said Gavin.

Nicole shot him a look that said *I'll do the talking.*

Jack rolled with it. "I understand that Aquinnah sat for a polygraph this morning."

"Which she failed," said Nicole.

Jack nodded. "I'm not surprised, given the examiner you hired."

"She failed because she was lying to you," said Gavin.

Nicole was about to chide her client again, but Jack took her by surprise.

"I agree," said Jack.

Lawyer and client exchanged a quick glance, pleased. "Well," said Gavin. "I'm glad we're all in agreement."

"Partial agreement," said Jack. "Aquinnah was lying *only* when she told me that she got rid of Sashi's body by herself, before you came home. She didn't do it without help."

"She didn't do it with or without help," said Gavin. "Your client murdered Sashi."

"Let me tell you why you're wrong, Gavin."

"I'm sorry," said Nicole. "We really don't have time for this. The reason we invited you over here, Jack, is to talk about the overtures DCFS has been making toward my client, and the future custody arrangements for Alexander."

"Wait a minute," said Gavin. "I want to hear what Swyteck has to say."

"Gavin, I don't recommend that you—"

"Nicole, I got this," he said firmly. "Go ahead, Swyteck. This should be interesting."

Nicole sighed. "I advise you to just listen, Gavin. Don't let him engage you."

Jack was tempted to borrow the line she'd used on him: *Good luck with that.*

"Let me start with the little things," said Jack. "Something that didn't compute for me was when you were in court and you accused Debra of rehoming Sashi. Now, you had to know that was a lie."

"No, I was beginning to think it was true."

"Gavin, just listen," said Nicole.

"Or maybe you just panicked," said Jack. "For a time, the case before Judge Frederick was going well for Dylan Reeves. It was starting to look as though he didn't do it. But if he didn't do it, who did? Stepdads are almost always suspects when seventeen-year-old daughters disappear."

"You think I accused my wife of rehoming Sashi so that the spotlight wouldn't shine on me?"

"Gavin, for the last time: just listen."

"Yeah, listen good, Gavin. Because you've done a lot of talking. You talk a lot about how much you love your son, but you know what? I went to your apartment. Not a single photograph of your son anywhere. Not a single photo of any of your children. I talked with Alexander when he came by the Freedom Institute. Says he does nothing but watch TV and play video games at your house. I heard you talking to Debra last night. You bought tickets for you and Nicole to watch a movie while Alexander was supposed to go with the sitter. When we searched the house, you didn't even know if he owns a bicycle."

"I don't live there. How would I know?"

Jack stayed with it. "And to be honest, you didn't seem all that eager to call nine-one-one. You seemed more keen on finding a way to blame Debra for his disappearance."

"Gavin, I don't see this as productive," said Nicole.

Jack kept going. "And then I talked to Aquinnah. I heard what I heard. My client is innocent."

Gavin was getting that look on his face that Jack had seen at their first meeting—when Gavin had threatened to punch him out. "What you heard," says Gavin, "is a twenty-year-old woman with the emotional maturity of a seventeen-year-old girl who is still not over her parents' divorce and will do anything to get her mother's love and attention. It's like the old joke, Swyteck. How many seventeen-year-old girls does it take to change a lightbulb? One: she stands still, and the rest of the world revolves around her."

"I've heard it," Jack said drily, staying on task. "Here's the bottom line, Gavin. I believe Aquinnah gave her sister those pills. And I *don't* believe you would have let my client die for a murder he didn't commit just to keep it a secret that Aquinnah encouraged her sister to commit suicide."

"I would never let anyone die for a murder he didn't commit."

"You might," said Jack. "To save yourself."

"That's fantasy."

"Is it?" asked Jack. "Here's my theory on why Aquinnah took Alexander. She was worried that her father was going to take him and rehome him."

"That's such a stupid thing to say," said Gavin. "Anyone who was even halfway paying attention at the hearing would know that one parent can't rehome a child. It takes both."

"Not if the mother has lost custody," said Jack, tightening his glare. "That's why you sicced DCFS on Debra, isn't it? Did you do it anonymously, Gavin? What horrendous lies did you pass along to the department to make those social workers drive out to Debra's house and threaten to take away her son after all the suffering she's been through?"

Jack noted the suspicious glance that Nicole suddenly shot in her client's direction. Gavin was simply glowering.

"Really, Swyteck? What conceivable reason would I have to rehome a perfect son like Alexander?"

"Because your perfect son was home on that Friday night," said Jack, leveling his gaze—ready to take his shot. "He was no sleeping baby. He was a very smart six-year-old. Old enough and smart enough to know that you killed Sashi."

"What?"

"Okay, that is *it!*" said Nicole as she rose from behind her desk. "This meeting is officially over. Gavin, do not say another word. Mr. Swyteck, the only thing further that I want to hear from you is 'goodbye.'"

Gavin remained in his chair, fuming. Nicole walked around her desk, as if ready to lift Jack from his chair if he didn't move fast enough. Jack rose, locking eyes with Gavin, reading what nearly two decades of experience in criminal law had taught him to read.

"I'm right," Jack said—and he knew he was.

Jack turned and showed himself to the door.

ndie's talk with Alexander was at the one-hour mark.
She'd tried to keep his recounting of the day of Sashi's disappearance on some semblance of a timeline, starting with when he'd arrived home from school that afternoon. But he kept getting ahead of things. Each time Andie brought him back to the chronology, he'd skip ahead again. It was obviously painful for him; yet a part of him seemed eager to tell them—to finally tell *someone*—about the last time he saw Sashi.

They were just passing the point when Aquinnah had burst into Sashi's bedroom and thrown something at her. He didn't know that it had been his mother's sleeping pills—but Andie did.

"Where were you, Alexander, when that happened?"

"In the bathroom—the one between our bedrooms."

They'd covered the upstairs floor plan earlier. Debra had originally divided the "Jack and Jill" bedrooms between Sashi and Aquinnah, but the wars over the common bathroom, which was accessible from either room, eventually became epic. Aquinnah had moved to the room down the hall. Alexander became "Jack"; Sashi was "Jill."

"Could you see anything from inside the bathroom?" asked Andie.

He nodded. "Through the crack. The door doesn't slide all the way closed."

There was a pocket door, Andie inferred, between Sashi's room and the bathroom. "What did you see?"

He swallowed the little lump in his throat. "Sashi. She was crying."

"Do you know why?"

"They were fighting."

"Arguing? Or fighting?"

He blinked, as if fending off a bad memory. "Yelling. There was a lot of yelling. I was scared. So I hid in the bathroom."

"What did you do?"

"I just stayed in the bathroom."

"How long?"

"A long time."

"Did you see anything else?"

He nodded. "After a while, I looked through the crack again. I saw Sashi."

"What was she doing?"

"Sleeping."

"Did you see anything else?"

He paused for a minute, seeming to gather his thoughts. "Yes. Later. After my dad came home."

"What did you see?"

"I heard him first."

"Okay. What did you hear?"

"He came up the steps. Real fast. Real hard."

"Like he was running?"

"Yeah. In the hall, too. Sounded like running."

"Then what?"

"I heard Sashi's door open."

"You didn't hear a knock first?"

He twisted his mouth, thinking. "No. No knock. It was like the door flew open. And then he started yelling, 'Sashi! Sashi! Wake up, Sashi!'"

"What were you doing then? When he was yelling at Sashi to wake up."

"I was so scared. I was still in the bathroom. But I peeked out the crack."

"What did you see?"

His voice shook as he answered. "Sashi was on the bed. She was kind of sitting up, but slouchy, like she was still sleeping. Dad was holding her up, but it was like she kept wanting to fall back."

Andie paused to let the image in her mind come into focus. "What else did you see?"

He looked at Andie and then at the psychiatrist. The words seemed trapped in his mouth.

Dr. Cohen brought out the doll they'd been using before— the Sashi doll—and gave it to Andie, who placed the doll on the blanket. The three of them formed the points of a surrounding triangle.

"Okay, Alexander. So this is Sashi lying on her bed," Andie said. "Where was your father?"

He pointed, indicating the spot next to Sashi. "He was standing right there."

"Standing up in the bed?" asked Andie.

Alexander shook his head. "No. Sashi was in the bed. He was standing on the floor. Over Sashi."

"Okay? What did you see next?"

Alexander focused his gaze on the doll. "He . . . reached toward Sashi."

"With one hand or two hands?"

"Two hands."

"Show me how he held his hands," said Andie.

Alexander laid the left palm over the back of his right hand.

"Good," said Andie. "Did he touch Sashi?"

He nodded slowly.

Andie paused, trying extra hard to tread gently. "Show me how he touched her."

Alexander kept his hands as they were as he rose up on both knees. Then he leaned toward the doll. Slowly, his hands moved toward the doll's face. He placed both hands over the doll and pressed down—and not just for an instant.

"How long did he keep his hands there?" asked Andie.

Alexander kept pressing. Tears started to fall. "A long, long time."

"Did Sashi move?"

A teardrop fell from his chin and landed on the doll. "Just her leg. A little."

"What did your dad do when her leg moved?"

"Nothing. He just kept pressing. And then her leg stopped."

Andie quietly drew a breath. "Then what did he do?"

Alexander eased up on the pressure he was putting on the doll's face. "Dad took his hands away."

Andie gave him a few seconds. "Then what?"

Alexander sat back on his haunches, staring down at the doll on the blanket. "Sashi didn't move."

An eerie silence came over the room. Andie could only imagine what Debra was going through in the next room, behind the one-way mirror.

"Do you want to take a break now, Alexander?"

He sniffled back his tears and nodded.

Andie had seen a lot with the Bureau, heard too many horrible stories, and thought she'd gone tough on the inside. But she had to fight the urge to hug this boy—and fight hard she did. They were being videotaped, and in her world, a display of affection or even of concern would only have given Gavin Burgette's future criminal defense lawyer a basis to argue that a pregnant FBI agent had co-opted this child and planted a story in his head.

"Thank you, Alexander," she said in an approving tone. "You're a very brave boy."

CHAPTER 70

Jack crossed the palm-tree-lined median on Bayshore Drive and continued toward the parking lot across from Nicole's law office. Thunderclouds were rolling in from the bay, and in the afternoon air Jack detected a mixed scent of seawater and the coming rain. Coconut Grove Marina was nearby, and beneath the threatening cloud cover the tall and steely assortment of gray and barren masts was probably Miami's closest cousin to a windswept, wintry forest.

"Swyteck!"

Jack was on the sidewalk at the parking lot's edge. He stopped, turned, and saw Gavin Burgette walking toward him. If Jack had left a smoldering ember in Nicole's office, it was now a raging fire. Jack could see it in his eyes.

"Something you need from me, Gavin?"

Burgette didn't even acknowledge the pleasantry. He came right up to Jack, standing so close that both men were within the same square of sidewalk. Jack didn't back away, but he prepared himself for a verbal encounter that could instantly turn physical.

"You are so fucking smug, aren't you?"

"You need to watch your tone, Gavin."

"You think you and your pretty pregnant wife have it all, don't you? You're going to have this wonderful child who will love you and make your life all you ever wanted it to be. Well, I got news for you, pal. That isn't the real world."

"Gavin, you're bothering me."

"I'm doing you a favor here, Swyteck. Because you know who else had it all? I did. For thirteen years, Debra, Aquinnah, and I did. And we still would, if Debra had listened to me and drawn the line on adoption with Alexander. But we made one mistake—one too many kids from Russia—and it was *all* fucked. For *all* of us. Do you have any idea what it's like to have a kid like Sashi? A daughter who destroys your wife, your marriage, your other children?"

"I admit, I don't know what I would do if I found myself in that situation. But I know what I *wouldn't* do."

Gavin shook his head, and the anger he exuded hung over them like the worsening weather. "You really think I did it, don't you?"

"I do."

"Well, you can poke and jab like a world-class middleweight all you want. But you can't get me to go there."

Jack knew he could—if he could just navigate this growing storm. "I had a talk this morning with a sleep-disorder specialist," said Jack. "Funny thing: we don't live in the world of Marilyn Monroe anymore. Unless you buy from a pill mill or hire a personal pusher like Michael Jackson did, it's really, really hard to die from an overdose of the pills that doctors prescribe these days for common sleeping problems. You might end up with brain damage, but the chances of surviving are pretty damn good. Isn't that interesting?"

Gavin was silent. He also seemed to deflate just a bit—his confidence, not his anger.

"So here's the timeline in my head," said Jack. "Sashi swallowed those pills right after dark. We have your Porsche going through Golden Glades turnpike interchange in time to put you at home just after six. It's a virtual medical certainty that Sashi was still alive when you got home. She was, wasn't she, Gavin?"

He didn't respond right away, but Jack saw the first crack in the granite facade.

"But she was dead and gone—literally—by the time Debra came home at around eight," said Jack. "We know that."

Another crack. Jack didn't expect a full confession, but he could see something building inside this man—something that he'd been living with longer than anyone with a conscience could. Finally, he spoke.

"Aquinnah didn't kill her."

"I know she didn't. But you let her believe that Sashi died from an overdose. That was quite a handy way to keep her under your thumb, wasn't it? Let her think that the police could swoop in at any moment and throw her in jail for causing Sashi's death."

Gavin was clearly struggling to show no reaction, but he was failing.

Jack kept at it. "That's why Aquinnah won't give me an affidavit and tell the court what she told me last night. You and Nicole have her believing that she'll go to jail for giving Sashi those pills."

Gavin closed his eyes tightly, then opened them. It surprised Jack a little to see that he apparently had *some* shame.

"What did you do, Gavin? Go upstairs and finish Sashi off, and then bring her downstairs? Or did you stuff her in the trunk of your car, still breathing but unconscious, and let the Everglades do the job for you?"

Gavin took a telling step back, giving Jack his own square of sidewalk. The afternoon sun had completely disappeared. Jack felt a raindrop on the back of his neck. And then he heard the sirens blaring in the distance.

Police sirens.

For an instant, Jack wondered if Gavin would make a run for it, but he must have seen the futility of it. Two lines of MDPD squad cars, one from each direction on Bayshore Drive, were speeding toward them. Police beacons swirled and sirens screamed as the show of force squealed into the parking lot, jumped the curb onto the grassy swale, and blocked off the sidewalk at both ends. Jack and Sashi's killer were surrounded.

The first pair of MDPD officers jumped out of their vehicle and assumed the stance, pistols drawn: "Hands over your head! Now!"

Jack complied immediately, locking eyes with Gavin, who stared right back at him.

"Hands up! Both of you! Right now!"

Gavin stared for a moment longer at Jack, and, slowly raising his arms, he spoke in a low, angry tone.

"You're dead wrong, Swyteck."

Jack was expecting another lame denial, but that wasn't what he got.

"Nobody knows what he *wouldn't* do," said Gavin.

Two MDPD officers hurried toward them. They grabbed the suspect and quickly cuffed his hands behind his back.

"Don't forget to Mirandize him," said Jack.

The senior cop did it, and Jack made damn sure he didn't miss even one constitutionally required word of it. The officers took Gavin straight to the squad car, and Jack watched as they shoved him into the backseat and slammed the door shut. The squad car sped away. Two more vehicles were right behind it. Jack's gaze followed the blurring line of police lights until they rounded the bend and the flashing orange faded into a gray afternoon.

Another MDPD officer approached with an umbrella. The rain was falling a little harder. "Are you all right, Mr. Swyteck?"

Jack reached for his cell phone to dial the warden's office at Florida State Prison.

"We are now," said Jack.

Dylan Reeves' execution date came and went. No lethal cocktails were served. Nor were there any hugs or high fives with Jack at the prison gates to mark his release. He was moved up one floor in Q-wing, from death row to gen-pop, where he would serve out his sentence for the aggravated sexual assault of Sashi Burgette.

Jack would probably never hear from him again—unless he and Carlos "Bad Boy" Mendoza failed to get along.

"I give it a fifty-fifty shot that one of 'em ends up stabbed," said Theo.

Jack was sitting on a bar stool at Cy's Place, cashing in once again on that promise Theo had made to him upon his release from death row: free beer for life.

"Could happen," said Jack. He didn't know if the bad blood between Mendoza and Volkov had spilled over to Reeves, but having any kind of a past with a thug like Mendoza was hardly a plus behind prison walls. While the Miami-Dade state attorney and the Florida attorney general's office had joined in Jack's motion to vacate his client's murder conviction and death sentence, Reeves was on his own when it came to a change of correctional facility.

"Could be real fireworks if Volkov ends up back at FSP for stalking Debra."

"Stalking?"

"I'm sure his lawyer will argue that making those phone calls on Sashi's birthday is more harassment than stalking. Not sure a jury would agree. Especially after Debra saw him watching her outside some Russian deli."

"Piece a shit."

"Yup."

"Speaking of . . . what's the word on Mr. Wall Street?"

Gavin had never actually worked on Wall Street, but since he was clearly going to prison, Theo figured that he had earned the title.

"He's cooked. Aquinnah cut a deal and will testify against him."

"What'll happen to her?"

"Throwing sleeping pills at someone from across the room isn't a Dr. Kevorkian assisted-suicide situation. I don't know the details of her deal with Carmichael. My guess: no jail time. But she won't be voting in any future elections. At least not in Florida."

"And Debra?"

"Don't know if she'll ever speak to Aquinnah again. But she's got Alexander. The Department of Children and Family Services backed off its investigation. Debra wasn't paranoid: Gavin *was* pumping those social workers with lies to get full custody of Alexander."

"So he could rehome him, too?"

"More likely control him—remind him on a daily basis that if he ever opens his mouth, he's going back to Russia."

"Gavin'll be the one openin' his mouth—on a daily basis."

"Is that your crude attempt at irony?"

"If irony means payback's a bitch, then yeah." Theo wiped down the bartop and took Jack's empty glass. "Refill?"

"No, one is my limit. Gotta keep alert. I'm on Riley watch. We're at thirty weeks now."

"That's still early, right?"

"Yeah, but it's pretty safe territory. The doctor has Andie checking her blood pressure every two hours. If it goes up and stays there, it's time to check into the hospital and make it happen."

Jack's phone rang. He checked the number and looked at Theo.

"You kiddin' me?" asked Theo.

It was Andie. Jack answered. "Hey, honey. We were just talking about you. Your ear must be buzzing."

"That's definitely not my ear buzzing, Jack."

Jack gripped his cell. "Holy crap."

"I know, right? Dr. Starkey said to meet her at the hospital at seven."

Jack drew a breath. He could almost feel her smile coming through the phone, but there had been a hint of something else in her voice.

"So this is it?"

"Uh-huh," said Andie. "This is really it."

ACKNOWLEDGMENTS

*G*one Again is my thirteenth Jack Swyteck novel. Jack came to life as a young lawyer defending death row inmates at the Freedom Institute in *The Pardon* (1994). It's been quite a journey back to his roots in *Gone Again*, but I can't say that coming full circle was part of a grand artistic plan. When I wrote *The Pardon*, I had no idea that it would become a series. I was equally surprised when I started typing more than two decades later, only to find that Jack was suddenly back where it all began, standing on the familiar steps of that historic house along the Miami River. (The house is real, by the way, owned by friends of mine.)

I don't know where Jack will go from here, but I'm grateful to the dynamic duo that has brought him this far: my editor of twenty years, Carolyn Marino, and my agent of almost twenty-five, Richard Pine. My beta readers, Janis Koch and Gloria Villa, have left their mark on more than a dozen Grippando novels. The mistakes are mine, but Janis and Gloria have saved me from even more serious embarrassment.

Finally, I'm grateful to my wife, Tiffany. Books and the book industry have changed so much since the first Swyteck novel. Your love and support have never wavered.

ABOUT THE AUTHOR

JAMES GRIPPANDO is a *New York Times* bestselling author of suspense. *Gone Again* is his twenty-fourth novel. He was a trial lawyer for twelve years before the publication of his first novel, *The Pardon*, in 1994, and now serves as counsel to Boies Schiller & Flexner LLP. He lives in south Florida with his wife, three children, two cats, and a golden retriever named Max who has no idea he's a dog.